T0077404

Different Hearts Walk Longer Miles

A Novel by
V. Austin Koch

Order this book online at www.trafford.com
or email orders@trafford.com

Most Trafford titles are also available at major online book retailers.

© Copyright 2013 V. Austin Koch.
All rights reserved. No part of this publication may be reproduced, stored in a retrieval
system, or transmitted, in any form or by any means, electronic, mechanical, photocopying,
recording, or otherwise, without the written prior permission of the author.

This novel is a work of fiction. The situations are fictional. No character is
intended to portray any person or combination of persons living or dead.

Printed in the United States of America.

ISBN: 978-1-4269-1778-3 (sc)

Trafford rev. 03/05/2013

 www.trafford.com

North America & international
toll-free: 1 888 232 4444 (USA & Canada)
phone: 250 383 6864 ♦ fax: 812 355 4082

Because of my friend Libby . . .
The motor in motivation!

Chapter One

The decrepit Model-A Ford stopped at the curb, the slight drizzle giving it a false shine. Getting out on the curb side a young woman hurried a small boy and a suitcase up the steps of a house. It was midnight when she rang the bell; the child staring up at her. How does a three year old handle something he knows nothing about? With fear! And little Jerry Foley was filled with it. The door opened a crack then, upon recognition, all the way.

"Carol! What are you doing here at this hour?"

Knowing her sister; Mary Waters knew another human sensation . . . dread!

"Mary," Carol said excitedly; "keep Jerry here for a couple of days, please, I have a chance for a good job as hostess; but I have to work late night hours; the money is good and I'll come for him as soon as I get set up."

It was hard for Mary to say no; she really never had the opportunity. In one moment Carol turned and was out the door with a *call you tomorrow* thrown over her shoulder. She did not even kiss her child goodbye. It really was goodbye; neither of them ever saw her again. Now she had to face her spouse!

Mary's husband had never wanted children of his own; he damn sure did not want someone else's bastard! It was an uphill fight for Mary. She suffered a year and a half of agony; then she gave in. Finally, at a Catholic orphanage; the nuns relieved her of the child's physical presence . . . but she could never erase him from her mind. Her spouse said; "back to normal."

Years later Mary made a successful effort to track Jerry down; he had no recollection of her. He had a vague memory of his mother

1

leaving him and somehow had blanked out the rest. It was awfully painful for Mary.

As far as Jerry Foley was concerned his life began when he enlisted in the Army in 1941. At first it was difficult for him to adjust to Army routine and regulation; but the barracks life was not unlike the orphanage and he didn't have the adjustment problems that those who had left the comfort of their homes had. He was quick to see opportunity and in three months he was made Corporal; simply by reading his Army manual. He impressed his buddies . . . and also his officers with his knowledge. Though he was unaware of his ability to lead men the cadre saw it and quietly began to groom him for leadership.

Standing six feet tall with good shoulders and a muscular body that was developed doing hard construction work; he had the appearance that men envy and women admire. On the surface he was happy-go-lucky with eyes that seemed always about to laugh. But there were deep-seated uncertainties that his sub-conscious pushed even deeper. The Army posed one problem for him. In his teen-age years he had developed an almost constant thirst for beer. Many GIs complained about the weak PX beer; Jerry simply drank more of it! Fortunately they kept him so busy he didn't have time to seek it out. If he had the opportunity; he would be drinking. And there were times; especially over seas, when he had the opportunity . . . and he waded in!

Jerry was discharged from the Army in 1944. Behind him was life in the Infantry; his stint in the ETO and for the first time in his life, very close friends, some of them killed during the war. His hairline had receded, ageing him a little but adding to his appeal. He had always had a 'devil-may-care attitude'; now he had a hairline to match. His buddy Pete use to say; "No matter how he looks; women chase him."

Everyone was going home; he was sick of hearing about it. Re-enlisting in the Army had entered his mind but he didn't think he could handle the stateside regulation. Life overseas offered much more freedom than strict stateside protocol. Jerry had a hard time coping with what's been termed *chicken-shit* by the GIs. Pete Conway had been urging him to come and stay with him and his widowed mother. Pete assured him that there was plenty of room and Long Island was a great place to live. After spending an hour at a bar discussing the matter; Jerry was convinced and they made their way to the unsuspecting widow. Pete embraced Rose "I'm home Mom."

Rose Conway was so happy to have her son home she would have welcomed a rattlesnake with him if necessary. She opened her home to Jerry; hoping her misgivings did not show. For the first time in his life Jerry lived in an organized home. The first month was one long party. The two of them were out almost every night and the beer flowed all day long at home. Rose tried to be patient but one morning, holding her breath; she took her son aside and began asking him about his plans for his future. She mentioned the *GI BILL OF RIGHTS* and all of the advantages he was entitled to; there were ways that would enable him to buy his own home, if he chose to do so. He and Jerry were collecting the twenty dollar a week benefits which were intended to help them get started on a career of some sort. Rose worried about all the drinking and wasting of money. Pete laughingly told his mother they went job hunting every day; with his arm around her shoulder he assured her he was thinking of his future and she needn't be worried about him. His arm felt reassuring; but the worry did not go away. She was sure that she would have worries as long as Jerry was about!

There was one thing about Jerry she did like; he was immensely helpful around the house. He perceived when something needed to be done and in a flash . . . it was done. She never had to ask him to do anything. That did not change the fact that she felt he was a bad influence on her son; being his mother; she could not imagine her son was eager for all this carousing. The truth being he loved it!

As time wore on Rose became convinced that Jerry had to go. She began rehearsing the way she would discuss it with Pete. It never occurred to her that she was about to grab quite a tiger by the tail! Men who serve in combat together create a bond that defies description; it is a place that only those who were there can enter and that includes mothers and wives. Her son's welfare was all that Rose concerned herself with and it never entered her mind that there could be such an attachment. Being so naïve was going to cause her a lot of pain; as if worrying about Pete all the time he was in the Army wasn't enough pain. She became obsessed with the idea and it occupied her thoughts all the time; it was destined to come to a head and it was only a matter of time until the day of doom! And it wasn't going to be a long time, either.

One evening Jerry and Pete sat Rose down; they were in a jovial mood, boosted by a few beers.

"Well Mom, you are going to like what we have to tell you." Pete was beaming and very pleased with himself. "Jerry and I have joined the Police Force and we're going to be in the motorcycle branch. There is a better chance for quicker advancement in that section and we want to get ahead fast!"

They were laughing and thrilled with their recent decision; you can bet that Rose was not thrilled; she was horrified! She rose up from the chair as if she were fired from a cannon. She was sure Jerry instigated this nonsense!

"Are you both insane? You were lucky enough to make it through that damn war and now you want to risk your lives again!"

She could not hold back the tears; she knew her words fell on deaf ears and her days of worrying were far from over.

Three years later Pete met Anne and soon after they married. Everyone worked but Rose and they all lived together to keep down the expenses. Jerry was now faced with a big decision; he was uncomfortable with the arrangement; the laughs were gone and the closeness that he shared with Pete was relegated to their time on the job. He could not find fault with the ambience of the home; even Rose was more pleasant because her son was no longer bar hopping every night; she liked Anne and enjoyed the feminine company in her home. Jerry did not resent Anne; he didn't like what she represented. He began staying in the City in cheap hotels or the "Y." He told Pete he had a broad on the string and she wasn't exactly what he would bring into his mother's home.

He said, "I respect Rose too much."

Finally, at a bar, he looked at Pete saying; "I'm moving in with the broad, pal."

"If that's what you want, buddy, but we are all going to miss you. It's a bit of a shock to me."

Pete wondered about the girl; Jerry was not one to ever get entangled. He usually sought out a hooker or a girl who hung out at bars and was easy. He could not recall seeing Jerry with the same girl twice. Even overseas where many GIs had steady girls, Jerry patronized the brothels; and always alone. Plenty of girls tried to latch on to Jerry but he was very slippery.

Lying to Pete was not something he was comfortable with; telling him he just wanted to get out after being welcomed into his first real home was totally impossible. He chalked it up as a white lie. The search for a small, reasonable apartment in New York City became quite a challenge. He quickly realized how good a situation he had left. Temporarily he was renting a unit in a cheap motel in New Jersey which was owned by two retired cops and they gave him a good price. The place was just a cut above a flop house; but at least it was clean and bug-free! He was also not tied to a lease and that gave him the freedom to move quickly, should he find an apartment.

Jerry had had himself transferred to the vice squad and didn't see Pete very often. One day they met accidentally and Pete extracted a promise from him that he would come out and have a Sunday dinner with them. Jerry kept his promise and had a great meal and a really enjoyable day. Rose had relaxed into a state of contentment. Anne had persuaded Pete to get out of the bike squad and he was, in fact, on a job at a desk and was now moved up in rank. All of this was pure heaven to Rose; she never interfered in their marriage, if she sensed a quarrel she went to her room and never asked questions. Cooking and caring for them was a pleasure and Anne had insisted on a weekly cleaning woman to relieve her of any heavy, difficult work. Rose was glad Jerry was gone.

* * *

Tony Castaldo put the last clean glass on the shelf; now he could go home. He had closed his bar at two a.m. which was ritual; and it was three a.m. now. From noon to three a.m. are enough hours and anyone who owns a business knows that the boss works the longest hours. Well, Tony was certainly his own boss because he had no hired help. He handled the cash and there were never any shortages! Tony's Place, a name selected without too much strain on his imagination, was open seven days a week. That did not leave any time for a social life and that was just what he wanted. Tony had been in the social world when he was younger and he didn't handle it very well; he had a quirk that he didn't understand and he suppressed thinking about it. "My business is my life."

The experience he had in his youth still had a grip on him. It held him back.

Looking in the back bar mirror he ran a comb through his thick, wavy hair. The gray hair was sneaking in and while it was attractive, it reminded him that time was passing; and not slowly! He toyed with the idea of touching up the gray hair but it seemed to be a lot of bother; he chose not to be bothered. Actually, it added to his good looks. By the calendar he was fifty-two but he looked much younger. His height was about five feet nine inches; a trim body was kept that way simply by avoiding excesses. He was especially careful about drinking; overdoing his own products was not on his agenda. When your business involves people who are drinking your head has to be clear and Tony never forgot that. As he looked at his reflection in the mirror he paused and said aloud, *God's gift to woman; what a joke!*

There was a brooding sadness in his dark eyes and not without reason. Growing up in Brooklyn, New York had made him street-wise very young. With it came pre-exposure to sex; most of the guys liked to appear experienced and knowing; privately they were insecure. Tony was well-endowed and both admired and envied by his pals. Girls openly pursued him and when he was about sixteen his libido took command and he tried to have his first experience. He wanted to have a story to tell his pals.

He had a very willing partner and during foreplay he was proudly erect and rigid. When he attempted penetration; something his partner was passionately demanding; his erection drooped . . . completely! After several of these experiences (he covered up by feigning pre-ejaculation); he began avoiding girls. It was a time when girls kept their trysts secret; his problem was not an item for gossip. Once, he spoke his thoughts aloud. "If they talk about me; I'll have to move."

One afternoon when he was walking home from school alone a pretty blond girl fell in step with him and asked if she could accompany him. He had no reason to refuse and she was pretty and had a certain effervescence about her.

"Sure," he said; not wishing to appear eager.

They walked along engaging in chit chat, it was a lovely day; a gentle breeze stirring the air.

"Have you got time to walk through the park? It's so nice today I hate to get home too early." As she spoke she took his hand and smiled; warmly.

"I have time," he answered; "plenty of time."

They came to the park and entered; it was heavily treed with tall maples and oaks, there were many dogwoods and pines. The pines scented the air and it was delightful and surprisingly, there were very few people around. As they went deeper into the woods they came to a trail that was really like a boardwalk through the thickest part of the woodlands. If it weren't for the boardwalk they could not have made it through here. The breeze played through the leaves and every now and then a bird had something to add.

They stopped and leaned against the railing; Sylvia had been holding his hand and there had been no conversation but there was a growing attraction; Tony felt a rising desire for her; she seemed to dispel his fear and he began kissing her. She kissed him as no other girl had ever kissed him and he was wildly aroused. He dropped his pants and she hungrily reached for that throbbing erection; she was delighted with what she found.

"I have to be a virgin when I marry," she whispered, "I know what to do." Her head slid down his body and she took him in her mouth! Tony was wild with passion and nothing drooped! Sylvia Miller was the solution for Tony; she became his steady girl and not without protests from his Catholic parents and Sylvia had to cope with a very angry Jewish father.

"You're in love with his pecker!" he had railed at her.

"You should see it, Daddy," she added fuel to the fire.

The romance went on for over a year and Tony began to feel trapped. The sexual pleasure was being overshadowed by Sylvia's demands; she wanted to get out from under her father's yoke and to her, marriage was the solution. Tony knew he would never wed her and his protests that he could not afford to get married were drowned out by her going on about the inheritance that would come from her deceased maternal grandmother. She was already researching the kinds of business they could get into. Some of Tony's friends were in the Navy and it began to look like a good idea to Tony. Since the United States was at war he knew he would be drafted anyway. One week after his nineteenth birthday Tony enlisted in the Navy. His mother's hysteria was mild compared to Sylvia's wrath. She cried, she screamed, she threatened and she even did a bit of pummeling. Tony remained fairly calm and he simply told her he would be drafted anyway. He had told his parents after the fact, his mother getting hysterical at the news; he told Sylvia Miller about being drafted into the Army eventually and he did not want to be in the Army. He walked her home that night, there wasn't even a goodbye kiss, he never heard from her again; but she had let him know how rotten he was and her words stayed with him for a long time.

He liked life in the Navy and his industrious nature and his habit of being neat and clean about everything would help him advance while serving. On his off time he went out on pass with his mates; drinking and woman chasing seem to have top priority and he was introduced to brothels by the 'old timers' in his group. Even with prostitutes his old problem prevailed and his only satisfaction was with oral sex. He never confided in anyone and he felt very inadequate in his inability to perform. One hooker suggested that he might want to try it with a guy and he was very angry with her. He stormed out of the room; forgetting about the sex . . . he just got drunk.

Tony put four years in the Navy and came out in one piece; in good health and with money he had saved. He never threw his money away foolishly, and while he was in the service both of his parents had died. His father went first, the victim of a blood clot. The following year his mother died; Tony felt she just could not make it without her husband; the only man she had ever loved. He was surprised at the amount of money they had left him; he never dreamed they had saved so much. Another surprise he got was that they did not own the house they lived in; they had rented it all those years! They never talked about finances in front of Tony; if there ever were any difficulties, he was not made aware of them. His uncle had power of attorney and took care of all the details. Tony had been given leave to go home for the funeral but he did not have to get involved with funeral arrangements. He was an only child and his parents loved him more than he realized. They had made it possible for him to open his bar business.

Tony had a small apartment four blocks from his bar. It was a short walk but he welcomed it after so many hours indoors. Sometimes he walked home along Third Avenue; he wouldn't readily admit it to himself but he was well aware that at that hour of the morning gay guys cruised the area subtly offering oral sex. This was his secret outlet; a guy would make a gesture and Tony would nod his head in agreement then, in some secluded spot, he was satisfied. It was impersonal; without involvement, often without a word. He didn't consider himself a homo; it was an enjoyable convenience that did not complicate his life. And most certainly the price was right! But there was one guy, a customer who came to his bar and, over time, had gotten to Tony's core; he loved Brian McHugh. He would not allow himself to feel it was a sexual thing; he loved to give him a hug or touch him in some superficial way. After all; he was Italian! Brian was special.

"Who the hell is coming?" Jerry Foley demanded of Tony.

Tony had lowered the hinged section of the bar, placed a bar stool there and cleaned an already clean ash tray. After putting a place mat and a cocktail napkin in front of the stool he began to assemble a lethal-looking martini.

"This is my ten o'clock reservation, Jerry," he spoke down his nose, "a real gentleman; maybe a bit too cultured for you."

He laughed devilishly as he poured the drink over the ice. The *reservation* walked in and took the seat as though it was his living room.

"Hi, Tony, how goes it?"

The smile was genuine and though meant for Tony it did not exclude Jerry. Jerry felt he had also been greeted. It was a pleasant feeling and Jerry had to admit this guy had personality.

"Top of the evening to you, Brian." Tony smiled in return.

"You make a piss-poor Irishman, Tony; stay the Sicilian that you are."

Jerry was trying to be funny and Tony laughed; half-heartedly. Brian was not amused; at first he thought Jerry was attractive; now he appeared crude.

"Oh," from Jerry, "are you Irish?"

"Is he Irish? Have you looked at that face? Tony was incredulous.

Jerry made an attempt to open his eyes very wide in a mock examination of Brian's face, but after drinking most of the day, they didn't open very wide.

"Ye-e-e-s, I guess you could say he qualifies." Jerry was grinning.

Tony filled Jerry's shot glass and put a head on his beer. Then he moved down the bar, checking the needs of his customers, making pleasant small talk as he went. It was a close relationship he enjoyed with his customers.

Jerry leaned into the bar, he felt good. He drank a lot but he could handle it and he did not forget to eat; when you drink a lot and don't eat you are headed for trouble. He was naturally curious and being a detective on top of that just intensified his need to know. Brian tweaked his interest; one thing you learn about asking questions . . . you invite being questioned in return. Jerry did not like people to know he was in police work. It seemed there was always a change in demeanor when people became aware of his job.

"Tony was telling me what a nice guy you are, Brian, and I agree with him; on top of that, you have class, a nice kind of class, not snooty class." The boiler makers had lulled him into a cozy, uninhibited state; he added, "I just met you tonight and I've really enjoyed your company."

Brian didn't know Jerry Foley; he had just paid him a big compliment.

"Did Tony say I had class? That's a nice compliment, but somehow I don't like the word. Well, at least he had something good to say; he can be pretty critical of people sometimes."

"Oh, he thinks a lot of you; before you came he fussed around getting your drink ready. I even asked him who was coming."

"Well, I like Tony a lot. I come here quite often directly from work and have a few drinks and relax; sometimes I have supper while I'm here; his food is simple, but it's good."

Jerry's curiosity finally won over; "What do you do, Brian?"

"I'm a hairstylist."

Jerry flinched inwardly; "this guy is a hairdresser!" His thoughts raced on; "he must be a faggot! Aren't they all faggots?"

"What's your line, Jerry?"

"I'm a detective;" his voice was flat; "Vice Squad."

"Oh boy;" Brian said, sympathetically; "you get the seamy side of life."

"Sometimes it gets me very fucked up; please pardon my language."

"I think I've heard just about everything and survived."

Brian didn't like the tone of his voice. Jerry felt betrayed; he had warmed up to Brian readily, but if he was a faggot! He was drunk now; it didn't show, but he was and his reasoning was affected.

"I've got to go." Jerry stood up; he took his leave saying; "Be good."

"Good night, Jerry." Brian said to his back.

Tony returned to Brian and asked; "What blew Jerry out?"

"He just said he had to go."

"Probably heard the call of the wild and went to find a broad. He's got quite a rep with the ladies . . . and he gets it for free!"

"He's a good-looking guy." Brian commented.

"I've never seen Jerry get chummy with any of the guys in here. Not like he did with you. It must be a secret society you Irishmen have." They both laughed.

Brian smiled, "I don't know how secret it is." He continued; "I like his sense of humor and he has a great laugh. He's quick and it's fun to get a rise out of him." Brian meant what he said.

"Did he tell you he was a cop?"

"Yes; a detective."

"Oh, excuse me, I didn't mean to demote him!" Again; they laughed.

"Are you hungry, Brian? "I've got some meatballs and sauce warming in the kitchen; you need something to soak up that gin."

"You won't find me refusing your cooking, Tony."

He went down the bar and checked everyone's drink; then he disappeared into the kitchen. He returned shortly with two platters and some napkins. He would eat with Brian.

"Gino," he called to one of his regulars. "See who wants a hero and fix 'em up." Tony took Jerry's seat; "Sorry to disturb you, baby, but I can't eat standing up."

Brian grinned at him; getting a kick out of the unnecessary apology.

"Welcome aboard!"

They ate in silence; Tony guardedly studied Brian's face. He had dark curly hair, cut on the short side; no hippy crap here, and big blue eyes that seemed to have a touch of sadness. His smooth skin was always clean-shaven and that knock-out smile completed a very nice picture. There was a special presence about him, a kind of dignity that was not stuffy or stiff. Brian looked younger than his thirty-six years; he would always have that boyish appearance. He rarely used profanity and Tony loved his company; he was drawn to Brian and Brian was oblivious to it. Most people reacted to his charm and always treated him nicely; he was accustomed to that and he did not feel that Tony gave him special treatment. The general intercourse he had with his clients, elegant, wealthy ladies, primarily, was gracious and mannerly and very pleasant; he tried to treat everyone the same way. His clients doted on him and his co-workers liked him and respected the high quality of his work. It never made him a Prima Dona. Being the oldest of six children also had humbled him a bit. He had been brought up in a home of much hospitality and family involvement; his father had many proverbs . . . self-composed, and used them to lay down the law. His favorite was; "*if you live here; you work here . . . your Mother is not your servant!*" There were no male or female chores; everyone helped with everything and that was why Brian excelled at cooking. Sometimes he resented his father's thumb, as most teenagers do, but his mother had ingrained respect for their father in all her children; she had a sweet, cheerful disposition, but it was not a good idea to get her riled up! When he was thirty years old his parents took their first plane trip to Ireland; they were both killed when the plane crashed; it tore the heart out of him. It brought the family even closer than they had been; ironically, as they married, they were spread out all over the country and as they had children it became difficult and expensive to get together. Brian was the only one unmarried and he knew he would stay that way. He did, however, write a lot of checks and his nephews and nieces loved their Uncle Brian. His life-style was naturally very different from his siblings; while he skied in Aspen or Austria, they took their kids to local parks.

Closing the door of his apartment Brian groaned aloud; "God, I'll be a mess in the morning; why the hell didn't I get out of there?" He knew well the answer to that question; Jerry Foley. The story of Brian's life; being attracted to men who liked woman; it was a stone wall he kept banging his head against; never seeming to learn. Men that he could have, readily, didn't interest him. His dream was that he would meet *him* someday; and not in a gay bar. Brian went to gay bars occasionally to meet up with friends and gab away the hours about very important nothings! It was fun for a while; but it got stale quickly. He would rather go to Tony's and meet guys like Jerry; even though it didn't go anywhere at least he had the pleasure of the company he liked. There were a few times Brian was surprised to learn that some of these guys were bi-sexual and they ended up at his place. It did not happen often and it was almost always a one-night stand, but it was nice; and it was what he felt comfortable with. Occasionally there might be a call back, sometimes months after a first encounter, and probably at one in the morning; Brian's door was open. He had never had a bad experience; the men were happy to be in his company and treated him fondly. Being with him gave them a much needed release; most of them were married . . . because society said they must marry; but as they got older the homosexual side became more dominant and many wives thought they had married alcoholics who couldn't drink at home; what they needed was not to be found at home.

It was after three a.m. as Jerry made his way along a seemingly deserted street. He had quite a buzz on; no staggering though, he could handle a lot of liquor. In the doorway of a closed store two young girls hung back in the shadows.

"What are you two doing in there?" His voice was firm with authority.

"We ain't doin' nothin' wrong." They knew it was the 'fuzz'.

"One of you come out here." They had to comply . . . this was nothing new. The little blond moved very slowly toward him.

"Move it!" He hissed through his teeth; what are you up to?"

"Nuthin' we're waitin' for our boyfriends; they're late."

"Don't bullshit me; boyfriends! He said with much scorn, "Johns is more like it!"

She stopped about two feet from him and then edged a little closer. She was accustomed to rough treatment, she had no fear for her person; she was trying to figure out his game.

"Tell your friend to beat it," he whispered to her; she knew what he wanted; and she was willing. The blond obeyed his command and the friend understood. He backed her into the entryway he took her hand and put it on his shield.

"You know what that is?

"Yes." Her voice was barely audible. He pulled down his zipper, still holding her hand. "I know you know what this is . . . kneel down."

Tony closed at two a.m. now, at three he was ready to go home. Everything was shining and ready for tomorrow; taking the money he went to the freezer in the kitchen and unwrapped a frozen turkey breast. After inserting the wrapped money inside the breast he re-wrapped the breast and put it back in the freezer. Exiting from his back door he secured two padlocks in addition to the door locks. He started his walk home and he re-ran the events of his day as he went. Brian had seemed a little dejected as he said goodnight; despite the smile and thank you for the food, he was certain that he hadn't said anything to offend him; he wasn't so sure about that lug Jerry. They appeared to enjoy each other's company, though. When you have liquor in the equation it changes everything. It was a short walk to his apartment; he was home in fifteen minutes. As soon as he unlocked his door he eased off his shoes; "oh, God, does that feel better!" he sighed aloud; after regulating a hot shower he stripped off his clothes and hopped in. "The end of a long day," he was still talking aloud; "a long, long day." He reveled in the hot suds; his entire day was cleansed away. Later, bath towel over his shoulder, he entered the living room with a plastic pan of hot water in which he had dissolved a package of Johnson's Foot Soap. Settling into his lounge chair Tony put some mellow music on the radio and gingerly eased his feet into the water. From the drawer in the end table he took out a joint; his only bad habit. A habit that he was gradually weaning himself away from. For two reasons: he knew it was bad for his health and he knew he was giving criminals money. It also gave him a craving for sweets and he watched his weight closely; the extra calories he could do without. He was in good shape and he intended to stay that way. Letting his mind just wander his thoughts settled on Brian; here in this quiet place he could admit to himself that he had a physical yen for him. Brian was not in the category of his quick stops on the avenue; Brian was someone worthwhile.

For the past year Jerry had been living with a sassy old lady named Nora Hennessy. She had been at the station with a complaint and, though she wasn't his case; he was taken in by her moxie and offered to see her home. He had acquired a second-hand car. He had just finished a tough all-night shift made tougher by a hang-over from the night before. They arrived at her house, a tidy wood-framed bungalow, and were standing at the front door.

"Let me get me keys out," she said, more thinking out loud than to him.

He made the offer; "Give them to me; I'll open it."

"I guess I'm able to open me own door!" Her independence bristled.

Nora was cut with many facets and indeed, she was a jewel. They chatted for a while and she eventually invited him to stay for beef stew. After consuming the two bottles of beer Nora had; Jerry went out for a couple more, the liquor he bought was for Jerry; Nora drank beer only.

He awoke about four a.m. At first he wasn't sure of his whereabouts; he knew he wasn't home. Still in half a stupor he sat up and rubbed his hands, gently through his hair. Gently, because that head was hurting. His shoes were off and he was covered with a fresh-smelling blanket.

"Christ, I'm still at Nora's!" He moaned aloud. Nora heard him.

"Are ye awake?" She spoke in a soft voice, sensing he was hung over.

"Awake yes; alive no." She smiled at his humor.

"I'm heating the coffee; you wouldn't drink it at supper time."

"Oh, don't bother, Nora, let me get the hell out of your way." He was embarrassed.

"It's no bother; I'll join you. I'm awake now and there's no way I'll go back to sleep."

They had coffee and English muffins with orange marmalade. They lit cigarettes; he was surprised that she smoked.

"You sure can talk, lad, and you sure can drink!' Her eyes rested on him.

"You're no slouch, sweetheart; do you keep all your men overnight?"

"Only when they make lovely promises; like you do."

"Promises; what promises?"

"Like fixin' up me back bedroom and painting and all the wonderful things you can do when you're in your cups!"

"I'll take the fifth," he smiled.

"You drank the fifth!" She banged the table.

"If I made you a promise; I'll keep it.

"You also said you'd rent it from me 'cause you're miserable livin' alone."

He stared at her and wondered how much he had said to her.

"Would you like to have a boarder?" His tone was serious.

"I'd like to have *you* for a boarder; but you better not be a slob! I'm nobody's maid."

He moved into her home and into her heart. She had never had a child; but she certainly married one. All her married life Nora had catered to an immature fool; after his death she wondered why she had stayed with him.

* * *

Jerry let himself in quietly, Nora would not awaken; she was accustomed to his crazy hours. He undressed and went to the bathroom; after relieving his bladder he turned to the sink and washed his privates. "You're wearing lipstick," he whispered to his prized possession, "that's not nice!" He grinned at his reflection in the mirror. A shower would have been his preference; but that might wake Nora. Jerry had come to love Nora; this was a new experience for him and it was a genuine feeling he had for no one before. This was how he came home on many occasions; it was how he got by, although society had quite a different impression of his persona.

Some of his fellow officers were discussing him before his arrival one morning; it was Tom Nesbitt, his partner on the job who was speaking.

"With Nora to fuss over him at home and so many broads willing to get under him just about anywhere; we'll never be able to get him married off into slavery like the rest of us!"

There was a chorus of laughter and heads nodding in agreement. At that moment Jerry walked in, red-eyed and chewing Cloret gum.

"Is it a private joke or can anyone have a laugh?" His eyes were very red.

"You look adorable, darling," ribbed Tom.

"Lay off! I met some married dame whose husband was out of town; God! She drained me dry. I don't even want to talk about it."

He fervently wished it were true. Making up these stories did not seem like a lie to him; he had an image to live up to and he preferred his image to what he was really all about. They were outside now, he and Tom,

"I think I'll drive," smiled Tom, "self-preservation first! We have to sniff out some people who are in the 'white powder' business."

"Lead on." Jerry was docile.

Just about five that afternoon he returned home. No stops. He was aching for a beer but if he hit some gin mill he would be off and running. An uneasiness had nagged at him all day. It wasn't the liquor; Brian had surfaced in his thoughts and he had regrets about branding him a faggot off handedly. Jerry had avoided going back to

Tony's because he knew he had acted badly. *Innocent 'til proven guilty*; how many times had he heard that! It rolled around in his mind.

"Hello, sweetheart," Forcing himself to be jovial, he kissed Nora on the nape of her neck. "I'll have a beer," he grinned, "and you can tell me all about your day."

He never discussed his job with Nora; very early in their relationship he realized it upset her to learn of the filth he dealt with on his tour of duty.

"My day is just like Eleanor Roosevelt's, "she quipped; "and I've told me secretary to hold all calls." She hugged him and they laughed.

"It sure smells good in your office; my belly is growlin'!"

"It's just pot roast," she said, modestly.

"Just pot roast; how about heavenly pot roast, my dear?"

Her heart swelled with pride; how she loved to do for him!

Nora had cooked for various well-to-do people for many years. By word of mouth she had built up a clientele of some very well-known people; mostly professionals and all of them childless. Their schedules varied; for some she prepared breakfast, others might require just lunch, and then there were the dinner people. She didn't like to work full time for the same people; Nora never got into their private lives; her own was unhappy enough. Although she didn't plan her routine to make more money; she made quite a bit more. Christmas gifts from her busy clients were generous checks; they didn't have time to shop! Nora worked hard six full days a week; Sunday was for Mass and catching up on her own work and unfortunately, seeing what her worthless husband was up to. He was always seeing important people; who evidently conducted their business in sleazy bars and who might properly be called bookies. When he did manage to get some kind of work Nora never saw a dime from him. Early in their marriage a friend's nephew convinced her to take out a good-sized life insurance policy on him; good advice which she heeded and it would be the only time he gave her anything.

Nora had one couple that she prepared dinner for three times a week. Clifford Haley was a stock broker and Diane, his wife, was an attorney. Though Nora did not become involved, personally with clients, the Haleys were of Irish decent and they were warm, down-to-earth people. They became interested in Nora and very often would have their martinis in the kitchen as she prepared dinner. She always had attractive, delicious hors d'oeuvres and though invited, she never drank with them. Over time Clifford asked her if she was planning for her retirement, financially, Diane realized from sketchy replies to her ordinary questions, that Nora's husband was a non-provider. He gained her confidence. Nora admired him a great deal, and he worked out a plan that accumulated far beyond her expectations. Nora was worth a lot more than she showed. The Haleys had put five thousand dollars to what Nora was able to spare for her plan; they thought that much of her. Nora cooked for them for twelve years; when Diane told her of the divorce she broke down and cried.

"I never noticed a thing at all," she wept. They had a good cry together.

"I suppose you would call us 'civilized people,' Nora,"

When they were saying their final goodbyes; it was only Diane, she never saw Clifford again. Nora hugged Diane;

"I'll only say one thing; he'll be sorry."

Nora had finished in the kitchen; shooing Jerry and his offer to help into the living room. She was surprised to see him still there, slouched in a chair; his long legs stretched out in front of him.

"You're so quiet I didn't know ye were here."

"Just tired, Nora," He sat up and stretched.

"You really should take one night of rest, Jerry,

"You're right, gorgeous." He sighed and ran his hand over his chin; "I think I'll shower and shave."

"To be sure; and then it will be out the door and hooray!" The look she gave him said it all. She didn't like the way he looked. "You should take a night's rest, Jerry;" she scolded him good-naturedly; "You burn those candle ends too much!"

"No," He shook his head from side to side, close to her; "I don't think so."

"We'll see;" she picked up the paper he had brought in. "We'll see."

Nora went to her room to watch television about seven o'clock; she didn't hear him go out at eight; but she felt she was alone.

Tony saw Jerry come in the door and he asked two men to move over so he could give him a seat at the end of the bar. Jerry did not like to sit in the middle of the bar.

"Well, hello Studs; should I alert all the fair ladies in town that you're here and all polished up and ready to roll?" Tony was grinning as he put a coaster in front of Jerry. He did it with a flourish.

"Hi Tony," Jerry replied in a low voice.

"Very low-keyed, baby; considering how glossy you look!"

"Just fresh from the shower; you're obviously not use to clean people." He raised his brows looking down the bar at the pot-pourri of humanity collected there.

"Easy on my clientele;" Tony whispered, "they're very sensitive."

Now he raised a laugh out of Jerry. Most of Tony's customers were regulars; some every night, or day, depending on their habits and their jobs. It was their place to be who they wanted to be. The conversations went from broads, to sports, to money and, in season, politics; the sound level went from quiet to loud . . . depending on how much liquor was consumed. It was a warm atmosphere if you were a regular; a chance customer dropping in for a drink would be warmly welcomed by Tony; the regulars would consider it an intrusion. Jerry always talked with Tony; those in close proximity were given a nod in greeting, if he caught their eye. Once in a while he might find someone he felt comfortable with, as he did in Brian's case; then, especially if he had consumed enough alcohol he was congenial. When it was learned he was a detective most of the regulars were content to *leave him be.*

"Eight to four tomorrow?" Tony asked, referring to the hours he worked.

"Off tomorrow; it's my swing." Meaning he had three days off.

"Nipping off to Bermuda, maybe?" Tony loved to needle Jerry, good-naturedly.

"Margaret Truman wants me to come over and give her a voice lesson,"

"Somebody should!" quipped Tony. They laughed together.

Jerry stayed on beer for about two hours; "pour me a shooter with that," he told Tony as he was getting him a fresh beer.

"Your wish is my command," said Tony as he put the shot glass in front of Jerry. "I am at your service."

"Go pat your cash register," Jerry teased him about the money he made.

"That's my love; see how she shines!"

"What are you doing with all your money? Buying up Rome?"

Tony smiled. *You should know,* he thought, *not Rome; the Hamptons!*

Years ago on a fishing trip to Montauk, Long Island with two of his regulars; they stopped at a real estate office where one of the guys was buying a lot. Tony went in with him and became interested in the process. He did not know you could buy a lot with some cash down and monthly payments for the balance. Tony had a fair amount of cash he took out of his business that he forgot to tell the IRS about. He kept it in his apartment and was uneasy about that after it became a substantial amount; this seemed like a good place to put his money. He liked the agent he had been talking to and walked out with his card and some brochures about the *East End*. That was the beginning of his accumulation of land; his secret pre-occupation. He kept in touch with the broker he liked and over the years they became friends and Tony was well rewarded with being the first to be offered exceptionally good deals. Eventually the agent sent him copies of his maps and most of the transactions were done by telephone until the finalizing required meeting in person. By taking his broker's advice Tony learned to stop hiding his money; he became aware of what tax shelters were all about and he was on his way to making real money. His customers assumed he had more money than they; he was their banker, lender, lecturer and sympathetic listener. Tony's Bar was a closely knit society and none of them wanted to be excluded from the *membership* . . . it was part of their existence. There was one particular customer who had become a close friend and confidant; Gino Merino helped with the general running of the place. He was especially good in the kitchen and though the menu was simple; the quality was that of home cooking.

Tony turned his attention back to Jerry.

"Has your friend been in?" Jerry asked the question in an off handed way. "Who?" Tony replied in kind.

"Your *reservation* customer; I forget his name." He asked himself why he was lying.

"You mean Brian? No, I haven't seen him; we must have wrecked him with those martinis, he doesn't drink that many; ordinarily. He works from nine to nine on Thursdays and the salon is like a zoo on Fridays; he's probably home; taking oxygen!"

* * *

Brian looked at the clock; it was twenty after five.

"If she doesn't let me cut that hair shorter she's not getting any more Friday afternoon appointments; one hour under the dryer and she's still not dry!"

"Easy love, she'll hear you; you're her little genius, you know, you must not spoil the illusion!"

Eleanor teased him; they had worked together for five years and like most people who knew him; she was very fond of him. He was a real friend. When her husband was terminal with cancer her family and friends were wonderful. Brian was incredible! He was there and he was there and she didn't have to think when he was around. So many little things that he would simply take care of and big things, as well. When her husband died Brian was a rock; she needed him then; and she leaned.

When the apartment next to his became available he convinced her to sell her house on Long Island and move next to him. He had always hated the fact that she had to commute back and forth to work, spending hours every day in that mad crush. Being in a whole new environment would also be a good thing for her; too many memories and agonies were in that house. She and Ted, her husband, hard a warm, loving relationship; it would be hard for her to find a replacement; she was a young forty years old and childless. Her life seemed to be over. As time went by she dated; if a man attempted to touch her affectionately, she froze. Needless to say they didn't call again. Her best evenings on the town were with Brian; they both loved piano bars and they never ran out of conversation. Eleanor knew that Brian was gay but she never quizzed him about it. If he wished to tell her anything, she listened; if he seemed to want her advice or opinion, it was forthcoming. None of their co-workers ever made any derogatory remarks about him to her; they would have deeply regretted it if they had.

Brian didn't really care for *gay bars* but there was one he liked and he had friends who frequented the place. It was called 'Goosies' and once in a while he took Eleanor there and she enjoyed the repartee that was very witty and sometimes quite bawdy. Eleanor took it all in stride and she was very well liked. She received advice on how to use make-up and how to do her hair. She found this very amusing since she made her living giving just such advice!

"I'll see if she's done." Eleanor smiled at him.

"Stick a fork in her!"

"Come over here Lydia; I'll take your rollers out."

"Where is my master? She cooed.

"Having a cup of coffee; he needs a hypo of caffeine to get ready for the unveiling."

"He's our Michelangelo, Eleanor."

"Indeed he is!" Eleanor could hear Brian's '*my God*' from inside.

"Is she really gone?" Brian had finally finished with Lydia.

Eleanor was laughing; "well the perfume certainly lingers on!"

"Lingers? The wallpaper is going to peel off!"

"Darling, it wasn't a total loss; that was a ten spot I saw her put in your little pocket; wasn't it?"

"Oh; she's good there's no doubt about that!"

"You looked a little drawn all day; if I had the time I would have warmed the cream of chicken soup!"

They laughed knowingly; cream of chicken soup was his hangover cure. She had heated a can or two for him over the years.

"I was out a little late last night."

"Where?" She knew she could ask.

"I went to Tony's bar; and maybe it was a mistake."

"Come home with me; I have meatballs and sauce made with my own two hands while you were out dissipating."

"Sounds good to me; can I bring something with me?"

"Just your gorgeous self; I'll make you a nice martini."

"You really know how to hurt a guy, don't you?"

"A little bit of the hair of the dog, darling!" She stressed the *r* in darling.

After Eleanor had moved next door to him Brian got the bright idea to have a connecting door put in. There was a perfect spot since each apartment had a small foyer back to back. They could hop back and forth and look in on each other; but never without a knock. "We can't keep locking and unlocking all our front door locks when we want to see each other," Brian had reasoned. He came in that door now, having gone into Eleanor's place first. He called back to her; over his shoulder,

"A fifteen minute nap and a quick shower and I'll be back for that martini; heat up your balls, mother."

"Pig!" She threw at him.

Eleanor went to the refrigerator and took out a bottle of skin freshener. Getting a small pad of cotton from her bathroom she soaked it in the cold solution and pressed it over her face. "From Heaven," she sighed. The dinner only needed heating up; she busied herself putting together a green salad; then she would make the martinis, Eleanor was quite sure he would skip the fifteen minute nap; it would probably end up in an all night collapse! A luscious cheese cake was in the refrigerator; they would both say it was not on their diets and then they would promptly dig in. Who could refuse New York cheese cake?

"It smells wonderful in here!" He didn't knock; he knew she was waiting.

"You look positively glowing; what miracle are you hiding from me?"

"Four gallons of Visene!"

"Only four gallons did all that?"

"Bitch!" They laughed together and she relaxed for the first time all day.

"Thank God for Saturday and Sunday," Brian groaned; "we need it."

"Does that mean baby stays in tonight?"

"Absolutely!"

"Mother has a smidgeon of doubt."

"A good mother would not be suspicious of her baby."

"This mother *knows* her baby!" And mother turned out to be right.

Brian woke up from nap number two; he always felt a little drowsy after dinner so he had dozed off. The stereo still played soft music. "Eleven-thirty and I am wide awake; I might as well face it; I guess I am going out!" He was talking in a soft voice; if Eleanor was awake he didn't want her to think he had company. The sleep had recharged his battery and that eternal curiosity of what was out there created a slight tingle in his being.

* * *

Tony's Bar was a fairly good walk from Brian's place but it was such a pleasant night and he had a fully charged battery; so he opted to walk. He enjoyed walking along and checking out the shop windows. Some were done so attractively and others were the pits. A friend of Brian's was a window dresser for Lord and Taylor's department store and he was a first class designer; as he would have to be, to work for that company. Brian was gifted with excellent taste and this quality was recognized by his wealthy clientele; they were not about to entrust their crowning glories to someone who would mess them up! Not likely! In a half hour he was arriving at Tony's.

"Here's our boy now," Tony was all smiles;

"George, move over please; we need this seat." He had to make sure Brian had his favorite place. There was a half-full glass of beer in front of the seat next to him and an empty shot glass next to it. He wondered if it was Jerry; he didn't have to wonder for long. Jerry came out of the men's room, half in his cups and feeling good.

"Hi, Brian, how you doin?"

"Good, Jerry, how goes it with you?" A sensation went through Brian and he reminded himself not to be foolish.

"Well, it looks like we survived last night; you look chipper."

At that moment Tony leaned over the bar; "Shall I make a nice martini?"

"Not on your life! Gin and tonic, please, and heavy on the tonic!"

"Coward." Tony smiled as he made the drink.

"You should find a drink that's good for you; then stick to it." Jerry advised.

"Like those boiler makers?"

"This is a smart drink," Jerry insisted."

"Of course," Brian replied; condescendingly.

Jerry went into a discourse on the food value in beer and a few well-placed shots.

"You're not serious?" Brian asked as he finished; "you really don't mean all that?"

"Sure I do;" Jerry came back very positive.

"They are suicide!" Brian reasoned.

"Bullshit!"

"They would kill me, I know that!"

"I'll buy you one." Jerry grinned.

"I'll pass, thank you." Brian half-closed his eyes to express hauteur.

"Tony's right; you are a coward!"

"I'll be alive tomorrow; coward or not."

"You're off tomorrow."

"How did you know that?" Knowing full well it had to be from Tony.

"I'm a detective; I'm supposed to know a lot of things."

"Here you are; complete with a slice of lime. That takes care of your vitamin C." Tony set the drink in front of Brian.

"That's good," Brian commented after his first sip; and very sensible." He looked down his nose at Jerry.

"Coward," Jerry whispered.

When it was about one-fifteen Jerry began to itch; he wanted a change of scenery.

"Let's go somewhere else; I feel like traveling."

Brian was taken aback by the suddenness of his request.

"Where do you want to go?"

He was also trying to absorb the thrill of being included.

"Don't you have any other haunts? Jerry asked.

Brian had a quick mental picture of taking him to Goosies! Of course Jerry's job made him familiar with all the gay bars and many other dives in the city.

"I like Asti's; I like the singing there."

"High-brow."

"It is not," Brian protested.

Jerry nodded his head solemnly; "yes it is."

"You pick a spot; I'm flexible." He passed the buck.

"O.K., come on."

"You guys leavin' me?" Tony showed his disappointment.

He really felt very disappointed. Friday night was busy; he hadn't had much time to kid around with them. Tony came up from the middle of the bar.

"We're gonna hunt up some broads." Jerry gave Tony a knowing look.

Brian felt a sense of panic; he hoped he wasn't in for a big embarrassment.

"Don't try to ruin my prize customer." Tony smiled, but it was an empty smile. He didn't like this development.

Jerry took Brian on a tour of bars; they all knew him well. He was impressed with the free drinks that came their way; not because he was a cop, they just liked him. Brian was included because he was with him. So far there was no mention of 'broads' and Brian had ceased to be concerned about that.

"Jerry, let's go have some breakfast."

He knew Jerry had a lot to drink and so far his driving was good. At least Jerry had eased off the shots and was just drinking beer.

"It's still night time; breakfast is daytime food."

"It would be a good idea to soak up some of this alcohol we're drinking."

"That's a bad idea; I have a lot invested in this buzz and I don't intend to spoil it."

"Famous last words; it is three-thirty in the morning, they're going to close soon anyway." Brian tried to reason with him.

"I can get a drink any time, any day."

"I don't doubt that."

There would be no breakfast in the immediate future.

"You know where I want to go, Brian?"

"No; I couldn't even begin to imagine."

"Jones Beach."

"Jones Beach!" Brian was incredulous; "You're mad, Mr. Foley!"

"This is the middle of May and I want to watch the sun come up over the ocean. I've done it before with a buddy of mine; he didn't think I was mad."

"Seriously, Jerry, don't you think you've had a little too much of your 'high food value' boiler makers to be driving all the way out to Jones Beach?"

"That's why I'm not hungry; will you go with me?"

"If you promise me you will listen to me if I tell you your driving is bad and turn around and head home; I'll go."

"I give you my word." He was serious.

Jerry secured a six-pack of beer from the bartender and they got into his used, but well cared-for car. Jerry drove very well and he was not a speed-demon; that wasn't his mood, he was feeling mellow and also excited because he was going to the beach. Soon they were on the amber-lit Belt Parkway; traffic was light and it was a clear, starry night.

"What a beautiful night," Brian had some enthusiasm about the trip now, "it is so clear; you can see a million stars!"

"Wait until you get to the beach; that's where you really can see them."

Jerry had asked Brian to open a can of beer for him; he sipped it as he drove.

"Have one yourself, he had invited, it will wash out that gin you had."

He teased Brian, good-naturedly, and was not surprised at the polite refusal. They were on the Causeway and almost to Jerry's destination; Parking Field Nine, located right on the ocean-front. They pulled into the large parking lot and parked, facing the Atlantic Ocean. It was low tide; the small waves were dropping gently on the shore. A few cars were scattered throughout the lot; lovers, no doubt, hoping the troopers were 'cooped up' and catching a little nap.

"Let's get out and walk along the beach," Jerry suggested.

He opened a fresh beer and held one up toward Brian.

"No thanks," was the expected reply.

Taking off their shoes and socks and rolling up their pants, they walked the edge of the shore where the breakers ended. The salt water felt cold, at first, but was invigorating as they got use to it.

"I'm surprised that I can see so well, even though it is night time; what's left of it."

Brian thought they might need flash lights. It was really invigorating and he felt his lungs expanding.

"Your eyes adjust to the dark and the white sand is in sharp contrast to the water; unless you're feeble, walking is no problem." He spoke with authority and Brian found it amusing.

Down along the horizon dawn was beginning to fuse its light with the starry night. It happened slowly at first, then, as if controlled by some master rheostat, it spread along the horizon in the East. They had arrived back where the car was parked.

"Is that ever beautiful!" Brian's voice was full of awe.

"We need a fresh beer." Jerry said, dryly.

"I thought you wanted to watch the sun come up?" There was a hint of impatience in Brian's tone.

"Not without a beer." They sat in the car and eventually dozed off. Jerry awoke first; "It's ten after seven."

He made sure he spoke loud enough to wake Brian.

"What about that breakfast you were talking about?"

"Good idea," Brian stretched his arms out; "this sea air makes you hungry."

While they were sitting in the car, before they dozed off, Jerry had begun talking about his time in the Army. He barely touched on the combat rigors preferring to relate some of the outrageous things he and his buddies used to do. These were the memories he cherished; his animation and the slight smile that turned up the corners of his mouth added much interest for the listener. He would have gone on for a lot longer than he did but, boiler makers eventually take their toll and sleep takes over.

"I know a good diner that's on our way back; how does that sound to you?"

"I love diners," enthused Brian; "especially if they are run by Greeks!"

"Trust me; this is as Greek as you can get!"

They laughed, and suddenly coffee seemed like a better idea than beer; even to Jerry.

It was almost eleven o'clock when Jerry pulled to the curb in front of Brian's apartment. As he got out of the car he thanked Jerry and waved him off; Eleanor was opening a window and did a double-take. "Well, well," she was talking aloud, "I certainly have to hear what this is all about." Going into her kitchen she prepared a pot of coffee and got ready for the inquisition. It was one flight up and Eleanor was standing in her open doorway.

"This way, Sweetie," she beckoned; "I don't care how exhausted you are; I have to hear about this! Can't you smell the coffee?"

She wore an emerald green housecoat, no make-up and her Titian red hair was brushed loosely from its usual coif. Eleanor had a lovely face; high cheek bones, a fair complexion and warm, brown eyes with a lot of sparkle!

"We just got back from Jones Beach!" He said in hushed excitement.

"We?"

She took his hand and led him into her apartment. They sat at the small kitchen table and she poured the coffee; a basket of mini-muffins was on the table.

"Sit yourself down, darling," she cooed. "Don't keep me in suspense! I'm bursting with curiosity!"

He filled her in on all the details and she was as excited as he. Some concern for her friend was forming in her mind;

"This Jerry does not sound gay," she said.

"I'm not kidding myself, Eleanor, Jerry likes to do spur of the moment things and I happened to be next to him. It was company he wanted; it could have been anybody else. He was also full of boiler makers. I enjoy his company so much, I saw no reason not to join him; at first I thought he was crazy to want to drive all the way out to the beach, but it turned out to be a really invigorating trip. Watching that sun rise out of the ocean was spectacular!"

Eleanor had a few questions but she didn't think this was the time for them; besides, the blue eyes across the table were at half-mast and it was time to send him off to dreamland before he laid his head down on her table. At least he wasn't carrying on as if he had met the love of his life. She shooed him off to bed with a kiss and a hug. She said; "Go to your crib!"

As tired as Brian was it didn't keep him from taking a shower and getting rid of the sand he had accumulated at the beach. Sand at the beach was beautiful; on hard wood floors it was a disaster. He was asleep before he hit the pillow.

Eleanor finished sprucing up her place and stood looking out her window; she was bored. Sighing, she went to the phone and dialed a familiar number.

"Hello, Edith, it's Eleanor; how are you? I've got an itch to go out for dinner tonight and if you're free I'd love to have your company."

"I hate to admit it but I haven't a damn thing planned. I have not heard a word from Jim; the louse."

Edith had a 'thing' for married men; getting herself involved and then making demands that a married man could not comply with and then the inevitable break-up and all that went with it. Turmoil was a good description for Edith.

"Do you feel in the mood for a little Italian?"

"Eleanor, when would I not be in the mood for an Italian? Not necessarily a little one!" Eleanor laughed at her quick humor.

"It's a 'yes'; I could use some good company and I promise you I won't bore you with any gripes about Jim."

"Wonderful; come to my place about seven and we'll have a drink and decide which establishment will have the pleasure of two New York knockouts!"

"Honey, when they see a gorgeous red head and a perfect silver blond make their entrance they won't dare bring us a check!"

Edith was a hair colorist and an expert in her field; Eleanor's red-blond Titian locks were created by Edith. Eleanor had always been low-keyed about hair color and she was mighty nervous when Edith told her what she wanted to do to her hair. Knowing Edith's talents she closed her eyes and was thrilled with the results.

"I'll see you at seven, dear," Edith hung up.

Shortly after seven Edith arrived. She was wearing a pale blue suit over a soft peacock blue blouse; her silver blond hair was smartly arranged in an up do; she looked stunning. Eleanor greeted her and commented on how lovely she looked.

"Edith; you're a knockout!"

"Thanks love, how about that drink? I'm not counting calories tonight!"

Having a tendency toward plumpness; she had to watch her weight constantly.

"Once in a while a girl has to be good to herself."

"Follow me and name your poison, darling, I don't have the *Heinz fifty-seven Variety*; but what I have can cause you enough trouble."

They enjoyed a couple of drinks and decided to go to Armando's for dinner; that is, Edith decided. *Every waiter in the place is handsome*; she had cooed. Eleanor could not disagree with her. They had no trouble getting a table and the dinner turned out to be perfect. As they were leaving the restaurant Edith groaned;

"Oh, Lord, I am really stuffed."

"Darling, you didn't miss a course; I was really surprised when you passed up the dessert."

Eleanor was teasing her; she had ordered a salad and an entrée and that was more than enough for her.

"Let's walk a bit," Eleanor suggested.

"Let's walk forever!" Edith added. Twenty minutes later Edith stopped.

"Enough is enough! I'm built for cabs."

"It's early," Eleanor didn't feel like going home; "do you want to leave?"

"No. let's find some place where we can have a brandy and not get raped or arrested for loitering."

"We could go to Tony's; I've been there with Brian a few times, it's not fancy but Tony is a doll and we could have a drink in peace."

"I don't mind being swept off my feet if I like the broom; I think you know I'm not exactly unavailable."

A cruising taxi stopped quickly; he knew a good tip when he saw one. They were at Tony's in a trice; Edith sighed, "Oh Lord."

"It doesn't look elegant," Eleanor explained, "but it's homey and Tony is a gentleman."

They entered and Edith realized there were very few women present; a big plus;

"Law of Averages," she smiled at Eleanor, "that's good!"

They chose a table in a corner with a good view of the place.

"Now," said Eleanor, "We can see everything that happens from here."

"I dare you to make something happen here;" whispered Edith, "I just dare you!"

Tony saw them come in as did every other guy in the place; he recognized Eleanor but couldn't remember her name. He was annoyed with himself.

"Good evening ladies," his hands held up in a gesture of welcome. "Any friend of Brian's is always welcome here."

"You remembered," she gave him a warm smile; "It's been a while since I've been here; I am sorry to say."

Tony leaned over and kissed her softly, close to her ear;

"Everything but the name," he whispered.

"Eleanor," she whispered back, with the trace of a smile; as though they shared a secret.

"This is my good friend Edith; she works with Brian and me."

"This place has never had this much beauty," Tony beamed; "I'm going to have to chain some of these guys to the bar!"

"Now don't tamper with the clientele, Tony, you'll give them a complex; its better they spend their money here than with an analyst." Edith smiled at him; she liked him. He leaned over and kissed the side of her brow.

"Anyone who looks after my cash register is definitely in the will!"

A sense of well-being eased over them; they ordered two snifters of brandy and Tony walked toward the bar thanking God that someone had given him a gift of brandy; two handsome snifters were included in the box. The glasses were about to have their first baptism! Jerry was at his usual spot at the bar.

"Classy broads," he commented.

"They both work with Brian; they are having an after dinner brandy like many of my high-class customers. I have a lot of people who do that." Tony did not look Jerry's way.

"You dreamer;" Jerry was laughing, "you can't even look at me and say that! Put their drinks on my tab."

"Do you know what you're doing? These drinks are two bucks apiece!"

"Did I ask you how much they were?" Jerry was miffed.

"I just don't want to hand you any surprises, Jerry."

"Okay, Tony, I understand," he was himself again.

Tony served the drinks;

"There's a friend of Brian's at the bar; he would like you to have your drinks with him. His name is Jerry Foley."

"Tony, I don't think we should let him do this;" Eleanor spoke up.

"He wants to Eleanor; he's pretty stubborn, sometimes."

"Tell the gentleman we are delighted, Tony, and when he has his next drink put it on our bill."

Edith stepped in and solved the dilemma for Eleanor.

"We have to think of Tony's register!"

"Thank you, Edith," Tony saluted and Eleanor asked;

"Is this fellow Jerry a detective?"

Tony was taken by surprise;

"Yes he is."

She nodded her thanks.

"Brian has a detective friend?" Edith was very curious; "I've never heard about him!"

"He met him here at the bar and they kind of hit it off well; he's very interesting, according to Brian." Eleanor explained.

"He sounds *very* interesting," said Edith; with raised eyebrows.

"Oh, Edith, it's nothing like that."

"I wouldn't blame any guy for going for Brian; he's very special, he is not a silly queen like some gay guys. We certainly have our share in the hair bending business!"

"It's not that kind of friendship; Brian told me about him!"

Eleanor did not want to pursue the subject any further. Brian was in a class by himself in her book.

"End of story."

Edith knew better than to push this; they chatted for a while about other things and Eleanor was even willing to endure some of the *Jim* saga for a bit as long as she stayed off Brian.

"I came over to say cheers and thanks for the drink."

Jerry was standing there with a shot glass and a glass of beer.

Edith quickly invited him to sit; "Pull up a chair and join us."

Edith liked what she saw; *this is some hunk of man*, she thought. He proved to be delightful company. Eleanor was impressed; she thought he might be on the crude side; but he was witty and charming and quite a gentleman; Edith also thought him charming but, along very different lines. She was not what you would call inhibited and with a substantial amount of alcohol in her well-heated blood; she was ready for action. Jerry was quick to sense this; he liked Eleanor, but he knew where his success would be if it came to sex. Edith was leaning in his direction and Jerry liked those vibrations! An hour passed.

"I think we should call it a night, Edith, it is getting a little late."

"I think we have a Cinderella in our midst." Edith poked Jerry.

"Let me finish my drink, dear." Eleanor gave her a super-sweet smile.

"Of course, dear."

"Finish your drinks and I'll drop you off at your apartments."

Jerry rose and excused himself and headed for the rest room. By the time he returned they had taken care of their bill; Tony refusing to accept the tip that was offered.

He watched them leave; scratching his head.

Out on the street Jerry unlocked the passenger door and like a rush of wind Edith was in the front seat. Eleanor and Jerry exchanged glances and she sat in the back seat after he opened the rear door. Edith gave Jerry directions; she wanted to be sure Eleanor was taken home first. At Eleanor's place Jerry insisted on seeing her to her door; as she unlocked her door she nodded toward Brian's door; "Brian lives in twenty-two."

He made no reply; they were both being very quiet because of the late hour. She opened her door;

"You think a lot of him, don't you?" He was whispering.

"Oh, yes, he's my best friend and he is a real friend."

He went down to his car and who knows what?

As soon as he got behind the wheel Edith moved close to him and rested her head on his shoulder.

"Tired? He asked softly.

"Not at all; you give me all kinds of energy."

She moved her hand along his thigh; there was magic in her knowing touch. Turning her head up to his she locked him in a rousing kiss; there was a growing response in his crotch and her hand found it and then there was a surge of passion. He undid his zipper, the sound was electric; he slid the car seat back as she freed his growing rod from its cage. Edith moaned in appreciation; she knew he had it. "What a man;" she sighed "and what a stud!"

"It's beautiful," she whispered. "You're magic," he gasped as he put his hand on the back of her neck, exerting a gentle pressure. She resisted, slightly, but between the desire and the drink, she really had no resistance. She took him to Paradise with expertise that rivaled anything he had ever had. He drove her home and said he'd walk her up. "Which way?"

The heat of the passion subdued, at least for him; he got out of the car to see her to her door. That is not what Edith was expecting;

they had the appetizer, now should come the entrée. She clung to him as they entered the building and when she opened her door he bent down and kissed her quickly.

"A perfect end to a great evening," he whispered.

"You've got to come in, Jerry! I need you . . . all the way; you can't leave me like this!" She had a strangle hold on him. "You mustn't go!"

"I've had it, babe; between the booze and that beautiful thing in the car I'm done. But it was terrific!"

She tried to drag him into the apartment but he held her at arms length and then, giving her a quick kiss on the top of her head; he was gone.

"I'll call you," he threw over his shoulder . . . he didn't have her number!

Edith locked her door; she was hurt, she felt used; she had been stupid and she was god-damn mad! There is nothing more demeaning than being used! Getting into a hot shower kept her occupied; she wanted to cleanse her body of Jerry Foley; she loathed him! Edith wasn't the type to shrug this off; it would smolder within her and it would never be her fault. The fact that Jerry was so entwined with Brian was a great dissatisfaction to Edith.

Brian came into Tony's about one a.m.

"You missed the party, Brian; they haven't been gone that long."

"What party?"

"Your friend Eleanor was here with a blond named Edith."

"Oh, I am sorry I missed them; they must have gone out for dinner."

"Right on the money; but guess who was the *party boy?*"

"Couldn't I have a drink before I go through the quiz session?"

"Oh, I'm sorry, it's getting near the end of my night; I'm getting old."

"That will be the day!; a gin and tonic, please."

"Comin' up."

He made the drink and placed it in front of Brian; "There you go."

He tasted it and smiled; "really refreshing; well done." Tony pressed him.

"Are you ready with your answer? Can't you see I'm excited?"

"Why don't you end your misery and just tell me?"

"Okay; they got wound up with Jerry, Edith seemed to go for him; Jerry is always interested in a hot broad. He gave them a lift home; I bet Eleanor got dropped off first."

"Edith is a bit on the lusty side; she usually messes up with men."

Brian felt uneasy about the party . . . he didn't really know why.

Tony was giving last call; he needed to give his customers plenty of final notice because they never wanted to go home.

"You take your time, enjoy your drink; I have a lot to do before I get out of here. You can keep me company."

"I'll help you close up; I'm a good cleaner-upper. When my friends invite me to a dinner party they always make sure I stay to the end; so I can help with the clean up. I'm famous for that."

"Some friends; if you help me I'll take you for breakfast."

"You've just hired yourself a busboy."

They laughed and Tony began talking about Jerry and the brandy; he knew he'd get a laugh out of Brian when he said he only had two snifters Brian made a mental note for his Christmas list. Tony was giving final drinks now; this was the end of last call. He picked up Brian's glass Brian raised his hand.

"I don't need another one; I'll start to straighten the chairs and tables."

"Sit still and have a drink; we have time, believe me, they will nurse those last drinks! I should enlarge the place and rent rooms."

It was a little after three when they came out of the bar.

"Where would you like to go for breakfast," Tony asked.

"I know a place called Zum Zum; their food is good and it is an easy walk from here."

"Sounds good; a little walk would be nice."

It was only a fifteen minute walk and the place was really jumping with patrons. The mix of people was fascinating; some were very well dressed, many in jeans, a few were almost undressed. It was a human stew of the contents of the various night spots that were closing for the night. Brian always found this atmosphere very exciting; he liked the contrasts that resulted from the mix. There were rarely any confrontations at this place; the management knew their business. They were lucky to get a table without waiting long; a carafe of coffee was served at once; their order was taken and Brian said they would have time for a cigarette. That translated to *there will be a bit of a wait*. It gave them time to talk in a more relaxed way than at the bar. Their food was served and the wait was just about a cigarette long; not bad considering how busy they were. It was, indeed; a well run place. They finished breakfast without much conversation; both of them were considerate in nature and business minded; they did not want to tie up a table with chit chat. Tony yawned and said; "That hit the spot."

Stepping out into the early morning they both had a feeling of well-being; and also of being tired. Tony had a long, busy day and his body was demanding the feel of a mattress. He didn't want to part with Brian's good company.

"Brian, my place is kind of small, I could only offer you the living room couch but I would feel better if you didn't walk home alone at this hour."

"It's not that far; I'll enjoy the walk." Brian tried to put him at ease.

"There are a lot of creeps crawling at this hour; I don't have to tell you that you've lived in this city long enough to know it."

"Nobody ever bothers me, Tony, I'll be alright."

"Nobody bothers you because you're so ugly; is that it? Come to my place; I can make you comfortable and then I won't be worried. If anything ever happened to you after you stayed and helped me; I'd never forgive myself for letting you go home."

"Okay, Tony," Brian gave in, "there's no reason why I have to be home."

They were at Tony's after the brief walk; Brian looked about the small apartment and it was no surprise it was spotless and neat. *Just like his bar*, thought Brian.

"Would you like a night cap?" Tony held up a glass.

"No thanks, I've just about had it, I'm sure you must be worn out; you've had a long day."

"I can't argue with that; I am bushed."

He began making up the couch with some sheets and Brian stopped him; taking over the chore and ordering Tony to bed. They were both off to sleep; almost as soon as they hit the pillow. Tony went to his room with a "G'night Brian."

Brian awoke with a start, for an instant he was confused; then he remembered where he was. *Two o'clock! My God, I didn't sleep... I died!* Tony was gone; a note invited him to anything in the refrigerator; it ended with *stop around tonight.* He dressed, he would shower at home; he folded the bedding and had a glass of juice; and then he headed home. There was a taxi outside; he hopped in; he wanted to get home quickly.

* * *

Jerry had been out all night. He made a breakfast stop (which consisted of coffee) and it was about twenty of seven on a Sunday morning when he let himself in.

"Just comin' from six o'clock Mass are ye? What a fine boy I have here!"

Nora was on her way to seven o'clock Mass when he entered.

"On your way St. Nora; you have enough religion for both of us."

"Are ye hungry?"

"No, thanks, Nora, I had some breakfast."

"I'm havin' pot roast, if you're stayin' in."

"I'll be here; I'll see you later, Sweetie."

He gave her a kiss on the cheek and remembering Edith's tongue in his mouth, he felt he had sullied Nora. He felt lousy; the shower helped and he piled into bed. Looking at the ceiling his mind drifted back over the evening. *Why am I so fucked up? He asked himself; I should have a girl like Eleanor!* Sleep came, blissfully; without dreams.

Toward the end of the week Brian had a cancellation near lunch time. He offered to pick up lunches for any of his co-workers who wanted take-out food and shortly he was handed a list and money in an envelope. He stepped out into the spring day and was delighted with the brief liberty; it was a rare occurrence. Pearson's was a fast food place with a long counter and a few tables. The take-out was the big thing here and they did a lot of take-out. Brian made his way along the counter heading for the take-out section; he saw Jerry talking to some guys and tapped him on the shoulder saying hello. Jerry blanched and seemed non-plussed;

"Oh, hello there, how are you? Say hello to Eleanor for me." He turned back to his conversation. "He lives next to a red-head I know," he explained to the guys.

Brian was stunned; he moved along the counter like a robot; he had been dismissed! He remembered the night at Tony's when he told Jerry he was a hairdresser; this was the same behavior . . . only a bit worse. He was hurt; he wished he wasn't so fond of this guy. It took some time to get his order and as soon as he settled the bill he headed back to the salon. Out on the street he saw Jerry coming in his direction on the same side of the street; quickly he crossed over and avoided passing him. He sensed Jerry staring at him; he could see that he had stopped. Brian kept his eyes straight ahead and made his way through the crowd; from now on it would be hello Jerry; goodbye Jerry whenever they chanced to meet. A determination that would dissolve with a short explanation.

Eleanor and Edith sat in the day room waiting for Brian and lunch.

"That touch-up has to come off in fifteen minutes; I hope he gets here soon I am past being hungry."

She was acting as if nothing had happened; Eleanor had called her Sunday evening to see how she survived Saturday night and Edith told her she had invited Jerry for a night cap but he took a rain check; Edith was going to leave it all at that. She had had enough of Jerry Foley!

"Here's our delivery boy now," she smiled at her cherished neighbor.

"Don't forget I accept gratuities, girls!"

He sounded more jovial than he felt inwardly. They busied themselves with the food; in their business lunch is an elusive thing and sometimes you don't get to have it at all. A timer rang and Edith jumped up.

"That's me," she groaned.

"I saw Jerry in Pearson's with some guys; probably other detectives, he said to say hello to you." He was not going to mention the off-hand greeting he received.

"That was nice of him;" she had already told Brian how charming and generous he had been; she even mentioned that she was somewhat surprised (and impressed!). Brian had reminded her of his reputation and concluded with *leave him to Edith!* She didn't tell Brian that Jerry had refused Edith's invitation; she also didn't tell him she found Jerry interesting and she also found him attractive!

Eleanor let herself into her apartment; it was a little after five-thirty. The rest of the staff worked until nine p.m. on Thursday but Eleanor had an agreement with Cleo, the manager and she did not work the long shift on Thursday evening. Her co-workers did not resent her being off early. The salon was elegantly decorated with flattering shades of peach, pale blue and silver. Tall, fluted columns were used effectively as accents throughout the spacious establishment. There were twelve employees plus Justine, a full-time maid. The actual owner of the place was a mystery; there was a persistent rumor that placed a wealthy lover of Cleo's as the financial backer of the salon. It certainly never came from Cleo; she was a clam about her personal life. It happened to be fact; not rumor. Cleo lived in a beautiful condominium which she owned; a gift from her lover. It was difficult to guess her age; she was lovely to look at and she kept herself in top condition. That included plastic surgery when required. Her business sense was top-drawer and the salon made a handsome profit on a regular basis. Cleo had no problems!

Eleanor came out of her bathroom in a white, terry cloth robe; feeling refreshed she headed for the kitchen and poured a cold glass of V-8 juice, a favorite pick-me-up. What she would make for dinner was running through her thoughts when her door chimes startled her. *Who could that be?* She hurried to the door, "Who's there?"

"It's me; Jerry Foley."

It was a surprise and a little thrill went through her. She unlocked the three locks and let him in.

"I'll just lock one lock since I have one of New York's finest here." Her smile was warm and genuine; he knew she was glad to see him; he relaxed.

"I know it's not good manners to come without calling but I didn't know your number and I would like to take you out for dinner; if you have the evening free. I'm really sorry for not giving you more notice."

"Why don't we have a drink and discuss it?" She entered the living room.

"I've got mine already; fix one for yourself while I change."

"It will be my first today; you don't know how unusual that is."

"There's a bucket of ice cubes in the freezer," she called to him as she left.

He made his drink and shortly Eleanor was back in an emerald green housecoat that fitted her figure becomingly. Her hair had been brushed and there was a touch of color on her lips. She had retrieved her drink and she sat in the chair opposite to his.

"I live with a sweetheart of an old lady," he began, "and she's always telling me to bring some nice young lady home for dinner and for the first time, I would like to make her happy and bring you home with me. I promise you, Eleanor, you will have the best pot roast you have ever had in your life!"

"Oh," she exclaimed, "absolutely one of my very favorite meals! How can I say no?" Getting up, Jerry showed his delight;

"Does that mean you'll go with me?"

"Yes it does; just give me some time to get dressed, I won't be long."

She arose and went toward her bedroom; he headed for the phone to tell Nora she was having company.

"The first time ye bring somebody here and for *dinner* and ye give me such short notice! Have you no consideration for anybody?"

She was really riled up. He placated her and he assured her no fussing was necessary and told her Eleanor was down to earth and did not stand on ceremony; it ended with him being told not to appear before one hour. He put the phone down with a sigh of relief and a feeling of elation. Nora put her phone down filled with curiosity and excitement and the need to get a move on!

Eleanor came into the living room; she was wearing a two-piece beige suit with a blue satin blouse and beige shoes. She looked lovely.

"You're a knockout in no time," his enthusiasm was genuine and she relished his appreciation.

"Let's finish our drinks," she suggested and he held his up; empty!

"You got me started; I'm your responsibility,"

"I'd rather be in Philadelphia," she replied, archly.

"Let's stop at Tony's for one drink; I want to show you off."

"There is no such thing as one drink at Tony's; you'll get wound up."

"I give you my word, one drink; I want to show you off."

"If you try to have a second drink or if someone buys you one I am getting a taxi! Do you understand me? I didn't get dressed to go to Tony's."

He made a sweeping bow. "You have my word."

They arrived at Tony's; as he held the door for her he asked,

"Bar or table?"

"I don't mind the bar; and we can talk with Tony."

He grinned at her; "that could make me jealous."

"Maybe by the time we sit down you might manage to grow up."

"You play a lot of musical chairs, don't you Tony?" Jerry smiled.

"I'm working on my first symphony," he rejoined laughingly. He turned to speak to Eleanor.

"I'm blinded by all this beauty! But why this beast?"

"I'm working with the humane society, Tony, will you help me?"

Jerry gave her a feigned hurt look and an indignant look to Tony.

"We only have time for one drink, sir; do you think you could take care of us? I hate to say it but we are in a bit of a rush."

"One drink? Are you going to share it?"

"My goodness! You're not only musical; you're comical!" Jerry retorted. Tony felt that Jerry had enough teasing; he turned barkeep and made the drinks they had ordered.

"This place actually gleams," Eleanor commented by way of making conversation; she had also sensed the edge on Jerry's reply. An admiration for Tony's tact arose in her.

"He does most of the work himself; Gino is a friend of his and this place is his second home. He's a big help to Tony; he can even handle the bar if Tony wants some time off. That doesn't happen often; there are other guys who help out, too."

"He's obviously well-liked; you can see it."

"They love him; he's also their bank and general advisor."

One of those moments of pause occurred; neither had anything to say. They just sat there; looking at each other.

Jerry put his hand on hers; "I'm so glad you are going with me. You will love Nora, I promise you."

"She certainly sounds like a delight and it also sounds like she has adopted you."

When he put his hand on hers a sensation went through her that she had not felt for a long time. It thrilled her; and it frightened her. Remembering his reputation her inner spirit was saying; *there had better be a Nora when we get there!*

"She's given me the first real home I've ever had; she doesn't know how much I love her."

Eleanor was taken with the emotion in his voice; she fought the urge to hug him, and that urge gave her cause to think about where she was heading.

Nora was glad she had made the pot roast; it wasn't what she would normally select for *company* but she knew most people loved pot roast. The aroma of the pot roast and the red cabbage filled her kitchen and would have activated the taste buds of the most select gourmets. Raspberry sherbet was for desert; no time to fuss with that. Most girls were always watching their weight anyway. Nora had enjoyed setting the table; it had been a long time since she had used any of the lovely things in her closet and she took a lot of pride in her accomplishments. The people she cooked for always complimented her on the beautiful tables she laid. All the while she was preparing dinner her thoughts kept going back to her guest. Nora was trying to imagine what type of girl she would be. *For the life o' me I can't see where he would meet a nice girl; he spends all his time working or in gin mills! He better not bring some floozie here!*

Eleanor had insisted on stopping to get a bouquet for Nora. Jerry told her that Nora never had flowers and it wasn't necessary. She suggested it might be a nice thing for him to do once in a while. He had a twinge of conscience and shut up. They arrived at Nora's and Jerry opened the door calling her name. Wearing a crisp, pale yellow dress, her lovely white hair brushed to a silvery sheen; she was the Hollywood version of a mother. It was sad that she had never been one. Nora took an instant liking to Eleanor; she greeted them warmly and hugged Eleanor as if she had known her a long time. Jerry knew Nora was not a demonstrative person; he knew the affection was real. It was most certainly mutual and Eleanor was quick to compliment her on her beautiful hair. Nora was quietly vain about her hair and enjoyed being told it was lovely; but she would never admit it. Eleanor sighed; and looked directly at Nora;

"I thought these flowers smelled beautiful; but the aroma from that kitchen is much more appealing!" She handed the bouquet to Nora. "Thank you for inviting me, Nora, career girls don't get many home-cooked meals; especially meals that have the aroma of this one." Nora beamed.

"Bless ye for these lovely flowers; now I can make a center piece for me table, me dinner will be complete after all. No matter how beautiful your dinner things are, if you don't have fresh flowers on your table; your table is not complete. Thank you again, dear, you're very thoughtful. Jerry, take Eleanor into the living room and fix a drink. I have a few things to do. Excuse me, Eleanor dear, I'll be with ye shortly."

Eleanor offered to help but was assured everything was just about ready. Jerry saw to the drinks and Eleanor amused herself admiring the lovely things Nora had. There were a pair of antique ladies chairs that caught her eye; they were exquisitely made and as delicate as crystal. Upon close inspection they proved to be very sturdy; but who would dare to sit on one?

The dinner and the evening were very much enjoyed by all. Jerry made a mental note to bring flowers to Nora at least once a week; he never gave it a thought and when he saw how much she enjoyed them and how pretty she made the arrangement; he wanted to see that pleased expression on her face more often. He gave Nora a very generous rent every month; she protested at first, and then decided to put the money away for him.

"I hate to be the one to say I have to go; but I am a working girl and I have to give these feet their proper rest if I am going to stand on them all day. It has been such a wonderful evening and the dinner so delicious plus the pleasure of your company Nora; it is easy to call it a perfect evening. I hope you will come to my home and let me entertain you some day." Nora was beaming;

"I would love to visit you, dear."

Jerry was surprised; Nora never wanted to go anywhere but church!

"Well, you ladies work out the dates and I'll be happy to be the chauffeur; I want to be sure that I get invited!"

He stood up; he knew Eleanor's work kept her on her feet all day and he knew Nora would not let her help tidy up. As soon as Eleanor offered to help Nora she was assured there was practically nothing to do. They said their goodbyes and Nora gave Eleanor a very sincere hug.

"No hug for me?" Jerry tilted his head, quizzically; Nora laughed.

"No hugs for lugs!"

Jerry started the car and before he made a move he asked her if she would like to stop for a nightcap.

"I can't take the time tonight," Jerry, "I really do want to get a decent night's sleep. Honestly; it has been such an enjoyable evening; anything more would be anticlimactic."

"Well," he laughed, "that certainly sounds final."

"Oh, shut up, you." She poked him in the shoulder and he liked the feeling.

He walked her to her door and made no effort to enter. She did not ask him in and they stood in the doorway saying good night.

"It's been lovely, Jerry, I want to have you and Nora here soon."

Before she could continue he took her hand and looked into her eyes.

"When? I don't want this to be for Christmas."

"Very soon I promise you; if you don't hear from me in five days you can call me and bawl me out. I'll give you my number right now!"

"Three days." He took her face in his hands and gave her a gentle, tender kiss. In almost a whisper he said, "good night," and he was gone.

Locking her locks she gave into a bit of fantasy; could she be falling in love with Jerry? A knock on the connecting door snapped her from these reveries.

"Come in, love," she hugged Brian as he entered.

"Would it be rude to ask you where the hell you have been?" He had both hands on her shoulders, "you look radiant, darling."

"You're going to die when I tell you."

"Kill me," he laughed . . . and kill him she did!

As she relived the unexpected invitation for him and he noticed that she was flushed with pleasure as she went on; he died inside. Brian was well aware that his fantasy for Jerry was pretty far-fetched and could only cause him pain; but that did not stop the dream. Now, this lovely lady he cared so much for was telling him the last thing he wanted to hear. Knowing Jerry's reputation with women *and really only knowing the tip of the iceberg;* he was genuinely concerned for her being hurt; and badly hurt.

She ended by saying what a perfect gentleman he had been all evening and his obvious caring for Nora touched her deeply.

"I'm going to have them here for dinner and maybe you will see he is different when he is not in a barroom."

"Please," Brian held up his hand; "spare me all that! I don't want any part of it! Let me know when you are going to have them and I will go to a long movie!"

"If mother says you come . . . you come!"

He kissed her brow; "I know you're tired; I'll let you hit the hay."

Brian was filled with mixed emotions and he knew he could not sit home. It was almost midnight; he decided to grab a cab and go to Tony's. His morale needed some serious boosting and he was sure that talking with Tony would make him feel better. In ten minutes he was opening the door at the bar and his heart almost stopped! There was Jerry down at the end of the bar where Brian always sat! He had to go there or Tony would be asking him why he didn't sit where he usually sat. This was the last thing he wanted. An uneasy feeling gripped him and he knew he brought it on himself. Taking a stool at the end of the bar sat him looking right at Jerry; who was seated at the corner of the bar, a couple of stools away. Jerry was involved in conversation with the man on his right and he did not look Brian's way.

"Where were you tonight?" Tony had his elbows on the bar looking straight at him. "I made veal and peppers and no Brian!"

"I'm sorry Tony, I should have called you; I fell asleep and when I woke up I just fixed something at home; not as good as your veal and peppers; that is for sure."

"I can warm some up for you; if you're hungry."

"No thanks, Tony, I'll just have a gin and tonic."

Tony began mixing his drink. Brian still felt uncomfortable about Jerry's attitude in Pearsons and he now found himself in an awkward situation. He was honest enough to admit he created this, but he was not going to talk to Jerry unless he opened the conversation. Jerry did that; almost on cue. "Hi Brian," the stool next to Jerry was now empty; his voice was subdued. He knew he had given Brian short shrift that day and he, too, felt uneasy. Brian acknowledged the greeting with a similar *hi* and Tony came with the drink. He smiled; warmly,

"Here you are, sir, can I get you anything else?"

"You can refill mine if you have the time." Jerry twitted Tony.

"I'm on a very tight schedule; but for special customers we make time."

He took Jerry's glass; he was only drinking beer, and went to fill it. Jerry spoke to Brian.

"We had Eleanor at the house for dinner tonight; Nora loved meeting her."

"I know," said Brian, "I talked with her just before I left home."

"She's very fine people, Brian."

"I'm well aware of that; she's my closest friend." His voice was flat.

"She's a real lady; I have a lot of respect for her."

"I'm glad to hear that." In the same flat tone.

"Brian, I think I owe you an explanation about the day we met in Pearson's. I was with other guys from my job and we are watching an employee there; I couldn't explain it to you there; I really couldn't even talk to you. I saw you on the street later; but you seemed to be in a hurry and you headed back to work."

"I wondered what was wrong; I couldn't think of anything I did to offend you."

He grabbed at the explanation so eagerly; it was pathetic. They were soon back at the usual banter kidding with Tony and enjoying their repartee.

"Are you goin' home?"

"I have to, Jerry, Fridays are heavy and I've been here too long as it is."

"Okay."

He said his goodnights and was gone. Brian did the same. He would like to have walked home but it made more sense to take a cab and get the extra sleep. Riding in the cab he thought of Jerry and Eleanor; if they became a serious item it was going to be a difficult thing for him. Well, if it made Eleanor happy that would please him; he knew from experience that he would get over Jerry. He would have no other choice.

Jerry let himself in and went quietly to bed. He stretched out and had a feeling of well-being; he wasn't drunk, he was relaxed and that was unusual. Sleep was just about taking hold of him when it started. Nora had been having coughing spells for the last six months and they were getting worse; especially at night. He could hear the dry hacking and even though she muffled her face with a thick, Turkish towel he could hear her. Laying there he tensed up; it was such a helpless feeling; not being able to help her. He got out of bed and put on his robe; his first one, a gift from Nora. Tapping on her door he opened it slightly and softly called her name,

"Nora, are you alright?"

"Oh, for Hevvins sake; I woke ye!" She was sitting on the bed, her face strained from the spell. "I'm sorry, Jerry."

"Don't be silly, I just got home a few minutes ago."

"I'm goin' to make meself a cup of tea with honey; that will soothe it. Would you like a cup, dear?"

"Yes, thanks, I'll join you."

He didn't want to leave her alone. He didn't like the way she looked. They walked into the kitchen; he made her sit down and he fixed the tea.

"Nora, sweetheart, you have to go see a doctor; I'm going to take you. You've been knockin' off this honey and tea for six months and you're getting worse. I'm worried and I do not want any arguments from you."

"I will, dear, I will."

"Damn right you will; and you're going this morning, with a police escort!"

"I'll have to call and make an appointment; you just can't march in there."

"You just watch me; you won't need any damn appointment."

She was warmed by his attention and care but doctors frightened her. However, she had a feeling that she was going to see the doctor!

"You don't look too boozed up, darlin' your eyes are actually round!"

"Don't try to change the subject, smarty, I'm wise to you!"

The kettle began to whistle and she started to rise; "Stay where you are." He was on his feet and even remembered to pre-heat the pot! He put the honey on the table and they waited while the tea steeped.

"Would you like honey in your tea?" She asked him like a little minx.

"Why not? It's a magic cure-all isn't it? Maybe you should quit the cigarettes" . . . he gave her a sly look.

"Fifteen minutes after you quit, darlin' . . . or even ten minutes!"

"You're impossible," he sighed. He smiled at her, in spite of himself.

He poured the tea waiting until she put the honey in first; her method.

"I hope I'm goin' to see Eleanor again."

"She's going to have us over for dinner soon; she's afraid to cook for you . . . you're such an expert."

"I'd be happy with a hamburger from her."

"That's just what I told her!"

In her heart she felt God had sent her a son and words could not explain the joy he gave her. Taking care of him was automatic for her; he was learning to care for her and it was something new for him; and he knew it was also something very good for him. A nagging worry stirred in him.

Chapter Two

Eleanor was stymied; she wanted to arrange the dinner party but she did not have Jerry's phone number. He unknowingly came to her rescue by calling her; they worked out a Sunday with him checking the complicated schedule he had.

"I don't want to wait until then to see you," he added;

"Let's go to a movie or something you might like to do."

The thought of Jerry sitting at a movie would be very amusing to those who knew him well. If they served beer it might keep him from twitching.

"I'd like that; something that would not make it too late getting home. But, let's not make it a dinner date; it would be easier."

"Give me a day or two; I'll come up with something."

They said goodbye; Eleanor sending her regards to Nora.

She had given Jerry a lot of thought and regardless of his reputation and judging him by how he acted around her she was going to date him if he asked her. Watching his attention to Nora and the affection Nora held for him put her mind at ease.

One day during lunch Eleanor finally told Edith about having dinner at Nora's with Jerry. Edith could not hide her surprise;

"I never thought you would bother with him! He's strictly out for flesh!"

"He was every bit a gentleman; and Nora, his landlady, is an absolute joy. On top of that; she is one fabulous cook! It was a lovely evening." She hoped she didn't overdo it; Edith was staring at her.

"He must have stayed sober." Her anger showed; but it was not at Eleanor. *He uses me then takes Eleanor home to Nora!*

Eleanor didn't mention she was entertaining them; the expression on Edith's face made her think better of saying anything more.

In a few days she received a call from Jerry and he asked her if she would enjoy taking a ride out along the North Shore of Long Island. He mentioned the beautiful estates along the way and the spring flowers would be in bloom.

"Oh! I would love that!" she enthused.

"I have a big surprise for you." He was smiling; enjoying this.

"What is it?" She was excited. "What a silly question!" He said.

"I'll see you Wednesday, bye-bye!"

She was full of curiosity and never had a chance to ask what she should wear . . . and she still did not have his phone number!

Jerry called for Eleanor at exactly five, p.m. She was ready; dressed in a smart sweater set and skirt, comfortable shoes and a short coat over her arm. He escorted her to the street; she sensed his repressed excitement and when he opened the door to a beautiful, gleaming Cadillac she knew why!

"Enter Cinderella and we'll search for your glass slipper."

"Oh, Jerry! It's gorgeous! I hope you didn't rent it; and if you bought it I'm going to have you investigated."

They were both laughing as he got in.

"It's a bit of a story, but first, you haven't had dinner, have you?"

"I had a late lunch; I told you we didn't have to make this a dinner thing." She was really trying to be an inexpensive date.

"Well, Nora has been feeling poorly on and off lately and I got her some Chinese take-out; I didn't want her to cook. She has a persistent cough and I don't like it; I took her to the doctor and she wouldn't let me go in when he examined her. Mules are lambs compared to her! He gave her a prescription and I had it filled right away. It's a cough medicine and she is getting a good night's sleep now."

"She should quit smoking," said Eleanor, "but of course we all should." There was a faint "no comment" next to her.

"About the car; it belongs to a politician that I have done favors for and when he is out of town I have the use of it. He has a beautiful estate on a secluded lake upstate; I can use that, too, I never have but I've been thinking it would be nice to take Nora there for a week-end; I'd like you to join us."

"I'd like to; I can take care of the food end and see that she does nothing but breathe in the rarified air."

"I appreciate that, Eleanor; she's never had much attention in her life. The people she cooked for cared about her; her husband gave her nothing."

"I think it's wonderful that you two found each other; she really loves you, I can see it. And I can see how much you care for her."

"She means a lot to me; I'd do anything for her!"

"This car rides so smoothly! It's a dream, as we say on Park Avenue; *It carries well!*"

"Oh, is that what we say? I must remember that."

Jerry drove out to Long Island with ease and at moderate speed; it was his intention that this be enjoyable for her and he was not about to create any tension with unnecessary speed; not that he wouldn't have loved to put his foot down and let those eight cylinders do their thing. He took a back road that wound through the waterfront estates nestled among tall, old magnificent trees. As the day drew near sunset he found a small public beach and parked to watch the sun set over Long Island Sound. There were thin, wispy clouds near the horizon edged in bright gold and colors from violet to orange and crimson.

"I called the weather bureau and arranged this sunset; I knew you would appreciate it."

"You must have a lot of influence there; this is absolutely stunning. Let's get out and enjoy this wonderful air; too."

They walked near the beach and sat on a picnic bench; the sign indicated that you had to be a town resident to use the facilities. Eleanor called his attention to the sign asking him if they were breaking the law.

"When they see that license plate there won't be any questions."

"Is he that important?" Jerry smiled;

"He's very important!"

He didn't elaborate and she changed the subject mentioning the other people enjoying the sunset also. Some people were fishing along the shore and off a small pier that was there. The area seemed very well maintained and she felt it would be nice to have a picnic here. A gentle breeze was keeping the gnats under control. There was something about looking at water that tranquilized.

He took her hand; then he put his other hand under her chin.

"Why don't we look for a place and get bite to eat? A small place; like a mom and pop kind of thing."

"That sounds great; my sweaters will be acceptable there."

"You could walk into the Russian Tea Room and knock them dead."

"Well, let's not put the Russians to the test!"

As she stood up he put his arm around her waist and they walked back to the car. They made an attractive couple and other occupants of the park assumed they were lovers. They found a small restaurant, a converted cottage called The Secret Road Inn and it was just what they wanted. It was about ten o'clock when they came to her door.

"What can I say to such a perfect evening? Thank you is so inadequate. And the elegant transportation! It takes a lot to render a girl speechless; especially a hairdresser!"

"I'll give you another reason not to talk," he whispered; he held her close and kissed her; there was more passion this time, but it was not demanding. He released her and kissed her forehead gently.

"Jerry, I don't have your phone number."

He opened his wallet and gave her a business card.

"This has all the numbers you can reach me at; just use the number in red for emergencies."

She thanked him; "Jerry, would it be alright with you if I have Brian for dinner when you and Nora come? I'd like him to meet her; I've told him about her."

"Of course; I think they will like each other."

"Oh, I know they will! Brian will love her dry wit."

"I don't know how dry it is; she always has to have a couple of beers!" She kissed him; "She deserves them if she wants them!"

They said their good nights and with a farewell hug; he hit the road.

After Eleanor locked her door she waited to see if Brian would knock on the connecting door; all was quiet so she went to her bedroom and prepared to turn in. Her mind retraced the evening and she found it flawless. It was a perfect date; the more she saw of him the more she felt that people who saw him as a user of women just didn't know him . . . she was falling in love!

The date of the Sunday dinner arrived and Brian was helping Eleanor with the preparation. She had settled on a recipe for country ribs because they were always full of flavor and very tender; her special mashed potatoes were an excellent accompaniment and Brian had made the salad; a big help, he made it in his own kitchen and brought it in an attractive bowl. That is a friend, indeed! A Russian Cream dessert with fresh raspberries would top it off. She felt confident they would enjoy it. And they relished it!

"You're guests are going to want to sit right down to eat when the aroma of this place hits them; it is sensational!"

Brian had just finished setting the table; he wanted to bring flowers but Eleanor told him she was sure Jerry would bring them so he selected a bottle of wine.

"I think the kitchen crew deserves a nice cold drink, Brian, would you do the honors? They won't be here until two and it's just a little after one. We need something to keep us going."

"How about a well-chilled martini?"

"Sounds perfect, dear!"

He put two cocktail glasses in the freezer and began to make the drinks.

"I'm so glad you decided to join us today; I was afraid you might resent my dating Jerry; not that I think it will go anywhere."

"Do you want it to go anywhere? You need to give it some serious thought; you could be playing with dynamite, however, I know he respects you and has a high opinion of you."

"Has he talked to you about me?" *She's like a school girl!* He mused. "Just that much; he didn't do a character study."

"Is there a touch of sarcasm in the air? I seem to sense it!"

"You seem to *nonsense* it would be more accurate."

"Oh! We have our clever cap on today!"

"I am never without my clever cap; that's common knowledge."

"Oh, excuse me!" She apologized through her laughter.

Nora and Jerry were right punctual; she had a lovely bouquet and Jerry carried a bag which was an ample supply of beer; beer drinkers have a latent fear that the supply might run out.

They enjoyed canapés and drinks and about three Eleanor and Brian readied the dinner and quickly they were all seated at the table. The time seemed to just evaporate and Brian had to admit Jerry was a different person in this setting. He was very helpful when they were clearing the table and his caring for Nora was quite evident. He began to understand why Eleanor was falling in love; that was something he saw very clearly. It was also clear to him that it was not a one-way street; Jerry was just as interested in her! He wasn't jealous; but he did have an uneasy feeling about it. It was obvious that Nora was happy with what was happening and Brian could see that she liked Eleanor a great deal. And she liked her for her Jerry! A family aura was beginning to gel and Brian found himself being drawn into it. Like Eleanor, he had warmed up to Nora and he loved her sharp, dry wit. And she was so quick! During dinner Jerry talked about the lake house his friend had and he explained his plans for a week-end stay. He asked Brian to join the party and when he began to hesitate Eleanor chimed in and said *of course he will go with us; we will need an extra pair of hands because we are not going to allow Nora to do anything but relax.* He gave her a raised eyebrow look and knew he had been tricked into joining them. What Eleanor did not know was that he really wanted to go! Jerry spent some time describing the place and created a growing interest in all of them.

"It will probably be short notice," he concluded, "I can only use it when he is out of town."

After Nora and Jerry took their leave Brian and Eleanor cleared the table and made short work of getting the kitchen back in order.

Brian poured a couple of brandies and they put their feet up in the living room and listened to music and had some light conversation; their subject was not about the dinner, they were discussing the coming month of June. The salon would be a bee hive all month! Weddings, graduations and clients making plans for summer vacations; name it! It seemed to happen in June. Needless to say no employee in the salon ever took vacations in June. Brian mentioned that they probably couldn't manage a week-end in June with Jerry because it was not unusual to take appointments on Saturdays.

"I don't think we will be hearing from him about the lake house that soon anyway. I would think the owner would be using it in the warm weather; it will probably be in the colder weather when he can use it."

Eleanor got up; "What's so terrible about a crisp, cold day on a lake? Think of how invigorating it will be!"

"Indeed! I bet we will have to pry you away from the fireside!"

Brian arose and made ready to leave. He gave her a warm hug and thanked her for an enjoyable dinner.

"Are you going to Tony's?" She was smiling at him.

"No, dear, this was a very satisfying day; I'm going to turn in early."

"Thank you for all the help; it made it pleasant and easy."

"The pleasure was all mine; love you, darlin' good night."

Finally the month of June was over and it had been a banner month. Cleo was delighted with the amount of money they took in and also with the increase in new clients. Brian and Eleanor were arriving home together; they had both worked on this last Saturday in June and were in a celebrating mood. They were tired but that didn't mean they were dead.

"Come into my parlor, little fly, and I'll fix you a tall one."

Brian demonstrated with his hands an exaggerated size of a drink.

"Just let me throw some cold water on my face and I'll be in."

Going to his bath room Brian did as Eleanor was doing; before he came into his bath room he had put two tall glasses in the freezer. It just seemed to be a good day for a Tom Collins. He discovered that he was out of cherries but he peeled and sliced a navel orange, sprinkled the slices with powdered sugar and put them in the freezer. They will add something to the drink he thought. *Maybe I've just invented a Timothy Collins.* He couldn't wait to tell her how clever he was!

"I tossed a little snack together; sorry but I'm fresh out of crackers."

She came in with a plate of pepperoni rounds and cubes of cheese.

"Who's worrying about crackers? We are not out of gin; that is critical!" He handed her the tall glass with a cocktail napkin.

"Tell me what you think of this; your first Timothy Collins."

They toasted each other and she found the drink delicious and refreshing.

"You're so clever; how do you stand yourself?"

"One doesn't even notice it when one is always clever."

She shook her head and they laughed; as they so often did. They were sitting in the living room which was tastefully done in an eclectic way that was attractive and comfortable. Brian's taste was masculine; not on the arty side.

"After I've had some breathing time I'm going to have you and your new family here for dinner. We should invite Edith; to add spice!"

"I don't think that is a good mix; I know you are kidding but the thought makes me cringe." Eleanor had grown serious.

"Please! Get that somber look off your face; you *know* I'm kidding."

She bounced back and they waxed into talking shop and made plans to go out for dinner close to home; let's keep it all simple was Eleanor's wish.

Later that evening when they were out for dinner Eleanor asked Brian when he was taking his vacation.

"Not until October; and just one week then. I want to save a couple of weeks to go skiing in February."

"Are you going to Austria?"

"I guess so; you can't beat the skiing there and the club gets us such good flying rates that I can go to Austria cheaper than any nice ski resorts in the U.S. First class accommodations and food are really inexpensive in Austria."

"Because the working class gets paid peanuts." Eleanor expounded.

"Am I responsible for their economy? If I didn't go the working class would get nothing! And remember; Americans are very good tippers."

"I wasn't blaming you, darling, I was editorializing!"

"Oh, is that what that was? Did you take a course in that?"

"You know I'm involved in international affairs."

"If you mean those foreign clients you have who tip you so well, Sweetie, I certainly am aware of that. I've seen you spend eons discussing nail polish shades!"

"That is so low class I wouldn't have any kind of reply!"

"You certainly know when to be speechless . . . that's détente!"

They were both laughing hard and abandoned the topic, willingly. It seemed like it was going home time; their tired bodies were demanding some respite. After settling their bill, they left the place arm in arm, homeward ho!

On the way home Brian suddenly stopped and faced her, his hands on her shoulders. "By the way, darling, we didn't get to your vacation."

"That's simple, dear; at home, could it be any simpler?"

"It seems to me from what I hear that Jerry is taking some of his time while you are off. Have you heard anything like that?"

"Oh, have you turned detective all of a sudden? You must hang out at the right gin mills. Why don't you get involved in charity work?"

"I was only asking you a simple question! You gave a simple answer, that's for sure; why so touchy?" They had continued walking and were almost home. "You're acting like a teen age boy! Get with it!"

"I'm sorry; I was just teasing you and I should know better."

"You above all people should know better; Jerry is no joke."

"I promise you; there will be no more silliness."

They were in front of their building; he gave her a hug and they went up the one flight to their doorways. Eleanor was herself again; she hugged him.

"Why don't you come in with me and you won't have to unlock all those locks of yours? He already had his door open. "Good idea," she said.

With a quick kiss on the cheek and a good night; she went into her digs. She felt that she had been a bit silly about Jerry . . . too much school girl!

It was almost mid-night the time café society wakes up. Brian had a second wind; he didn't feel like going to Tony's and he hadn't been to Goosie's for quite a while. He didn't have many gay friends; he eschewed the kind who talked constantly about their rights while they trampled over the rights of others. He had a few friends who could talk without their hands and who had something to say when they talked. Ronnie was one of these friends; he usually hung out at Goosie's and Brian was sure he would find him there. So, he hailed a cab and just as he hoped Ronnie was at the bar; not in conversation with anyone; which was most unusual. They greeted each other; happy to meet after not meeting for some time. There was no stool available and Brian assured him he'd rather stand up. Ronnie was prepared to chastise him.

"Well, give an account of yourself; I've called you and left messages on your machine but you never get back to me! I would never bother you at the salon; I know how busy the star is."

"My answering machine was on the blink and I didn't realize it right away. I called you a few times and you weren't home. Of course you won't spend a few bucks and get a machine (because they are toys) so I can keep in touch with you. You do your receiving here, in your private office."

"Oh, we haven't lost our sharp tongue; have we?" Ronnie countered.

"Just keeping things clear, bon ami."

"The French will get you nowhere, darling."

"Perhaps not here; but in the circle I revolve in it is readily noted."

"I've missed our repartee; it is so mentally invigorating!"

They were both laughing; always seeking one-upmanship.

"Did I hear something French?" Brian asked.

The laughing resumed. Brian ordered drinks for both of them and in response to Ronnie's request for an account went through the whole Jerry story, including the sojourn to Jones Beach, and right up to Eleanor and the new *family.*

"My God, Brian, get the story on TV; it's a soap!"

"It would be a bore to most people."

"You know, Brian, we've been friends for quite a while and I've listened to your various trysts with guys you are never going to go anywhere with and threaded through this saga is a guy who really cares about you. You don't seem to have a clue about him! I'm talking about Tony; I've never met him but with all the different guys you talk about, not that there are scads of them; Tony is woven through the theme as always doing something nice and always being supportive. From your description he's not bad to look at, either; doesn't that tell you anything?"

"I don't think he thinks of me *that* way; he's nice to everyone."

"Brian! He's in his early fifties, he's Italian, he's never been married and to top it off . . . he doesn't have a girl friend! He's in the closet! Do you need a hammer to get that into your head? And, I forgot! He was in the Navy! He is waiting for you! He probably hasn't made a move on you because he thinks you're so refined. He doesn't know what a trollop you are!"

Brian reacted quickly and poked Ronnie in the shoulder; he was shaking him.

"I'll give you trollop! Talk about the kettle calling the pot black!"

"Seriously, Brian, you should concentrate on him; you could have a life with him! Tony has his own business; he's not a drunk, he doesn't gamble, from what you tell me he works long hours all the time. That means he's saving his money. Just what the hell do you want? A white horse?"

"Let's change the subject; what's happening with you?"

"What can happen when you work in a museum? You dust!"

"Don't give me that stuff! Browsers go to museums; you specialize in browsers! And, of course, any man that is breathing!"

They were both laughing and trying to drink their drinks. Brian mentioned how Jerry and Eleanor were trying to include him in their social plans and how uncomfortable he felt; even though he had a good time. He would rather not be around it all. Ronnie was quick to give him advice.

"Stay with them and get your belly full; then you'll be rid of Foley!"

"I'm well aware there's nothing for me with him."

"Yes, but he's a stud and you love being around him; just in case!"

"Oh, that's all you think of; there's more to life than that!"

"If there is, you haven't discovered it yet; it's waiting for you."

"You must have had a very busy June, Brian, I hear they had to open the bank on Sunday for you; I should have gone to cosmetology school instead of college."

"There is a small matter of creative talent involved, precious!"

"Aren't we sensitive tonight? You've been under too much stress."

They could rib each other this way because they were friends; anyone who attempted this in a derogatory way had better be prepared for a scathing shredding! They were both able to defend themselves quite well . . . indeed!

Ronnie had a rough childhood. He lived in fear of his father, who was very strict and unloving. Ronnie, an only child was not the son he wanted; he was a tall, robust man who loved sports and excelled in them. His son was a bit on the pudgy side and preferred books. He had a fair complexion with smooth, white, creamy skin; the kind women spend a ransom on attaining. His thick, dark hair was close-cropped primarily to avoid any annoyance to his father. When a young man with long hair crossed "Daddy's" path he became instantly enraged and didn't hesitate to show his displeasure. Ronnie's mother gave him encouragement but she also feared her husband and always deferred to him. While in college Ronnie became involved with a student and thought he had found true love with someone who understood him. It was a time when well-known people were coming out of the closet and celebrating their homosexuality; Ronnie decided to join them and told his parents about himself and tried to introduce his partner. The rage shown by his father had his wife fearing he would have a stroke! Ronnie was kicked out of the house and the family and disowned. He had to work his way through his last year in college; his mother helped him when she could, secretly, or there would have been heavy consequences from her unforgiving spouse. He never saw his father again and after his death he had a reunion with his mother who died three years later. His big love affair lasted two years and left Ronnie with a lot of doubts. He had romances here and there, but he did not believe he could ever trust anyone in a serious relationship. He relished listening to Brian's experiences and offered him advice and caution when he saw fit. He was all ears as Brian related his sojourn to Jones Beach with Jerry.

"You're trying to tell me he drove you out to Jones Beach in the wee hours and nothing happened? And you were both full of booze? I don't buy it, sweetie, you must have been numb! You both must have been numb!"

"It's not like that, Ronnie, he likes my company, and he is a ladies man; not that I think his conquests are in that category. He's been dating Eleanor for about a month and I am not too comfortable with that."

"That cop stud dating Eleanor! Has she turned over a new libido?

"He's impressed with how nice she is; it's something new for him, he has always chased after hookers or girls of that ilk."

"That's why he likes you sweetie . . . you're of that ilk!"

"Watch yourself, chubby, you're on dangerous ground!"

They laughed together and turned to their drinks. Brian sighed; looking downcast.

"Well anyway we are becoming one big happy family; not that I like the idea . . . they pressure me into it."

"You're a fool to bother with him; Tony is the one who really cares for you and you are oblivious to the fact. He is an Italian without a girl friend, he treats you like a king, he lives alone and he has his own thriving business. Open those big blues and mind the store. You would have a future with Tony; don't forget he spent a few years in the Navy . . . we do know about sailors!"

"Tony is a real nice guy, Ronnie."

"Mother of God! Everyone you know is sanctified! Brian get with it and drop that cop and concentrate on Tony! I'll bet if you gave him just a little encouragement he would have a lot to say to you. From what you tell me he's already trying to lay the ground work but he has his work cut out for himself dealing with someone as dense as you!"

"Enough! Lets drop the subject; I have to hit the road and say bye-bye and we must do this again sometime . . . minus the advice!"

"Not so fast," piped up Ronnie, I've invited Budd and Eddie to have breakfast at my place and I've already told them you are coming. They'll be here in five minutes."

"I would like to get home before daylight; you're breakfasts are good for hours!"

"Oh, when you go joy riding with the cop and get home just before noon that's perfectly okay! You can leave at your own convenience."

"Don't get upset, darling, I'm just joshing."

The foursome went to Ronnie's and listened to music and the chit chat never ceased. The breakfast was wonderful and Brian made it home wearily late.

Brian slept until almost three in the afternoon; he got up and went sleepily into the kitchen in search for something very cold. The V-8 label caught his eye and he poured some in a tall glass over ice. Its healthy contents made him feel he was doing his body some good. Not a bad idea after all the alcohol he had consumed at the bar. He decided to call Eleanor.

"Good morning, glory, it's your neighbor."

"Good afternoon; from someone who wasn't out all night."

"I had to celebrate having a Saturday off; didn't you go out?"

"No I made a light supper and caught up on loose ends in the house."

"Are you free to go out for dinner tonight?" Brian asked.

"Are you inviting me?"

"Certainly! Is it something I've never done before?"

"Don't get peevish; I want to be sure you are fully awake. What did you have in mind?"

"I just thought of asking you this minute; that's as far as I got."

"Come to my place around six," she suggested, "we'll decide."

"You'll maybe buy me a drink?"

"Do you think that is wise?" She loved to needle him; "Or what?"

"Not to do so would be otherwise!"

They laughed together and agreed to meet at six.

She ended with; "Try ice water on your eyes . . . it's a great refresher!"

He knocked on the connecting door and let himself into her apartment; calling her name he made his way to the living room. Eleanor had just put down a tray with the makings for drinks; since they were going out for dinner she skipped snacks.

"Hello, darling, what can I fix for you? Or would you prefer a little chicken soup to line your stomach?"

"There is nothing wrong with my stomach, thank you, a little gin and tonic will do very nicely. You do everything so well . . . it will be perfect!"

"I wouldn't dare present Mr. Wonderful with anything but perfection. I'd be afraid of losing my social status."

"It's refreshing to be treated with the proper deference one deserves; too many people are so lax in social graces!"

They laughed as they hugged; enjoying the regard they held for each other. Both of them were dressed casually, but smartly, they would be admired in any setting.

"We will have our pick of tables tonight," Brian noted; most of New York disappears to the mountains or the beaches on Fourth of July week-end."

"Can you imagine those beaches out on Long Island? You won't even be able to see the sand!" Eleanor shuddered as she sat down.

"That is not for me, thank you, but people seem to love being packed like sardines!" Brian continued.

"You can't pack New Yorkers close enough! They love it! Look at the hoard that does the subway rush hours every day . . . you have to be made of steel to weather that! Then you have the stalwart ones who drive in and out of the city every day! They are the unsung heroes."

Brian raised both arms above his head as he finished.

They had just the one drink at Eleanor's and decided to walk around town and wait until their instincts chose the restaurant. Eventually it was a small Italian place that looked interesting; it was not overly busy and had a certain charm about it. They had no trouble selecting a table. The waiter took care of them promptly and with comfortable expertise. Brian looked over the wine list and they had a wonderful meal. They enjoyed a very good espresso and that topped off their dinner; neither of them had dessert, Eleanor put her hand on Brian's arm and looked at him.

"Brian," her voice was soft, "I'm so happy that we have the friendship we enjoy. It means so much to me to have you close and to be able to rely on you. I've never had a friend like you."

"Are you bent on reducing me to tears, madam? I'll have to blame it on the cigarette smoke; there aren't any onions around."

"Oh, can't you be serious! Not even for two minutes?"

"I don't think serious is going to be in my life; it is not for me."

"Don't think that way, Brian, you have so much to offer; it will happen, I know it will because I know you!"

They left the restaurant and enjoyed the walk home. When they were in front of their digs Eleanor released his arm; she felt he was going to go out and he wanted to go alone.

"I think I will sort of drift with the wind."

"Maybe sail to Tony's?"

"I don't know; I might end up there."

She kissed his cheek, "Just be careful." She went into the doorway refusing his offer to walk her up.

Brian's adventurous feet carried him to Tony's; the walk had invigorated him and he got rid of the slightly stuffed feeling dinner had left him with. Tony's was very busy and he noticed quite a few women were present; that was unusual. It dawned on him that he rarely came here on Saturday nights because he worked many Saturdays. So this was the Saturday night crowd. There were no empty stools so he made his way to the corner at the end where Tony was working; Gino was bar keeping on the other end.

"Busy where you work," quipped Brian.

"Tell me about it," Tony answered with a grimace; he didn't like it this busy.

"Gin and tonic and lime, please," Brian ordered his drink.

"Summer is here," Tony smiled as he made the drink; "Stay in the corner; someone is bound to leave soon." He was glad to see Brian. Brian had never seen quite as many women in the place; part of Saturday night, he surmised. The man seated in front of him turned and said, "You're welcome to this stool; I've been sitting here for a couple of hours and it's time I made a move."

"Oh, no thanks, I just finished dinner and standing up seems like a good idea."

"I know what you mean," he extended his hand, "my name is Frank Vargas I've seen you in here a couple of times; we never got into any conversation though."

Brian introduced himself and it was like pressing a button. Frank began talking about himself and mostly about the impossible woman he lived with who happened to be his wife. It wasn't boring because he had a wonderful sense of humor and one realized he ranted about his wife in good spirit and really cared for her. If his wife ever heard him he would have a tough time getting in the front door! After about an hour he stood up and announced, "Well, I've got to be getting home; regardless of what I've said my wife is terrific in bed and I am getting horny!" He gave Brian a broad grin, clapped him on the shoulder and was gone. Brian took Frank's stool.

"Now it looks like home," Tony smiled coming in front of him. "Did Vargas bend your ear too much?"

"No, he seems like a very pleasant guy . . . he's funny."

"I'm sure you heard about his wife; nobody escapes that."

"Oh yes," said Brian, smiling, "everything!"

There was a gradual exodus from the bar; the married couples seem to leave first, then the others straggled out and they all seemed to regret leaving. The good-nights were lenghthy. Tony made a drink for Brian and one for himself then he sat next to him, sighing heavily.

"It's been like this all day; I don't think we have enough in the kitchen to even make one sandwich. I am bushed!"

"Don't ever complain about business being good . . . it's bad luck!"

"Why not? Everybody else does!"

"Tony, who ever complains about business being too good?"

"Okay, I'll change the subject; you look pretty spiffy, Brian, did you get dressed up to come here?" He poked him; laughing.

"I took Eleanor out for dinner and we talked each others ears off; she's such a good friend and I'm lucky to have her living next to me. If we need each other we're right there. We're very close."

"How about me? Am I on that friendship list?"

"You're way up on that list . . . you know that."

"Well, it's nice to hear it."

"Jerry is working twelve to eights he was here earlier with his partner Tom; do you know him?"

"No, I don't," Brian replied.

"He's a real nice guy; I like him. He had a couple of cokes; Jerry had a couple of shooters! Before going to work; I think he's slipping."

"A couple of shots mean nothing to Jerry; he's immune!"

"Believe me Brian; Jerry is a drinking Mick and booze is the first priority on his list. He's a pub Irishman, forever!"

Tony decided to change the subject.

"You're on vacation; or do I remember that wrong?"

"You have it right . . . two weeks."

"Are you going away?"

"No I'm just going to hang around here. I have things to do at home; that will take up some of my time and I'll wing it from there."

"It must be nice to have a vacation; I never do."

"Whose fault is that? You're your own boss!"

"The worst kind of boss to have; you just never go."

"Tony, that is absurd! You just don't want to go."

"Well, I don't want to go anywhere alone; I'd be lost!"

"Now we get to the root of the problem; I understand that."

He got up and fixed a drink for a customer and came back and sat down. He put his hand on Brian's shoulder and smiled.

"I'm not a complete waste," Brian, "I'm taking Monday off and I'm going out to East Hampton."

"East Hampton!" Brian sat upright. "Whatever brings you out there? Do you have friends there?"

"A little business; I bought a piece of waterfront some time ago and the agent told me there's a cottage on the property; right on the water."

"Didn't you see it when you bought it?"

"I've never seen the property." Tony waited for his reaction.

"You have bought waterfront property without seeing it? Are you crazy? It could be underwater property!"

Brian could not believe what he was hearing. Who in the world would do that? Well, he was sitting right next to him; the proprietor!

Tony explained that he had been buying land out that way for years and had a trustworthy agent who had put him on to many good deals and had increased the value of his investments. He was a rarity. This was a new Tony!

An idea was growing in Tony's mind. *What a nice trip it would be if Brian could go with him!* The two of them could have a great time together; Tony could show Brian other land he owned out there and Brian was to be his guest for the whole trip. He would insist. Tony had asked Brian to keep what he had told him a secret. He never discussed his investment with anyone at the bar. He gave Brian a cat that ate the cream look and put his hand on his shoulder again.

"I have an idea . . . tell me what you think of it."

"How would you like to come to East Hampton with me? I'd like to show you the property I have out there."

The invitation took Brian by surprise; he hedged for time to think about this.

"I've never been there; I've heard a lot about the place, of course."

"Come with me, Brian," Tony coaxed, "I'm going to rent a car and drive there."

"You know how to drive! I'm impressed!"

"Of course I do; don't you?"

"No, I've never had the occasion to learn."

Well, I'll teach you; it's easy."

"I would like to learn; some day I want to own a car when I don't live in the city. A car is a liability in the city."

"What do you say, kid, will you make the trip with me?"

"Sure I'll go; I know it will be fun and I couldn't have better company!"

"Tell you what, Brian; if Gino can work tomorrow for me I'll take off and we'll go tomorrow. I could use a couple of days out of this coop."

"Why not; I'm available and very willing!"

His excitement grew at once; Tony went behind the bar and spoke quietly to Gino. Brian could see Gino nodding his head agreeably and his anticipation increased. Tony also asked Gino about Tuesday and Gino was available.

"Go for a week I don't care; you need it. I can always use the extra money."

They sat and planned their excursion unaware of their folly. To plan to drive out to the Hamptons right before the Fourth of July without a reservation was sheer lunacy. They were to learn that there wasn't a motel room available from Hampton Bays to Montauk for the entire week! They wouldn't learn this until they had driven out there. Another problem was getting the rental car a day ahead; the manager of the Hertz place stopped at Tony's almost every day after work, Tony had helped him with loans many times to help him hide his horse-playing habit from his wife. Tony leaned on him and didn't hesitate to remind him that he owed him a favor. He wanted that car for three days and was determined to get it! Suddenly, the trip was very important. It was four a.m. when he got into his bed; at eight a.m. he was on the phone with George, the manager; with only four hours sleep he was in no mood for refusals. Refusals were not an option!

"I'll call you back in fifteen minutes, Tony."

"Fifteen; not twenty, George!"

He got the car but had to promise to return it Tuesday night, no matter how late. Tony felt that was reasonable and agreed. He hadn't mentioned Tuesday to Brian; he would spring that on him after they were there. They delivered the car; a beautiful white Ford hardtop with only six hundred miles on it Tony called Brian; he was very excited and couldn't remember when he ever knew such anticipation.

"I can pick you up in twenty minutes; you ready?"

"I'm in bed!" Brian was trying to wake up; "let me think!"

"So, ten minutes to dress and ten minutes to do whatever you want. Please be down on the street in case I can't park."

"Do you have my address? I think I'm awake now."

"You gave it to me last night. What's the matter; senility?"

"Let me wash up, will you? I'll be downstairs waiting."

He popped into the shower thanking God he had packed last night. He was downstairs waiting, just minutes before Tony drove up. He double-parked and put Brian's bag in the trunk. Cars came up behind them blasting their horns because he was blocking traffic. Tony shouted a few appropriate obscenities and got slowly into the car. He started the engine and they were off!

"Mid-town Tunnel here we come! How do you like these wheels, Brian? It's practically new!"

"Beautiful, Tony, it still smells new!"

"Well, you can catch up on your sleep if you want."

"Sleep! I'm too excited to think of sleep!"

Traffic on the Long Island Expressway was fairly light and moving; it was Sunday morning . . . no business traffic and it was still early. In a couple of hours it would be bumper to bumper; no express here! They drove for almost two hours and stopped for breakfast. Brian had dozed off a little despite his attempt to stay awake. They finished their coffee and Tony decided to try and call his broker, who expected him the next day. He came back annoyed because he got one of those answering machines he detested; the anger increased.

"Let's go; I'll try him later, after all, it is Sunday morning."

"He's probably still asleep; if he has any sense."

"Well, you got in a few winks; with the seat back down you could have gotten an hour's rest easily."

"I didn't want to sleep; I have to watch you!"

Tony laughed, he was so happy Brian came; "*you* watch *me*?"

As they left Southampton and were starting through Watermill the lovely pastoral views began to unfold. The lush, green farms stretched away on both sides of Route 27. To the north the farms rolled gracefully with ponds and stands of trees breaking the green of the potato crop. In the distance hills were in silhouette, a glacial ridge that ran East and West along the North side of the South shore of Long Island. On the South side of the highway the farms seemed flat to the eye although they had a continuous undulation. The farms on the South side ended at the Atlantic Ocean and this gave the acreage a very high market value. The old-time farmers loved the land and would not sell to developers for any price. But that blood was dieing off and their heirs had trouble resisting the money. Large, expensive contemporary homes were beginning to appear on one or two acre plots. The designs confounded the locals who knew only traditional type houses and they had a bit of contempt for the occupants. However, these occupants were their bread and butter so most of the comments were at home or at the local's bars. In time more and more of these houses would appear and the locals would have difficulty buying a house in their own town!

"These big old homes are magnificent," Brian enthused over the design and landscaping, "they obviously have had excellent care and maintenance through the years. The trees are so huge and seem to protect the houses in some way."

"Unless a big storm knocks one over on your roof!"

Tony gave Brian a wry look and Brian just looked away; eyebrows raised. Tony was immensely pleased with the way things were going and he congratulated himself for inviting Brian; whose pleasure was visible.

"I wonder what my shack looks like; my broker said it needs work but it has a one of a kind location. I want to show you some of the other land I own."

"You own more land out here? You're pretty smart, Mr. Tony! This is better than the stock market."

"I'm going to have my broker take us around; he'll bring maps; I could never find the sites by myself. I feel stupid about that. I should have located them long ago; I'm not good at doing things like that alone."

"Tony! Don't ever call yourself stupid; you have real smarts! And you are very modest; you never brag about any of this. How many people you know have any investments in real estate? They're all rent payers; like me."

They were turning east from Route 27 onto Main Street in East Hampton and Brian was so impressed with the natural beauty of the Village. Large elm trees lined the broad street and a sparkling pond was lined with huge chestnut trees; there were gracious homes, then they passed the John Drew Theater; Brian had heard of it many times. Next came the shops on both sides of the street and some were smart and attractive; others looked unimaginative and a bit seedy, this surprised Brian; they seemed to be misfits. He made no comment about them; he didn't want to taint the moment. There was a movie and it looked just like a movie; much needed by the natives!

"Now I see why they rave about East Hampton; and to think it is fronted on the Atlantic Ocean! What a location; as they say."

"Wait until I show you the estates along that ocean front! You will really see what money can do . . . lots of money!"

Tony found a place to park; he had spotted a public phone and he needed to contact that broker. He wanted some suggestions as to where they could get a room. Seeing the amount of cars and people gave him some concern . . . there might be more people than rooms! He was waking up a bit late. Brian stayed by the car and stretched his legs. Glancing over the parked cars he was awed by the many expensive models both foreign and domestic; *don't come here without money* ran through his mind. He enjoyed seeing the smart looking people, marveling at the deep golden tan so many sported. It was easy for him to pick out the natives who lived there all year round; they dressed differently and if they had a deep tan they got it while working! Tony returned looking perplexed; Brian was worried.

"I got him this time; he's on his way here. We're going to have some difficulty getting a room; he's making some inquiries, we may have to go out to Montauk. I should have called him sooner."

"We'll find something," Brian tried to cheer him up; "we just can't be fussy, as long as it is clean I don't care where it is. We won't be in the room much anyway . . . there's too much to see!"

Tony appreciated his attitude; he would feel rotten if Brian appeared to be unhappy about coming his broker had to come through. He told him he would like something on the waterfront; his reply was not encouraging.

"We'll have to take what we can get and probably pay more than it's worth. It's the Fourth of July week-end!"

Brian agreed that they would have to be satisfied with what is on hand. A patrol car, with two officers; stopped to question two would-be hitch hikers; as soon as they were free Tony went over to see if they could help him. Cops have a lot of information. They didn't give them much hope saying you couldn't rent a dog house this week. The suggestion was to try Montauk where most of the motels were located. The officer thought it would be a good idea to stop in a bar at the docks; bartenders can be very helpful. Tony rejoined Brian; not smiling!

"The cops think we should try Montauk; that's where most of the motels are . . . I think we should ride out there and see what we can do; I'm not going to sit and wait for Ed Gunther."

"Do you know how to get there?"

"The highway ends there; if you don't stop you're in the ocean!"

They were in Montauk in twenty minutes and Tony got directions to the fishing docks. There were many motels right in Montauk, some were ocean front; but they were surrounded by cars and people, it was not encouraging and the cops had suggested the docks. One savvy bartender could save a lot of hopeless looking. There were many bars at the docks; one place, not very large, was next to a huge waterfront restaurant and shoppe complex and it was drawing Tony in.

"Let's try this Kincaid's place; I get good vibes from it."

"I'm with you," Brian said agreeably, "good vibes suit me."

The entire area was alive with people; there seemed to be a boat in every slip and the crowd had a merry demeanor that was infectious. A honky-tonk piano player greeted them as they came in the door and the next problem was to find a seat or a place at the bar. After all the driving, standing would not be a difficulty. Tony moved into a spot at the end of the bar near the kitchen; not a popular spot, he knew, but they had a toe-hold. Brian stood behind him and Tony was looking up at a lanky, gray-haired man who was at least six feet six inches tall. Tony was sure he owned the place; he wasn't as groomed as most bartenders are.

"What'll you have?" his raspy voice booming. Tony ordered;

"Two bloody Marys, please."

Kincaid laughed; "my Bloody Marys are hot blooded!"

"You're the doctor, whatever you prescribe!"

It was instant accord; they were friends. He moved down to make the drinks.

"Bloody Mary okay with you; Brian?" He had turned around.

"Excellent! Especially a hot-blooded one!"

Both of them had picked up on the general well-being that was the ambience of this place and Tony was certain that Bob Kincaid would find a room for them. When he returned with the drinks Tony was going to enlist his help immediately. First he would tell him he owned a bar in New York City. Some people had gathered around the piano and were singing; Brian loved piano bars and he drifted down by the music. He sensed that Tony was going to engage Bob in conversation and he wouldn't be missed. After listening to the music for a while Brian went to the bar and ordered a gin and tonic; he also ordered a drink for the piano player. The bartender was fast; and he had to be to keep up with the clientele! This was a drinking crowd! He carried the drinks back to the piano and luckily, his seat was still unoccupied. Actually; there was no luck involved; the piano player had saved it for him. He was taking his break and very much appreciated Brian's thoughtfulness. They both said 'cheers' as they sipped the drinks. Bob Ayers, the piano player came to Montauk with his wife for a two week vacation. He fell in love with the place and the wife went back to Scotland minus a husband. His first love was scotch and then music and he discovered he could make more money in Montauk than back home. She was a nurse and she had two daughters from a previous marriage; she had to go home and now she had to face the fact that this marriage was on the rocks. Bob sent money to her but he wasn't leaving Montauk.

It was a drinking town and he was right at home. When he came to Montauk he had latent homosexual tendencies; he had his first homosexual experience there and that was the end of the already shaky marriage. Bob Kincaid gave him a steady job and found a reasonable studio apartment for him. Kincaid seemed to be able to help everyone but himself; his personal life was a riotous mess!

"We have to go right away; Bob found a room for us; I'll tell you about it along the way." They got into the car and Tony continued;

"The place is an old hotel it's up high on a cliff overlooking Long Island Sound. It's old and not too well maintained but the food is excellent and it's clean."

"Well, we got our waterfront wish, the food is good and it is also clean! We're lucky! Is it far?"

"Only about a mile; Bob gave me directions, it is a little tricky to find. The owner is supposed to be a character."

"It seems that Montauk has a collection of characters! I was talking to the piano player; he came here from Scotland for a two week vacation and never went back! His wife went home; she has two daughters; that was almost two years ago."

They were going up a hill toward the Sound there was a lot of thick greenery around them; Brian could not identify the plants but they were wild! Suddenly it was there on a ridge; a white clapboard structure of no particular design, but quite large, and a few out-buildings, one a garage made up the complex. Everything seemed to need a bit of paint. There was plenty of room to park and quite a few cars, none fancy, and several pick-up trucks. This was not East Hampton! It was honky-tonk but it had something!

They entered and were looking at a long bar and instead of the usual back-bar with shelves of liquor displayed and large mirrors; there was a continuous run of large windows; for a very good reason. The view of the Sound was spectacular! People would sit here and enjoy their favorite drink and gaze at something wonderful that TV just didn't have! If the outside needed paint did it really matter? In addition to this; the aroma of well prepared food drifted through the place. Their spirits were soaring! They sat the bar and ordered drinks; when they were served Tony asked to see Gus, as per Bob's instruction. The bar maid, his daughter, nodded and disappeared. Shortly he came to them, a husky, garrulous type of man who greeted them pleasantly. When Tony said Bob Kincaid sent him he nodded his head, saying;

"I've been expecting you; I've got a room for you, I had a cancellation, it's a front room; so you get a water view. You have to take it for the three day week-end; I told Bob to make that clear."

"That's fine with us, we'll be happy to get settled."

Tony took out his wallet and paid him in advance in cash. Gus was pleased with that and he showed them the room personally. It was clean; and it had only what was necessary. Twin beds, a dresser, two chairs and a stand for a suit case made up most of the décor; there was a closet with wire coat hangers, and it was so narrow one had to hang clothes frontward or you couldn't close the door. Nails driven into the back wall of the closet were provided for the hangers.

"If you need anything stop at the bar and tell them. And, oh yes, your bath is down the hall on the right; you share with one other room. Please don't leave personal gear there."

He was gone; they stood and looked at each other, this was not what Tony had planned, he was embarrassed. Brian sensed this and quickly began to enthuse over their luck in getting the room. "We won't be in it that much," he concluded. He made Tony feel better and Tony liked that. Gus had told Tony he would have to go down to the desk and sign the register; Ridge Top had its regulations! Brian unpacked and just putting some personal things on the dresser and having their bags in the room made it look a bit more livable. Tony had paid for three days; Brian wondered if they were staying that long; it was okay with him! Watching how Tony handled things had increased Brian's opinion of his competency; his steady way of doing things gave Brian a secure feeling and he found it all very appealing. He remembered Ronnie's advice about Tony. Brian changed into shorts, a tee shirt and moccasins. He then went to inspect the bathroom; it was old but it was clean and it had a shower! It would be just fine. When he returned to the room Tony was changing his clothes.

"You're one step ahead of me, you've changed already. Now we look like the other tourists here. I called Ed and we are going to meet him for breakfast tomorrow and have a tour of my stuff. Especially that cottage; if it's livable I'll be able to stay there when I come out here. How do you feel about staying the three days, Brian, is that okay with you?"

"Perfectly! I am enjoying every minute of this trip. Now that we have a place to hang our hats we can explore the area. I checked the bathroom; it's clean and it has a shower."

"You're really good company Brian, I'm so glad you could come with me."

"And I am very happy to be here; and the company could not be better!" Tony filled with satisfaction.

"Would you like to go back to Kincaid's for a couple of drinks? I know you liked the music and I'd like to thank him for his help; he was a godsend!"

"I am ready, captain, anywhere you steer the ship!"

"Let's go mate!"

They made the short ride to Kincaid's and it was still busy; Bob saw them enter and he made room for them at the end of the bar. He was smiling as he pointed to where he wanted them to go.

"How did you make out," he asked.

"We're all set and we owe you a big thank you."

"You owe me nothing!"

"At least have a drink with us!"

"I could be persuaded to do that."

Once again they got head to head and Brian made his way to the piano. There were different people around it now but they were in the same mood as the previous customers. Good spirits and sing-a-long . . . whether you could sing or not! Bob, the piano player smiled and nodded to Brian as he approached.

"How have you been?" Brian asked.

"Hanging in; just hanging." He laughed.

After awhile Tony came and joined him and Tony revealed yet another facet; he could sing! Bob recognized it immediately and soon coaxed him to do a solo. Tony had no inhibitions and sang a couple of popular songs to the delight of the crowd. Tony noticed a table for two being vacated; he leaned over to Brian.

"How about getting something to eat; you must be hungry and we've had a bit of booze already!"

Brian nodded in agreement. "Good idea."

He followed Tony and they sat at the table. A couple were seated at the bar waiting for a table and never noticed their loss. They seemed to be drinking their dinner. A lovely looking young girl came to take their order; she had a charming Irish brogue and, as they learned later, came to Montauk to work for the season. Montauk had a longer season than the Hamptons due to the numerous boats catering to fishermen. Some boats operated all year round. They ordered there food and both decided to just drink water. The meal was excellent and it surprised both of them. They would have been satisfied with plain, good food; the dinner was excellent. They had coffee laced with amoretto for dessert. Maureen, the waitress was well rewarded for her attentive service. It was getting dark and Bob had told Tony to be sure and ride out to the Point and see the light house; they headed that way, about a three mile ride. They parked in the parking lot and walked to the light house; the sun was just about to the horizon and the sky was a panorama of color. Toward the east the darkness was setting in but the western sky was clinging to the light; it was spectacular! The light in the light house was lit and it turned faithfully warning seamen of the rocks beneath it.

"Tony, did you ever see anything like this! It is wonderful! And listen to that surf against those rocks!"

"It is beautiful, Brian." He put his hand on his shoulder; "really unusual."

When the sun disappeared from view they went back to the car and started out to the hotel. Tony found it without any trouble and Brian admired his sense of direction; Brian was certain that he could not have found it, especially at dark. They entered the room and found extra towels had been placed there in their absence. That was nice. Brian always slept in the nude so he undressed to his briefs and sat on his bed. Tony did the same and was in boxer shorts.

"How about a night cap?"

Tony produced a leather case that held two bottles of liquor and two glasses. He handled them with exaggerated care, joshing.

"You have such good ideas! I love that case you have."

He poured two drinks and they drank a toast to their day. The room was lit by one small lamp; if you liked to read you had to do it in day light. They finished their drinks and Tony put his arm around Brian's shoulder. "It's been wonderful having you with me; you've made this trip special for me."

"I'm so glad I came; it's been one great thing after another; and we've been so lucky with everything!"

Neither one knew quite how it happened; but they only needed to get in one of the beds that night. Tony had found what he needed all of his life; he just wasn't fully aware of it. During their lovemaking he whispered to Brian that he felt like a complete man for the first time in his life . . . Brian didn't know what he meant. But Brian had never felt such complete satisfaction. He had the feeling of really being loved . . . not just used. Ronnie's advice ran through his mind.

Tony was the first to awaken; he eased carefully out of the bed and went to the dresser. Looking at his watch he saw it was a little after eight. He looked in the mirror and really thought he would look different; last night had been a new awakening experience. Wrapping a bath towel about his middle he headed for the bathroom; Gus had told him there were all men in the wing where their room was like barracks, he said. There was an ample supply of soap so he put his toilet article bag on the shelf and hopped into the shower. Plenty of hot water he luxuriated in the hot suds. After shaving and dabbing himself with after-shave lotion; he went back to the room. Brian was curled up and sound asleep. He dressed and quietly left the room and went downstairs; he asked the bartender if he could get a container of coffee to take outside and was told there was a complimentary coffee bar in the dining room. He really was starting to like Ridge Top! The coffee was excellent and he went out to the front of the hotel and into a glorious morning. The salt air was cool and refreshing, a gentle breeze added to that. There was a huge rock that was rather flat on top; he climbed up on it and looked out over the Sound. There were many boats of many descriptions on the water. They seemed to be going in all directions but the main course was due east . . . toward the Atlantic Ocean; the area was a famous fishing ground and the day was perfect! He sipped his coffee and let his mind retrace last night. He thought of how they had made love; he could not say Brian initiated things; he was a very willing partner. It all seemed natural to him; he never desired a man before. He had let gay guys have their way and they gave him oral sex on his way home occasionally; that was for immediate gratification and meant nothing. But he loved Brian! He realized he had loved him for a long time; and it first was apparent to him when Brian took that sojourn with Jerry to Jones Beach . . . he was envious and resented Jerry. Brian seemed to care for him; but it might just be a fling for him. This was all so alien to Tony but he was totally honest with himself; he loved this guy! He had never loved anyone in his life! Here he was; in his fifties, he had plenty of money, a good business and owned a good deal of valuable real estate. He had more where-with-all than anyone knew about; but he had no life. The action happening at the bar gave him an interest, but he was outside of the mix. If Brian was in the same boat and wanted to have a life with him he was certain they could make it work. But, how did Brian feel? This was supposed to be a fun trip; he would not start any serious talk and perhaps frighten Brian away. What people would say didn't bother him; what had *people* ever given him? He was more anxious than ever to see that cottage! If it needed upgrading he would get right to it; he would ask Brian to help him. Maybe he could finally get some happiness from his money. He couldn't stop his brain from spinning fantasies. Entering the hotel he stopped a waitress and asked if there was room service. She informed him that Gus only allowed non-breakable cups, glasses and plates in the rooms; she asked him what he wanted. He mentioned black coffee and if possible, some Danish, or anything that would go with the coffee; even just toast and jam would do. Suzie, the waitress asked him to wait where he was; she indicated a chair and invited him to sit. Tony was very impressed with her and her cheerful demeanor. Suzie returned with a carafe of coffee, two plastic cups and some mini blue berry muffins, fresh from the oven, and several napkins on a tray. It all had an inviting aroma.

"Will this be enough for you," she asked.

"Perfect, Suzie!" He had noticed her name tag pinned on her blouse. "What do I owe you?"

"Just a dollar for the coffee," she smiled, "I swiped the muffins!"

Tony laughed and gave her two dollars. "How late do you serve breakfast?"

"You can have breakfast any time the kitchen is open."

Tony thanked her and she thanked him and they went their separate ways. Brian was up, showered and dressed and he made room on the dresser for the tray.

"Oh, does that smell good! The coffee is much needed!"

"You look like a million bucks . . . no hangover that I can see!" Tony gave him a soft punch.

"It was quite a day." Brian said as he moved his head from side to side; slowly.

"It was quite a night," Tony said softly; "the most wonderful one ever! All my life I've been barking up the wrong tree . . . not any more!"

Brian sighed; "I was wondering how you would feel today; I was afraid you might have regrets. If it lowered your opinion of me I'd feel awful."

"I love you Brian; I realize now that I have for a long time. It's something I never dreamed would happen to me; but I'm very happy with it. This is supposed to be a fun trip; I won't do any serious talking now, let's enjoy each other; just know that you've made me happy and I hope I've done the same for you."

"I've never felt so completely happy, Tony." Tony hugged him; closely.

They finished the coffee and muffins and walked around the waterfront of the hotel. Tony showed Brian his rock and they sat there and admired the view and the perfect day. Soon it was time to call Ed Gunther. He told them he would pick them up in half an hour; he had borrowed his wife's convertible so they could have three hundred and sixty degree sightseeing. Both of them were delighted; they never got to ride in a convertible; there were no convertible taxis in New York!

Ed drove to route 27 and headed back toward East Hampton; they came to an area where the trees disappeared and the road began to go downhill. The ocean was on the south side and it spread out as far as you could see; the north side was undulating and covered with a variety of vegetation and scrub pine. From their high position they could see two enormous radio towers in the distance and Napeague Harbor nestled safely in the dunes. Long Island Sound was visible in the background.

"What a beautiful view from up here," Tony exclaimed, "it's a great spot for a home."

"Not while New York State owns it!" Ed laughed.

The highway was now heading west, it was low and flat, the narrowest part of Long Island, the Atlantic on one side and the Sound on the other. They came to a side road where Ed turned and crossed the Long Island Railroad which ran parallel to the highway and back to the City. After a short distance he turned onto a narrow lane which one could easily pass without noticing it; if you didn't know it was there.

"Where the hell are we going?" Tony asked.

"To your cottage, sir," Ed was smiling, "Do you see that big white building up ahead; it's right on the waterfront."

"I see it," a puzzled Tony said.

"Now, do you see that smaller structure near it?"

"Yes," Tony answered.

"That is your place. The white building is actually a barge that was beached there and made into an art school. The Museum of Modern Art owns it; Mrs. Nelson Rockefeller, the first, raised the money for them.

"It has a history!" piped Brian.

"It really does; the barge has a name . . . the Kearsage, and I wish I knew the rest; but I'm afraid I don't. I'll have to do some research!"

They all laughed, heartily.

"See that you do." Tony admonished.

Ed parked in front of the cottage which was up on a rise of dune. It was surrounded by beach plum and they were bearing fruit. The natives who were aware of this treasure came and picked them when no one was around and made beach plum jelly.

Taking out the keys Ed walked toward the front door. It was a hip roof construction with what looked like an attached garage but was used as a boat house. A small shed-like structure was on the other side and turned out to be the well house. The roof was cedar shingled and looked sound. The house was actually constructed of all cedar when it was built, some fifty years before, but a subsequent owner had re-sided it with asbestos shingles and destroyed its charm. As far as design goes it was simply utilitarian. The windows were all double-hung and you would think the builder was totally unaware that this was waterfront. What view? They went inside and Brian was sure it was going to smell musty and damp but the cedar offset that. The two bedrooms were small; so was the kitchen. The kitchen looked like the nineteen thirties, with very basic, old equipment. There was a porch, built into the house to fend off the foul weather. If you were sitting in the living room you had to stand up to see the harbor in front of you. The occupants were fishermen who were on the water most of the time; it wasn't necessary for them to look at it when they were home! But the living room held a gem! A stone fireplace, built by a mason who knew what he was doing, had a built-in Heatalator on each side to circulate the heat out into the room. The mantel was a slab of solid oak planed smooth, exposing the grain, and marine varnished so expertly that it still had a handsome sheen after these many years. There was a full bath and a breezeway to the boat house. An exposed stairway in the living room went up to an attic that ran the full length of the house. Lots of possibilities; and a lot of work! Tony was embarrassed; he had envisioned something quite different. Brian was excited. The location was sensational! Fifty acres of land zoned for wild life! That meant no other structure of any kind could be built there! This place was grandfathered in because it was built before the zoning change. The closest house was over a mile down the beach! Ed had been explaining all this but it hadn't registered with Tony . . . he was busy being dismayed.

"I guess we could have it burned down," Tony moaned; "I think it's insured."

"Tony!" Brian hooted, "This place is wonderful! Look at that beach! The sand is pure white and the harbor is pristine; there are so few houses around it. I love it!" Tony was floored; he was sure Brian would hate it. He suddenly began to feel relieved; he looked at it with new eyes.

"It needs a lot of fixing up, Brian."

"I'll help you; it will be fun!"

Ed had been silent for a while; he knew from experience that there were times when his opinion didn't matter . . . you just listen . . . and learn!

"Tony, this is a valuable piece of property," Ed finally spoke;

"You only own a half acre but you are surrounded by over fifty acres of preserved land. You even have those two radio towers nearby!"

Ed was hugging him, laughing. It was a well-chosen interjection; it changed the mood to one of enthusiasm. He gave Tony the keys;

"I have another set in the office in case you call me to do something here. I don't mean work, of course!" Again they all laughed.

"Let's show Brian your other properties; then I want to take you out for lunch to my favorite restaurant. You have to get to know these places; it looks like you may be spending more time out here."

Brian was completely knocked out by Tony's accumulation of property. He had been doing this for years and never told anyone about it. Brian could see how lonely Tony was . . . he also began to see that he, himself, was lonely even though he appeared to keep himself busy. Again Ronnie's words came back to him; Ronnie was wiser than Brian had thought. If Tony wanted a life with him, Brian was ready. They had an enjoyable lunch with Ed and the conversation was all about the cottage. Ed assured them that he could get reliable contractors to do any work that would be needed; he used them himself, they were skilled locals who didn't charge an arm and a leg. Back at Ridge Top they said goodbye to Ed and got into the Ford.

"I feel like celebrating," Tony exclaimed, "let's go see Kincaid and have a couple of drinks!"

"I'm with you," Brian was full of enthusiasm.

On arrival Tony parked the car and they went inside. No music! Bob had a bad hangover from the long day before; Kincaid excused that, readily; he was well aware of the ravages of a hangover. There were two empty stools at the end of the bar and they made a bee line for them.

"Well, what have you two been up to; have you been sight-seeing?"

Tony filled him in on the cottage and this time Brian was able to enter into the conversation. Bob rose up to his full height when they described the location.

"You own that shack at Napeague Harbor? That's my favorite clamming spot! Now I can go there and camp on your deck; since we are such good buddies."

Laughter as usual and Bob was annoyed when a customer wanted a drink and took him away from his interesting conversation. He knew a lot about the place, especially the fireplace; Bob was an accomplished stone mason himself and he had nothing but praise for the workmanship in its construction. When he learned they intended to restore the place he was delighted and he, too, had guys who were good workers and would put them in touch when needed.

"I'll let them know you are good friends so the prices will be right!"

The mood was definitely up!

"You are welcome there anytime, Bob, you've been an instant friend to us and we won't forget it. My clams are your clams;" laughter; encore.

They would have had dinner there but Tony wanted to try the food at Ridge Top; so they went back to the hotel after a couple of hours at Kincaid's. It was good to get back in their room and as sparse as it was; it was it was a comfortable feeling to be there. They stretched out on their beds and in no time both dozed off. Between the excitement and the drinks it was no surprise. Brian awoke first; it was dark and he was confused as to where he was, it took a minute or so to orient himself. Getting out of bed he lit the lamp and Tony began to rouse.

"Where am I?" He was pretending to be lost.

"You're at the *Chez Gus* in wonderful Montauk. Are you hungry?"

"I think I am; what about you?"

"I could eat; I'm going to wash up."

"I don't think we could share that sink so I'll wait until you finish."

"I won't be long . . . two shakes!"

"Take your time; there's no rush."

When Brian returned Tony went and cleaned up and was back in a few minutes. They went down to the dining room and were fortunate in getting a small table for two. The place was busy and the diners didn't look like the general run of the guests in the hotel. Most were very nicely dressed and there was no boisterous conversation at all. They had heard the food was good here and moderately priced; the busy dining room was a testimonial to that fact. Neither felt like drinking and they decided a glass of wine would be the best choice. Looking over the menu, which was extensive, they concluded it certainly was moderately priced. If the food was really good this place was nice to know about. Tony had secured Suzie as their server and Brian marveled at how he was able to get around and meet these people who all seemed to like him. She came to the table and took their orders commenting on a few of the entrees. Brian liked her and admired her friendly, but, professional, approach. When she brought the salad Tony ordered two more glasses of wine. The entrees came, piping hot, something Brian liked very much; and the dinner was delicious. Brian was accustomed to eating out often and in very good restaurants; this chef could hold his own with any of them. The chef happened to be the wife of Gus, the owner. No hired chef was going to walk out and open his own place and steal the customers from Ridge Top!

"Well, this place is everything they say and then some." Tony said.

"It's as good as I've had in the City and for much less money!"

"Well, Brian the rent in New York is kind of stiff."

"I know, but this business is seasonal; they have about four months."

"Not Gus; Bob Kincaid said he has the fishermen all year round. Some of those party boats sail year round. There are guys who come in my bar who fish out here and they come here in the winter, too.

They get a special train in New York and it gets them here at five a.m.; needless to say it has a bar car! A lot of the motels close so he has it made."

"Well, he certainly seems satisfied; and he doesn't spend a lot on décor."

Tony laughed and shook his head, "Décor; that is really funny."

"Well, Brian, what do you feel like doing; any place you'd like to go?"

"I would really like to go upstairs and just relax and talk about your cottage. I've had enough to drink today and it seems everywhere we go out here drinking is a part of it."

It's a resort, Brian, that's what vacationers do! Please don't rule out drinking; where would I be without it?"

"I'm not trying to eliminate drinking; God forbid! I've just had enough."

"Okay, we'll go up and see what ideas we can work up with the shack."

"Don't call it a shack! You forget where it's located; Paradise, Tony."

"I'm glad you feel that way; it makes me feel good."

They went upstairs and talked for quite a while; Tony began to realize that Brian had a talent for remodeling and he had the ability to imagine how the finished project would look. He was very impressed with the way he had retained how the place was laid out and how he knocked out walls.

"Brian, tomorrow we'll get some pads and go out to the cottage and make notes and take measurements. Right now I'd like to hit the hay."

"That's a good idea; let's go out early and bring breakfast with us."

"And *that* is a good idea," smiled Tony; "I also have another idea; let's push these two beds together and make a little elbow room. We can separate them in the morning before the maid comes in."

"My God! The good ideas are flying around here." Brian was laughing. They fixed the beds and it worked out comfortably. Another night of getting acquainted and there was no doubt this attraction was growing in depth. The physical need was wonderful;

but the magic was the ease with which their personalities clicked; a very important component of a relationship.

The sun was just about fully over the horizon when they left the hotel. Tony stopped at a diner in Montauk and Brian went in and ordered take-out food for their breakfast. It was only about a four mile ride to the cottage. The day looked like it was going to be as beautiful as they enjoyed previous days; they had been so lucky with the weather. Tony parked the car and went up the steps to the front door; once inside he began opening windows and doors to let the fresh morning air in. Brian brought in the food and a legal pad. They ate out of the plastic containers; sharing the breakfast. Fancy? No; wonderful fun? Yes! There were two large containers of coffee and the coffee was still hot. They enjoyed the view; the mix of birds was awesome! This was a section of Paradise and it was theirs to enjoy privately. Their conversation was confined to the upgrading of the cottage and they went from one idea to another making decisions and then scrapping them for something that seemed better. The time melted away and it was a keen enjoyment for them. Tony put his hand on Brian's shoulder and looked directly at him;

"Brian, do you think you could live out here all the time . . . year 'round I mean . . . with me?"

Brian returned his gaze. "Do you mean in the near future or eventually?"

"I guess I mean whenever."

"Of course I could! Don't you know that?"

"We'll talk about it, kid, I want to make some plans."

Chapter Three

Jerry Foley and his partner Tom Nesbitt had just finished an eight p.m. to four a.m. tour of duty. Tom looked like he could do another shift; one would not say the same about Jerry; he looked a bit haggard; he needed rest.

"Well that is that for a couple of weeks," said Jerry.

"For you; but not for me," lamented Tom. "What am I going to do without you?" Tom was sincerely unhappy about not working with him.

"I'll be back before you know it; two weeks goes buy fast."

"Yeah; when you're having fun; not when you're working. How come you changed your time? We always go on vacation the same weeks."

Jerry hedged;

"I guess I just wanted some kind of a change; I don't know." Tom knew his partner too well; this had to be a dame!

"It wouldn't be a dame," He grinned at Jerry "Now would it?"

"Well, it could be that; I wouldn't call her a dame, though."

"Oh!" Tom sat erect on the diner stool, "This is someone special! Now I have to hear about this! Don't tell me you've found a nice girl. Lucille will be ecstatic!"

"You ought to quit the job and write soap operas. Don't start ringing bells; it hurts my ears."

The owner of the diner came to chat with them, briefly,

"Like a special coffee? He smiled. Jerry looked at Tom.

"That would be nice," he said.

It surprised Jerry; a special coffee was a double shot of whiskey in a coffee mug. Tom drank very little on the job and rarely before he went home. He didn't seem in his usual hurry to get home; it puzzled Jerry; it didn't add up!

He would wonder a lot more when Tom accepted a second drink. This was definitely not his buddy Tom. He was also smoking more; it didn't jibe.

"Aren't you going to tell me about this new flame. Tom poked Jerry kidding.

Jerry did not want to talk about Eleanor; he wanted to end it pronto!

"Now you have something to look forward to; I'll fill you in . . . later."

"Oh, mystery! I love mysteries; is it going to be a serial or one story?" Jerry gave Tom a look of displeasure; he didn't like what he was mouthing. "Could we change the subject? I've had enough of this."

Tom knew it was time to quit needling Jerry; he didn't want to annoy him. He also knew that this lady must mean something to Jerry; he always talked openly about the one-night stands he frequently had. At least he said he had them; many times they were manufactured affairs to keep his image firm. They were very close friends; if Tom needed money, Jerry was right there. He lived half way out on Long Island in a nice development because he didn't want his children growing up in the city. Lucille was a devoted wife and mother and they seemed to have a good marriage. Jerry never had this nagging feeling about them before but it was haunting him. Because they were so close he decided to throw out a feeler.

"How is Lucille?

"She's okay . . . why?"

"What do you mean . . . why? Can't I ask for your wife?"

"Oh, sure; of course."

"If something is bothering you I'm willing to listen; you know it won't go any further than me. Sometimes it helps just to talk about it."

"I do need to talk, Jerry, I know you will understand."

Jerry never expected the problem to be what it was; Tom continued; heavily.

"It's Lucille and me," he went on with difficulty, "we're married twenty years and she's still uptight about sex; it's the religion really; things that I need she feels are sinful or dirty. The Catholic Church is always in our bed! I use condoms because I don't want a house full of kids that I can't afford. The priest finally told her it was my sin, not hers, so that was one big hurdle cleared. I love her, Jerry, but I'm walking around like a horny teenager because I'm not satisfied. It gives me a guilt complex yet I don't really think it's my fault. I am not looking for another woman; I want my wife, but she is firm in her beliefs. One night, about a year ago, we were at a party and she got a bit high on some wine that she liked; she's no drinker, when we got in bed I started making love to her and I could tell she was really horny. I was kissing her everywhere and I got down there where she never let me kiss her. She went wild! I took advantage of her mood and I slid up on top of her and put it in her mouth. It was something I needed so bad and I just went at it! I made the big mistake of coming in her mouth; that brought her back to reality and she ran into the bathroom sobbing her heart out. I could hear the water running but I knew she would never be able to get her mouth clean; as far as she was concerned. The next day I apologized and I told her it would never happen again. Our sex life has been pretty stiff since then."

"That is heavy stuff," Jerry commiserated, "you can't fight the church."

"I'm forty-five years old, Jerry, and I lust like I was twenty-five. I've never touched another woman since I've been married and God knows I had plenty before. When I was in the Navy and I had shore leave; my clothes were off more than they were on. I learned a lot of fun things; things that most women would enjoy; but not *my* wife."

Jerry knew this was serious business; this could wreck their marriage. All Tom needed now was the right female who had an active libido and could sense his needs and he would be her slave. He felt helpless.

"Well Jerry, I've got to get going; thanks for listening, it really helped."

Jerry and Eleanor went out on a few dates during their vacation; Nora joined them twice; once when they went to Jones Beach. She had a persistent cough and Jerry thought the sea air would do her some good. Seeing him with Eleanor made Nora very happy; it was just what Nora wanted for Jerry. One afternoon Jerry dropped in at Tony's about five in the afternoon and to his surprise Tom was there; he was doing day shifts. Taking a stool next to him Jerry spoke.

"What are you doing here? Shouldn't you be on your way out to Long Island?"

"Didn't you ever hear of saying, *hello?*"

"Oh, hello," said Jerry, "Do you feel better now?"

"Much better, dear." Tom nudged Jerry's shoulder.

"Lucille and the kids are spending a couple of weeks in Hampton Bays with her parents at their summer home. They came and picked her up yesterday; the kids have a ball when they go out there."

"So, you are foot loose, Tommy boy!"

"That I am; that I am." Tom ordered drinks for both of them while Jerry was saying hello to Tony. Gino was working the bar with Tony. Tom spoke,

"So how is your vacation going; are you seeing this mystery woman?"

"As a matter of fact I am. A few times; as a matter of fact."

"Well, I like to work with facts," Tom was grinning, "it's easier."

They sat for an hour drinking and talking. Tom had been in a down mood before Jerry came in but now he had perked up a bit. Jerry sensed that he was still not his usual self. He was thinking they ought to eat something because of the drinks they had consumed and he got the idea of calling Eleanor to see if he could bring Tom to her place for dinner. He wanted them to meet and he would stop and pick up whatever Eleanor wanted to prepare. The fact that he had a few drinks made it seem like a wonderful idea; it never occurred to him that he would be imposing. After telling Tom about his wonderful idea he went to the phone and called her. He was cheery

"Hello gorgeous, it's Dick Tracy."

"What a nice surprise; where are you?" He told her about his wonderful idea and really expected an immediate *come right on over!* She hesitated and then in a low voice said, "Edith is here."

"You're kidding," he breathed, "tell me you are."

"No, my dear I am not." Jerry asked; "Would that bother you?"

"Not really, I thought you might not like it." "I don't care," he lied, "Tom needs some cheering up and I know you are expert at that."

She laughed and shook her head, "Just bring some steaks; I have enough food in to do the rest. It's going to be very simple." He thanked her and told her he would call her when they were on their way. He went back to the bar.

"We're all set; she's looking forward to meeting you. One of the girls who works with her is there so you will have a dinner partner."

Suddenly the idea of Tom meeting Edith didn't seem like a smart idea. Knowing the state of mind Tom was in and knowing full well Edith's bent it might be like playing with matches next to gasoline. Well, the die was cast and he would have to sweat it out. He hoped Edith wouldn't get loaded. His unease stayed.

When they were leaving Tony's Tom elected to take his car and follow Jerry so they wouldn't have to come back for it later. Jerry went to Nora's butcher who stayed open until nine o'clock. He did a lively business from five to nine; mostly people on their way home form work. They usually knew what they wanted, didn't haggle about price or go on about their kids or grandkids or their aches and pains. They just wanted to get home! He recommended New York strip steaks and selected four choice ones for Jerry. Jerry asked to use his phone and he called Eleanor to alert her. The evening to end all evenings was about to begin . . . and so was deep trouble!

Eleanor had invited Edith over and she was hesitant about accepting at first; she had been stand-offish for a while; it was the reason Eleanor was asking her over, they hadn't done anything together for some time. There was no way for Eleanor to know of Edith's experience with Jerry and she was biting the bullet at the thought of seeing him again; she was determined not to let him mess up her life. A more timid woman would have made her exit; Edith was not timid! Not by a damn sight! They had a few cocktails while they waited; Edith made sure she was well fortified. Jerry Foley would never know that she was trembling inside! Edith would not allow it!

"Thank God he's bringing a friend; Eleanor, it will be nice to have someone to talk to; you and Jerry will probably be making plans."

"Edith! You know I have better manners than that! I'm afraid his partner is married, though."

"Since when has that been a problem?" Edith tilted her head, with lowered eyes, "Just let him be attractive and good company, please, God!"

"I haven't met him yet so I can't give you any clues. Jerry is fond of him; he often speaks of how close they are.

"Close! Cops who work together are joined at the hip! The partner comes before anyone else; a woman should be so lucky to get such love!"

"Well, it is a close relationship and it is a dangerous job."

The door bell rang and they came in with the steaks and a bottle of vodka and it sounded like there were four of them. They were very jolly! Edith was extremely pleased with what she was looking at and she found it easy to be cordial to Jerry because he brought along a real hunk of a man. It just might turn out to be a pleasant evening. Jerry was introducing Tom and Eleanor then Tom came to her and introduced himself as Jerry and Eleanor went into the kitchen.

"This turns out to be an evening of pleasant surprises," Tom smiled at her," I thought I was going to be on my own."

"Well, you've rescued us from boring each other to death; we work together all week and we still have to get together and talk some more. The curse of womanhood; we can't stop talking!"

She was glad she did her hair. He was drawn toward her and he could smell her subtle scent; there was a sensation in his groin. If he hadn't been drinking he might have been on guard; but he was drinking; and he wasn't on guard. Edith had all her guns out; she was loaded for bear and this was no grizzly; this was a big Teddy bear. They were called to the kitchen for drinks; he took her arm; she leaned against him, feeling the lean hardness of this body. Edith felt like a teenager!

"Step right up, folks," Jerry had glasses and the liquor laid out on a small table, "let me fix you something cold; we're not serving wine with dinner so choose your drink accordingly."

Eleanor had just put the steaks under the broiler and the room was beginning to take on that wonderful aroma. Edith had made an attractive salad and they used a potatoes au gratin packaged concoction that was a success. The table was set and as soon as the steaks were done they sat down and enjoyed themselves. Jerry saw the chemistry between Tom and Edith and he was worried. If these two became an item he would blame himself. Eleanor noticed the attraction, also, but she thought it was just one evening and they would go their separate ways. She couldn't have been more mistaken! This fire was just starting and there was plenty of fuel to keep it going; and it was going to burn hotly! After dinner was over and the kitchen cleaned up they had a couple of drinks and it was Edith who said she had to call it a night.

"I will drop you off if you like; I've got to get moving too."

Tom had stood up and Eleanor was impressed with how fresh and sober he looked. Jerry didn't like this one bit and Edith sensed it and she wallowed in her revenge; she loved seeing his disapproval. They said their goodnights and Jerry and Eleanor were alone. He didn't say anything to her about how he felt. They had previously made plans for the next evening to take Nora out to dinner and they began discussing where they would go. They lit cigarettes and she asked him if he would like a cup of coffee.

"I made it for dinner but I had no takers; it's still fresh."

"Sounds like a good idea," he smiled at her.

She went to the kitchen and his mind went to Tom and Edith; *it won't take her long to pull down his zipper!* And he had a hunch there would be no stopping her! Tom pulled up in front of Edith's place and parked; that pleased her. Then he went around and opened the door; "I'll see you to your apartment; is it ground floor?"

"It's one flight up; I don't feel safe on ground floors."

"You're a hundred percent right," he said.

She opened the door and turned; they went right into each others arms. He kissed her passionately and she responded with all the gusto in her. *Oh, God this is my kind of man,* she thought. He was getting excited; she felt it . . . *"Oh!"*

"I don't have too much time; I have a long drive."

"Let's not waste a minute; come into the bedroom."

They undressed feverishly and their mutual needs cast off any inhibitions that might have existed. What he couldn't have at home was at his disposal here. She gave him what he craved and he was consumed with it. Needless to say he didn't have a long ride home; he had a long ride . . . in Edith's arms!

The next morning Tom came out of the bathroom freshly showered. He was physically sated; but his emotions were in somewhat of a turmoil. One thing he was certain of; this was going to be handled with complete honesty as far as Edith was concerned. How he would handle the home front was another matter. Edith was sitting on the bed brushing her pale gold hair; she was still in a euphoria she had never experienced before. Seeing him again was of the utmost importance; and it could be on any terms Tom required. This was her man! He came over and kissed her brow, tenderly, she purred like a kitten full of cream.

"You have beautiful hair, Edith, it's so soft."

"If anyone should have nice hair it should be me . . . it's my job!"

They laughed and he began getting dressed; she hated the idea of his need to go . . . but there wasn't going to be any foolish emotions about making him stay. Above all, she was not doing anything to destroy what they had found; it was too important to her. He had already effected a change in her; she was in love, this was not the usual toss in the hay. Putting on her robe she went to him.

"Would you like some coffee? It won't take long and I have a thermos; you can have it on the ride out to Long Island."

"That would be great! I'd save time and I need the coffee."

"Come and keep me company while I make it, you're so good for me."

"I hope I can see you again, Edith, I need you; you're magic for me."

"I appreciate your situation; I'll be here for you whenever you can manage it. Do something for me Tom; don't tell me anything about your family life. When you can be here it will be "us" . . . that's all I want."

"I was going to tell you that I never could discuss my family; we have ESP."

He kissed her and held her close; she floated in his soapy scent. The word no was not in Edith's vocabulary where Tom was concerned.

He made no sexual demands on Lucille; he was affectionate with her for he still loved her. He wasn't in love with her but their years together and the fact that she was a fine person was not overlooked by Tom. In his mind he was giving her what she needed and he was taking care of his needs. He really thought he had worked it all out for everyone . . . Lucille was well aware of the change in him; being a woman she missed his intense passion. Even though she felt she must resist some of his desires she still thrilled at the pursuit; that was gone; their love-making, which was infrequent, was of habit. The church would have approved of it; and Lucille was beginning to foster a resentment toward her religion. If Tom had lost his desire for her she was not blaming him; she was placing it squarely at the feet of the Hierarchy and their *head in the sand* attitude about marital sex. She could find no fault with his behavior; he was the perfect husband. But she had lost her lover and how could she complain when she had constantly put him off when he got a bit frisky. Could she now ask him why he had stopped? Not very likely! If she asked her confessor for his help he would tell her to pray to the Virgin Mary or maybe St. Jude, the patron of difficult cases. Lucille was in a very difficult position; she could not complain about getting what she asked for! Her mother was very religious and would be of no help. Lucille was a very private person and had no close women friends to discuss this with; going to a marriage counselor was also something she wouldn't consider. On the surface they still appeared to be the wonderful couple people knew them to be. Only Lucille knew; and she began to wonder if someone else was giving Tom what he seemed so desperately in need of. Dare she pose such a question? Where would she begin? It could never happen; not from Lucille! In living up to the demands of her church she had so far kept her husband; but she had lost her lover to a Venus fly trap who would do anything to keep him!

Jerry picked Eleanor up the following afternoon; they decided to make an early day and take Nora for a drive out on Long Island and find a waterfront restaurant for dinner. It was a mild day and with the car windows open Nora enjoyed the fresh air. She sat in the back seat like a queen and looked very smart in a pale blue suit. Eleanor had persuaded her to take off her hat and her silver hair looked elegant. They took the North Shore route and Nora exclaimed over the foliage and beautiful estates. Jerry had made a turn toward the Sound and quite by accident they found a country inn right on the water. It had been a private home years before and it was the only building in the area. It was exciting for each of them and he parked close to the entrance. There were several cars parked and they were beautiful cars; an indication of the clientele. It was quite breezy and they hurried inside. The place had a European aura, heavy, carved beams and stucco walls. There was a huge fireplace opposite a semi-circular bar where a few people were enjoying cocktails and the view. The view! It was panoramic! The waves in the dark blue water seemed crested with thin edges of silver and the sun shone brightly overhead. An assortment of boats were sailing or docked and some were farther out, looking like toys and all of it was beautiful. Nora was speechless. A waiter came and suggested a table in the large bow window facing the water. It was perfect. They seated themselves and Jerry made sure Nora had an unobstructed view. The curve in the window assured everyone a good vista. "Are you drinking, Nora?"

"Jerry dear, is the sun shining outside?"

"Don't let him tease you Nora; let's ask him if he's drinking!"

"Sure we know there's no doubt of that!" Nora rejoined.

The waiter brought menus and took the drink order leaving a plate of canapés. Eleanor looked at the menu; she knew it would be expensive and it was. She wanted to split the tab with Jerry without insulting him. Nora rose and said she was going to the ladies room declining Eleanor's offer to go with her. This was a good time to talk about the tab. She was graciously refused; he assured her he was not insulted and the matter was closed; tight!!

"What a find this place is, Jerry."

"I should do this with Nora more often; she does so much for me and I do things around the house but this is a treat for her." Nora returned and he held her chair as she sat down. She smiled,

"My; the grand manners come out in grand places," she said wryly, "you don't do that in a diner."

"Now Nora, don't tease him when he's doing nice things; he's a gentleman at heart and sometimes he just can't hide it."

"I'll thank you both to cut out the cute stuff; it's time to be ladies."

They laughed together and the waiter arrived with the tray of drinks, smiling;

"If you need more time to look at the menu I'll check back."

"Thank you, Bruno," Jerry noticed his name-tag, "I think we do."

It was most enjoyable for all of them and Nora was having difficulty staying awake on the ride home. Between the motion of the car, the fresh air, and the beer; it was like a sleeping pill to her. Jerry took her home first and they both made sure she was safely in her bed before they left. On the way Eleanor went over the day telling him how much she enjoyed it. Then she started talking about Tom and Edith, mentioning that she felt uncomfortable with what was happening.

"I know it's none of my business and I would never say anything to Edith, but I have a feeling we might be seeing them socially a lot. Who are they going to have for friends with their situation? From what you tell me about Tom he's going to be mighty protective of his family life. I'm glad to hear that; for his children's sake."

"Tom and I are closer than brothers; I am behind him all the way. No one knows what goes on between two people; they have to settle it whatever way they can. Not to satisfy other people; it's their lives. I don't question him; why should I? If you are a friend you are there when he wants to talk . . . and you listen!"

Eleanor admired his loyalty; she couldn't ask any questions; they weren't going steady or in a serious relationship although she found herself getting in deeper as they were seeing each other. He was affectionate but he never pressed her for intimacy; contrary to his reputation he showed her respect and was very thoughtful. But she was afraid they might become a foursome; going on dates together frequently; it made her uncomfortable and she knew how Edith could flare up. She had to work with her so keeping things smooth was important. Talking to Brian would help; he always made a situation less stressful than it seemed. Of course nothing's a snap with Edith.

They arrived at Eleanor's and he walked her to her door. "Nightcap, dear?"

"Just one, I don't want to let you go;" hugging her, kissing her brow.

They sat on the couch with their drinks and he put his arm around her as she settled in close to him. He began kissing her softly, exploring her face and it was firing up her desire. She felt comfortable with him and trusted him; Eleanor was in a vulnerable state with a man who had never had a commitment of any kind with any woman. His passion began to grow and his hand was gently caressing her breast; he had never gone this far before and she made no effort to stop him. He kissed her deeply, his tongue sought hers and she responded; he was getting fully aroused and suddenly he drew back and felt an unexplainable sense of fear. She sighed; "What's wrong,"

"I don't know; I'm getting carried away . . . it's too soon for that."

He knew he sounded ridiculous, even juvenile, but he had to leave! He stood up and excused himself heading toward the bathroom. After throwing cold water on his face and getting his breathing back to normal he returned to her. She was standing; obviously embarrassed;

"I'm sorry, Eleanor, I . . ."

"Please don't explain," she interrupted him, "you better go; its better."

He kissed her brow and was gone. Once again she was left with that uneasy feeling; *what did he really want? Where was this going?*

He went to a dive in the seedy side of town and had a couple of shots and a beer. He had taken a stool at the end of the bar to avoid looking in the mirror. He knew why he had brought things to a halt with Eleanor; he didn't want to face it. After a few beers he walked out and went down a side street that not many people would care to be on. He noticed a young girl standing by some steps that led down to a basement apartment; he spoke.

"Want some business, Sweetie?"

"What's on your mind, Bo?"

He moved closer to her, taking her hand and putting it on his crotch. "Kneel down and take care of this; there's nothing to be afraid of, I'm vice-squad."

She performed well and he rewarded her with money; he also thanked her, there was a change in his attitude and he was no longer rough with these girls. Walking away he felt physically better but his mind was very unsettled. If he had continued making love to Eleanor and reached the peak of his passion he would have wanted her to satisfy him like this girl just did . . . he was sure it would be a big *no!* How could he keep on seeing her? Being with her was wonderful and he was aware she was good for him; and she loved Nora. He got into his car and headed home; he was really upset and mixed up; facing a stone wall.

Arriving home he let himself in being very quiet; then it started. Nora was coughing that hacking cough and it was getting worse. He called to her at her door;

"Nora, can I come in?" She kept coughing, so he went in; she was sitting on the edge of her bed; she looked drained and terribly pale. He was frightened and got her medicine and gave it to her. The syrup gave her some relief and she wanted to stand up. He helped her and put her robe around her shoulders.

"Come into the kitchen and I'll make you some tea and honey; you're miracle cure for everything."

"Ye can stop your smart talk; it's worked fine for many years."

"Tomorrow I'm taking you to the doctor; I want to tell him just how bad this cough is; I know you don't tell him everything."

"I don't need no doctor; he'll tell me the same thing and give me the same dope!"

"You're going just to give me peace of mind; I'll even pay for the visit!"

"You'll do no such thing! I'll pay me own bills! And speaking of bills I want to give you something toward that dinner today. That place was dear . . . . don't get me wrong; it was worth every penny!"

"I don't want to hear another word about that; understand?"

He poured her tea and she pouted; having been silenced. He forgot the lemon and was curtly reminded of his carelessness. She looked better and her color was better, but he was still very concerned about this. They talked until Nora said she was tired. He saw her to her bed; quietly heading for his. The helpless feeling gnawed at him; he wanted to get her to a specialist who might diagnose her problem and help her. He refused to think about lung cancer. She had good health insurance and he made up his mind that somehow he was going to get her to see the kind of specialist who might help her. Her condition preyed on his mind. If he had to use knock-out drops he was getting her examined!

After taking care of some simple household chores Brian showered and dressed and the wander-lust immediately set in. All he could think of was what was happening with Tony and he was aching to talk to him about it. Going to the bar didn't seem like a good idea because they were not able to talk freely. The last thing he wanted to do was embarrass Tony at his place of business. Calling him on the phone was not an option so he decided to say;

"To Hell with all this thinking; I'm going to Tony's!"

Brian went into Tony's and took his regular stool; it was early afternoon and not overly busy. Tony was working the bar alone and he came over as soon as he was free.

"Gin and tonic?" Brian nodded.

"Ed sent me some names of contractors out East and he called me about a guy who would go in there and make the place inhabitable for now. How does that sound to you?"

"I think I would want to know what kind of money he wants. He might be one of those self-styled designers who think they are worth top dollar."

"If Gino will work for a week here would you go out there with me?"

"Sure I will; we could do a lot ourselves. Could you find a nicer place to work? I don't think so! When do you want to go?"

"As soon as Gino is free; I'll call him and ask him to come here now."

He went to the phone and as he picked it up Gino walked in the door; he had a friend with him.

"Here he is now, he just came in!"

"Mental telepathy! I was just calling you."

"Well, here I am . . . but we don't have a drink!"

They all laughed and Gino introduced Mario; a very pleasant man; who might be in his fifties. Tony made drinks and Brian talked with the two men.

"Gino," said Tony, "would you be able to give me a week here; I want to go out east again?" Gino looked at him; "When do you want to go?"

"As soon as I can; it's up to you."

Mario is going to be with me for a few days . . . "I'll help you," Mario interrupted; "we have nothing special to do."

"I'll pay both of you." Tony looked at Gino; who said,

"How about the day after tomorrow?" Tony looked at Brian who nodded yes;

"I appreciate this, Gino, it helps me a lot. I've got some things to take care of and the quicker the better. Come here tomorrow for dinner and we'll arrange everything."

Are you going to go with him, Brian?" Gino asked.

"Yes," he replied, "I'm on vacation and have no plans so this is a real treat; I love it out there! Especially Montauk, it's so different,"

"I know Montauk, Brian, I go on fishing trips out there; there's no place like it! They have some great party boats there and plenty of them." Gino enthused.

"We had a few drinks in a bar at the docks; the place is a bee hive! The bar owner was the one who found us a hotel to stay in." Brian was excited.

"I know, Tony told me about it."

"Do you ever go out there, Mario?" Brian included him in the conversation. "No, I'm not into fishing or boats; give me the beach."

"Oh, Mario the beach out there is sensational! Pure white sand." Brian brightened up with enthusiasm. Mario smiled;

"I'll have to check it out;"

Brian stayed until closing and helped Tony wrap the place up. With his help it did not take long. They went out the back door; Tony locking both locks securely.

"It's kind of dark back here Tony; don't you think that's a bit risky? You always leave here alone; you are in New York City, you know."

"They don't even know I exist; I'm small potatoes."

"Tony; people get killed for a couple of dollars here!"

"Not to worry, pal, let's grab a cab I don't feel like walking,"

Entering Tony's apartment he lit some lamps and put some papers in his desk.

"I'm going to take a quick shower; you look like you just had one. Do you want anything before I go into the bathroom? Do you want to use it?"

"No, go ahead, I'll get ready for bed; you must be tired."

"Not as tired as you think!"

Brian went into the bedroom and undressed; he turned down the bed and got into it. He stretched out and it felt good; shortly Tony came in and crawled in next to him, sighing in comfort. The clean, soapy scent of him filled the air and they rediscovered each other. There was no conversation; only murmurs. Later they would have cigarettes and discuss the coming trip out East. Tony shied away from talking about their relationship. He was moving slowly.

In the morning Brian went home to get ready for the trip and to tell Eleanor all about it. He had called her and she was making breakfast and was anxious to see what her friend was up to. She was happy for him and there seemed to be a good feeling about all this. Maybe he had finally found a guy who appreciated him. When she first learned about Tony she was very surprised; it never dawned on her that Tony could be homosexual; he was completely masculine and it had puzzled her. Eleanor had a lot to learn and there were many lessons in store for her. She heard him come in from his apartment and she went to meet him.

"Tell me all about this, boy; pronto!"

"Did you ever hear of the expression 'good morning,' madam?"

"Oh, ceremony today," she kissed him, "good morning, darling."

"That's a little more civilized; I don't feel like I'm being accosted!"

"Oh, God forbid!" She was laughing heartily, "We can't have that!"

"Come into the kitchen and I will give you sustenance."

"A cup of that coffee I smell would be wonderful."

"No orange juice? Fresh squeezed!"

"Coffee first, if I may; I'm not accustomed to regimen."

"If you keep putting your eyebrows up there they may stay there!"

"Are you opening a finishing school here?" He lowered his eyes, disdainly, "I don't recall filling out an application; are there uniforms?"

"You my dear, would be expelled before you were admitted!"

They were laughing; happy to be in each others company. It was a comfort to have a friend with whom you could relax, feeling really close. He filled her in on all the property Tony had accumulated and asked her not to mention it to anyone; especially Jerry, who might tease him about being a rich land owner. He explained how private Tony was about his personal business.

"He doesn't tell anyone anything."

"And so he should be; it's nobody's business what he owns."

"That's how I feel," agreed Brian, "I was floored by what we saw!"

"Well, you two will have a great time fixing up that place; you'll be a big help to him, you have good ideas and wonderful taste. And I might add you know how to do it without spending a lot of money. You have acquired some lovely things and at prices I could hardly believe. I've learned a lot about where to shop from you."

"And I don't even have a school!"

"I'll box your ears; you imp!"

He told her of their plans to drive out the next day and spend a week making the cottage inhabitable; later on, in the fall, Tony wanted to remodel the whole place. Bob Kincaid had told him to wait until the fall and winter months because the contractors didn't have as much business and he would get better prices.

"Does it have heat?" Eleanor asked.

Brian described the fireplace and said it would heat the living room comfortably. Tony would put in central heat in the fall when remodeling.

"All of a sudden you have a lot happening in your life, Brian."

"As do you," madam, "Jerry took his vacation to match yours."

She told him about the delightful drive out on Long Island and finding the wonderful restaurant. Because they were so close she told him about the romance that was blooming with Tom and Edith and how it upset her; sensing she and Jerry would be seeing a lot of them. It wasn't necessary to tell him about Edith's temperament; he had seen her in heat.

"I'm surprised to hear that about Tom; I don't know him but Jerry always said he was a terrific father and husband. Well, it's just starting up; maybe it will fizzle. Why does Edith always get involved with a married man?"

Eleanor shrugged, "That is the sixty-four dollar question, dear."

"If she starts making demands and throwing tantrums it won't last."

Eleanor raised her brows, "It's been her modus operandi so far."

They were going to see a re-born Edith; it would amaze them! She had found all that she craved in a man and would do anything to prevail! If Tom wanted her; that was all that mattered and she found him at the right time in his life. She was at his disposal and his pleasure dominated!

"All you can do is swing with it and ask Jerry to cool it with them."

"I already know that won't happen; they are too close."

"Just when your life was getting interesting this thing comes up!"

"I don't know," Brian; "I don't think there's a future with Jerry."

"He's showing you attention no other girl ever got from him."

"There's something missing . . . I can't explain it."

"I can see that it troubles you; don't get in too deep."

"Thank you for caring," her hand brushed his cheek; "it helps."

He offered to help clean up; she sent him on his way; "get packing!"

Brian headed for his pad and did just as Eleanor had ordered. He was all packed and in shape so Tony would not have to wait for him.

Brian stayed at Tony's the night before the trip because they agreed to start out at four a.m. before the heavy traffic. Tony had rented a car and they were on their way just about on time. When hunger set in they could stop for breakfast. Tony had brought a thermos of coffee and some plastic cups to give them a jump start. Eschewing drinks the night before they were bright-eyed and bushy-tailed at the outset. It made more sense.

Traffic was light and thankfully it wasn't Friday; when there is a mass exodus out of the city in the summertime. To the shore or the mountains! They were on the Long Island Expressway and moving at a nice pace; something you could do in the wee hours. Tony gave Brian a gentle poke in the ribs; he teased him about not being able to drive; leaving it all to him.

"We've got to get you a learner's permit so I can teach you to drive. I'm going to get a post office box so we have an address out East and you can get the permit wherever we have to go to get it. There are a lot of back roads that you can use to get experience and you won't be risking your life like you would in the city."

Brian smiled. "And maybe a lot of other peoples' lives!"

"Nonsense," Tony came to his defense; "you'll learn fast!"

"Thanks for the support; I am going to need it and you'll need patience. I've never even been behind a steering wheel except in the Dodge-Em cars at Coney Island."

"Well, that's good experience! You have to be alert in those things."

They laughed at that and Brian poured some coffee and handed a cup to Tony.

"Thank you, sir, it's easy to manage this when there are so few cars; in another hour this will be a bee hive."

When they reached Hampton Bays they stopped at a diner and had breakfast; the sun had risen and it looked like a beautiful day was ahead. The conversation was primarily about what they would do when they arrived at the cottage.

"I called Ed and he told me to call him when we were in Amagansett; I think he wants us to meet the guy who does those quick fix-ups he was talking about. I still want to ask Bob Kincaid who he has in mind; he always seems to try and save our money."

"You definitely get that feeling when he's talking . . . he's for real."

"You're right about that, Brian; we've made a friend there."

The rest of the trip was not as easy going as the first half. The two lane highway was not adequate to handle the morning traffic. The combination of the residents, the business people and the tourists was too much for the narrow road. For years factions were trying to build a by-pass so that traffic going to Montauk and the other eastern most villages could be expressed there. But narrow-minded business people who had political clout always defeated the attempts. They thought there would be a loss of income for them if the traffic were rerouted. The fact that the people heading east never stopped in those villages; they shopped at home and brought everything with them, never penetrated these narrow thinkers. As the years went by and the property value escalated it became prohibitive to contemplate such an enterprise. It would cost the tax payers too much money and the politicians shied away from the idea as if it were the plague! So the congestion was something they had to live with and complain about; and blame on the tourists; their bread and butter! Many locals celebrated the end of the season and the absence of the *summer people* not realizing they were complaining about the very ones who enabled them to live a securer life!

Finally they reached the cottage and went in and opened windows and doors to let the wonderful air circulate through it. After bringing their gear in and leaving it in the living room, temporarily, Brian looked at Tony and exclaimed;

"Tony! The place has been cleaned up! I just looked at the kitchen and it's shining. Did you ask Ed to have it done?"

"No; I never gave it a thought or I would have. Only he has a key."

"What a thoughtful thing to do; I brought cleaning stuff."

"Well, don't unpack it; you don't need it!"

"I'm going to leave it here; when don't you need cleaning stuff?"

They checked the other rooms and all were cleaned. It lifted their spirits.

"Brian, let's change into shorts and take a walk on the beach. I want to walk barefoot in the water to soothe my aching toes."

"Do you have a problem with your feet?"

"No; but I want to soothe them anyway."

"By all means! Let us be off and get to soothe your feet!"

They stopped at the water's edge, barefoot, Brian noticed there were people at the barge next to them. They had built a two-storied structure on the barge and there were decks all around it. The view was excellent from the top deck; they would get up there in the future. The frontage on the water was built up with railroad ties and afforded a strong protection from erosion. Tony would meet the man who conducted the school and he would be instrumental in getting the same protection for them as well.

"Let's go," said Tony, "look at all those birds down along the shore!"

"I'm going to get a bird book," Brian enthused, "and binoculars!"

"You're going to look like a scientist; you'll need a pith helmet!"

"You will use them also; you'll see!"

Brian started running Tony followed him calling; "Remember my age!"

Tony had gone over to the restaurant across the highway and called Ed. He was the one who had the place cleaned for them. They made a date to meet for lunch in Amagansett; Ed was bringing the handy man with him. Coming back into the cottage he found Brian busy organizing the kitchen. He had brought paper plates and utensils for temporary use and easy disposal. When his eyes fell on a small Hibachi charcoal grill in the store he purchased it; a wise move, they would use it often. There was room to put a portable dishwasher in the kitchen and as soon as Tony returned it was the first thing Brian mentioned. He explained how it hooked up to the faucet easily and was on casters for easy moving.

"We have enough room for it," he concluded, "and they're not expensive."

"You've been busy! Where did you get all this stuff?"

"It was all in that black duffel bag."

"You're really efficient!" Tony smiled at him. "We need a phone; I'll get one put in. When the real work starts here it will be a must! Hopping over to that restaurant won't cut it."

"They might be closed in the winter; it's kind of like a stand."

"I think you are right, Brian, it probably doesn't have heat."

They met Ed and David and there was a cursory discussion about a temporary fix. David had seen the cottage; it was his wife who had done the cleaning. It was decided that David would follow them back to the cottage and they could discuss things on site. During the conversation David repeatedly said *it all depends on what you want to spend* and Brian found this annoying. He had nothing to say during the meet leaving that to Tony. It had given him the feeling that David might have a high price tag clipped to his ideas; Brian didn't have good vibes about David; he'd get Tony's aspect and see.

As soon as they were inside the cottage David seemed to take charge. It sounded like the major renovations were being done. Tony was ill at ease and already had decided to go out to see Bob Kincaid as soon as David left. He noticed that Brian had no suggestions or any comments at all; he got the feeling Brian wasn't well-impressed!

"Okay," David, "let me think about what we've discussed and I'll get back to you soon. Good-by and thank your wife for me."

"Well, he's gone, Brian, and I think we both feel the same way."

"It felt like we were going to tear the place down and start over!"

"I say let's go see Bob Kincaid . . . right now!"

"I'm with you!" Brian was hugging him, "Let's go!"

Tony locked up and they headed for Montauk; good music on the radio, a perfect day and the feeling that they made a wonderful decision! As they walked through the open door, the honky-tonk piano music and the general ambience felt like coming home. Bob gave them a warm greeting and made room at the corner of the bar. He had a bartender working so he was having some of his own product. His eyes showed the result of quite a few vodkas.

"Did you just get here? How long are you staying? Are you at Ridge Top? Speak to me!"

"Can we get a drink in this place?" Tony smiled at him.

"Talk to the bartender! I'm off. You didn't answer my questions."

"Our throats are too dry; we need to oil them."

"Danny! Come here and make some drinks! It's an emergency!"

Everyone in the vicinity was laughing and it felt good to be part of it. Tony engaged Bob in conversation and Brian drifted down to the piano to enjoy the music and talk to Bob; the Scot who didn't go home.

"Welcome back; are you staying longer this time?"

"We have a week this time; can I get you a drink?"

Bob nodded his head; "That would be much appreciated."

Brian went to the bar and ordered two drinks; he took them back to the piano and placed Bob's drink on a cocktail napkin in front of him within easy reach. He was playing a few requests; people were gathered around him, some were singing, others just humming along. The place had a good crowd; but it wasn't jammed. It was enjoyable.

Brian was just finishing his drink when Tony approached; hurriedly! "We have to go; it's important, I'll explain outside."

"I didn't want to try to talk over the music," he explained outside, "I just got a big wake-up call from Bob; we have no water!"

"You can tell we're city people," said Brian, "we just turn it on."

"He told me about a plumber who lives in Amagansett and he is familiar with the cottage; he has put wells there in the past. Bob called him and he is going to meet us there."

"Thank God for Bob Kincaid! David never mentioned water!"

"You're right, Brian, he is definitely not for us."

They were not in the cottage five minutes when the truck pulled up. A tall, man unfolded from the cab and at first sight he seemed to be about thirty years old. He was about fifty; it certainly didn't show! They met and exchanged handshakes; Tony felt an instant confidence; Jim Devlin was his kind of man. While they were outside he showed them the well-house and suggested they get a new pump. "This one still has some life in it; but you're better off with a new one; especially when you are going to drive a new well." They went into the cottage and sat out on the deck. Jim explained that the underground water by the cottage was brackish and not potable. Years ago he had dug a well for the owner of the cottage and he ran the line across the meadow over to the railroad property. It was a long haul; most well-drillers would never do it. The reward was sweet water and it was only necessary to go down ten feet. He could do it by hand; it wouldn't be wise to have heavy duty equipment on railroad property; somebody would get curious and the Long Island Railroad might send him packing. Nothing would show above ground and in fifty acres of meadows who would really care? It was not an expensive operation as wells go and it was easy to do a new well when the old one went dry. He could do it in a day. Tony had heard enough. He gave him money to get the new pump and told him to do it as quickly as possible. Jim told them to buy some five gallon water cans; they could get water at Hither Hills State Park, so they could use the toilet. The Park also had a bath house where they could shower at a nominal fee. They walked him to his truck; he would start working early tomorrow, he had assured them. He headed off out the long driveway and he was on the highway pronto!

"I have a good feeling about him; Bob Kincaid swears by him."

"Bob knows these people," Brian added, "we're safe with him."

There was a well-stocked hardware store in Amagansett and they were able to get lined five gallon cans made to hold water. They could drink the water from the State Park, they were told. They went to the Park; it was a short ride from the cottage and right on the ocean. The bath house was clean and had several showers and many lockers. There was no hot water supplied! Brian hated cold showers!

"It won't be for long; Brian. Jim says our hot water heater is o.k.; it seemed to be about a couple of years old."

"Don't worry about me, Tony. I'll survive."

"Let's go to Riverhead and get a mattress for the bed." The man in the hardware store gave me a card for the Big Barn Furniture store. He said they deliver and they carry sheets and blankets, too. I'm glad he suggested the Coleman lamp we will need that until the electric is turned on."

"Are we going to cook on the Hibachi tonight?"

"No, Brian, let's go to Bob's place; his food is good."

"I guess it's better if we give ourselves more time here."

Once again they were in the car and on their way. When they went to the hardware store Brian had told Tony to look at his gas gauge; it was on empty! Luckily there was a service station in town and they filled the tank. Because of the traffic it took almost an hour to get to Riverhead; there were many stores of every description and even a Sears! They went on a spree and filled the car with things they would need. Tony paid for everything with cash and it seemed as though his wallet was a bottomless pit. The first thing purchased was the mattress and delivery was assured the next day. The Barn had three floors of all kinds of furniture and Tony told the owner they would be back after things settled down. It was Christmas-like!

"We better be getting back, Brian, if we want to take a shower we need to get to the bath house before dark; it might close at dark."

"Good thinking, Tony, it never entered my mind."

Traffic was not too bad and they made good time; stopping at the cottage for toilet articles and fresh clothes they went to the Park. Brian remembered to put the water cans in the car so they could fill them. They were in time to take showers but the showers had gotten a lot of use and the water was really cold. Welcome to camping joys!

They put the water in the trunk and headed for Bob's place. The brisk, cold showers had given them both a shot of energy in addition to a hearty appetite; the conversation was mostly about what they would order for dinner. Tony was anxious to thank Bob for steering them to Jim Devlin; Tony had a feeling he was going to be a main figure in the remodeling in the fall. Jim would know the reliable local guys to hire. David had left them with misgivings; Jim had left them with a comfortable sense of satisfaction.

"Here we are," said Tony; "I hope we can get a booth so we have some room. Those tables for two are okay if you're having a sandwich."

"People eat late when it's nice at the beach; we'll get a booth."

They did get a booth but it was the only one vacant. The people who had occupied it had just left and it wasn't completely ready but Tony sat down quickly and claimed it. Now he was sure he would enjoy his dinner. It was away from the piano so it would not be very noisy.

As soon as Brian was seated Tony got up and invited Bob to join them; he wanted to fill him in on their progress and he wanted information about getting the power turned on as quickly as possible. Kincaid sat down, his eyes a little beady and his unruly gray hair looking like it had never known a comb or brush. Actually, it was the damp sea air that made his hair a problem; not that it irked him at all!

"So how did you make out with Jim," he asked, "was he okay?"

Tony related their experience with him and sang his praises as Bob beamed; then he got right to the electric and Bob went to the kitchen and returned with a telephone number. He handed it to Tony and gave him instructions.

"Go to the wall phone by the kitchen and call this number; you will reach the garage where the trucks are kept. Ask for Phil, tell him I gave you his number and explain that you just opened your house and discovered you had no power. Tell him the real estate agent neglected to take care of it . . . don't mention names."

"What are you drinking, Bob?" Tony asked.

"Vodka and tonic;" Came the quick reply.

A waiter came and cleaned the table and Bob instructed him to pick up the drinks. He chatted with Brian cordially until Tony returned to the table. When he came he was beaming and obviously happy.

"You are a miracle worker, Mr. Kincaid, they are coming to the cottage in the morning and we will have power before noon! How does it feel to have so much clout where you live?"

"Just remember those guys all drink here when they work Montauk; and on cold winter days that big pot-bellied stove keeps them toasty-warm and so does my booze and home made soup!"

"As soon as I mentioned your name Phil became my friend."

"Phil is a good friend to have; and he doesn't have his hand out."

"What do I do tomorrow; I want to show my appreciation."

"He'll send two guys on the truck; is it worth two twenties?"

"Any day," said Tony, "what about Phil?"

"I always send Phil a Christmas present; you can add to it."

"Do you send him a check?"

"Cash is always preferred," grinned Bob, "I have couriers!"

They all laughed and the discussion was all about the cottage. Bob reminded them that he had clamming rights along their beach. Brian promised him a life-time clamming certificate and he knew of a place in the city where they made up ornate certificates of any description; he would have one made for Bob; they were a lot of fun. Bob would end up hanging it behind his bar. When he was asked where the place was located he said it was absolutely very top secret! They left Bob feeling elated; knowing the power was coming and having enjoyed an excellent dinner. When they arrived home they got busy getting the bedroom set up; having the Coleman lamp was a godsend, it lit up the whole room. The rest of their time there was spent making the place livable and they accomplished a great deal. Both of them were resourceful and they worked well together . . . so far.

* * *

Jerry had taken Eleanor to do some shopping; a couple of her purchases were on the heavy side; that is why she enlisted his aid. Nora told Jerry to bring Eleanor to her house for lunch; as Jerry told Eleanor about the invitation he said he was *ordered* to bring her to lunch. They arrived after shopping, stopping at Eleanor's place to leave the parcels. Making one stop at a flower market Eleanor had selected a variety of blooms for Nora.

"She'll say you shouldn't have," Jerry admonished.

"Let her say anything she likes; she'll love them!"

And indeed she did! And she went quickly to arrange them for her table. Jerry made some drinks and they sat down to a lovely luncheon. Nora made a fruit compote for desert and then they had coffee and lit up their cigarettes.

"I thought you were kicking the smoking habit, Miss Nora," Jerry chided her, "isn't that so?"

"And what is that thing in your hand, detective; a flower?"

"I'm not the one with the cough; and I spoke to your doctor."

"He has to pry even off duty, Eleanor, like an old Harpy."

"He worries about you, Nora, you're important to him."

"Oh, I see he has had your ear; two against one!"

They laughed and Jerry asked them to listen. "I have news for you!"

"What have ye got up yer sleeve now?" Nora eyed him narrowly.

"The politico I know has a place up on a lake and I can use it when he isn't there. He is in Europe for two weeks so I want to take you two girls up there for three days. Eleanor and I are on vacation and I'm hoping Miss Nora can work it in to her schedule."

"I don't need to be traipsin' on some trip to no lake!" Nora protested; "you two go and leave me in peace."

"It's you I want to get up there and get some fresh air into you."

"Indeed!" Nora bristled; "You're fresh enough as it 'tis."

"Nora," Eleanor smiled; "you have to go; you're my duena!"

"And what the hell are ye callin' me?"

"It's Spanish for chaperone, dear, it's nothing bad."

Jerry was laughing hard; the look on Nora's face was priceless!

"I'm going to take his Caddie so you'll be comfortable."

"Don't be usin' no foreign words on me; English is enough."

"It sounds wonderful; I can't go without you, Nora."

"He's put you up to sayin' that; I know."

"Not true; dear, I'm hearing it for the first time; honestly."

She eyed Eleanor and smiled; "I know ye wouldn't lie to me."

"When are you planning this nonsense?" Nora asked Jerry.

"Tomorrow; the weather forecast is good; so we should go."

"Are ye daft sonny? I have to get my clothes ready."

"We're not going to Ethiopia, darling, just two hours away upstate; you don't even need your passport."

The two of them convinced her it could be done; Nora sighed; heavily!

The next morning Jerry picked up the car and drove to Eleanor's apartment. She was ready and looked charming in a sweater and skirt. Jerry was relieved that she didn't have a ton of luggage; some ladies pack everything but the kitchen sink. He put her things in the spacious trunk and they went to get Nora. She had been ready for an hour and was up at five o'clock to give her enough time. Nora, like Eleanor, did not have too much baggage. When they arrived Nora wanted to fix something to eat and she was promptly over-ruled. Jerry looked at her;

"You're all dressed up in your yellow suit and little white hat; looking so pretty; and you want to cook? Never!"

"We can stop and have a bite on our way," Eleanor said, "we will want to do some food shopping before we get there so we can do both at the same stop. I'm sure we will all want to stretch our legs."

Off they went; Nora commenting on the beautiful car and how clean it was; running her hand over the upholstery.

"It's like going to a funeral," she said, "Or a weddin'."

"Well, I'm glad you added the wedding;" chided Jerry, "we can do without the funeral stuff!"

"I've been to funerals in cars like this one."

Eleanor looked back at her; "We must not upset our chauffeur, Nora, you know the help today can be very independent."

"Especially the Puerto Ricans." Her eyes were half closed and *avec hauteur.*

Jerry was laughing; he had never heard her disparage anyone! This remark really surprised him. He knew she was being cute; to irk him!

Eleanor looked at Jerry and squeezed his arm; "this trip was a great idea."

About half way there Jerry stopped at a quaint little shopping plaza designed after an alpine village. It was on a small lake and was a charming sight. They had breakfast in a Swiss-type restaurant and the food was first rate. Later they went to an immaculate food market and though they tried to get Nora to wait in the car (she would have none of that!) the three of them food shopped. Eleanor told Nora she would do all the kitchen work and Nora could just rest. Nora had a basket and was making selections for her menus! She wanted Eleanor to be free to spend time with Jerry; she prayed that something would develop with them. The courtship would get all the help she could give. With the shopping done they were on the road again. Nora had much praise for the market.

"We have an hour to go." Jerry gave Nora a quick look; "Why don't you take a nap?"

"Take a nap! Indeed! Just keep your eyes on the road!"

Eleanor and Jerry were enjoying her quick come-backs and she actually did doze off in spite of herself. She sat there so like a queen! They were in the mountains now; this was emphasized by an occasional sign warning motorists to watch out for rock slides. A rather ominous announcement! There was so much open space; a city dweller is so accustomed to everything being close together that huge expanses of open land tend to overwhelm them. They require the places they use to be within a couple of blocks from their residence. God forbid they have to walk three or four! Except of course when they went *shopping!* That was different; they enjoyed touring all the stores. Naturally it would take all day and a tasty lunch!

"There's so much undeveloped land outside of the city," Eleanor marveled, "it really takes your breath away! Everyone should get out of the city more often; especially in a luxurious car!"

She looked at Jerry, laughing. He gave her a quick glance; laughing along with her;

"We would be moving at a snails pace if they did!"

"It's so lovely; you relax whether you want to or not."

"Like that one in the back seat!" He whispered, "She's out!"

"We mustn't wake her," Eleanor cautioned, "She needs rest."

"I think she looks better already," noted Jerry, "She ate well."

"Oh, that was a good lunch she had," agreed Eleanor, "Indeed!"

Suddenly Jerry turned off the highway onto a side road; it was narrower and wooded on both sides.

"We're nearly there."

"I didn't realize we were this close," exclaimed Eleanor, "Gee!"

He drove about three miles and turned into a driveway marked private; it was crushed gravel and made a luxurious crunch under the tires.

"I've never been on a private driveway before; I should wake Nora so she can experience it. I don't want her to miss it!"

"Nora is not asleep! Nor has she been; and I've seen many private driveways and entrances and everything private!" The voice came from the rear; "It means nothin' to me; ye still have to tend to it! Everythin' ye own needs to be taken care of."

"That is the truth, Nora," agreed Jerry, "you can't escape it."

"If I said it; you know it's true," very much awake now; "Amen."

The driveway curved and there was the house, a lodge actually, made of logs and gleaming with marine varnish! The driveway became circular in front of it with beautiful plantings in the center. It was a large structure and certainly not a log cabin! Behind this wonderful looking place was a pristine lake, dark blue and sparkling in the bright sunshine. The owner had bought all this acreage around the lake and with three other political cronies had divided it for four residences and no more. There were homes built in north, east, south and west sites on the lakefront and the woodland remained in its natural state. All four owners occasionally entertained the under privileged and religious groups for days outings. It was a deductible!

Entering the lodge there were all sorts of exclamations from the two ladies. The living room was immense with a great stone fireplace centered between glass walls facing the lake. A well-equipped kitchen was at one end opened to a spacious dining area; there was a long pine table that could seat fourteen people, surrounded by comfortable chairs. It would be easy to sit there and enjoy a nice dinner with a sensational view. At the other end was the master bedroom suite; it held two king-size beds. Eleanor had never seen a bedroom this size; or even close to it! The bath had a Jacuzzi tub and a large separate shower that was glass-walled to afford a view of the lake while showering. It was rustic; but luxuriously so! The other bedrooms were on the upper floor as were three additional baths. A bedroom and bath were off the kitchen with a small living room. This was designed for a house-keeper or caretaker. Jerry opened one of the large sliding glass doors and they went out on the large deck with a covered barbeque outdoor kitchen. Nora was impressed;

"They didn't forget a thing in this place; I'll bet they throw some parties in here! You could handle a hundred people!"

"That's what politicians do, Sweetie, but you can bet they have paying guests most of the time." Jerry had his arm around her, "Now, madam, tell me; aren't you glad you came, honestly?"

"Of course I am! I'm no ingrate! It's a fine, grand treat."

They toured the outside for a while and Nora started to worry about the food in the car so Jerry and Eleanor unloaded while Nora made tea. It was decided that Nora and Eleanor would share the master suite and Jerry would take the caretaker's bedroom. This would make it unnecessary to use the upper floor. Eleanor thought it would be a good idea if she were close to Nora should she need anything during the night. Jerry loved the attention she gave Nora. When everything was inside and put away Nora announced that tea was ready and thought it would be nice to have it on the deck. There was a round table with a bright yellow umbrella, Jerry opened it up and they brought the tea there. Now they knew why Nora did her own shopping at the market. She bought out the gourmet section! The tray of goodies she prepared needed the years of experience she had doing things like this. How it was all accomplished baffled Jerry and Eleanor; who were too busy enjoying the treats to give it too much thought! Nora was enjoying all this more than they realized; having the pair of them together in this family atmosphere was part of her dearest wish . . . to have them linked permanently! She plotted without a conscience. After the tea was cleared away Nora announced that she would like to take a nap and then prepare dinner when she awoke. Jerry suggested she use one of the lounge chairs on the deck and take advantage of the mountain air; it would do her good!

"Oh dear God! Will you ever stop doin' me good?"

"Let me fix the lounge for you, Nora, it is a good idea," said Eleanor.

She went to the bedroom and came out with a blanket and pillows and with her arm around her escorted Nora out on the deck and soon had her in her crib . . . as Nora described it. Eleanor had noticed an old school bell on one of the shelves; she gave it to Nora; a disbelieving Nora.

"If you need us just ring it; the sound will carry up here; we're going to walk down to the dock and look at the boat."

"Glory be what else is goin' to happen to me?"

"Have a good nap," Jerry smiled, "you need strength to cook!"

"Indeed? Since when can't I cook? Go chase yourself."

They walked toward the dock, hand in hand, Nora beamed, gleefully. As they walked out on the dock they neared where the row boat was tied up;

"The oars are probably in that little boat house;" Jerry got down into the boat; "this is really nice, Eleanor, I know how to row we can take it out tomorrow; maybe we can get her ladyship to come with us. I wouldn't bet money on that though."

"I think she would give you an argument there, Jerry, I don't think she would be comfortable getting off terra firma."

"It won't hurt to ask; it might get a rise out of her!"

"Oh, Jerry, you will certainly do that!"

He came up on the dock, "That boat is nice and dry; no leaks."

"That's good to hear, dear, I'm not much of a swimmer."

"I'm sure he has life preservers in the boat house."

"Bring a dozen," she laughed softly; "I might need them."

"You won't drown while I'm around," hugging her, "don't fret."

"You can teach me to row; I can use the exercise."

"I'll do the rowing; you can navigate."

"God knows where we'll end up; on the rocks I'm sure."

They laughed together; he put his arm around her and Nora would have loved seeing this but she was in a nice relaxed sleep. They walked along the shore; a gentle breeze coming across the lake caused small ripples that glistened in the sunlight; it was beautifully quiet an occasional chirp from a bird could hardly be called a noise. They paused near a magnificent blue spruce tree; he drew her close and kissed her tenderly. A strong sensation coursed through her and it was clear to her that she was falling in love with him; the wisdom of that was another story. People weren't known to bother much with wisdom when they were falling in love! The spot had a magic of its own and they stayed there; she resting in his arms while he caressed her and neither bothered with words. Eventually she broke away, gently.

"We better get back and see how Nora is doing; I want to help her with the dinner. The menu is top secret so far; if it is anything like the tea she fixed we'll be in luck. She loves to cook and she sure knows how!"

Taking her hand they headed back toward the house; Nora not about.

"I'll bet she's in the kitchen already, Jerry."

"She sure is!" As he opened the door the aroma hit both of them!

"Do you think we should have a drink, cookie?"

"I'll give ye cookie! I have a perfectly good name; use it! If you were making those drinks ye wouldn't have time to be so funny."

"I'll get busy this very second; whatever you say."

"I want to give you a hand, Nora," Eleanor washed her hands, "Just tell me what to do but please don't tell me you don't need me."

"I'd love your company, dear, I can keep you busy."

"Wonderful!" Eleanor had expected to be sent on her way; "maybe I can learn something; like making what smells so good!"

"That's only a sauce simmerin', love, it's simple."

"Here are your drinks ladies; I'll go watch television."

"You do that, darlin', you can tell us the news at dinner."

"You just want to get rid of me; I know."

"Nothin' of the sort, dear, we'll call you if we need a drink."

There was much laughter as he gave Nora a sidelong look; "Bye."

Nora and Eleanor got on well in the kitchen and Eleanor was learning a few things about adding flavor to food. New York strip steaks were on the menu; they were in a marinade and were going to be grilled out on the deck; by Nora not by his nibs! There was a warm camaraderie developing between them and Nora looked really well and had nice color. The nap and the air were good for her; and the company was all she wanted. She was happier than she had been for many years and she wanted this until she died. Jerry had brought love into her life and it was sorely missing for so long; she felt lucky.

The dinner was a huge success and Eleanor insisted on taking care of the cleaning up. Cleaning up after Nora was easy; she was neat in the kitchen and incredibly organized. When Eleanor came into the living room, Jerry had made a fire, it was a homey scene. He served an after dinner drink and Eleanor suggested they play cards. Nora chirped up happily saying she loved cards. They played longer than expected and suddenly the long day caught up with all of them. It was time to call it a night. Nora kissed them and went to the bedroom; Jerry held Eleanor and kissed her good night and retired to his room. He had let the fire burn out but he checked it again. Eleanor left one lamp lit and went to bed. Nora was already tucked in and she would have a restful night with no coughing. She had taken a good dose of her medicine; she didn't want to disturb Eleanor's rest. Between the medicine and the drinks she was well sedated. It had been an enjoyable day and they were all pleasantly tired and contented. Tomorrow was another day and nice weather was in store.

They enjoyed another nice day at the lodge but Nora was not to have the peaceful night she had the night before. The coughing began about midnight and Jerry awoke and came to help Eleanor. It was the worst spell Jerry had ever known her to have and he was frightened. He found some honey in the kitchen and made some tea. They had her out of bed sitting in an easy chair, a blanket tucked around her. He wasn't sure if the tea was actually a benefit or if it was mental; but she improved after the second cup. It was close to two-thirty before she dozed off; they made her comfortable in the chair and let her sleep where she was. They went to the kitchen and lit cigarettes.

"Would you like some coffee?"

"That's a good idea, Eleanor, I'm wide awake."

"So am I; she gave me an awful scare; has she seen a doctor?"

"Yes; I went with her last time and he just tells her to take her medicine and stop smoking. She's not an easy patient!"

"That doesn't surprise me; she is a bit head-strong!"

"Oh yes! Just a bit!"

Eleanor smiled even though she felt his concern; he cared about Nora and she sensed his feeling of being helpless; especially up here!

"Do you think we should leave in the morning, Jerry?"

"Let's see how she is tomorrow; she bounces back fast."

"If you feel uneasy don't hesitate to take her home."

"That won't be easy! She won't want to spoil it for us; other people always come first with her. Nora has very good insurance; but she hates going to a doctor and a hospital . . . she thinks you go there to die!"

"You can't take the Irish out of her, Jerry."

"Lord; I know that! I wouldn't want to, El."

"It's part of her charm; she is so nice to be with and that lively wit she has keeps you laughing all the time. Nora is more fun than a lot of young women that I know; she is good company, Jerry."

"I love her, Eleanor, I've never had anyone close to me in my life and it was a lucky day for me that I met her."

"It was for her, too, you're like a son to her and she feels so secure with you living with her; it's so good for both of you."

"Let's get dressed and walk down to the dock."

Eleanor stood up; "I'd love to; "I'll be back tout de suite!"

"Put a sweater on, it's chilly at night up here."

It was a beautiful night; because there were no street lights and it was really dark the sky seemed to be made up of stars. They seemed so close and the lake was calm with gently flowing currents that reflected the lights from the houses; like slowly turning jewels. They sat on a bench on the dock; his arm was around her holding her close and the only sound was the water gently lapping against the dock. For a few minutes neither spoke; then Jerry broke the silence.

"I feel like I should be quiet; it's sort of like a church here." He kissed her tenderly; "I'm glad you're here, I've been thinking about coming up here with you for a long time. He picked a good time to go to Europe."

"Who is he Jerry, he must be wealthy?"

"He's a politician; of course he's got money! He knows a lot of people and none of them are poor. I do favors for him; sometimes

Tom helps me. He depends on us to keep quiet about this place; not very many people know he owns it. I don't question him about why he has the place; it's none of my business. I don't do anything illegal for him; just some errands and chauffeuring. I just don't tell anyone that I do it. I have a hunch he runs some big card games here; but I'm not sure of that; it's just a hunch."

"Well, it's nice to know the right people; he trusts you, for sure."

The conversation got back to Nora and she tried to comfort him seeing he cared a great deal for her. He felt helpless; it was always on his mind.

"She should see a lung specialist, Jerry, she is right where the finest of doctors are located."

"Nora has a peasant way of looking at doctors; the best thing is not to go near them, in her book!"

"You're going to have to grab her by the back of the neck and get her to one; she'll listen to you."

"I wish I could give her a pill, Eleanor, and knock her out until the examination was over! That would be wonderful."

"I can picture that!" Eleanor laughed, "And when she awoke?"

"Oh, there would be hell to pay; I'm sure of that."

They started back to the house; he gave her a long kiss when they stood up. She welcomed his attentions now and desire was warming! Where this was going was a mystery; she had to let him find his way.

"Is it okay with you if we leave the day after tomorrow, El?"

"Whenever you wish Jerry; tomorrow, if you're worried."

"We'll see how she is; she won't complain . . . you have to watch."

"I know; she'd suffer before she would spoil our fun."

They were at the house; "That's Nora; completely unselfish."

He kissed her goodnight.

"I'll have a look at her when I go in." Eleanor eased his mind.

"Thanks, sweetheart, I know you will."

Nora seemed better; but she didn't bounce back as usual. They decided to stay one more day and head home. Nora had no comment.

* * *

Brian was walking to Tony's place. He had dinner with Eleanor and they had talked about three hours rehashing their trips. It certainly seemed as though Jerry was getting serious with Eleanor. Brian knew Eleanor was smitten and he still felt uneasy about it. Somehow it didn't just fit. In the beginning he might have been a bit envious; since his involvement with Tony that could be factored out. He just did not believe Jerry could live the way Eleanor needed to live.

"Well, look who's here!" Tony smiled, broadly;

"Nice to see you." They shook hands enjoying the charade.

"Nice to see you, too."

It was the first time they had seen each other since they returned from the Hamptons. It was all of three days; both of them were still quite tan and Tony had gotten a deep tan quickly. It accented the silver streaks in his hair and was very attractive. He had never looked so good and all of his customers where quick to notice.

"I've had a few phone calls; I have to fill you in . . . gin and tonic?"

"Please; and a twist of lime." He was back quickly,

"For you, sir." Brian put money on the bar and Tony frowned.

"I said that was for you; meaning on me!"

"We have discussed this and you agreed to what I wanted; when I come here . . . I pay for my drinks!" They were speaking in low tones;

"I buy a lot of drinks for people; not just you."

"Case closed, Tony, we have an agreement; take the money!"

Tony was not pleased; but he had made the agreement. "Okay."

"Now tell me about the calls; who called you?"

"Jim Devlin; we have water! He had it tested and it is fine! He is going to clean out the faucets and the shower head; there's sediment from not being used and some other things to shape up the plumbing. The new pump is great and we have good pressure."

"Well, you're nobody if you don't have good pressure!"

"Especially in the Hamptons!" Quipped Tony, "It's a must!"

They laughed and Tony had to attend to some customers. The door opened and in walked Jerry; there was an empty stool next to Brian and Jerry sat down exchanging greetings and immediately noticing Brian's tan . . . and then Tony's tan. You didn't need to be a detective to put two and two together.

"Well, you two look mighty healthy . . . did you get all this color in the same place?"

"What are you drinking, sir? Beer, shooter or both?"

"I'll try both for openers." Tony smiled; "Comin' up!"

Brian did not want to answer his question; he didn't know how Tony felt about discussing things out East.

"I hear you had a nice trip up to the mountains; I had dinner with Eleanor and she told me how beautiful the place is. She really enjoyed it."

"I asked you a question." Jerry smiled a curious smile. "You seem to be avoiding it."

"What was the question?" Tony was close enough to pick up the conversation; he always kept an ear out when Jerry sat next to Brian he didn't trust Jerry.

"Brian was telling me you have a beautiful spot up in the mountains." Tony butted in to get Brian off the hook.

"We were interrupted and I am filled with curiosity and frustration. I didn't know you had a place upstate."

"I don't own it; I know the owner and he allows me the use of it sometimes." Jerry was annoyed; he knew Tony was going to infer he bought the place with *funny* money and cops hate this kind of talk even if it's joking.

"Is it a relative who owns it?" Tony feigned an innocent look; he loved putting Jerry on the spot.

"I don't have any relatives and damn well you know it! There are other bars in town! They have paid entertainers!"

Jerry grabbed his money off the bar and stormed out.

"Now what got into him? Tony looked at Brian and smiled.

"He wasn't even drunk!"

The rest of the night dragged for Tony and Brian; they had things to talk about and they wanted to be alone together. Finally it was closing time and Brian helped clean up. They took a cab to Tony's apartment there was no mention of breakfast. Tony was filled with elation and anxious to be alone with Brian. As soon as they entered the apartment Tony went to the bedroom and stripped off his clothes he came out into the living room and hugged Brian.

"Let's take a shower together and in two shakes Brian was following him into the bathroom. They renewed their new-found affection and in after-glow conversation their commitment deepened.

"You've given me a life Brian; it is something I never thought I'd have. It's new to me and I hope you will be patient with me. I don't want to lose you."

"Tony, for the first time in my life I feel that I belong to someone; I don't think I realized how much I needed it. You are fine the way you are; don't think you have to act gay; you are not gay. You are a homosexual but you are not gay. Just be yourself; that's who I love."

Tony held him close; there was no more conversation necessary.

Edith and Eleanor were enjoying coffee in the staff room before their day began at the salon. Eleanor had been telling her about her trip with Jerry and Nora; Edith's idea of doing some sort of penance! She would never get involved with an old lady.

"It sounds like you had a wonderful little trip but speaking for 'moi' I would be more than ticked off if any guy toted along his nanny on a cozy venture like that." Edith sipped her black coffee the usual Danish pastry not in sight. She was out to lose pounds; she was feeling much desired and very satisfied. Tom had been at her door every night since their first union; he came at odd hours depending on how the job was going and he left her spent and very much in love. This gave her enormous will power and the weight was dropping off; she had even joined a gym and had never been so determined to get in shape in her entire life. No man had ever reached her as he did and she was not about to lose him. Not Edith!

Her life revolved around him now and she learned his likes and dislikes and catered to them. It was the first time she ever put another person's desires before her own . . . Edith was deeply into this. They never talked about his marriage; "that's his business."

"You couldn't possibly resent Nora!" Eleanor was offended, "She is good company and very witty and I love talking with her. They are so good for each other! Nora never makes any demands." Eleanor would not allow Edith to make a shrew out of Nora; Edith had a history of being a shrew . . . . and then some! "I love her."

"Well you're not as selfish as I, happily, am." Edith smiled a genuine smile; "I think I'm getting better, though." Content in her new-found attachment she wasn't about to worry about this old saga.

"I hope you don't get serious with that Foley; you're much too good for him and he would never appreciate your qualities. I don't want to see you humiliated."

"There is nothing serious going on; I'm a big girl if I get hurt it will be my own fault."

Eleanor wondered why she used the word humiliated; it seemed odd to her. Edith remembered her night with Jerry vividly! She would never forget the humiliation; she hated him. Eleanor continued; it was a good thing she couldn't read Edith's mind!

"I think it is wonderful how they have found each other; she is so happy to have him in her life . . . he is like a son to her. I don't think Jerry has ever had a home like he has now; he really cares for her; taking her to the doctor or anywhere she has to go . . . and he does it very willingly."

Edith arched her eyebrows; "Where does that leave Eleanor?"

Eleanor bristled; she was not letting Edith put her down.

"I am perfectly contented the way things are; I'm not looking to wear a veil; he takes me to nice places and he is good company."

Edith felt a sense of dread; Eleanor had struck a nerve! It was as if Eleanor had read her mind . . . for she would love to marry Tom!

Edith decided it was time to change the subject; "I've got to get ready."

Edith prepared for her first appointment and was feeling sorry that she had rattled Eleanor's cage; before the day was over she would ask her to go out for dinner after work and try and make it up to her without saying she was sorry . . . Edith would treat for dinner that would be her apology. Later that day when they were squeezing in some time for a sandwich Eleanor agreed to join her for dinner and they settled on a small Italian bistro near the salon. The food was excellent and Edith loved the waiters; she chortled, "Each one is a stud."

"If you shampoo and set my hair I'll do yours."

Edith made the offer to Eleanor and later; beautifully coiffed they were on their way to Luigi's. They made quite an impression . . . a lovely Titian haired lady and a sexy blond. Adolfo who had served them many times bore down on them knowing they were excellent tippers and much fun. He flashed his piano smile and selected a perfect table for them. It had good privacy and they could observe most of the clientele. They were both people watchers and their commentary, always in fun; was deadly for the tasteless outfits and badly done hair. Well turned out ladies on the other hand were given proper praise.

"Martini, El?"

"Yes, that sounds great; straight up I think."

Edith agreed; "Exactly what we both need."

Adolfo brought ice water and menus and a plate of canapés. He took the drink order and said he would mark them 'emergency' and scurried away; he didn't even take time to flash them that bright grin.

"That's what you call a fine waiter; and handsome to boot!"

Eleanor laughed at Edith's enthusiasm; a waitress with a high up-do and spike heels plus rhinestone ankle straps went by the table.

"Oh God! She must be right off a slave ship!" Edith raised her eyes to heaven and Eleanor convulsed with laughter.

"Oh Edith, stop!"

They had finished an enjoyable dinner and were having black coffee; Edith feeling very proud that she ignored the dessert menu. When Eleanor came back to work Edith would leave on her vacation.

"Are you going anywhere on your vacation?" Eleanor asked, "Or are you staying around town like Brian?"

"I have to get some dental work done; this would be a good time to get it over with. I'll give the dentist the money instead of some hotel. There are some good sales on now, maybe I'll shop a little."

"Edith, there is no such thing as a little shopping!"

They laughed, knowing this was so true. Edith said, "I'll try."

The check came; Eleanor wanted to split it but Edith insisted on paying . . . including the tip. She quipped, "I want to see that smile!"

Outside the bistro Eleanor hailed a cab.

"Come on Edith, I'll drop you off; it's not that much out of my way. Don't give me a story!"

"Whatever you say; I'm too full to walk, anyway!"

The next morning she called Brian.

"Am I calling too early? I hope I didn't wake you."

"Not at all; I was just going to make coffee." He yawned deeply.

"Don't! I've already started a pot."

"I was hoping you would say that."

"You little devil! You're using me!"

"Using is better than abusing."

"Waxing poetical at this hour is absolutely déclassé."

"Can you spell that? I know I taught you that word but I bet you can't spell it!" She was irked, because she couldn't!

"Damn you!"

"O moi fois! What language to use on a boy!"

"Some boy! Get over here so I can box your ears!"

"At least gift wrap, darling, don't be chintzy!"

"I'm hanging up; get over here!"

"My, my she is so bossy." He was talking aloud "But I better go!"

He came in wearing a white terry robe to point up his tan. "I'm here!"

Eleanor whisked into the room and almost shrieked.

"Look at you! You look absolutely Hollywood! Give me a hug, gorgeous!"

They talked about their trips for a short while then Brian asked;

"What is it I am to assist you with, precious one, choosing a bridal gown?"

Eleanor looked toward the heavens. "Don't you start; I've had enough of that with Miss Edith! I want to get Jerry a gift for taking me up to the country; I want it to say thank you but I don't want to go overboard. You have excellent judgment so I would love to have you help me; if you have time."

"For you there is always time; I guess we will rule out a fine Swiss watch?" She poked him playfully.

"Be serious, please, I want a simple gift; let's not go overboard."

"I know two guys who have a nice men's shop just off Madison Avenue; they really know how to buy and they have merchandise you don't see everywhere. It's not 'way out' stuff; Jerry is on the conservative side and you will surely find something suitable. I don't see Jerry in anything cashmere; do you?"

"Hardly; his fellow officers might have a lot of ribbing to amuse themselves with."

"After we finish breakfast we'll go there first; if you don't see anything you like there; there is always Bloomingdales!"

They enjoyed a leisurely meal and much coffee and cigarettes and Brian confided in Eleanor about how serious his relationship with Tony was getting. She did not go into her feelings about Jerry; mostly because she didn't have a clear picture of where they were going . . . or if they were going anywhere. At this point Eleanor wasn't about to say how much she was starting to care for Jerry; she had experienced a marriage with a man who loved her; she knew the confidence of that kind of relationship; she did not have that feeling as yet. There was something missing; it was troubling her; it nagged. They went shopping and selected a fine wallet; Eleanor smiled;

"This is it; this will do the job perfectly."

* * *

It was after five and Tom had just come off the day shift; Shannon's bar was a bee hive they were two deep at he bar so they bought drinks and found a small bistro table. Jerry had met Tom and they were going to have a couple of drinks together at Shannon's bar.

"It's good to come to a halt," sighed Tom, "All the weird ones were out today; I think they had a convention here."

"How come you're drinking the hard stuff?" asked Jerry; "You always drink beer."

"Blame it on our weird targets; I need a fix."

Tom inquired about Jerry's trip up state and they talked about it for quite a while. Tom continued to drink highballs and Jerry was very surprised at this; he knew something was up so he asked;

"Tom why are you hitting the hard stuff; what's wrong?"

"I've gotten involved with Edith; I'm really hooked on her."

"You're seeing her regularly?"

"Any time I can make it work; Lucille and the kids are out in Hampton Bays visiting her parents so I'm at Edith's every night. I can't get enough of her! She is what I need."

Jerry dreaded this; he had a low opinion of Edith and he could see the possibility of a ruined marriage and family. He knew he had to be careful of what he said; Tom was too far gone to listen to any adverse talk about her.

"When that bug hits you it really takes over."

"She's all woman, Jerry, she has the same needs I have."

Jerry was very well aware of her talent just from one experience; he was not bringing that up. He never thought anything could disrupt Tom's family life; he used to envy the solid relationship they had. He didn't like Edith; now he felt a smoldering hatred building up inside himself.

He patted Tom's shoulder; "It will cool down."

Tom gazed toward the back bar; "I don't think so, Jerry, I don't think so."

Jerry felt a cold shudder run through his body saying "Give it time."

They parted company; Jerry went home, Tom went to see Edith! Jerry continued to brood over the turn of events in Tom's life. There was no doubt in his mind that Edith was totally responsible for everything. He fantasized about her having a fatal accident and a happy ending would take place for all. Cold reality told him otherwise.

Chapter Four

Nora had changed her clothes and put on a comfortable house dress. It was a cheerful floral design but it didn't do much cheering up for her. She was very depressed. "I'll have a cup o' tea," she said aloud. As she waited for the water to boil she sat staring into space. Her visit to the doctor upset her. Nora went alone purposely; she wanted any bad news to be her secret. "All them big words," she said to her twisting hands, "and more damn questions than a district attorney!" She rose and poured the water into the teapot; she put a cozy on it. "And don't they go after the cigarettes!" She looked upwards as if consulting heaven still talking aloud. "X rays and tests and I had emphysema; that caused my shortness of breath . . . of course livin' seventy-five years doesn't shorten your breath," she said sarcastically. There was no real question in her mind; she knew he was right. The coughing spells were getting worse; if Jerry was home she muffled her mouth in a doubled Turkish towel so he wouldn't hear her cough. The over-the-counter medicine no longer gave her relief she fingered the prescription package she had brought home; "Dope I'm sure!" The tea was ready and she added a little honey and sat down looking out her kitchen window at a tree that she loved. She spoke aloud. "This is the happiest time of my life; I hope I'm not goin' t'die." The thought brought tears to her tired eyes. "Well if I am . . . I am."

After he left Tom Jerry wandered to the sleazy part of town and went into a dive and had several boiler makers. He was depressed about Tom and thoughts of Edith and Eleanor were rolling around in his head. He knew he should not see Eleanor; there was no real future with her. He was what he was . . . when he was drunk he saw himself better; when he was sober he never looked into himself. That was a no-no. He left the bar and walked along the shabby street; a young girl was approaching from the other direction, she sidled toward him. She wore tight white shorts and a black tee shirt and needless to say, very high heels. The make-up was heavy and bizarre and her eyes were glassy.

"You need some help, hon?"

Acting dumb he asked, "Help with what?"

She moved her mouth as though she missed her bubble-gum. "Whatever."

"Tell me; I'm shy."

She moved very close to him. "Oh, you're very shy, I know."

He pulled down his zipper moving her to the shadows; she began stroking him;

"You're hung, baby."

"It's all yours" he murmured.

He put his hands on her shoulders and pressed her, gently, downward to his aching point of need. She immediately complied;

"Beautiful;" he sighed, "really beautiful.

For the first time in his life he couldn't respond; she made every effort to arouse him but there was no response. He pushed her away and began to masturbate furiously; sinking to his knees.

"You just drank too much, hon."

He hissed at her; "Get the fuck out of here! You're an amateur."

She was gone in a flash; "I don't need no beatin'!"

He continued his efforts futilely; slumping forward on his knees he sobbed softly . . . tightly. He stayed there whispering "Oh my God."

Tony and Brian had gone to Brian's apartment after closing the bar. It was the first time Tony had been there. Sharing a V-8 drink they were propped up in bed enjoying a warm after-glow. It was early morning;

"I've got something I want to run in front of you, Brian."

"Run it!"

"How about me getting Gino to run my place until the end of your vacation and we go out East to the shack? He did a great job while we were away three days."

"That's a prima idea" Brian enthused; "do you think he's available?" "I know he is . . . I've already asked him."

Brian was filled with excitement; "When can we go?"

"As soon as you get your ass out of this bed!

Tony was grinning broadly; "I bought a used station wagon and it's full of groceries and booze and stuff. You couldn't say no . . . you just couldn't!"

"*Me* say *no*? Mrs. Mc Hugh didn't raise an idiot!"

Brian flew out of the bed and into the shower. He was dressed and started packing in a fury.

"Easy boy, it's early you don't have to break a speed record."

"Where is this wagon you bought? Can I bring anything; like bed linen and blankets?"

"The wagon is in a friend's garage not far from here and I forgot about bed linen. I'll go get the wagon while you pack. I've got plenty of cash on me don't worry about money."

By seven o'clock they were on their way; both so elated that not even the morning business traffic could annoy them. The sun was rising brightly promising a beautiful day. They stopped for breakfast in Hampton Bays and finally made it to the shack.

"Here we are!" Tony was smiling, "Ed Gunther had some people come and clean the place up." He spoke to Brian as he unlocked the door immediately noticing the improvement in the place.

"I'll go bring some stuff in."

Brian's arms were full and he went in to unload and then went out for more. The place smelled a bit stuffy from being closed up but the odor of cleaning solvents was noticeable. They spent the day getting the cottage in order stopping for a quick bite at LUNCH; the restaurant out on the highway. When it got to be five o'clock Tony blew the whistle.

"Enough for today; it's cocktail time! Then we'll clean up and go see our friend Bob in Montauk and have dinner. We have to catch up on the local gossip and he's the one to go to for that!"

"I'll drink to that!" Brian was drying his hands. "I'm glad we thought about ice and stopped to get a bag. Cocktail hour without ice is not a pleasant experience. What can I make for you?"

"I'll have what you're having; keep it simple."

"I was thinking martini; is that okay with you?"

"That sounds simple enough." They laughed and Tony hugged him. Brian picked out two glasses;

"I'm good at simple."

They had dinner at Kincaid's; Bob sat with them and drank and told them about Henry, a free-lance builder who was there having dinner with his wife. He wanted them to meet. When all of them had finished eating Tony asked Bob to invite Henry and Techla, his wife, to come to his table for an after-dinner drink. Bob brought them to the table, made the introductions and then took his leave of them. He had the sense and courtesy to know it was going to be a private meeting. He had simply said; "I'll leave you with each other."

There was the usual small talk; Tony was surprised that both of them still had pronounced German accents although they had lived in the States for many years. Henry was tall and well built; he was probably in his early sixties but he was strong and still could perform as well as any of his younger competitors; and then some! He took much pride in his work and he was a perfectionist. Henry had worked for wealthy people and still had customers in East Hampton who owned large estates and would only have Henry do their work. Techla was a haus frau and taking care of Henry was her career; as she put it; "Dat's my chob." They talked for an hour and agreed to meet at the cottage the next morning. Henry knew exactly where it was . . . he clammed there with Bob. He told them; "You have a gold mine on that beach."

Henry was there next morning right on schedule and ready to go to work. Brian made a pot of coffee and the heads went together. They were immediately comfortable with Henry and quickly saw his ability to listen and comprehend. He excused himself to go to his van and get some equipment.

"This is our man," Tony exclaimed gleefully; "he listens to us Brian."

Brian agreed; "I feel good with him."

Henry returned and they spent a couple of hours discussing the work to be done. Henry called a lumber yard and ordered what he needed; he told them to open an account for Tony and put Tony on the phone to give his information. There was no credit check . . . Henry had spoken! The cottage had been built of cedar wood but someone had later covered the outside with asbestos shingles. These had to be removed and would be replaced with thick # one Perfection cedar shingles. They last a lifetime near salt water. He was going to employ two young fellows who were good workers to do that job. The place buzzed with activity all day long; it was music to their ears. Tony and Brian made lunch and a couple of cold beers where much appreciated. Jim and George, who were stripping off the old shingles, were especially happy with the beers. Sitting by the waterfront sipping beer they could do all day . . . but not on Henry's watch! They knew that even if another beer was offered they had better give a polite 'no thanks'. Everybody was busy and by four o'clock much progress was made.

"We will work until six," announced Henry.

The next day Henry told them that Techla was going to make a dinner for them on Saturday night; "we eat early so come about four o'clock. I will write directions for you . . . it's easy to find."

"Well, that was a command performance invitation!" Brian was smiling; Tony along with him. "They're German, Brian!"

"Bob told me she's a fabulous cook so we are in for a treat."

Brian smiled; "That I am sure of . . . we'll have to bring something."

"I brought a few bottles of wine we can bring a couple."

"They probably have plenty of wine; let's bring flowers. I have a feeling Techla doesn't get a lot of bouquets; she will be pleased. Remember, Tony, I work with women every day . . . I know them."

"I bow to experience; the women who come to my place would rather have booze anytime!" Brian enjoyed a hearty laugh.

"I have no doubts about that!"

Saturday came and they found the house easily; it was on a small hillside facing west overlooking Fort Pond. This fresh water lake in

Montauk was between the Atlantic Ocean and Long Island Sound; two huge bodies of salt water and yet this lake had pure, soft fresh water. So soft that those who knew washed their hair in it for beautiful soft hair. It was a closely kept secret. Not easily done here!

"This is it! There's the sign 'Keppler' by the driveway."

Tony turned into the drive and went up a gradual rise to the bungalow; there was ample parking space and beautiful landscaping. Brian was right about Techla; there were flower beds all over the place in a well-tended plan. A deck went around the whole house and the view of the Pond was lovely.

"What a party you could have out here," Tony sighed; "what a deck!"

"Can you imagine the sunsets from here? You can see Fort Pond Bay in the distance." Brian loved the place. "I want to see inside."

"Well get up to the door before those flowers die!"

"I think we're bringing coal to New Castle."

Henry opened the door and greeted them warmly; the aroma from the kitchen was heavenly and Tony was ready to sit down at the table that moment. The hospitality seemed to wrap around you.

"It smells awfully good in here, Henry, no wonder you look so good . . . you're fed the best meals in town!"

"I've got no complaint with anything in this house; my wife takes good care of me; we take care of each other."

Techla came in from the kitchen; she had removed her apron and wore a very pretty dress. She looked fresh and composed, not like a lot of cooks who work up a sweat when cooking.

"Velcome," she smiled and hugged them.

Henry took them on a tour of the immaculate home pointing out the various pieces of furniture he had skillfully made. This was a social call but he was too German to pass up this golden opportunity to dramatize his ability. He was too modest to verbalize his talent.

"Come now, we have a drink; I'll show you my bar and you make what you like. We drink beer and wine; I don't know how to mix cocktails."

They had a wonderful dinner of pork cooked with apples and onions and heaven only knows what gave it all such savory flavor.

She made the best red cabbage Brian had ever tasted and he made a mental note to get some of her recipes after he knew her better. He had a hunch that nothing was written down. The dessert was a knock-out; an applesauce cake with a brandy sauce that was outstanding. Brian had to know how to make that sauce! After a truly charming evening they said their goodnights; Techla still thanking them for the lovely flowers. She couldn't speak English fluently but she had an endearing way of expressing herself. Of course sometimes Henry had to step in to explain her point. When this happened she would shake her head at her ignorance and he would hug her and kiss her brow. There was a deep love between them.

After they had departed and the two of them cleaned up the kitchen; which was not very messed up, Henry poured two glasses of wine and they sat in the living room comfortably talking in German. Techla looked at her husband after a while and said;

"Do you think they are a couple? The way Tony looks at Brian is not how a man looks at another man."

Henry had worked for many gay men in the area and he found most of them excellent to do business with. And they knew what they wanted!

"It could be; they are fine fellows and I like working with them so far. Tony seems to have money and Brian is not lazy he is busy all the time. It is nothing new to me."

"I'm not finding fault! I like them very much; I just don't understand how two men can care about each other that way. Maybe if they went to a whore house they could change."

Henry shook his head; "Tony was in the Navy for some years . . . you think he doesn't know about whore houses? Let's go to bed!"

Tony and Brian returned home and sat on the deck steps having a drink and looking out over the harbor. There was an old, small trailer park across the harbor tucked in the dunes. It was a pretty ordinary place in daylight but the magic of nightfall and the soft twinkling lights made it beautiful. There was no wind and the water was still and sparkled where any lights hit it. They could hear the surf across the highway and it sounded like traffic on the road.

But there were very few cars on it. Mother Nature was just cleaning her beaches.

The time would go fast and once Henry got going things started to happen. It was gratifying to see what a contractor who knew what he was doing could accomplish; especially when he had workers who liked their work and really put a day's effort into it. The walls came down and there were glass sliding doors on three sides of the living room. Everywhere you looked there was a marvelous view. The old flooring was replaced with random pine boards and just that much of a change made a drastic difference. The room was opened up to the outdoors and they vowed that no curtains or drapes or blinds were going to curtail that view. The weather remained clear and much progress was made. They got tanner and spent most of the time working on the cottage. Brian had informed Tony that he would have to cease calling it a shack!

Jerry ground out another cigarette. It was four in the afternoon and he still hadn't had a drink . . . not even a beer. He was parked in a small park near the river; he needed to be alone and he needed to dry out. "I've got to dry out," he said aloud, "at least for twenty-four hours." His eyes were red and swollen, he needed a shave and it seemed that every line in his face was pressing to be noticed. One look in his rear-view mirror said it all! "What a mess I am! What the hell is wrong with me?" He summed up the things he had going for himself; talking aloud. "I should be happy; but I'm screwed up!" Eleanor had made inroads. "She wants me to make a move; she's looking for a nest. God! I'm not ready for that. I can't leave Nora; she needs me. Now more than ever; she isn't well." There was another voice speaking that was kept low and not really listened to; "who needs who?" He went home.

Nora was in the living room when he came in; he had hoped to avoid her seeing him. She came close to him.

"I don't think ye could win first prize in a beauty contest, love."

"I'm damn sure I couldn't!"

"Why don't you take a nice hot shower and shave and I'll fix you a bite to eat? I made some chicken soup; that will do you good."

"I'll shower and shave but let me take you out to the Chinks."

She enjoyed Chinese food.

"You don't have to do that."

"I know I don't; I want to take you out."

"Well, that will be lovely; I'll get dressed."

"Wear some of your crown jewels."

"I'll wear me rosary around me neck."

He smiled; "You'll scare the Chinks!"

They had an enjoyable dinner; he was glad he could eat and she ate very well. She loved Chinese tea and could never make it herself. They were in the living room and he asked her to sit down. She was concerned for him but she would not ask any questions.

"Nora, would you do me a big favor? Will you go up to the lake with me? Just the two of us."

"Sure I will . . . what's wrong darlin'?"

"I want to get off the booze . . . I need to get away to do it. I'd like to get going now; would that be alright with you?"

"Yes, I'll get some things together; how long will we stay?"

"Probably three or four days."

"Come into the kitchen with me; I have cooked food and we can take other food that I have. It will go to waste here."

He followed her into the kitchen, docilely, and they packed what she wanted to take.

They arrived about midnight Nora had dozed along the way; he had brought a blanket and pillow for her comfort. He took her bags into the master bedroom and she followed him.

"I'll help you make the bed if you like."

"No dear I can handle that; you see to yerself."

Nora heard a clinking of bottles, knowing only too well what kind of bottles; she began to panic. Jerry came into the room with all the whiskey in the house.

"Keep this in here, lock your door and don't let me in if I beg you on my knees. I don't think I'll bother you . . . it's just a precaution."

Nora was up early, just after dawn; he was not in the house. She had a good night, not much coughing her new medicine showing some benefit. She put on her robe and went out on the deck; at first she didn't see him then she saw the boat moving through the water; he was rowing rapidly and did so for about two hours. He came in exhausted, and she started his breakfast while he showered. When he came into the kitchen Nora was amazed at the change in him already; it didn't seem possible that he could bounce back so quickly. She wondered what he would be like if he didn't drink at all.

"Today you could get first prize; you look wonderful!"

"Mr. Wonderful is hungry, madam!"

"Well, we can take care of that; sit ye down!"

And so it went for three days. They made a shopping trip into town; he was eating everything but the furniture, but he looked marvelous. He had a golden tan already and he looked really handsome.

"I've never seen yer blue eyes so clear, darlin' they really are blue aren't they?"

"Don't get smart; you're not too old to spank."

A couple of hours later Nora had a bad spell and he packed the car and headed home. He was very worried about her and if she needed attention he wanted her near her doctor.

Back in the city he called Eleanor; she had been trying to reach him and worried that something might have happened to Nora. He said he took her away and she was doing well until yesterday and he decided she should be near her doctor. Eleanor didn't press for more information and after some chit chat they hung up. She was more than a little puzzled.

Jerry was blaming the job for his excessive drinking; he had his twenty years in and he could retire if he chose that route. It would be good for him to work at something entirely different; exactly what he would do was a mystery at the moment. He knew for certain that he was better without the drinking; and he looked like a million bucks!

"When I do take another drink it's going to be beer and beer only; I'm finished with booze!" He said this aloud as he drove to Tony's; he had called Tom and arranged to meet him there when Tom finished his shift. He arrived first; Gino was behind the bar.

"Where's the boss?" He lit a cigarette while Gino finished washing some glasses.

"He took some time off; he's got a little business to take care of."

"Where did he go?"

"I didn't ask him and he didn't tell me." Gino was annoyed; he didn't especially like cops.

Tom came in and greeted Jerry he took a stool and looked at Gino. "Two beers, please, Gino."

Gino was drying his hands. "Comin' up!"

"Beer okay with you, Jerry?"

"Fine; did you have a crazy day?"

"Not really; I think all the perverts went to Coney Island. Maybe they chartered some buses and made a full day of it."

He sensed that Jerry was feeling low; but he certainly looked good. He patted his shoulder;

"Well, a little time off did a lot of good for you; you look terrific; I've never seen you with such healthy color!"

"I took Nora up to the lake; she hasn't been feeling too good. I did some rowing and a little outside work; that's where I got the sun."

Tom lit a cigarette; "She's been feeling poorly for a while, hasn't she?"

Jerry nodded, "I'm worried about her."

Tom stayed about an hour and said he had to go; Jerry asked no questions because he knew exactly where he was headed. It infuriated him that Edith had managed to get her hooks into Tom and the despise he harbored for her was mounting. He never thought that it takes two to tango; Tom never received any blame, it was Edith and Edith alone who engineered the affair in his mind. He had four beers; he was going to drink coke but when Tom ordered the beer he went along with it. Now he had to get out of there; he couldn't make conversation with Gino so he left a dollar on the bar and said good-by. Driving toward home he stopped at a pay phone and called Eleanor. They chatted for a while and he learned that Brian was away to the Hamptons again. He didn't ask if he was with Tony . . . he was sure of it! Something was going on with those two; his police instincts piqued his curiosity. "I'm going to have fun with Tony." He said this aloud to his windshield. "It's going to be interesting!"

He discovered something; if he tried not to drink he had nowhere to go. One afternoon Eleanor had lunch with him and they spent a few pleasant hours together. Nora was getting a little crazy trying to find things around the house for him to do. He had no whiskey . . . yet! Nora was a bit surprised that he seemed to be staying in for the evening. They had played cards for a couple of hours and had a few beers; she had not seen him drink any liquor since the trip to the lake. When she told him it was her bed time he got up and stretched.

"I might go out for a while and see what's going on at Tony's."

"Oh, I forgot to tell you Eleanor is coming for lunch tomorrow at about one o'clock. Will you be here?"

"Sure I'll be here . . . can I bring anything in for you?"

"A bottle of Chablis would be nice; I promised her I wouldn't fuss so it's going to be a cold buffet. I have everything else."

He chided her; "Do you have enough beer?"

"Why don't you just get goin'; if you're goin'?"

Jerry laughed as she pretended to slap him; he kissed her.

"I love you lady."

He didn't go Tony's; he wandered to one of his creepy dens near where his last sexual mishap occurred. After several beers he walked to the area where the little blonde plied her trade; he found her and with his arm around her shoulder he guided her near the dark stairway. His demeanor was gentle and considerate; she was quite surprised. This time as he left her she whispered; "You really are a stud." Pressing a generous amount of money in her hand he whispered; "Bye bye, baby."

Eleanor arrived for lunch and they spent several hours pleasantly; Nora had a couple of spells but the medicine seemed to work. She began to show signs of being sleepy and Eleanor figured the beer and the medicine combined was having an effect on her. Her diagnosis was right on the money and soon they were walking her to her room and Eleanor helped her to bed. Not without a proper amount of protest, of course! Jerry smiled; "She's a piece o' work!" They cleaned up the kitchen and Eleanor said she had to be going; he offered to drive her home but she insisted on a cab. He called one and paid the driver in advance under her protests. He hugged her and gave her a kiss and handed her into the cab. She settled back into the cab and once again that old confusion took hold of her. No woman could ask for better attention than he gave her; but something was missing and she flatly did not know how to handle it. To ask him what his intentions were was too antiquated for her; she had to smile at the thought of that conversation. He had tried to question her about Brian's whereabouts at lunch and she had avoided giving him an answer; it annoyed her . . . he seemed to have an ulterior motive and she would not tolerate any nonsense where such a good friend was concerned; she spoke aloud.

"It's none of his damn business!"

The cabby responded, "Pardon me, ma'am?"

She blanched, "Just thinking out loud . . . sorry."

"No problem ma'am . . . go easy on him."

She exited the cab and tried to tip him.

"All taken care of ma'am."

Edith got off the scale; she was ecstatic! "Six pounds in two weeks!" She sang to the four winds; "oh what love can do!" Dancing around her bedroom naked as a peeled shrimp pausing in front of her full length mirror; *not bad and getting better.* There was a cold supper in the fridge and plenty of booze and "these two lovin' arms" she sang aloud. Tom was coming; she didn't know exactly what time because he didn't know. He would call when he was on his way. Wrapping her hair in a turban of toilet tissue then covering it with a bouffant shower cap covered with small plastic daisies, she slid into a fragrant tub of suds; "I spent three hours on this hair today I will not steam it into nothing."

Lucille Nesbit spent three hours doing the floors in her house that day; she would, however, get a good nights rest with no man to keep her otherwise occupied. She would awaken ready for her next day.

Edith would not get much sleep but she would awaken ready to take on the world!

Tom came at nine thirty; he was on the job but he could steal some time; his buddies covered for him and they would not call him unless he was needed. He came in and she greeted him in a filmy negligee; they kissed hungrily, then he headed for the shower. He came into the bedroom she lay on the blue satin sheets her beautiful blonde hair a faint shimmer across the pillow. It was obvious that he was well on his way to a full erection and she tingled everywhere in her body. He slid onto the bed and lay against her kissing her deeply and rubbing his body slowly up and down on her. Her body craved for him everywhere and he slowly slid up and entered her capable mouth. Tom was pounding with passion, being careful to be gentle, and slowly slid down kissing her passionately and finally entering her where she needed him so much. They climaxed and collapsed wrapped in each others arms and lay there in the magic . . . the soft music framing the back-ground. They arose after a time she made some drinks while he used the bathroom; they toasted each other and she told him to raid the ice-box while she tidied up. He ate lightly and they had one more drink and headed back to the bedroom. He was able to stay for three hours and they made the most of it!

Jerry saw Edith as a whore; he had no idea she was capable of love to the degree where she put her needs second as long as her desires were fulfilled. Well, they were being fulfilled as like never before and Tom was her master; more than he realized. Jerry wanted Tom's marriage back the way it was; and that would never happen. His obligations to his family would never be neglected and Edith was in total agreement with that. Something Jerry did not believe possible. Wisdom was necessary here; Jerry did not have it where his partner was concerned. He should stay out of it . . . but could he? Unfortunately . . . he couldn't!

The vacations were nearing an end and in a couple of days he would not have the use of the Cadillac so he was taking Eleanor for a drive out along the North Shore of Long Island. Jerry wanted to find a nice water-front restaurant where they could enjoy a nice lunch. It was a beautiful day so he had the top down; he had called her to tell her she better have something to keep her hair in place. Eleanor laughed and said she just might let it blow wild in the wind. She was waiting down on the street in a white sharkskin shift; it had a square cut neckline with two emerald clips in the corners. Her hair was in a bouffant page boy and its Titian highlights shimmered in the sun; she looked lovely. He opened the door for her handing her into the seat.

"You are a knockout beautiful; really."

"Thank you, kind sir," she smiled as she fashioned an emerald green silk kerchief over her hair, "I'm ready for the open air!"

He pulled away from the curb "you look like an ad for expensive soap, sweetheart."

She threw her head back, laughing; "before or after usage?" she quipped.

"I refuse to comment." He said laughingly.

The drive along the shore was wonderful; it was refreshing to see the acres of huge trees with grand homes securely out of sight for the most part but occasionally catching a glimpse of one perched over-looking the Sound. The road wove its way along the shore and they came upon a discreet sign that simply said CAPTAIN'S NEST with an arrow pointing the way.

"Let's try it," Jerry showed some excitement.

"Oh yes" she answered, "It must be interesting!"

He turned down the not-so-wide lane and after a short time the trees faded away and Long Island Sound was in front of them. The lane ended and there was the restaurant up on a rise over-looking the water. Driving up the driveway they entered a spacious parking area and parked the car. The building was faced with cedar shingles and the trim and shutters were sparkling white. It was two-storied and had upper and lower decks; everything was freshly painted and in apple pie order.

"This might belong to a real captain," Jerry commented, "It sure is ship-shape!"

"It's so inviting; are we going to sit inside or outside?" Eleanor asked.

"There are some people outside but not many."

"Let's see what the inside looks like."

Jerry took her arm and walked toward the entrance. They entered and were charmed by the warm, inviting atmosphere and the heavenly aroma coming from the kitchen. It was a combination of light-grained paneling and sparkling white accents; a fire in the fireplace added a touch and they chose a table near it. It wasn't a chilly day but it was breezy and a bit cooler by the shore; the warmth of the fire was welcome. The place was busy but the ambiance seemed to keep the conversation level low. In fact there were mostly couples, of various ages, and a sort of intimacy prevailed.

"It's so inviting; wouldn't it be nice to have a home like this?"

"You couldn't want for more," he nodded his head; agreeing with her.

"I've almost got my twenty years in; it would be nice to retire to something like this, smaller of course, I don't think I'd want to maintain a place of this size."

The waiter came and Jerry ordered a glass of wine for her and a beer for himself. When the waiter returned they were ready to order and it was handled professionally and very cordially.

"This place is really well-run," he commented, "I have a feeling the kitchen is the same way; I think we are going to have a nice meal."

"If the aroma from that kitchen is an example of what is coming it's going to be super!"

She smiled at him and he reached for her hand; the light from the fire played over her hair and its red-gold highlights were softly beautiful.

"You really are lovely," he pressed her hand, "your hair looks absolutely beautiful."

"If it doesn't they should take my license away; after all I am a professional and it should look good!"

She squeezed his hand in appreciation. "Speaking of good looking, you look wonderful. You have such a healthy color I have never seen you look as good as you do."

"I've quit drinking the booze and I'm going to do my damnedest to stay off it!"

"Well, if it makes that much difference in how you look and I am sure you must feel a lot better; it would be worth the effort."

She didn't know just how much effort it took; those shooters had gotten to be a habit and foolishly; it seemed to make him feel manlier . . . or so he thought. The waiter served the salad.

"What a beautiful dish! It looks too nice to disturb." Eleanor was impressed with the presentation.

"You may feel that way but I am going to tear into this; my taste buds are working overtime just looking at it!"

They were silent as they enjoyed the delicious food; making low sounds of appreciation as they ate. The rest of the meal was excellent; they had another drink and neither had dessert. As they prepared to leave the waiter accompanied them to the entrance and gave Jerry a business card. If you would like to register in our book we have invitation only dinners on occasion and we will notify you to see if you would like to reserve. They are really quite nice; we have music and always a congenial group. I think you would enjoy it. Jerry signed the book and enjoyed that feeling of being special. It boosted his ego that this occurred while with Eleanor. She was indeed very impressed and the visit ended on a high note. It was late afternoon the sun was easing its way toward the horizon. Jerry put his arm around her and they walked down to the water's edge; gentle waves caressed the shore and the birds were feeding at nature's buffet. A flock of buffle-head ducks was busy doing their surface dives for food with the boundless energy they possess.

"What a picture!" Enthused Eleanor, "those little ducks are adorable; they seem to act on command."

"Maybe they do; there could be a number one duck that quacks *dive!* And all the little ducks dive."

She poked him as he laughed;

"They don't all go under at the same time! Look at them; they swim along and dive when they feel like diving. When they see a fish down there they dive. If they can't see the fish they have some sense of where they are; Mother Nature arranges all that."

"It must be so; they don't get all that energy from breathing salt air."

He turned her to him holding her close and kissed her. "I'm happy when I'm with you; I enjoy everything more."

Turning, they headed back toward the car.

"Do you want me to put the top up going back?"

"Oh no, let's try it down; I have my kerchief."

"That won't be too much help if it's cold."

"Doesn't that luxury liner have a heater?"

"Oh, you want to travel like the teenagers!"

"Why not? Those kids know more than we do!"

He drove homeward at an easy pace and it was just fine with the top down. There was a parking spot in front of her building; uncommon luck in New York.

"Do you want to come up for a cup of coffee?"

"I do but I better get home and see how Nora's doing."

She thanked him profusely; he kissed her and was gone.

He returned the Caddy and picked up his car; he would not have the use of the Caddy until the politico took another trip. He drove past Tony's and could see Gino behind the bar. "No thanks' he said aloud and headed home. It was dark now and there was a light in the kitchen; Nora was there and she heard him but couldn't get to her room without passing him. She had a bad spell and did not want him to see her.

"Hello sweetheart," he called as he went to the kitchen. He stopped cold when he saw her; she looked awful.

"Nora, you're not looking good. Did you have a spell?"

"Yes," she said weakly, a while ago. I came out to make some tea."

"I'll fix it for you; I'll even join you."

"Lord bless us! What it is the world comin' to?"

Though she felt poorly she couldn't resist her sense of humor; it was automatic. He put a pillow behind her back and she sighed in appreciation.

"Oh that's so much better; thank you Jerry." He came close to her;

"Did you take your medicine? Don't neglect it; it does give you relief."

"I took it; but it does make me sleepy."

"So what? If it makes you sleepy go to sleep! That's better than coughing and making yourself weak."

"Easy for you to say; I have things to do besides sleeping and being doped up."

"I can do anything that has to be done; and I want you to tell me anytime. You'll get better much faster if you get a lot of rest."

"Whatever you say; your lordship."

Jerry began preparing the tea pouring some of the hot water into the pot to preheat it. He knew her eye was on him to see if he overlooked this all important step. She raised her eyebrows as he did it correctly letting him know, tacitly, that she was surprised. Without saying a word she had let him know her thoughts; she twitted him devilishly. He was not about to let her get away with it.

"Everything going to your expectations, Madame?"

"What expectations? Am I supposed to have some?"

She half-closed her eyes rocking back and forth slightly against her pillow. It gave her a scheming appearance. He smiled; he loved her moxie.

"I want to be sure I do the tea correctly; I wouldn't want to give you a poor cup of tea."

"Yer doin' a lovely job; just lovely."

Nora looked better already and having him there was the best medicine anyone could give her. After the tea had steeped enough he poured her a cup and squeezed a few drops of lemon juice in with a half-teaspoon of honey.

"That's just perfect," she nodded to him as she sipped it, "it's as if I made it meself!"

"I couldn't ask for a better compliment than that!"

He made a cup for himself and toasted her when he tasted it; she returned his toast and it made him feel good to see her smile. He told her about his outing with Eleanor and this was music to her ears. How she would love to see him happily married to her. She prayed God would spare her until this happened. This was running through her mind as he spoke. Jerry had made some toast and he was surprised to see her eating it.

"Did you eat anything today? Tell the truth!"

"Indeed! Tell the truth is it? Since when did I start tellin' lies?"

"Now don't get your back up, sweetie, I just want to be sure you're taking care of yourself."

The tea seemed to revive her; she had perked up and had much better color. Jerry was relieved but he knew she was sliding down hill. Suddenly his eyes filled with stinging tears and he went to the bathroom quickly; he bathed his eyes with cold water. He certainly didn't want her to see him crying; he had to have as much moxie as she! They talked for a while and she started nodding and he knew he had to get her to bed; she would sleep now. He put his hand on her shoulder gently;

"Sweetie, let's get you propped up in bed where you'll get some rest." He knew enough not to tell her she needed sleep . . . that, for some mysterious reason, would bruise her delicate ego. Helping her to her bedroom he made her comfortable and arranged her three pillows to suit her. That alone was quite an accomplishment!

"I'll see you in the morning," he tidied her covers and kissed her brow; "Goodnight sweetie."

She was dozing off already; he was delighted.

He went to his room and got ready for bed; not that he was sleepy, he just wanted to think. It was a recurring thought about retiring. If he could convince Nora to sell her house they could go to Florida and get a place together. He knew from other detectives who had retired that you could buy a nice home in Florida for a low price. And the general living expenses were much less than New York. That wasn't the most important thing to him; it was the warm weather. If he could get her down there he was sure it would add years to her life. How could he get inside that stubborn head? He was sure the first thing she would say was that it would be impossible for her to leave her church. Not that there weren't Catholic churches all over the country; but *this* was *her* church! She went to the same confessor for more years than she would say. It would be a big hurdle to cross. He was hoping that she would want to be with him and that might make it easier for her. It never occurred to him that her unselfish reason for not going might have more to do with Eleanor and her desire to see them married. Nora had the instincts that many elderly people have; she knew she was on her way out. Her main desire was to see Jerry settled down with Eleanor; Jerry needed someone like Eleanor who had the right idea of living. She knew Jerry's background and the right kind of love could change his whole outlook on life. If only that could happen; she was leaving him all she owned and that would make them financially comfortable. If her money accomplished that she would die happy. Nora was positive that Jerry's job was a big reason for his excessive drinking; he saw nothing but the seamy side of life. Worse still he was exposed to the lowest form of womanhood that existed. If he had the security of her money he could retire nicely and live a more normal life. He would even have her house free and clear; she prayed he would get out of that job and live a normal life.

Tony and Brian were busy doing things to improve the interior of the cottage. The exterior was getting a complete re-do; the old asbestos shingles had been removed and the perfection cedar shingles were replacing them. It was a noisy proposition; but it was also a kind of music. Henry wasted no time and his workers followed his lead . . . or else! Tony was very impressed with the cleanliness of the job. When the men finished every day there was a clean up and no debris or nails were left outside. Any lumber that was outside was covered with tarps and Henry would tolerate nothing less. Bob Kincaid had come through again in his first class style. Each day brought Tony a renewed satisfaction and he was the happiest he had ever been in his life. At the outset his intention was to just fix up the place and make it comfortable and livable. Now he wanted to make it a show-place; not a fancy affair but a place that would bring a 'wow' when people entered. He had the right partner; Brian would come up with ideas that would enhance the place far beyond Tony's expectations. He would take Tony to places in New York where they could buy excellent paintings for bargain prices. Not that they would require many paintings; with all the glass walls there would be no place to hang them!

Tony went to answer the phone; Ed Gorman had secured a quick installation for them and it was he who was calling now. They had a five minute conversation.

"That was Ed on the phone; he wants me to come to his office about some land that I own. He says it's important, do you mind if I go right now?"

"Of course not; you don't need my permission."

"I thought you might not want to be alone."

"With all the racket going on outside and with what I have to do inside I won't have time to be lonely. "I'm cooking!"

Tony laughed. "You're cooking?"

"Don't get smart; bring a bottle of burgundy."

Tony hugged him; "At your service chef!"

He arrived at Ed's office; they greeted each other warmly.

"What's happening, Mr. Gorman, you've got my curiosity bug buzzing."

"I hope I can keep it buzzing; I have a proposition for you. It concerns the acreage you own in Northwest."

It was the northern area of East Hampton Township; hundreds and hundreds of wooded acres with waterfront areas and it still was rather sparsely settled. The average buyer of real estate wanted to be near the ocean. South of Montauk Highway was in big demand and it cost a lot of money. With prices starting to get higher each year developers from outside of the Hamptons were getting very interested in the north woods.

They went into Ed's private office; he closed the door.

"May I offer you some coffee?

"No thanks, Ed, I've had my quota of coffee for the day."

"How about a brandy?" Ed asked, smiling.

"Oh, this *is* going to be interesting!"

"I sincerely hope so."

He went to his liquor cabinet, a handsome antique, and selected a couple of snifters.

"There's a map spread on my desk; I've got a flag on the two hundred acres you own in Northwest. Locate them while I fix the drinks."

Tony went to the desk and was impressed with the large map. "I don't have one of these," he said admiringly, "this is some beautiful map!"

"You don't need one if I have one," Ed smiled. He handed Tony the snifter, "You're health, Tony."

Tony found the tiny green flag sticking up on the map. "Two hundred acres doesn't look like much when you see it on a map like this. Some of these tracts are huge."

"But it also matters where the property is located; notice the three hundred acres east of your land?"

"Yes, I see it."

"Now on the west side of your land is another tract of one hundred seventy-five acres."

"I see it." Tony was filled with curiosity; "So?"

"So, my friend, a big developer has purchased those two tracts; unfortunately not through my office, and now he is very interested in your property. I know the broker who sold him all that land and he has contacted me because he knows I handled the sale of your land. This investor does nice things. He's not greedy; he's classy and his developments are always beautiful. They are going to make you an offer on your land. First I want to ask you if I can represent you; they may go to you directly, this broker may not want me involved."

"Why did he call you if he doesn't want you involved?"

"To pick my brain; the call was just to say hello and touch base, then he mentioned the big sale he had and gradually got around to your land. He was actually trying to find out how savvy you were about real estate; that's how I can tell they are going to be after your land."

"Savvy I am not; of course I want you to represent me, Ed, we've come a long way and you have always given me the right advice. I'd be meat on the table for these guys."

"I was hoping you would feel that way; this is going to be a big thing, Tony, I'm talking about big money. It's my guess they were able to get that land at a very good price. That's why they went ahead on that without investigating your land. If they have to pay more for your land they can average it out. You are right smack between those tracts; they have to have your land to have continuity and to do it right. This developer does not think small. But my advice is going to be not to sell to them."

"Not to sell? You said this was big bucks!"

"If you make the right move; it's big bucks. You offer them a partnership; you will put in your land for a good piece of the action. They will do all the developing; you will not put up any money. You bought that land at the right time for the right price; now you can cash in; big time!"

"You've got my heart pumping, Ed."

"What's in it for me? Ed continued; I want to be sure that my office gets written listing rights when they start selling off the lots. This developer sells for small down payments and gives five year terms. It's a broker's dream. By the time the development is ready there is going to be much more interest in the Northwest. People who live in the city are more determined than ever to have a place to get away to. The Hamptons are easy access from the city; there is only so much property near the ocean and it is going to go sky high in value. When they realize how wonderful the woods are; the privacy one has in a wooded area and maybe if a few deer come grazing by while they are looking it might dawn on them that it is not such a big deal to jump in your car and drive fifteen minutes to the beach and shopping."

Tony was very excited. He couldn't wait to tell Brian. He tried to keep calm; he didn't want to look like a hick.

"I would like to get together with you and Brian so you can explain it to him before we go back to the city."

"How about early tomorrow; we can have breakfast here in my office. My wife will come over and rustle up something; she's a good cook and I would like her to meet you, I've told her about the cottage and what you are doing to it. She loves Napeague Harbor. She used to go hiking through the Walking Dunes years ago."

"Where are the Walking Dunes?"

"They're at the east end of the harbor and local folk lore has it that they are moving eastward gradually. They front on the Sound. My knowledge of them has been the fact that they are a marvelous retreat for lovers and nudists. There are all sorts of private nooks that Mother Nature has provided. God bless Mother Nature!"

"It sounds like you have first hand knowledge, Ed."

"Tony, I wasn't always married!"

They laughed and Ed said he would type up some information for them to study.

"See you about nine tomorrow." They shook hands. Tony scratched his head;

"I've got some thinking to do." Ed smiled; "Me too!"

In his excitement about the property he almost forgot the wine. Tony rang the bell as he entered the cottage, it startled Brian and he almost dropped what he was doing. He came into the kitchen and hugged Brian with all his gusto;

"Have I got news for you, buddy-boy, have I got news!"

"Well out with it! You've got me all worked up!"

"First I want to say this is all at the very beginning and may never happen; keep that in mind. He continued on and related the reason for his visit to Ed's office.

"Brian, if this happens we are going to do some real living! Get a calculator; I want to do some rough figures."

He made a rough guess as to how many half-acre lots they would realize from dividing the property and he was up in the millions of dollars. Many millions!

"Do you believe this? We will get a percentage of all this!"

"We have to be sure it's going to happen, Tony, if we get excited and it falls through we'll be down in the dumps forever. But I can't stop tingling all over!"

Tony hugged him again. "I'll sell my gin mill and you can quit your job and we can live out here year 'round. If you still want to be a hairstylist you can open your own place in East Hampton and write your own ticket!" Tony was going a mile-a-minute and his enthusiasm was contagious. Brian took the wine out of the bag and held it up.

"This certainly calls for a drink to celebrate! Keeping in mind, of course, that it might not happen."

At that moment they were both sure it was definitely going to happen. They had their meeting the next day and Tony was impressed with the sensible questions that Brian posed to Ed. Ed was also impressed and told him he should get a real estate salesman's license; he offered to be his broker to enable him to do so. He recognized talent when he saw it; Brian could sell!

"If you move out here I'll give you a job . . . you could sell a lot of real estate; I'm certain of that!"

It was going to be a waiting game with a lot of meetings and phone calls and intrigue. Ed had figured it all accurately and about a week later Tony received a letter from the broker asking him to call as he had some very important business to discuss with him. The letter stated that the broker would be willing to meet at any location Tony found convenient. Tony called Ed and he suggested Tony arrange a meeting at his cottage at the beach the following week-end.

"Make an early appointment in case it evolves into me getting into the act. That will give us all afternoon if any real talk is going to come out of it. The developer won't play games; but the broker will. He is not going to want me getting a piece of this action I'm sure of that! He will want you to sell your land to the developer securing himself that commission; then he will be sure he is the exclusive broker for the entire operation."

"Would you say he's a little greedy, Ed."

"A common ailment among a lot of brokers, Tony, but thank God there are quite a few who are not afflicted."

"I'll keep you posted Ed; we will see what we will see."

"I won't make any plans that week-end; just call me."

And so the waiting game had begun. Was the end a gold one?

Brian's vacation was almost over; they had come back into the city and all of their thoughts were about the meeting on the next week-end. Tony found it difficult to get back into his old routine and he began building a definite need for this deal to happen. It wasn't good for his nerves and he wasn't in the mood for a jokester like Jerry. And that's who came into the bar; looking tan and healthy and quite sober.

"Welcome back, boss, you look like you were on the beach everyday!"

"You look a little beachy yourself. You do have whites in your eyes . . . I never noticed them before. What'll you have?" Jerry smiled at him;

"Just a beer, no more hard stuff." Tony drew the beer and Brian came in the door in a white shirt that emphasized his deep tan. Jerry put two and two together in a fraction of a second!

"Well hello Brian!"

Brian sat on a stool and nodded to Tony;

"Hi Jerry, you're looking good." He looked at Tony; "Gin and tonic, please."

"I'm looking good?" Jerry exclaimed; "You and Tony look like you were ship-wrecked on some island! That color looks like it comes from the same place; were you away together?" His eyes were slits.

Tony took over the conversation. "I was doing some work on my place out East; Brian came along to give me a hand."

"Your place out East? I didn't know about this. What kind of a place?

"It's just an old shack, really, it needs a lot of work; I've had it for years and never bothered with it."

Jerry's wheels were spinning at mach speed; something was going on between these two; he was positive! He recalled asking Eleanor what Brian was doing with his vacation and now he remembered he got an evasive answer that amounted to no answer. So Eleanor knows all about this! What a clam she is he thought. More a good friend would be accurate.

"Tony, I'm pretty handy; if you ever can use my help I'd be glad to go out with you and pitch in. Just feed me and give me a couple of beers and a rug to sleep on."

"Thanks Jerry, I'll surely keep the offer in mind."

He refilled Jerry's glass but took no money. He was called away to the end of the bar. Jerry turned to Brian;

"I didn't know you were handy around the house."

"I'm the oldest of six kids; you get handy in a hurry."

"I didn't know you came from a big family; I came from nothing . . . that's what an orphanage is."

"That's rough, Jerry, we didn't have a lot of money but we had a good home. My parents lived for their family; they were very unselfish. They died in a plane crash when I was eighteen; I kind of became head of the family. There was a pretty good settlement from the accident and with the help of an old uncle I kept the family together. Most of them live in Ohio. We get together now and then; I'm an uncle!"

Jerry was very impressed and his opinion of Brian changed. Now he understood the close friendship between Eleanor and Brian. They both knew tragedy in their lives. He understood why Brian seemed so mature for his age.

"Tell me about this place Tony has, Brian, he sure has been closed-mouthed about it!"

"There isn't much to tell; it is an old fishing shack and he has decided to fix it up. I don't know exactly what he has in mind; I'm not sure that he knows exactly what he is going to do. He bought some land out there years ago and the shack was on the property; he never saw the shack until a month or so ago."

"You mean he bought some land and didn't look it over first?"

"That is exactly what I asked him!"

They both enjoyed a good laugh at that. Jerry pressed on;

"Brian, it's hard to believe he would do that; is it a nice piece of land?"

"Well" answered Brian, "It's a piece of waterfront on a beautiful harbor; it's on a white sandy beach and it is certainly worth fixing up!" Brian was getting annoyed with Jerry's quiz.

"If it was mine I would want to remodel the whole thing; it's very private; that makes it valuable." Brian felt the need to elaborate in Tony's defense.

Jerry's curiosity was boundless! Brian was a clam just like Eleanor; he would have to drag any information out of him. But Jerry was not about to give up; there was something going on with these two he was certain of that. He was determined to see if he was right!

"Are you two guys doing all the work or does he have a contractor helping?"

Brian was chafing at the bit! "Tony has a local fellow doing some work I'm not sure of the amount of work he will do; I don't pry into his plans."

Brian hoped Jerry would get the implied innuendo. Jerry picked it up immediately but he slid past it without any recognition.

"He must discuss his plans with you if you're helping him! Come on, Brian, that's just common sense!"

"So ask Tony directly and get it from the horse's mouth!" Brian had enough of him.

"Now don't get sore."

Jerry realized he had pushed too far. "I'm only curious!"

"You're asking me about things I know nothing about and that is very annoying . . . especially when you are implying that I do know something."

"Let's drop the subject Brian; I don't want to bug you."

There was a moment of quiet then they drifted into chatter about ordinary things. Brian relaxed and began to enjoy piquing Jerry's curiosity while telling him nothing; he felt an odd sense of power. His relationship with Tony had given him a new confidence he never had before; he felt on a par with other people and an inner strength was born in him. Jerry no longer attracted him as before and he could handle him without the smoldering desire he once felt for him.

"When are you going to the shack again Brian?"

Jerry was back on his hound-dogging; Brian was angry.

"When I have time off from work and if Tony needs me. Only Tony can answer that."

"Well I'm going to hit the road," Jerry sensed Brian's anger; "tell him I'm available if he can use another hand, he might be surprised at how handy I am." "Good night, Brian."

Brian was relieved to see him go; "Good night, Jerry."

Tony waved good night to Jerry and came back to check on Brian.

"What's the matter kid?"

"Oh, Jerry was giving me the third degree about the cottage."

"Don't let him bug you; he's snooping around, he can't stop being a cop. He might suspect there's something between you and me; let him snoop . . . tell him nothing."

He made a fresh drink for Brian.

"Cheer up! Are you going to help me close up tonight?"

"Sure I am! I don't want to lose my job!"

They laughed together and soon forgot about Jerry and the conversation was all about the cottage and what they would be doing to it. Brian remembered Jerry's offer and he told Tony.

"He mentioned that to me, too, maybe I'll take him up on it."

Brian blanched; "Are you serious? Would you?"

"Why not? Let him knock himself out snooping; I'm beginning to think he might be a bit jealous!"

"That would be the day!" Brian was shaking his head; "I can't imagine that!"

"Life is full of surprises, Brian, nothing is impossible; by the way that broker called me about the property, he started giving me a pitch and I told him Ed would represent me about any land deals. I know he was going to try and make an appointment to talk about it but he changed his tune when I mentioned Ed. He said the developer was out of town and he would get back to me. I don't like him; I see what Ed means by the waiting game. I called Ed and left a message.

"We just have to see what they do next." Brian's voice was a little sad.

* * *

Edith and Eleanor sat at a bistro table in a restaurant close to the salon. Edith was starting her vacation; Eleanor's was over.

"Lunch is on me, El, I feel like I was let out of a cage."

Edith stopped a waiter who wanted to keep on going but froze under her positive approach.

"Two marvelous martinis up, darling; dry, cold and quick! Show me how fast those dancing feet can move."

He was gone without a word; he smelled a good tipper.

"You frightened the poor guy, Edith."

"If he takes too long I'll put a dent in the top of his head so he can carry his soup bowls there!"

They laughed in unison both being in good humor.

"How was your first morning back? I hope it was as good as my first morning away."

"Oh, not bad at all; but tomorrow looks like an aching arch day the way the appointment book looks."

"I wish I were going to some place where everyone was bald; except me, of course. I need to be away from that book for a while. This vacation didn't come any too soon," said Edith.

"Are you sure you're not going to go anywhere?"

"Not while I have Tom; I can't be away from him."

Eleanor felt uneasy at the mention of Tom so openly.

"I love him, El, this may be the biggest mistake of all my mistakes but I have to have him and I'll settle for any conditions he makes; it is that bad!"

Eleanor looked quizzical; "Meaning?"

"Meaning him being married; he will never divorce her, he's too decent. Whenever she needs him he will be there; he loves her and respects her. She can't fill his needs; she is hung up on her religious convictions and she is frozen. It is no secret that I am well thawed out and I fill his needs with gusto and this time with a lot of love. If this involvement fails I am going to be one messed-up dame. I have to risk it; I need him more than I could ever explain . . . I am hooked."

"You certainly could get hurt; the kids are a big factor in his life. Jerry told me he is a devoted father; they might weigh on his conscience."

"We've discussed that; he will have to do whatever he decides. I am making no demands; I know that doesn't sound like me; but I am a new me where Tom is concerned."

The drinks came; they both ordered salads, Eleanor didn't have too much of a lunch period. The book was waiting.

"I can't help thinking of her position now; do you think she knows about you?"

"That's just what it is! She has her position and I have mine. We have agreed not to talk about his family affairs. When we're together it is just us; I will never have anything to say about her; never! I made that mistake once. It's me against her and may the best broad win!"

"Oh, Edith, it's not a boxing match!"

Edith was laughing; she said mischievously, "Isn't it, El?"

Eleanor didn't pick up the innuendo at first; then she colored, "Oh, Edith!"

The waiter came with a pot of coffee and two desserts.

"Coffee as ordered; dessert is on the house."

"You're adorable! You must have a happy girl friend."

The waiter blushed; "I hope so, miss."

As they were leaving the restaurant Edith put her hand on Eleanor's shoulder.

"I want to have you and Jerry over for dinner Sunday and Brian if he is loose."

Eleanor was stunned! "I'll have to check with them; I don't know Jerry's new schedule and I'll see Brian tonight."

"Tom said Jerry is off and he will invite him. Let me know, dear, as soon as you can."

She was gone. Eleanor was trying to get herself together; she was still in shock! This was something she had not anticipated; she really did not want to go but she would talk to Jerry quickly and get his feelings. Knowing how he felt about Edith she didn't think he would consider going; but there was his closeness to Tom involved. What a fix she thought; it bugged her all day. Eleanor called Jerry after she returned home from work. She had made a sandwich for dinner and some tea.

"Jerry this is Eleanor; I need to talk to you. Edith invited me to a dinner party next Sunday; she bowled me over! I was speechless. Did Tom talk to you about it? She said he was going to."

"Yes he did and I had the same reaction you did. I ended up accepting; he's my best buddy and I can't hurt him. I hope you will go."

"Yes, of course I will and I'll get Brian to go to; we will need help keeping the conversation going."

"I sure am glad to hear that. I hate to see what he is doing; especially with someone like Edith, but I have to support him. Maybe it will all peter out."

If he was not so concerned he might have noticed his pun.

"What should we bring, El; flowers?"

"I think she will do the flower thing; wine is probably our best bet. I'll pick a couple of bottles up Saturday."

"Keep the bill; I'll take care of it."

"Please, Jerry, let Brian and I do it; you're driving."

"Big deal; I'm driving."

"Well it is; taxis aren't cheap!"

"Are you calling me a taxi or calling me cheap?"

He made her laugh and it was much needed. She sighed. "Thank you Jerry, I needed that. We'll see you Sunday." Jerry smiled; "unless I turn up sooner."

Eleanor knocked on Brian's door and then poked her head in; "can I come in darling?"

"When you call me darling how can I say no?"

They hugged each other and Eleanor made her announcement. Brian stepped back and shook his head.

"Never in a trillion years! You must be off your rocker sweetheart! I'd rather a cup of cyanide!"

"Hear me out, please, none of us want to go; but Jerry feels he owes it to Tom and he would appreciate our moral support. You know, Brian, in a way we kind of owe it to Edith to give her a little support. After all we've worked together for years and this time she might be serious."

"You, madam, have taken complete leave of your senses! I can't believe my ears! She's busy using her wiles to take a devoted father and husband from his home for *her* pleasure and you think we should pat her on the back!"

"Brian! I am well aware of how wrong it is! But can we stop it? You might as well try to stop a tank with a sling shot! I'd like to help Jerry and I would be so grateful if you would too." Brian took a deep breath;

"Help Jerry indeed! He has been sticking his nose in Tony's business out East and he was giving me the third degree until I had to tell him off. He's making smart remarks about our tans looking like they came from the same place and we know he suspects something between us and he's playing detective to dig up evidence. I'm very disappointed in him."

"I'm sorry to hear that; try to ignore him and he will get tired of being a nuisance. Please say you'll go Sunday; it may turn out to be fun. Do it for me?"

"You really are possessed, woman! I cannot believe you are handing me this garbage! It might be fun? She wants to show off her new conquest and we have been selected as the audience! What an honor! The truth is she has no one else to invite and she is trying to tighten her grip on this guy by tossing in a bit of *family* atmosphere; and we are elected and this is what I can't believe; *you* want to help *her!*"

"No I do not want to help her; she already has helped herself! I do want to help Jerry; he has a deep feeling for Tom and how are we going to work with Edith if we turn her down. It is going to be edgy all the time. I don't want to do this Brian! I think we are obliged to!"

"Funny; I don't feel any obligation."

"You're not thinking ahead and you're sore at Jerry."

"I have a good reason to be!"

Eleanor looked distressed and Brian felt a pang of guilt; he couldn't allow himself to do this to her. He embraced her.

"I'm sorry, love, I don't want to hurt you; you know that. I'll go and I'll make myself like it."

She hugged him; "Thank you, darling, I really appreciate it, you are a very special friend."

They both had tears in their eyes. Brian kissed her brow; "I'm going back to my pad."

Edith was very excited about her dinner party. She was a reasonably good cook but she was not going to risk any failures in the kitchen; one wonderful thing about living in New York City was the variety of stores and restaurants and those marvelous caterers! Edith would cook nothing; she knew where to get everything needed for a gourmet dinner. All you had to do was pay for it and she was prepared to do exactly that. After spending a couple of hours with a caterer who had an excellent reputation the menu was arranged around a roast duck entrée and all the trimmings. That included canapés and dessert. Edith had the tableware and china to present an impressive feast. She would make coffee; and spend most of the morning making herself beautiful.

Sunday dawned a beautiful day and Edith rose and geared herself for the dinner party. By two in the afternoon she was ready; Brian and Eleanor arrived first bringing champagne which he had chilled at home.

"Oh, how sweet of you to do this;" Edith was really thrilled by their thoughtfulness, "I have wine but this is an elegant touch!"

"There's nothing like a little bubbly to warm up the festivities."

Eleanor hugged her; Brian followed suit but without much gusto. Edith escorted them to a bistro table she had set up as a bar and invited them to help themselves.

"I'll be your mixologist," Brian volunteered, "do martinis sound good?"

"Sounds wonderful!" The girls said in unison. They all laughed together.

"Let's sit down, El, while Brian works his magic." Edith led the way to the living room.

"The aroma is divine Edith, what are you cooking?"

"Roast duck; with some help from the 'Let Us Do It' people. Oh, they are wonderful caterers!"

Eleanor was impressed, "Many of my clients use them and they get raves."

"I'm not too swift in the kitchen so I decided to play it safe."

The door chime announced the arrival of Tom and Jerry. Edith jumped up;

"They're here!"

She ran to let them in smoothing her tight-fitting blue dress as she went.

"Welcome!" She greeted them warmly; "come on in."

Tom entered first and hugged her close, kissing her cheek. "Hello, sweetie."

Jerry followed saying "Hi, Edith," passing them as they embraced.

Eleanor was there and he hugged her and kissed her brow. Brian appeared with a tray carrying three martinis.

"If you gentlemen are drinking beer try the refrigerator; if you'd like a drink I'll take your order."

"I'll start with a beer," Tom smiled and headed for the kitchen Jerry following on his heels. "Me too."

The dinner went smoothly, everyone on their good behavior. Jerry drank only beer and he was spacing them. Eleanor noticed this and silently praised him for his good judgment; he didn't want to spoil Tom's day; Edith was not even a consideration. The only one who got a bit tipsy was Edith and the others simply ignored it. Tom didn't like seeing her that way but he made no comment; he assumed she was nervous and he was quite right. The dinner broke up fairly early; everyone glad that it was over, Edith happy it had been a success. They said their good-nights and suddenly Tom and Edith were alone. She looked at Tom, impishly;

"I need to finish in the kitchen."

"After I finish in the bedroom!"

Brian called Tony at the bar and gave him a run-down on the evening.

"You must be tired," Tony said caringly.

"Not anymore; how about you?"

"I'm numb; what I don't like is sleeping alone."

"Well, I wouldn't mind if my doorbell rang after you close."

Tony was delighted. "Are you sure?"

"I am very sure!"

They were having coffee in the morning; still naked after showering.

"You didn't get much sleep; it will be a hard day." Brian laughed; "I'll be so busy I won't know it!"

"You just don't complain; do you?"

"I have no complaints . . . I'm very happy."

"It may be too soon to talk about it, Brian, but I would love having you in my bed every night; it makes sense dollar-wise too; you wouldn't have to pay any rent."

"I would love that too; but you need to be very sure. Let's play it by ear; we're getting along swimmingly and if we give it time it will work out. Breaking up is tough, Tony, I have had one experience, years ago, and it really hurts. This is all new for you; you need to give it time."

"How does a young head get all that wisdom?"

"I prayed for it at my Conformation!"

"I was brought up Catholic; I know what you mean!"

They finished their coffee, dressed and Tony said he would get a cab and drop Brian off at work.

"I always walk, Tony, I need the air before I close myself up in all that perfume!"

"You used to walk!"

Brian knew better than to argue; they went by cab. In the taxi Brian told Tony he was going to have the 'family' at his place for dinner.

"I promised Eleanor I would go along with this drama and I'm going to live up to it."

"Do what you have to do; include me out!"

"I wouldn't get you involved; Jerry is bad enough as it is." Tony squeezed his shoulder; "Forget Jerry! We don't worry about him.

Nora had a cold supper for Jerry and she had also made a pot of pea soup. She had a ham bone left over and she could never throw it away without making soup. He had showered and came into the kitchen giving her a kiss.

"Smells good in here, sweetheart; but it's too hot to cook. Haven't you ever heard of cold suppers?"

"That's what we're havin'; and pea soup. I don't think it's hot in here." She sniffed at him. "Eleanor called today and her friend Brian wants us to come to dinner at his home. She would like you to call her to set up a date that you're available. That's very nice of that young man."

"That sounds like you want to go."

"I see no reason to say no; he's nice enough to ask us."

Nora would go anywhere that included him and Eleanor.

He wondered if Tony would be there "I'll call her."

He called Eleanor and looking at his schedule they set a date. After they made the arrangement she told him that Tom and Edith were coming. He felt betrayed.

"Now you tell me!" He growled. "Didn't we just do that dance?"

"I thought he was your best friend; why the objection?"

"Eleanor you know damn well why. You know what comes with him!"

"It was my understanding that we were all going to try to cope with this thing even though none of us like it. You're involved with Tom and Brian and I are involved with Edith. That is the fact; none of us like it!"

He pulled in his horns; he knew he was being unfair. "I'm sorry; I just hate facing that one! And why drag Nora into it? She's not use to people like Edith!"

"Jerry, Nora has lived a long time and she has dealt with all kinds of people! It gives her a chance to get out of the house; especially if she is with you."

He smiled at how convincing she was. He whispered, "And you."

"You better prepare her a little. She knows Tom's wife's name is Lucille; you know how outspoken she can be, she might start asking questions. That could get Edith riled if she's in her cups . . . a good possibility!"

"Thank you for my home work."

"There's nothing like being prepared."

"I must say Brian has some guts to take this on."

"There's nothing weak about Brian."

"Oh, I know how sacred he is."

"Careful Jerry; you're on dangerous ground."

"My lips are sealed."

"That's a good way to stay out of trouble!"

He knew it was time to end the call; she saved him the trouble with a brief "Talk to you later."

Jerry decided to talk to Nora immediately; he hoped she might opt out of going, feeling repulsed by it all. She was very fond of Tom and had thought him to be a wonderful husband and father; which he certainly had been. He went to Nora who was in her bedroom.

"Feel like a cup of tea, lady?"

She was surprised and sensed a problem. "That would be nice. I'll make it for ye."

"Indeed you will not! It was my invitation and I need the practice. Maybe someday you will have your church ladies here and I will have to make tea for them."

Nora was having a good laugh; she finally caught her breath and shook her head. "What I wouldn't give to see that!"

"Come into the kitchen and I'll give you a dress rehearsal. I'm not going to mess with your fine china, dear."

"That's a wise decision, dearie; very wise indeed."

He knew the *dearie* was a bit of her sarcasm because of the accent he had put on the word dear when he spoke to her. She was as sharp as a tack and as quick as a cobra. The tea over he put the dishes in the sink not without a sly look from Nora.

"I want to talk to you about something you might not like hearing."

She blanched; "You're not leavin' me?"

"Nothing like that! That is never going to happen. It's about Tom; he and Lucille are having problems; pretty serious problems, and Tom has become mixed up with another woman."

Nora blessed herself; "Oh, my dear Lord!"

"I'm afraid it gets worse, Nora, the woman is Edith, who works with Eleanor and Brian."

"Isn't *that* a nice kettle of fish?"

"Eleanor and Brian have talked this out; we all hate it, Nora, I've talked it over with Eleanor. I despise this Edith but I can't tell a grown man what to do. He's my closest friend and I have to support him. Eleanor feels the same way and she finally convinced Brian to be with her. They have known Edith for years and they all work together; it's not that we think what has happened is right; they know it is wrong but it's none of anybody's business. We have to stay friends and hope this thing fizzles out."

"I wonder if his wife has friends."

"She has the kids and her folks."

"Oh! Isn't she lucky! She has the kids and her folks! I'll not go anywhere with the likes of them."

"Nora; you can't make judgments! Where is all that religion you believe in?"

"Right where it belongs; I know right from wrong!"

"That's not for you to decide! Tom is my friend and partner; he can do no wrong in my eyes. Whatever has happened I know it was hard for him. He does not neglect Lucille; anything she asks of him he does. He loves his kids and he is still a good father. What happened between them is exactly that; between *them!* He will never divorce her."

"It's filth, just filth!"

"Nora, if we all opened our mouths and started telling them what we think they should do and then it did fizzle out nobody would be friends . . . there comes a time when you prove you are a friend. Especially in bad times!"

But Jerry was making points; she began to feel she was standing in judgment; that in her credo was wrong. She cried; he couldn't have felt worse.

"Nora don't cry; none of this is worth making you unhappy. I just wanted you to be aware of things when you go to Brian's party."

"I'm feelin' like I shouldn't go there."

"Would you do it for me? I want Tom to know we are his friends; if it all blows over he will know we stuck by him even if he was wrong."

Bingo! He had his arm around her shoulder; she looked up at him.

"I'll go, Jerry, thank ye for preparin' me."

He was so touched he had all he could do to keep the tears back. He loved this lady; at this moment he was awed by it. Her humility; a true humility, went right to his heart. He helped her stand and walked her to her room; he turned down her bed and said he would be back in a few minutes. In his room he sat on his bed and sobbed; so moved by her love. He never had love in his life; when he found it the quality was the finest. Indeed! He would never leave her!

They all agreed to a Wednesday evening for the dinner party; in retrospect Brian thought he should have his head examined since Thursday was his twelve hour day at work! He had decided on an Italian dinner because he could make it ahead and it always tasted better a day or two later. There was a recipe for a rolled stuffed veal in his mother's cook book and that was his choice. In a marinara sauce it would be easy to serve. He ordered a cheese cake from an Italian bakery and the rest was easy.

Wednesday evening came and Jerry and Nora where the first to arrive. Eleanor had come early and helped with the last minute preparations. They greeted Nora and Jerry and Brian graciously accepted the wine they brought. Nora looked very smart in a blue grosgrain suit and she admired Eleanor's mulberry and silver silk dress. They were just about seated when Tom and Edith rang the bell. Brian went to let them in and bid them welcome.

"Hello! Come right in."

They had a lovely bouquet and a bottle of Grand Marnier. Brian thanked them profusely and after he escorted them to the others he replaced the flowers on his table with theirs. The Grand Marnier went on the bar and it would be elegant with coffee.

Nora was extremely impressed with Brian's apartment. She had cooked for gay men; they were nothing new to her. It did not occur to her that Brian was gay and to see how attractive his place was earned her admiration. She owned nice things; some very good antiques and she had a sharp eye for quality. This apartment oozed with quality!

Everyone had a drink and canapés were dispersed about the living room. Edith appeared a bit nervous and she was drinking a martini. Jerry had a beer but there was a shot glass next to it. Brian was uneasy about this; it was a loaded gun! He shortened the cocktail hour and served dinner. It was all going smoothly; he noticed Edith ate very little, mixing the food around her plate to make it appear as though she had eaten some of everything. An old dieter's trick. Nora was very complimentary about the dinner and Brian was pleased. He noticed that Tom, Jerry and Edith were drinking quite a bit and it concerned him; he didn't want any blow-ups here! After coffee Jerry came to Brian and said that Nora was tired and he was going to take her home and he would come back. Tom heard him and offered to ride along. In a way Brian welcomed this; it sort of diffused things; or so he thought. As soon as the door closed Edith stood up and raised both hands to the ceiling;

"Well I got through that line of fire! That old lady has no use for me; I could feel the resentment across the room. She would like to see me burning in hell!"

"Nora was fine, Edith, you were on edge for no reason; I think you just felt ill at ease." Eleanor was annoyed with her.

"She was fine if you like icebergs! She barely noticed me."

Brian stood up; "she's from the old school, there is nothing sophisticated about her; we live in a different world."

Edith began to boil; "But why should I have to feel crumby in anybody's presence? If Tom needs someone else that is his affair! I didn't lasso him off the street."

They could not get her off the subject; the booze was showing and Eleanor knew how bad Edith could get when she was drunk. She was worse than Eleanor thought. The harangue continued even when Brian asked her to change the subject. The door bell rang and the boys returned; not without stopping and having a couple of fast shooters . . . which they did not need! They came in jolly and smiling until Tom took a good look at Edith. He started towards her, his arms opened wide.

"Come here, sweetie."

"Did your precious Nora have sweet things to say about Mary Magdalene on her way home?"

"Easy Edith; Tom held her, "she didn't say anything but that she had a wonderful evening. You're over-reacting hon."

She pushed him away; swaying as she walked. "My apologies, darling, you can't expect too much from a home-wrecker!"

Jerry was angry; "Edith, if Nora had anything against you she would not have come to dinner."

"Oh, I'm grateful to the Reverend Mother; and I think she is a *mother!*"

Edith's eyes were blazing; Jerry was taut. Eleanor turned to Edith; pleading,

"Edith do not ruin a nice evening; you wouldn't talk this way if you hadn't had too much to drink;" she spoke in a whisper.

"Shut up Snow White! Who are you to talk? You're letting Jerry use you and you're too stupid to realize it!"

Tom was at her side swiftly; "Come in the bedroom, honey, we need to talk."

"Tom darling, you know I can't talk with my mouth full!"

Brian went into the kitchen; he was sure if he said one word she would go off on a tirade about faggots. Eleanor followed him in tears; he tried to comfort her.

For a few seconds Tom was speechless then he turned to her; "Edith, I'm going for a short walk; when I come back I want this over with. If I say anything now it could ruin us!" He went out.

She went back into the living room. For a moment she was frightened and worried; then her eyes fell on Jerry who was standing with clenched fists.

"You misbegotten son of a bitch! You're the cause of all this! You had to tell Nora about us; we never had to be here with your precious *family*."

She said family with such scorn that Eleanor winced in the kitchen. But Edith wasn't the only one who had too much to drink! Jerry took three long strides and the slap sounded like a crack of lightning! Brian and Eleanor ran in and separated them. The welt rising across the side of her face would take a lot of make-up to cover. Jerry was breathing hard;

"You bitch I'll kill you!"

Eleanor screamed "Jerry!"

Edith held her face. "Big deal! Why don't you get lost, user?"

"You're a sewer," Jerry hissed; "a sewer!"

"Edith!" Eleanor was pleading; go and bathe your face."

To everyone's surprise; herself included, she did just that!

"Jerry; I want you to leave this minute! We can't have you here when Tom gets back and we'll never calm her down while you're here! She's drunk, Jerry, please go home."

"I know you're right, El, maybe I am too; where will I go?"

"Go home! Is that unheard of?"

"Okay; goodnight sweetie." He went out the door.

Brian came into the living room; they hugged each other.

"Too much booze, Brian, much too much."

"I saw it early and I started dinner ahead of time because of that! Edith ate almost nothing and Jerry was drinking shooters! I couldn't stop that without a fight."

"I'm not blaming you, darling; they should know better. Thank God Nora had gone home!"

"This isn't over yet; wait until Tom hears about that slap. Believe me Eleanor; there's going to be hell to pay!"

Suddenly there was a dull thud from the bathroom; they raced in as Edith was picking herself up. The door bell rang, Eleanor gasped;

"It must be Tom; what will we tell him?"

"Tell him I fell and hit my face on the sink."

As drunk as she was she didn't want to make trouble between Jerry and Tom; that would be bad for her.

"Go tell him!" Eleanor ran to the door;

"She's okay Tom, she fell and hit her face on the sink; I'll help her with it, Brian is getting ice. Give her a few minutes, Tom; I don't think she wants you to see her now. There's hot coffee in the kitchen."

Tom nodded and went there.

Eleanor got some witch hazel from Brian and soaked a hand towel with it; she took the ice cubes and folded them in it.

"Oh, that feels good; thank you Eleanor."

Tom finished his coffee and they went home. Edith kept the towel on her cheek hiding the swelling bruise. Edith was subdued. Whatever their conversation was about was never known. Neither of them ever mentioned it again. Jerry and Edith would take a long time to heal; if indeed it ever really happened. Eleanor helped Brian neaten-up the place then they had a night-cap.

"I don't foresee any social gatherings in the near future." Eleanor looked at Brian to get his reaction.

"Or even the far future; as far as I'm concerned!"

They had to laugh, in spite of themselves; they were drained.

"Sarah Bernhardt would envy that performance, El."

"I'm so disappointed with Jerry; he behaved horribly!"

"He was loaded too; and that was all pent up inside him."

"Even so; he was vile."

"They deserved each other tonight; I'm glad Nora missed it."

"She might have had a heart attack. It's a good thing Edith is on vacation; that face is going to have to stay in hiding for a while."

Eleanor was glad they wouldn't have to meet at work for now. This escapade needed time; lots of time. Suddenly Brian was laughing;

"She'll have to put her make-up on with a trowel if she even wants to go to the store."

"What will she do when Tom comes? They'll have to play Arabian Nights and she'll need a veil from the eyes down!" Eleanor grinned.

"And that's all she will wear," Brian added.

They where laughing hard and finally released the pent-up tension. It felt good; Eleanor hugged Brian,

"Thank you for a lovely time." She headed for her apartment both of them laughing.

Brian undressed and put on his robe. He put some mellow music on and sank into an easy chair. Sipping his night-cap he went through the evening like watching a movie. He knew he would never go to sleep; he was still keyed up from the fracas. He wondered if this was the death knell for Edith's romance. If so it would wreck her; he was certain of that. His door bell rang. He couldn't imagine who it was; he hoped Ronnie didn't decide to surprise him with some of his drunken, witty friends. He opened the door and there stood Jerry.

"Sorry Brian, can I come in please? I'm so rattled I don't want Nora to see me; if I go to a bar I'll just get bombed."

"Get bombed? You've already done that! You can come in on one condition: you don't ask me for a drink and you don't help yourself! I'm dead serious; if you come in here and then try to wheedle a drink out of me I'll just throw you out. I've had enough for one night and I have a long day at work tomorrow."

"I promise you I won't ask for booze. How about coffee; is that okay?"

"All you can hold and when I ask you to leave you go at once. Please remember I have a twelve hour day tomorrow."

"I give you my word and I'm not drunk now."

He came in and he did seem somewhat sober although that could be an act; drunks were good at that. Brian led the way to the kitchen and started to heat up some coffee.

"Are you hungry?"

"No thanks; black coffee will be fine. I'm sorry about all this crap we loaded on you tonight. You went to a lot of trouble; Nora loved the whole evening, and we had to mess it all up."

Brian knew he must be anxious about Tom and his reaction to him slapping Edith.

"Tom doesn't know you hit Edith; she covered it up and said she fell in the bathroom and hit her face on the sink. She actually did fall before he came back. She doesn't want to cause any trouble between you two; she's afraid she might lose him."

Jerry stared at Brian. "I guess you know that would break my heart. It would be wonderful except I know how hooked he is. She has a hold on him, right in his crotch, and she knows her way around that territory. He's an easy mark and she is an expert."

"She happens to be in love with him; this is a new Edith."

"I noticed she knocked off a bit of weight, she looks good; I'll give her that. I don't know how new she is though."

"You have a tendency to be hyper-critical of people without having much knowledge about them."

"I have a feeling you're talking about Tony."

"I am not! I'm talking about how you treat people generally. You seem to dwell on their bad points and ignore their good ones. No one knows better than I what Edith's bad points are; but Eleanor and I both agree that there has been a big change in her since she's been seeing Tom. There is no doubt that she is in love like she has never been before. It's not for any of us to say who is right and who is wrong; they are crazy about each other and if it lasts . . . so be it! If it doesn't pan out they will have to handle it. I don't want to be around Edith if there is ever a break-up because she will have one hell of a break-down!"

"Would you feel sorry for her?"

"In a way I would; but I'd never tell her I did."

"Why not? You're her friend; aren't you?"

"We work together; it's not a close friendship. I don't get involved with her personal life . . . she doesn't get involved in mine"

"Not like you and Eleanor; you're close."

"I love Eleanor; she's like a sister only closer; a friend."

"I wonder what Eleanor thinks of me now; I sure made a horse's ass out of myself tonight. I'm afraid to call her."

"The whole thing needs time; everyone has to get back to normal before there can be any talk. Otherwise it will be just arguments. It might help if you sent her a note telling her you regret the whole thing and mention that you would like to call her in the near future. At least you could get an apology in."

"I'm no letter writer; I'd make it worse!"

Brian laughed and poured more coffee for him. "Jerry I need to get some sleep; I'm sorry to throw you out but tomorrow is a tough day. We can talk another time." He stood up;

"I'm on my way and you are right. I shouldn't have stayed this long . . . I guess I needed a friend. Can I call you friend? It's a hell of a thing to ask after my performance."

"I'm your friend; but remember it's a two-way street."

They walked to the door; Jerry squeezed his shoulder. "G'bye."

He ceased quizzing Brian about Tony from that day forward.

Edith was suffering; some vacation! It wasn't just her face; her emotional misery surpassed her injury. She had called Tom and asked him to give her a few days to collect herself. He stopped her from apologizing and told her he loved her. She had a good cry over his being so wonderful. Then she called Eleanor and apologized for her foul mouth; promising it would never happen again. Eleanor being Eleanor let her off easy and changed the conversation to her injury telling her to call if she needed help. Edith was so touched by her thoughtfulness that she vowed never to make any smart remarks about her again. She had yet to call Brian and he was her host! "I'll get to it." She spoke to her pillow. But she never did apologize to Brian; she was certain he would not mention it.

Brian got through his Thursday ordeal and didn't need any rocking when his head hit the pillow. He vowed there would be no more Wednesday night dates. After a busy Friday he went home and had a nap. An hour later he awoke and felt a bit hungry; he was in the kitchen having a drink and looking at the stove. "I know one thing," he said to his stove, "I'm not touching you for my dinner!" He decided to go to Tony's and have pot luck; it would be good and required no labor on his part. The urge to see Tony also had something to do with his decision. After an invigorating shower he walked to the bar and was feeling just great; entering the place he found it quite busy; Gino was behind the bar helping Tony. As soon as Tony spotted Brian he made room for him at the end of the bar.

"Good evening sir, it's nice to see you again."

"And it's so nice to see you, sir; have you been well?"

"I was feeling a bit poorly; but I'm alright now."

They were laughing and the men close by thought them nuts.

"Now can I have a gin and tonic, *sir?*"

"But of course! That was my next question."

When Tony had a break he came up to Brian and after some chit chat he began to fill Tony in on his dinner party.

Tony laughed. "It sounds like I missed quite a show."

"I would have been happy to miss it; I can tell you!"

"Well, you did your duty; now you can give them a rest."

"You can say that again; a long rest!"

Tony looked at him; "When Edith picked on Nora she took her life in her hands; Jerry would kill for Nora."

"You are so right; he belted her in the face and she had one hell of a swollen puss!"

"He hit her?" Tony was filled with disbelief.

"It sounded like a crack of lightning! They were drunk."

Tony had to fill some glasses; he did with dispatch and returned.

"What did Tom do? Did they have a fight?"

"Tom had gone for a walk; he didn't want to get into a harangue with Edith he told her he wanted all the fuss ended.

"You mean she didn't tell him he hit her?"

"She was afraid to cause trouble between them."

"That surprises me; I'd think she'd like that."

"Not with Tom; she doesn't want to lose him."

Tony shook his head; "She must be nuts about him!"

"Edith is consumed by him; like never before!"

Tony smiled; "what a movie this would make!"

Brian gave him a side-long glance; "if you like horror stuff."

Tony shook Brian's shoulder gently; "let's change the subject."

"Gladly, oh gladly! What do you want to talk about?"

Tony looked at him with half-closed eyes; "take one guess."

"The cottage; maybe?"

"Excellent! When are you going to get your learner's permit so I can teach you to drive? You really need to do that."

"I know . . . I'll get on it; I promise."

"Do you feel like going out East tomorrow? Gino will take over for me. Do you think you could get Monday off?"

"I'm just getting back to work! There are other operators on vacation now; I have appointments booked all week!"

"I just thought I'd try! Don't get excited."

"You know I would love to take Monday; I can't!"

"Case closed; how about something to eat?"

"Now you're talking! I'm really hungry. Fix whatever you like but don't over-load the plate; forget you're Italian!"

"You might as well tell me to forget to breathe!"

Brian laughed; "I guess we all know that."

Tony returned in a few minutes with an antipasto platter. The bar was busy but Gino could handle it. He sat next to Brian and placed the dish between them;

"Eat up; it's good for you."

"It looks too nice to mess up; but mess it up I will!"

They ate in silence for a while then Brian spoke.

"Would it be okay with you if I invited Eleanor to go out East with us some week-end? I know the place isn't finished yet but that would never bother her."

"Any time you want to ask her you do so; you know I like her a lot; she's welcome anytime. Invite Jerry too, if you like. I don't mind having him around; maybe he will be of some use."

"I think it's much too soon for that; Eleanor is doing a lot of thinking about him; she is not over his demonstration at my place. He apologized to her with a lot of humility but that ploy is very popular with drunks . . . she is not stupid and she is not a teen-ager."

"I'll leave it in your hands; do whatever you like."

"I don't want to make you feel uncomfortable in your own place! It could spoil a whole week-end; I'd feel awful."

"Just talk to me before you invite anyone; and it isn't *my* place . . . it's our place; remember that!"

Brian looked at him and shook his head. "You're too much."

He stayed until closing and helped with the clean-up; Tony sent Gino home, he had worked hard all night. They went to Tony's apartment for the night and stopped at Brian's in the morning to pack some clothes for the week-end. Once more they were off. While they were at work Monday Brian told Eleanor of his conversation with Tony. She was alive with excitement.

"You're sure he doesn't mind? He's not just being Mr. Nice Guy is he?

Brian assured her she was most welcome.

"He said Jerry was also welcome; if you cared to bring him." Her face clouded over.

"No Brian; it's too soon for that; I don't know where I am with him right now. Have him out there without me and put him to work . . . he needs to be busy!"

"He claims to be a good worker."

"Let him prove it!" She bristled; and walked away.

They both had busy schedules and had no time for more talk. At closing time Eleanor asked Brian to have pot-luck supper with her and they went home together and raided her refrigerator. Brian made a couple of drinks and Eleanor started supper. He brought her a drink, they toasted each other and he helped her with the food. They ate in the kitchen and after clearing things away it was time to sit and have coffee and a cigarette. Ordinarily they probably would have rehashed their day at the salon but Edith and Jerry were still at the forefront.

"Do you think you and Jerry are finished? You are kind of mum about him; if you don't want to talk about it just say so, I don't want to bug you."

"I can't say anything because I don't have any answers for myself. I won't try to kid you; it's on my mind all the time. I can understand why Edith could get him so worked up; and if it was anyone else other than Tom involved I don't think it would bother him at all. The unfortunate thing is they were both drunk. Jerry hasn't touched the hard stuff in quite a while; it was a mistake to put them together."

"It was their mistake to get loaded; no one else did."

"I have to do some thinking; we didn't have anything serious going; I don't know what he wanted. He certainly treated me nicely; we always went to nice places. But there's a part of him that he keeps under wraps . . . from everyone I think. I never have that feeling of security that you get from someone who loves you; it's hard to explain, but I've had it in the past and I know how it feels."

Brian had that feeling with Tony but he wasn't going to start talking about that to her now. When you are in a confused relationship it doesn't help much to hear how wonderful someone else is doing.

"Give it time, you have a lot of common sense; just make sure you watch out for numero uno and don't end up a wreck."

She kissed him. "Thank you friend, I will keep that in mind."

He knew it was time to go; and that's what he did.

Labor Day was approaching and that was a three day week-end. There had been much progress made at the cottage; two beautiful new bathrooms were finished, the shingles were on, waiting now to weather and turn that lovely silver-gray. A re-modeled kitchen was most appreciated so they could turn out some good meals. Tony was so pleased; he had even been taking off during the week to supervise things being done and make selections. Brian was at the bar; he had just finished a long Thursday and came to have dinner. Tony was speaking to him.

"Now that the place is shaped-up we should have Eleanor out for a week-end; I'm thinking about Labor Day, it's a three day week-end. Does she have plans?"

"Not that I know of; she hasn't mentioned any. I'll ask her tomorrow, it would be great to have her along with us."

"You know Jerry hasn't been in here for quite a while; does she talk about him at all? I wonder what's up with him."

"She never mentions him and I don't ask anymore."

"That's being a good friend; she'll talk when she's ready."

He came around the bar next to Brian. "Are you ready to eat?"

"If you're ready; I'm ready."

The next day at work Brian invited Eleanor to spend Labor Day at the cottage.

"Brian! That would be lovely; I'll have to load up on sun tan lotion. You have to give me some hints on what I can bring; I don't know what you need out there."

"Just bring yourself and your bathing suit."

"We will discuss it, dear, I won't go empty-handed."

Brian executed a low bow; "as you wish, Madame."

Suddenly he decided to take a shot in the dark; "El, how would you feel about us asking Jerry to join us? Tell me exactly what you feel."

She backed up; staring at him. "I don't think I'm ready for that Brian . . . that would be close-quarters right now."

"I know he feels terrible about what happened El; he is so fond of Tom and he has no use for Edith . . . he just lost it that night. He hasn't touched the hard stuff since the blow-up; he sticks to beer and he's going easy on that! Give him a chance to talk to you. If you start to feel uncomfortable you can go for a walk on the beach . . . that will make you feel better right away."

"You don't know if he has the week-end off."

"He does and Nora is going on a week-end bus tour with the ladies from her church."

"Have you arranged this Brian?

"I wouldn't do that to you . . . how can you say that?"

"I'm sorry; I'm not myself, ask him if you like."

Jerry was thrilled with the invitation and jumped at the chance to go. He said he would bring his tool box in case they needed something fixed. Brian cautioned him to watch his drinking and explained that he had told Eleanor he was off the hard stuff.

"She's not over the mess yet Jerry; I'm just giving you the lay of the land."

"I understand Brian; I won't let you down. I appreciate what you are doing for me."

"It was Tony who told me to ask you to come."

"Please thank him for me."

"I will Jerry."

The big week-end was upon them; they had agreed to leave on Friday night around mid-night; the traffic would be very heavy earlier and also Saturday morning. Tony had called the cleaning woman who came every Friday morning and asked her to leave lights on in the house and outside the house. There were no street lights in those areas. Brian and Eleanor were all ready and down on the sidewalk when Tony arrived. He had already picked up Jerry. They put their things in the wagon and were on their way; a feeling of excitement shared by all. Eleanor and Jerry sat in the back seat and there was general chit-chat for a while; Brian noticed there was no commentary from the back seat and saw that Eleanor had dozed off. He shut off the radio and he and Tony spoke in low tones so as not to disturb her. Jerry dozed; or at least he made a stab at it. Eleanor roused a little before they got to Hampton Bays and Tony suggested they stop at the diner and stretch their legs and have a bite to eat. There was no dissent. They were there about half an hour then resumed the trip. When they entered Southampton Brian became the tour guide and began pointing various interesting land marks periodically adding;

"You have to see it in daylight." Tony finally chided him by saying;

"We definitely have to make the trip home in daylight!"

He and Eleanor laughed but Brian made a face at Tony and grunted. He refused to continue his tour guiding even when they pleaded with him. He lowered his eyes and raised his brows and with much hauteur said; "Wait until daylight." They were on Montauk Highway, Tony explaining; "this is the narrowest part of Long Island; only about a mile wide, the Atlantic Ocean is on your right and Long Island Sound is on your left. Napeague Harbor, where our place is located, is an inlet from the Sound. Suddenly Tony turned off the highway crossing a single railroad track and shortly turning down a narrow lane that crunched under the tires. It was the middle of nowhere!

"Where in heaven's name are we?" Eleanor asked incredulously; Tony laughed.

"This is our driveway; El, it's made of scallop shells the local fisherman dump here and they get crushed by the tires. Thanks to the Art Barge; our only neighbor. The director lives across the harbor where a lot of fishermen live. The shells crush down and make an excellent surface that drains very well; there are never any puddles. And you can't beat the price!" Even though it was dark she could make out the two tall radio towers and the barge picked up the outside lights from the cottage and was easy to discern. The driveway was long and curvy but at last they pulled up in front of their home. It was up on a dune about eight feet above sea level; at this point you couldn't see the harbor.They entered the cottage; Tony saying; "we'll get the luggage later." He pulled back one of the glass sliding doors and taking Eleanor by the arm walked her out on the deck.

She gasped. "Oh! This is so beautiful."

She could see the harbor even though it was dark. On the other side of the harbor there were lights that seemed to twinkle in what appeared to be a little village.

"You have Shangri-la here, Tony; it's priceless."

Jerry had very little to say; he was, in fact, stunned at what he was seeing. They went into the cottage and another tour began.

She was very impressed with the bathrooms; "they are so modern and elegant! And that kitchen is a New York City apartment dweller's dream! You have done a wonderful job on this place!"

"You should have seen it before," said Brian, "you would not believe it! We were lucky to meet Bob Kincaid out in Montauk; he steered us to the right contractors . . . the kind who do what they say they will do and on schedule."

"That is so true," added Tony, "if you fall into the wrong hands you can spend a lot of money and end up with inferior work. And you're usually stuck with it. These guys just disappear and there is nothing you can do about it."

He handed Eleanor a drink; she had been admiring the stone fireplace.

"This is certainly a plus; it looks old but capable."

"We'll have a fire tomorrow night at dinner time. It gets chilly at night and the fire feels good."

"It looks like it's all set to go . . . all you need is a match!"

"You've got that right, El; all you need is a match."

Brian walked over to her and handed her a match; "for tomorrow."

They finished their drinks and went to bed; they would rise early.

Brian and Tony were up before the sun; it was going to be a beautiful day, there were no clouds on the horizon; the sunrise ought to be magnificent. Brian wanted everything to be perfect for Eleanor. She appeared in a short, white terry robe; her Titian hair freshly brushed out softly.

She smiled; "mornin' all."

Tony handed her a glass of juice; "coffee in a few minutes; then we'll talk about breakfast. We can eat here or go to the diner at the docks in Montauk; it might be a zoo on Labor Day though."

"Let me make breakfast, please; piped up Eleanor."

Tony smiled at her. "You lady, are our guest; no chores for you!"

Brian stood up; "I will make breakfast and you take them for a walk down the beach and watch this sunrise; it's just coming up over the horizon now."

Eleanor walked to the window; "Oh! It's like a sliver of blazing gold!"

Tony took her arm; "Let's go, lovely, you can give that sun competition with that hair. Come on Jerry; we'll leave the chef to his kitchen!"

"Bacon and eggs plus . . . okay?"

Tony yelled back; "Perfect."

Brian got to work on the breakfast; he always cooked bacon in the oven so he started it right away as it took about forty-five minutes. Later on he would put some rolls in to warm up. The bacon taken care of he poured a mug of coffee and went out on the deck to watch the sunrise. He was delighted that it was so spectacular even though it didn't last long; Eleanor would really enjoy it. He re-entered the cottage and set the table and when he was ready to cook the eggs he went out on the deck and waved them on. They were on their way back but now they picked up the pace and hurried. They must not irritate the chef! They came in and raved about the aroma.

"We could smell the bacon down the beach and some seagulls wanted to come with us!" Tony tousled his hair, laughing.

"Why didn't you bring them; we'd be sure not to have leftovers."

Each fixed his own plate and sat at the table. Looking out over the harbor the water laid flat; there was no breeze, here and there where currents formed, the water reflected the rising sun and it looked like streaks of gold.

Eleanor looked at them. "The more you come out here the harder it is going to be to return to the city. This place offers a special kind of peace."

Tony squeezed her hand; "That has started already."

When breakfast was finished they all helped with the clean-up and the kitchen was shining in no time. "What a team!" Tony bragged. Brian suggested they take a ride through East Hampton and show Eleanor and Jerry the estates and introduce them to 'south of the highway' the magical place to live . . . for some people. All agreed and off they went. Driving through those lush lanes and seeing all those beautiful homes; many ocean-front and the gorgeous landscaping had Eleanor quickly running out of appropriate adjectives. She had heard about East Hampton; seeing it was spectacular.

Jerry shook his head; "There's a lot of money out here!"

Tony took them to where his land was located and Eleanor began to see a new Tony emerging. He was so laid back and seemingly simple she never dreamed he was so clever and farsighted. It dawned on her what was in store for Brian and this union took on a whole new meaning for her. Brian was in for a wonderful future!

Jerry continued to be amazed; he had a whole new opinion of Tony.

"Now I think we should show our guests a little honky-tonk and the other side of this world." Tony looked at Brian; I'm thinking about a Bloody Mary at Bob Kincaid's. How about it?"

"A capital idea! You will love this place, folks, I've told you about it so I'm not going to add anything . . . see for yourself!"

"We are putty in your hands," she quipped.

It was close to noon when they came into Kincaid's and the piano filled the air with honky-tonk. The tables were all occupied and there was chatter and laughter all giving the place its unique personality. Bob saw them come in and he had made room at the end of the bar. There were two bartenders and he was holding court at the end of the bar. Coming toward them with both arms raised he shook hands smilingly greeting them.

"And who is this lovely? He extended his hand and was surprisingly gentle as he pressed hers.

"I'd like you to meet Eleanor, Bob, she is a close friend of ours." Brian made the introduction.

"Well, if she was a friend of mine I'd keep her close too."

They all laughed at his wit and they both liked him. Tony introduced Jerry.

"Is it Bloody Mary time?" He asked devilishly.

"That's why we're here . . . and of course to see you; that is the main reason anyone comes to Montauk," Tony said wryly.

"Flattery will get you everywhere." Quipped Bob.

They chatted for a few minutes and some people left and a booth became available; Bob moved them into it quickly clearing the table then joining them. As the five of them sat talking the conversation centered on the progress at the cottage. Bob listened as Eleanor remarked at the improvement in the place and how excellent the workmanship was. He was staring at her and with an impish smile he said;

"I love red hair and you have the most beautiful red hair I have ever seen."

It was if he hadn't heard a word she had said and she was non-plussed. That was exactly what he wanted! There was more laughter and she caught on and poked him jovially.

They weren't really hungry and Tony suggested they have shrimp cocktails; he didn't want to occupy the booth and not spend some money. This was a big week-end for Bob . . . it would pay a lot of bills. All agreed and Bob went to the kitchen to make them himself. After a couple of hours they were ready to leave. Eleanor had two of those Bloody Marys and that was enough! Back at the cottage they changed into swim suits and enjoyed the sun and water. The time passed quickly and Brian started talking about dinner. They had brought steaks and he planned to grill them on the hibachi. He went to the kitchen to marinate them; Eleanor followed him in.

"Can I do anything?"

"Not now, El, I want to get the steaks in the marinade for at least an hour. Later on you could make the salad; that would be a big help. I'm just going to bake potatoes and sauté asparagus.

"Who could want more?"

She offered to scrub the potatoes and Jerry pitched in.

"Don't forget the cheese cake;" she added.

"Who could forget *that* cheese cake?"

The sun was setting over the harbor and it was a panorama of color; they were having dinner and Eleanor couldn't help comparing this view with dinner in her apartment looking at walls.

"Just imagine enjoying this everyday; everywhere you look there is natural beauty. I won't forget this week-end; believe me!"

Tony looked at her sincerely; "We hope there'll be many more."

Brian banged the table three times; "here; here!" He agreed.

Eleanor and Brian cleared away the dinner while Tony made coffee and then lit a fire. He set a bottle of brandy on the cocktail table and three large snifters; Jerry stayed with beer. It was dark now and the lights across the harbor twinkled; as they did every night. They sat around the fire with just one dim lamp lit in the living room. Tony served coffee and brandy. Eleanor sighed;

"Talk about atmosphere! Even the music is special!"

"Nothing is too special for our guests."

Tony and Brian toasted them; Brian nodding at Tony's remark. They settled back for a while; it didn't seem necessary to talk. They listened to the music; sometimes commenting on the selections. They were all at peace.

Eventually Tony asked; "Does anyone feel like doing some bar hopping? We could show them more of Montauk, Brian."

"It's up to you two; I'm for whatever you feel like doing. Personally; I think Montauk is better in daylight. I'd like them to see the lighthouse at night though." Brian offered his opinion to Jerry and Eleanor.

"Why don't we just take a ride to the lighthouse," she countered, "I would enjoy seeing that; it's famous!"

Tony arose from his chair and clapped his hands; "so be it!"

They filed out to the car and were on their way; once on the highway, with the windows open, they could hear the surf rolling onto the shore.

Eleanor piped up from the back seat; "It sounds like traffic!"

"Don't let the chamber of commerce hear that; they'll deport you!"

Tony glanced at her over his shoulder. As they drove out of the village Eleanor noticed they seemed to be going uphill as they progressed.

"Is it my imagination or are we getting into higher ground?"

Brian answered; "you are quite right; the end of Long Island is very high, the ocean bluffs are about one hundred feet above sea level. That's high in these parts. There is a big erosion problem out here; they've been fighting it for years."

They could see the beacon of the lighthouse slicing the air as it rotated. Suddenly the road curved and there it was, that grand structure poised high sending its warning to mariners.

"It's magnificent!" Cried Eleanor; "it takes your breath away! I've never seen a lighthouse before; except in magazines."

"Well now you can tell the world you've seen the Montauk Light, El; you can start with your clients Tuesday." Brian chuckled.

"You had to spoil all this by mentioning work!"

On the way back Brian pointed out the Dude Ranch that once housed Teddy Roosevelt and his Rough Riders.

"History included in this tour; how wonderful!" Eleanor teased him.

"Wait until we start on the Indians;" countered Tony.

The long day was catching up to them; when Tony suggested going home there was total agreement. Arriving back at the cottage Tony made sure the fire was out and all were happy to hit the sack. The next day they did tour Montauk and walked along the ocean shore wading in the surf and running from the big waves. The week-end melted; it was over so fast. Tony had taken a vote about leaving late in the evening; though it meant getting home in the wee hours the traffic would be very much lighter. They could avoid the aggravating stop and go of the two lane highway out of the Hamptons. Visitors arrived at different times; they all seemed to leave at the same time! They all agreed and packed everything early so they could leave when Tony was ready. So it was back to the city with great memories. Jerry and Eleanor made no references to the blow-up and Jerry had kept a very low profile being gracious and reserved. He was floored by it all!

Jerry had Nora to the doctor again and all he did was re-new the medicine. It annoyed him; he didn't think he was giving her the proper attention and he wanted to make a change. Nora had such a fear and mistrust of doctors that making a change horrified her.

"At least I'm used to this one;" she complained.

Jerry was frustrated and didn't know what to do. He had a deep feeling that the doctor knew there was no help for her and she was getting near her last days. The idea hit him in his very soul and he had to fight these thoughts and get rid of them. They were leaving the office, Jerry stopped;

"Let's go somewhere for lunch, Duchess, I don't feel like going home."

"I have so much food home; why spend money on goin' out?"

Just what he expected to hear. "It's nice to go out; it makes me feel good to take you out. Just please me!"

She wouldn't agree in words; she shrugged her shoulders and tilted her head; that was an okay. She had her stubborn streak! He took her to a small Mom and Pop kind of place; he knew the food to be like home cooking and he also knew she would order a bowl of soup and crackers. No matter how much he coaxed her; she was adamant about what she wanted. At least he was sure the soup was good. Sure enough! She ordered soup. He surprised her when he made no comment; if she ate a whole bowl of soup he would be happy. They had come home after lunch and Jerry busied himself outside the house. About six o'clock Nora made a light supper and they played cards. By eight o'clock she was all in and ready to go to her room.

"I don't know what's troublin' me I get tired so easy."

"That cough has made you a little weak; you need rest."

"If I get any more rest I'll get arrested!" She had her wit.

After she was set for the night he went to his room and undressed and picked up a book he was reading; it wasn't fiction it covered the effect of alcohol on the brain. He was about one third into it and it had him a bit scared. What he was reading did not please him but he couldn't stop reading it. Since the blow up at Brian's he had not touched the hard stuff and he had begun to drink his beer slower. Retirement appealed to him more and more. Tom was on vacation and he was relieved that he didn't have to face him for a while. Getting their friendship back on track was very important to him. He fell asleep while reading; when he awoke at about six o'clock his lamp was still lit. This surprised him; he spoke aloud; "I didn't sleep; I died!"

His shift began at eight so he jumped into the shower and got ready for work. Nora was in the kitchen making oatmeal; one hand holding her back while she stirred the meal. When he entered the kitchen he gave her a kiss and she enjoyed seeing him so clean and smelling so fresh. As he sat down she put a glass of juice in front of him and went for his oatmeal; "coffee's almost ready, dear." He patted her rump.

"You've not been yourself lately laddie; is there anythin' wrong?"

He looked at her; "with a breakfast like this what could be wrong?"

Maybe I'm worried about you; you keep doing too much."

"There's no need ta' worry about me . . . I'm okay."

"Sure you are; you just get yourself too tired. Try to take it easier and please ask me to do things for you."

"I will; I promise." He stood up and hugged her.

"I've got to get going; if you need me call!"

She was so glad that he had been away with Eleanor. He didn't say much about the week-end except that he had a wonderful time. Nora didn't press him for information although she was dying to hear more. He was gone and the house seemed empty. After cleaning the kitchen she took her rosary and sat in her bay window looking at her big oak tree and watching passers-by. She whispered aloud; "I wish he had told me more."

Eleanor had Jerry on her mind more than she wanted to; she tried not to dwell on her situation with him but it nagged at her. Her first day back at the Salon gave her something new to occupy her mind; Cleo had asked her into her office and closed the door.

"Sit down Eleanor I have something important to discuss with you." Eleanor sat down. "You've got my curiosity going!"

"I want to get your enthusiasm going. I'm getting married and I will not be working; I would like you to manage the salon; you are the most qualified in addition to having the perfect personality for the position . . . I imagine I've given you a bit of a shock."

"Cleo; first let me wish you all the happiness in the world!"

She rose and hugged her warmly; "I think it is wonderful for you. It's a big surprise but not a shock; you're a beautiful woman, it is perfectly reasonable that some lucky guy wants to marry you!"

"That's a lovely thing to say, Eleanor, thank you. I don't want you to give me an answer right now; take some time and think it over and please don't say no! I have a copy of our proposed contract in this folder; take it with you and read it. Get legal advice if you feel you wish to; when you are ready I would like you to come to my place for dinner and to meet my fiancé. We can discuss the deal then. Okay?"

Eleanor took the folder; "I'll say okay . . . I'm too stunned to add anything to that. You've really left me speechless."

"Good; that's how you should be right now. This is strictly *entre-nous* for the time being Eleanor; I don't want anyone to know my plans . . . that includes Brian."

"I understand Cleo; be assured I will say nothing."

They left the office; the wheels spinning in Eleanor's head. It wasn't going to be easy to keep this from Brian but she would keep her promise; there was no question about that. It would be a different life for her now; it should mean an increase in salary and that tickled her feminine heart.

Brian came into Tony's; he had a busy day and just wanted to have a couple of drinks and something to eat. He sat on a stool in his favorite corner and Gino came down the bar to him.

"Hello Brian; Tony is in the kitchen. What can I get you?"

"Gin on the rocks with a piece of lime, please. How goes it Gino; is the world treating you okay?"

"You know me Brian; I've got no complaints; who'd listen?"

Brian smiled; "I'll listen, Gino, I've got good ears."

He was making the drink;" I'll have to think up some troubles."

They laughed together and Brian felt a hand on his shoulder.

"Can anybody get in on the joke or is it private?"

"You have to have troubles; I'm listening tonight."

Tony squeezed Brian's shoulder and sat down; "pour me a beer, Gino."

Brian eyed him quizzically; "You don't say please?"

"I don't want to spoil him. I just took some lasagna out of the oven; you hungry?"

"I can smell that aroma and yes; I'm hungry."

"We'll let it rest for a few minutes; then we'll eat. It's too hot to eat it now. What's new with you, pal?"

"Not a thing; busy day, I don't feel like cooking."

"You came to the right place."

"It's a good feeling; knowing I can come here."

Tony gave the back of Brian's neck a squeeze.

"You belong here."

They talked about the cottage for a while Tony looked at Brian; smiling;

"I think we should have Eleanor and Jerry out East again."

"It went better than I thought it would;" said Brian, Jerry kept his word and he was really helpful."

"That's why I want to get him out there; he is very handy!"

They laughed and Tony continued; "before we know it the cold weather will be here; I want to get those railroad ties in place and I can use his strong back. He has some good ideas about placing them."

"I'll talk to Eleanor and see how she feels. I'll tell her we need her help and we can let her cook. She needs to be needed."

After they had eaten, Tony served Gino as well; he asked Gino to close up and they went home to Tony's place. Brian was surprised at how tired he *wasn't!*

They were able to work out a week-end in the first week of October when Jerry was off. Jerry arranged for one of Nora's lady friends at church to keep her company for the week-end. Needless to say it was not an easy accomplishment; Nora protested that she did not need a baby sitter and Jerry finally told her he would not go if she did not give him the peace of mind knowing she was not alone. With Eleanor's help she finally agreed; keeping Jerry and Eleanor together was worth any sacrifice. Besides, this lady played euchre and Nora did not have any other friends who knew that old card game.

The Friday night journey out East was pleasant; they each seemed to be in the right mood; Jerry was more relaxed and did not have the reservations that subdued him on the first trip. At Hampton Bays they made the usual stop at the diner and Eleanor and Jerry got a big surprise when Brian got behind the wheel and drove the rest of the way out to Amagansett . . . he had passed the test and now was a licensed driver! Tony said the traffic was not all that heavy and Brian had taken to driving quickly. He was a little nervous at first but the exhilaration and pride of being behind the wheel soon gave him a boost of confidence.

"I'm so proud of you, Brian," Eleanor gushed; "how could you keep this secret from me. *Me* of all people!"

"It wasn't easy, sweetheart, I wanted to surprise you."

"Well, you certainly did that!" They all laughed.

Arriving at the cottage, the lights creating a glow of welcome, Brian parked the car remembering to set the emergency brake as Tony taught him. He was exuberant with pride.

"Well done, pal, you drove like a pro!" Tony applauded him.

"I second that," Jerry shook his hand. "We'll celebrate this!"

They unloaded the car and Tony made a round of drinks. Brian lit a fire; the air was clear, crisp and *chilly!* Quickly the kindling caught on and the logs started burning, the scent and the sound creating a cozy ambience. They were all in great spirits. The freedom from the city gave them all a lift.

"I'd like to make an antipasto platter unless someone feels like eating heavier." Eleanor looked to see how her idea took.

"That sounds wonderful," Tony walked toward her; "I'll give you a hand. This is a treasure chest, Eleanor; you even have capers . . . I love them!"

He was going through the hamper like a kid on Christmas morning. He hugged her. Brian put on some mellow music and checked their drinks; Jerry stayed with beer and Brian gave him a big smile when he asked for it.

"I'm going out to get some logs," Brian headed for the front door; picking up the log basket on his way.

"I'll help you; Jerry rose and followed him outside.

"What a beautiful night!" Brian enthused; "look at those stars they really stand out when you don't have street lights and all the other city stuff that chokes Mother Nature."

"When you're over by the ocean at night it looks like there is no sky . . . just stars; everywhere." Brian continued.

"I believe it." Said Jerry.

They stayed up quite late; still toasting Brian's license, listening to music and chatting about random topics. It was a warm get together and they were developing a true sense of friendship. Jerry had done a lot of soul-searching since the blow-up and he was learning to appreciate what real friends are; he particularly had a completely different opinion of Tony and Brian and there would be no more smart remarks or innuendo. Tony had really shocked him with what he was doing out here and he was in awe of his accomplishments. It pointed up to him how little he had done and how stupid he was; "I laughed at Tony!" He had loosely computed how much money he wasted on drinking and smoking. Here he was ready to retire and he had made no provisions to make it a comfortable retirement. Tony could retire and live very well . . . and he had made fun of him and never dreamed that he was capable of doing what he, Jerry, had not a clue of doing! Eventually the yawning began and they all retired.

Despite going to bed late they were all up early. It was a glorious fall morning; the air was cool and crisp and Tony had made a fire as soon as he came into the living room. The scent of the burning logs and the aroma of the fresh coffee and bacon were absolutely heavenly. All ate a hearty breakfast and all pitched in and the kitchen was gleaming in very short order. They worked well together; enjoying it.

"Let's all take a walk down the beach," Tony suggested, "those cinnamon rolls were scrumptious but I need to walk them off."

"We better wear sweaters; it's pretty chilly out there."

Everyone went for sweaters and walking along the shore they were glad they did! The brisk breeze was ruffling the feathers of the birds and the gulls seemed to be shivering. Breathing the sea air was invigorating and the chill kept everyone moving at a lively pace.

"This is so wonderful!" Eleanor was bubbling over; her hair blowing wildly in the breeze; reflecting the bright sunlight.

"You look like Isadora Duncan, El, where's your scarf?"

"Would you like to get tossed into the harbor, sweetie?"

"What's wrong with Isadora? She was a dancer!"

"Quit while you're ahead, Brian, red-heads are dangerous!"

"Tony, do you think Eleanor would toss me into the sea?"

"She looks like she could, Brian," Jerry joined in.

Just then a small sail boat appeared; it was moving fast and the man at the helm really could sail. He maneuvered the craft expertly and despite the choppiness of the waves the boat followed his lead easily.

"He really can handle that boat; I'd love to do that." Brian was a little wistful; as though he was wishing the impossible!

"We can get a boat; you could learn to sail."

Brian looked at Tony. "I could never learn how to sail."

"You're driving a car, aren't you? You couldn't do that six months ago. You take lessons and you become a sailor!"

"Would you have the guts to sail with me?"

"I sure would! Don't forget I was a sailor!"

They were all laughing now and they turned back toward the cottage.

"Well, enough of this outdoor life; let's go and make some Bloody Marys!" Tony headed back at a trot.

"Get him!" Brian said, laughing.

Jerry followed suit and suddenly they were all a-trot! Back at the cottage Tony made a large pitcher of Bloody Marys and set it on the table with glasses and celery sticks. Brian was surprised and not too happy to see Jerry fix one for Eleanor and then one for himself! There was plenty of beer in the refrigerator. He hoped Jerry was not forgetting his promises. Well, maybe he was just having one . . . And maybe he wasn't!

"Brian and I are going to go to the Farm Store in Sagaponack to pick up some vegetables and things. You two can hit the beach and soak up the sun; the breeze will die down soon and the sun will be warm. The water is not too cold for swimming yet. We'll be back in a couple of hours."

They finished their drinks and took off.

Jerry and Eleanor talked for a while and then changed into swim suits.

He had purchased a new pair of swimming trunks and instead of the usual boxer short style that he wore the young clerk had suggested trying a tight Lastex style in a bright blue. When he put them on he was a little embarrassed at how tight the fit was at his groin . . . he was displaying quite a bulge. Looking in the mirror he was a bit pleased with what he saw and decided to be modern. When he came back to the living room Eleanor gave him a large beach towel. She certainly noticed the trunks but made no comment; she was surprised at the rush of excitement she felt seeing him in the revealing trunks. They went out on the deck and lay on the comfortable chaise lounges. There was still some breeze but they were sheltered from it on the deck.

After a few minutes Jerry rose and squeezed her shoulder; "I'll be right back." He went to the refrigerator and took the pitcher of Bloody Marys and poured two drinks. He picked up some napkins and went out and handed her a drink. He placed an ash tray on top of the napkins.

"It's a bit early to keep drinking," she warned.

He laughed and answered, "This is still breakfast."

She sipped the drink; "They really are delicious."

"They're more like food than a drink." He smiled at her.

"But a bit more lethal," she cautioned.

He shrugged his shoulders and sat down. Later they went in the water for a short dip; it really was a bit cold. Up on the deck he dried her back for her rubbing her gently with the thick, soft towel. She had taken off her bathing cap and was brushing her hair. The one-piece swim suit showed the curves of her beautiful body and his new trunks seemed to be getting tighter. They decided to go inside and used the pan of water by the door to rinse their feet. Inside she sat down and Jerry knelt in front of her and dried her feet. Eleanor was becoming aroused; she was surprised at herself, but she didn't stop him. After all; he was merely drying her feet. He went to the fireplace and put on a couple of logs; the coals were still glowing.

"Come over here by the fire El, I think you have a chill from the swim. That water was pretty chilly."

She came to him and he put a dry towel around her shoulders. The logs were catching on quickly and they were crackling. He was massaging her shoulders, gently, and gradually turned her to him and embraced her closely. He kissed her softly and, suddenly, pressing close to her, he began to get an erection. He kissed her more passionately, his tongue finding hers. Eleanor was responding without inhibition; he caressed her breasts and she was breathing hard. He pealed her out of her suit and dropped his to the floor. His throbbing hardness now released he held her to him and undulated his body into hers. Picking her up he went to the couch and laid her on it. Quickly he was beside her, kissing her deeply and pressing his hardness into her body. The passion so long kept under wraps was released from Eleanor and she clung to him; moaning sounds of satisfaction and asking for more. He was on top of her rubbing his body up and down her torso and he was close to climax. Suddenly he slid up her torso and tried to enter her mouth. She screamed and rolled out from under him;

"Oh God, not that way! Not that way!" She ran to her room.

"Oh, Jesus Christ!" He moaned.

He went out on the deck and taking some napkins he lay on the lounge and relieved himself. Eleanor lay on her bed frantically trying to cover her nakedness and sobbing while loathing herself. Jerry hung her suit on the door knob, telling her through the door that it was there. He had a shower and put on a shirt and pair of slacks. Barefooted, he walked along the beach in the shallow water; he had really done it this time. His mind ran in circles and he finally had to face himself. "I'm never going to have a normal life; it's not for me. I don't know what kind of a life *is* for me! She will never want to see me again; I'm sure of that! I am very damn sure of that!" He was talking aloud; the sea gulls quite indifferent to his problems; he was crying and he was unaware of it. They had to get through the rest of the week-end . . . he was sure she would not want to tell Brian and Tony what happened; she was made of good stuff and would see it through. He would take a back seat. After about twenty minutes he realized he had to speak with her. Tony and Brian would be back soon and he wanted to be sure of how she would act. Going to her bedroom door he knocked gently;

"Eleanor, can I poke my head in for a minute?"

"Yes," was the faint reply.

"I'm not going to go into how sorry I am right now; they will be back soon and I know how upset you are so I think I should tell them the drinks disagreed with you and you are not feeling well. That will give you a chance to get your bearings. We have to finish out the week-end and I'll try and stay out of your way without being obvious. I'm sure you don't want to tell them how stupid I was."

"Very well," was her only comment.

Presently Jerry heard the toot of the horn and he knew they were back. He went out to meet them and help them with their packages. They had several;

"You must have bought the place out!" Jerry laughed.

"Just a few things," replied Tony.

"We've got some fresh corn and some scrumptious beefsteak tomatoes grown right on that farm. The corn was picked this morning; that's how fresh it is!" Brian was very pleased with their shopping.

"And wait until you see the chicken pot pie we have; home-made at the farm . . . it is huge!"

"Eleanor is lying down; we went for a swim and then we had a couple more of those Bloody Marys and they seemed to disagree with her. I think a little rest will help her; she took some Maalox, I think; I haven't disturbed her."

"Let her rest," said Tony "I hope she will be able to eat dinner; this chicken pot pie is one of their specialties . . . it is gourmet!"

They stowed the groceries and the three of them took a walk along the beach. There was general comment about the great weather and the antics of the sea gulls. Jerry maintained good spirits despite the churning in his gut. He felt awful.

Eleanor had showered and dressed and appeared about an hour before dinner assuring them that she felt fine now. Knowing that ladies could have personal reasons for not feeling well they did not ask any questions. She was very grateful for that. Brian took her into the kitchen and showed her the tomatoes; she was very impressed with their size and color. He asked her to make a tomato salad; Jerry was out on the deck shucking the corn. Then he showed her the chicken pot pie he had on the counter and she could not believe how large it was. He explained that it was made at the farm with all of the ingredients grown right there. Almost everything there is home-made.

"How fresh can you get?" He asked her.

"Almost on a par with you!" She hugged him; laughing.

She had her equilibrium back and was glad she didn't have to face Jerry. There was no animosity toward him; she was ashamed at how she had lost control and stunned by the passion he had aroused in her. One thing was established . . . there could be nothing between them . . . ever! Now she knew where she was going with Jerry. Nowhere! It was a kind of relief among all the dismay. Eleanor would never be able to discuss this with anyone; Jerry did not have to say another word of apology to her . . . it was over, whatever they had. She was moving on and Cleo's offer now became extremely important. The new position was going to keep her very busy and there would be no time for social activity. There was a surprise in store for her on that subject.

Brian had warmed the pot pie in the oven and it was just about ready. He now was going to show them the proper way to cook corn on the cob. Bob Kincaid had bestowed this secret on him. It was the method the farmers used. Who should know better?

"You need a large pot almost filled with cold water; bring it to a rolling, boil and add salt to taste. Put the corn in the pot, cover it and turn off the heat leaving the corn on the burner for five minutes. Then slide the pot off the burner and serve with softened butter. You can hold the corn in the hot water for fifteen minutes and it will still taste freshly cooked. I am going to serve the corn as a last course by it self. I'm cooking two large ears apiece; you must finish the first ear before the fifteen minutes pass. We have to have our corn according to Kincaid."

They all laughed at the discourse and promised to comply. The corn was so delicious that they were all ready for the second ear much before the fifteen minute limit.

They were back in the city arriving very late Sunday night. Jerry saw Eleanor to her door; there had been little conversation on the way home. She opened her door and Jerry spoke.

"I'd like to get together with you and tell you how I feel; I don't want you to hate me . . . I hate myself right now."

"I don't hate you at all; it takes two to tango. We are not for each other; that's for sure. It is best we don't see each other; give me some time I think we can be friends and I want to continue seeing Nora with you. For the time being we had best let things cool."

He had so much respect for her. "You are one fine lady; El."

He was gone.

The only light in this small studio-type apartment was a plug-in night light. A Christmas tree bulb supplied the illumination. Lizzie Gilhooley lay on her couch-bed and began to awaken. This process would take some time because Lizzie was really 'coming to' rather than awakening. She had downed eight cans of beer with her cheese and cracker lunch and was not quite up to snuff. It was six o'clock in the evening but she didn't know the time or the day. Lizzie was a drunk. It was a call from nature that was arousing her and with some difficulty she got her obese body to sit up. With a lot of difficulty she weaved her way to the bathroom and was filled with gratitude when she landed on the toilet. Before she completed her mission she fell asleep. Twenty minutes later she roused again and after flushing, she washed her hands and face. Lizzie was particular about her toilette and the creative way she arranged her hair and clothes before appearing at any local bar; there were a few that denied her entry in the neighborhood. She needed to wear glasses and always carried them in her rhinestone studded purse. They were only used when she absolutely could not fathom what she was looking at. Her wardrobe consisted of a few dresses that had seen better days and had never seen a dry cleaner. Being artistic she loved color and her dresses had plenty of that; in addition to various adornments that she pinned to them. She had a special liking for cabbage roses and she had several of them. Not being able to afford hairdressers she styled her hair herself and this was unfortunate because she had no talent for it. Actually she wore turbans most of the time and of course, pinned a cabbage rose on them. Usually she would wear one of her many shawls that were trimmed with various kinds of fringes and always ankle-strap high-heeled shoes. Lizzie was a big woman but . . . she had small feet! In short; Lizzie was a pathetic character. Lost, lonely and still looking for the man of her dreams.

Her mother had died from excess drinking but her proud Irish father never admitted to that. He was quite a drinker himself and when he was seventy years old he was found dead in a ditch; dead from unknown causes. Lizzie had no idea where they were buried and the parents she talked about had a grand house in Dublin and both had been professional people. While she did a lot of talking; she rarely had a listener to her fantasies.

Before her sixteenth birthday her father came home one night, drunk as usual, and came into her bedroom, which was not usual. He undressed and got into bed with her. Lizzie was mesmerized and lay rigid while he clumsily fondled her breasts with one hand and sought her virginity with the other. She was both horrified and aroused at the same time. It was wrong; that was a certainty, but years of domination and fear held back any resistance. At the same time the stimulation and his eventual penetration gave her much physical pleasure. She pressed this into her subconscious and would never admit to herself that she enjoyed it. Lizzie never told anyone of this experience and he used her until the drink made it impossible for him to perform. They lived together until he died.

Lizzie carried a mixed bag of guilt; she felt guilty for not stopping him from raping her and for letting it continue on. The true fact that she enjoyed the sexual activity, though not in her conscious mind, added to the load she carried. Lizzie learned to solve everything the way her parents showed her; she drank beer constantly. For years she worked in a lamp shade factory and managed to hold her job until she was able to retire. Near the end it got very shaky; her last year of employment was accomplished only because her foreman felt sorry for her. He was aware of part of her life with two alcoholic parents. He did not know her father abused her. The drinking was getting the better of her and he covered up the work she did not produce. A few of her co-workers assisted him until she ceased working there.

Lizzie gave herself a sponge bath with a wash cloth and Ivory soap. She brushed her hair until it was a bush of fuzz atop her head. Then, shakily, she applied her make-up; each eyelash was coated heavily with mascara. Eyebrows were drawn in a thin Theda Bara fashion. A coat of foundation was spread over her face and a bright red lip rouge was not too artfully drawn. Getting into her clothes took some time; especially closing the ankle straps on her shoes. The final arrangement was the turban; made of a green velvet-like material she covered her bushy hair except for some fuzzy bangs pulled down over her forehead. With a faded red cabbage rose pinned on top of the turban she was ready. Her check had come a few days before so she had a five dollar bill and five singles in her rhinestone purse. The rest of her money was hidden in the refrigerator.

Down on the street she felt dressed up and with plenty of money in her purse she felt the need of new surroundings. After walking almost half an hour; she never walked that far from home, usually; she came in front of Tony's Bar. Peeking in the window she noticed there were mostly men at the bar and it appeared to be a congenial group. There was an empty stool near the end of the bar and she made her way toward it. When making these entries most drunks are able to get their adrenaline going and complete a fairly steady appearance. With a bit of effort she managed to get up on the stool and gradually got settled. Taking a dollar bill from her purse she placed it on the bar in front of her. Observing herself in the back bar mirror she waited for service.

What have we here? Thought Tony as he came in front of her.

"Good evening, my dear, what can I get for you?"

"Good evening, sir, I would like a glass of tap beer."

He placed a coaster in front of her; seeing no cigarettes he offered no ash tray.

"Do you have any special preference, madam?"

"I'll leave that to you," she smiled.

"I'll be back in a trice, madam." Lizzie nodded agreeably.

He served her beer and stayed for a little welcoming chit chat. As he spoke with her it didn't take him long to size up her situation. He felt genuinely sorry for her. He definitely did not want to hear her life story; it had to be bad!

Lizzie was on her third beer when Jerry came in. Unfortunately the only empty seat was next to Lizzie and Jerry gingerly sat down. One look at her and he was filled with revulsion; *"where did she escape from?"* He thought.

"Hello, Jerry boy, how are you doing?" Tony shook his hand.

"I was doing okay; now I don't know." Tony frowned his disapproval.

"Things are just fine, Jerry, look at the bright side."

Tony was asking Jerry not to make any trouble with his repulsive neighbor.

"Pour me a beer; that might help," Jerry gave Tony a sly look.

"It certainly helps to cheer me up;" came an unwelcome voice, "I don't know what I would do without it."

"You would probably weigh a lot less; that's for sure." Jerry grinned, nastily. Lizzie winced; she was deeply hurt.

"Mr. Foley is just trying to be funny, dear, don't take him seriously."

"I do have a strange sense of humor," said Jerry, "it's me Irish!"

"I'm Irish." Lizzie remarked in a low voice.

"What's your name?" Jerry asked.

"Lizzie Gilhooley." She answered in a louder voice this time.

"You can't get any more Irish than that!" Tony clapped his hands.

"I second that;" agreed Jerry, "that name is very green."

Lizzie was set back and although Jerry and Tony were smiling; she was not. When Jerry came in she thought he was so handsome and immediately began pulsing with excitement. Fantasies were already whirling in her brain; he shot them down in a hurry. Now she was reticent and afraid.

"Well, we Irish have to stick together,"

Jerry began, he was his old affable self; charming Lizzie into a warm, relaxed aura of well-being and she was quickly relieved of her tension. He bought her a beer; then he bought her another. She made an attempt to reciprocate but he would have none of it. Jerry had a couple of shooters along the way and Lizzie was positive he was interested in her. She revived her fantasies and was regretting not making up her bed before she left home. By now she had let her shawl drop down her back and her low cut décolletage revealed her ample bosom tight within the satiny fabric. Looking in the mirror she was pleased with what her dimmed vision allowed her to see. Jerry saw quite a different picture when he looked at her.

"I wonder what dairy she belongs to," he mused.

Jerry told her of some of his experiences during the war and she was a captivated audience. Tony had slid away adroitly leaving the Irish to commiserate and he was baffled by the turn of events. He couldn't wait to tell Brian about it. It was getting late and Jerry realized he had to get home. He had a buzz on and had not intended to let that happen.

"Well, it's time to go." He put his arms up and stretched.

"I'm ready," said Lizzie, "I've got some beer home; you can have what you want." She put her hand on his thigh and squeezed. She misinterpreted his intent.

Jerry reacted as if he had been touched by a decaying corpse! He pushed her. "You fat, slobby slut! Go back to the sewer you came from!"

He glared at Tony and he was gone.

Lizzie was devastated; the tears stung in her eyes and the mascara ran down her face. Everyone was looking at her and the humiliation and confusion engulfed her. Her body was shaking with short, heart-breaking sobs; Tony came to her, shooting meaningful looks at his customers to back off!

"It's alright, Lizzie, he's drunk; don't get upset."

She tried to explain but her voice was strained and taut. Tony walked her outside.

"I'll hail you a cab, honey." She shook her head.

"Let me walk; I need to walk!"

He didn't argue; he said good night. Lizzie headed home walking as though tacking like a sailboat crossing a lake. She bumped into trash baskets and bounced off light poles. The tears and the sobbing would not stop; somehow she made it to her building. A man was exiting and he held the door to let her in; she made it to her apartment door and now there was a new urgency . . . she had to get to the toilet! With some difficulty she got her purse open and discovered she had forgotten her key! It was the last straw. Uncontrollable sobs wracked her body; Lizzie was totally beaten. Her head eased against the door and she slowly slid down into a heaving heap of shiny fabric.

Early morning tenants going to work walked around her; hours later her next door neighbor got the Super to open her apartment. She zigzagged into her flat; she was hung over and distraught . . . and she smelled of urine. Lizzie never went to a bar again; all of her drinking was done at home . . . to what end?

* * *

It was a week before Jerry came back to Tony's. He was ashamed of his behavior but he felt justified to rebuke that repulsive broad. He had not given her any kind of encouragement and she nauseated him when she put her hand on him.

"Hello, stranger, I've missed you." Tony greeted him, smiling.

"I owe you an apology for the way I acted; that old broad turned my stomach and I just lost it . . . too many shooters."

"I thought you were going to stay off the booze. Would you like me to cut you off when you order it?"

"That would be a smart thing for me to do."

"Well, should I?"

"I'm not smart; you know that!"

"Case closed; what can I get for you now?"

"A beer will do just fine."

"As you wish, sir." Tony bowed his head slightly and drew the beer.

"Tony, if she comes in here again tell her I'm sorry."

"Jerry boy, she won't ever be in here again; rest assured."

"Well, in case she does come in." The apology made him feel better.

"Why don't you bring Nora out East for a week-end? The heat is in now."

"I'd like to; I've told her a lot about the place but it is really hard to get her to go anywhere . . . except church."

"We do have candles; that might make her comfortable."

Jerry laughed; in spite of the mood he was in. "I'm sure she would be impressed. She might get you to praying!"

It was Tony's turn to laugh. "That would surely get her canonized!"

Now they were both laughing and Jerry was feeling better; he had another beer.

"I'll talk to her about it and soon; we can't take her out there in the winter."

"Shoot for next week-end; we're not having any company."

He was able to get Nora to agree to go by saying Eleanor was going. A white lie for a good cause; he had no twinge of conscience. It was just managing Nora! Friday came and he told Nora that Eleanor had to do the hairstyling for a wedding on Saturday. He explained that the stylist scheduled for the job had a sudden appendix operation. He kept her busy getting ready and away from the phone; he didn't want her to call Eleanor to say she was sorry she would not see her. If she discovered his subterfuge after the trip he would handle it then.

It was daylight when they set out on their journey; it was very dark when they reached Amagansett. When Tony turned off the highway and crossed the railroad she thought she had never seen such wilderness. After he turned into the narrow driveway and she heard the crunch of the scallop shells she was sure the Indians would be next. When Jerry helped her out of the car and the wind hit her she held onto her hat with a "Glory be ta' God!"

Once inside the place Brian lit a fire quickly and Jerry gave her a beer standing her by the fireplace. He lit a cigarette for her and after Tony had lit some lamps she took in the room and was full of praise and when Brian showed her the kitchen Nora was bowled over!

"Who wouldn't love ta' cook in this kitchen? It has *everything!* You could not want for more. And Lord bless us . . . it certainly is cleaned and polished!"

Tony put his arm around her; "You can look at it all you want, Nora, but don't you dare to try and use it! You are our guest and we want you to rest and breathe in this salt air."

"We'll see about that," she flipped, "that's like showin' a baby a lollipop and then takin' it away."

They were all laughing and Tony was making drinks. Brian walked her to the glass sliding door facing the harbor and he asked Jerry to put out some of the lights so Nora could see the harbor. It's too windy to go out on the deck now; in the morning it will be calm. The weather looks good.

"I can see the water!" Nora exclaimed; "and there's lights way out . . . looks like a little village." She turned to Brian; all excited.

"I want to take you over there and show you that place. We'll go tomorrow if they will let us take the wheels for a few minutes." Jerry acted very excited.

"It's all yours," said Tony.

They had brought food with them and Brian and Tony fixed the dinner while Nora and Jerry sat by the fire. He made sure she had enough beer.

Early morning found everyone up and dressed and Brian had breakfast going. There was a big pot of coffee made and fruit juice. The weather was nice, as promised, and the sunrise a picture. There was a fire crackling but they had the heat on because it was a bit chilly; especially for Nora. When breakfast was over Brian shooed Jerry and Nora out to look at the 'village' across the harbor. As they drove away Nora could only think of this as a vast wilderness. Arriving at the 'village' and seeing a hodge-podge of old trailers nestled in the dunes she had the horrors!

"Who in the name of God lives there?" She exclaimed.

When Jerry suggested they look for a small place there for the summer and fix it up like Tony and Brian were doing she hit 'high C over C.'

"You have lost all your marbles if you think I could spend one hour in that place let alone live there! I'm sure there's rats there; as permanent residents!"

"I thought it would be a nice getaway for the summer; it wouldn't cost much to do it. I could do most of the work . . . I'd enjoy that."

"When you are not here can you see me alone in this God forsaken place? Do it for yerself, darlin'; include me out!"

Jerry was crestfallen but he realized he had not thought about her being alone there. He could understand her objection to that. So much for his idea!

The afternoon got cloudy and a bit raw; they decided to stay in and play cards; Nora brightened up at this idea and she took some of their money in a poker game. Tony was filled with admiration; "This lady knows how to play poker and then some! And she never gets tired!" He commented to Brian.

Sunday dawned a brilliant day which often happens after a storm. The harbor lay flat and was a deep blue; here and there where currents moved, silver sparkles reflected the sunlight. Jerry took Nora out on the deck carrying their mugs of coffee; it was so calm they were able to light cigarettes without sheltering them from the wind. He sat her on a lounge and gave her the coffee.

"Such a glorious place they have; when man-kind doesn't interfere God can do wonderful things. Just look at all those birds along the shore; they have plenty to eat and never have to cook or go shoppin'!" Nora shook her head in wonder.

"Are you sure you wouldn't like a little place out here?" Jerry smiled.

"It's enough to come and visit; you're not trickin' me, darlin' . . . I'm on to you and your tricky ways! You've got to get up real early to hoodwink me!"

"Nobody is trying to trick you; I'm trying to make your life a little nicer."

"And have you ever heard me complain about me life not bein' nice enough? I've told you more than once how much happier I am with you around."

"You win, madam, I'll never mention it again."

"Oh, how I'd like to believe that!" She banged the arm of her chair almost upsetting her coffee. Her eyes were slits; she wanted to show her suspicions.

Jerry rose and put his cigarette in the butt can. "You'll see; madam."

Brian opened the door and called them in for breakfast. It was after eleven by the time they headed toward Montauk and to take Nora to meet Bob Kincaid. First they would make a tour of the place including a ride out to see the lighthouse. Nora was impressed to learn Teddy Roosevelt had his Rough Riders at the ranch. She said she didn't know they had a war out here. No one made comment. By the time the tour was over it was almost two o'clock. Tony pulled the wagon to the side of the road by Lake Montauk. It was a fresh water lake until man-kind opened it to Long Island Sound and let the fish adjust on their own.

"We're going to Bob's place now; Brian and I think we should have our dinner here and have something light at home before we leave tonight. Is that okay with the rear seat?"

"Fine with me," said Jerry; "Nora, what say you?"

"A cup o' tea will suit me." She murmured.

"That means it is fine with her." Jerry interpreted.

"Oh, isn't he the quick one; with his smart remarks." Nora bristled.

As usual they laughed; but Nora feigned disdain looking at Jerry through slits. Kincaid's was busy but as soon as Bob saw them he readied a booth.

"Welcome! And how is everybody? And who is this silver-haired beauty?"

"Well, there's no way ye could be hidin' that *you're* a harp!"

She stopped Bob in his tracks with that quick wit; he blanched for a trice.

"And I'm pretty sure *you're* not from Sweden, my lovely."

They were all laughing, including the other diners close to them. Bob called a waiter and took the order for their drinks while the waiter brought the menus.

"We have a corned beef and cabbage special today." The waiter offered.

"That's for me!" Nora was enthusiastic.

"And I will go right along with you," said Jerry.

The others ordered and Bob brought their drinks and sat with them. Nora was formerly introduced and a good deal of repartee was flying around the table. Bob was smitten by Nora and continually tried to squeeze smart remarks from her. There was no lack of come backs and Nora was in her glory. None of them had ever seen her so alive and the enjoyment continued. Departing; Nora said to Bob;

"I've eaten fine food and I'm a cook meself; you're second ta' nobody!"

He hugged her and threatened to come and get her if she didn't come again.

"I'll see how me calendar is for the next few months."

He hugged her again, laughing all the while.

Back at the cottage Tony made a fire and everyone refused after dinner drinks. They had eaten well and had enough to drink at Bob's. Brian and Tony said they were going to take a nap; they would share the driving to the city. Nora and Jerry were going to sit by the fire and Jerry assured them he would make sure it was extinguished. They were leaving late to avoid the Sunday traffic. Nora and Jerry stayed awake; Nora reliving the fun at Bob's and pointing up his smart remarks and Jerry happy to listen and know she had such a good time. She had no coughing problems, so far, and that was reassuring. He was glad they came.

During the ride home Nora dozed into a deep sleep; she slept almost the whole trip and was actually embarrassed when she awoke. To her; it was a weakness. You had to be Irish to comprehend that logic! To her utter amazement; she went to bed when they arrived home and slept until seven in the morning.

"I must be gettin' sleepin' sickness." She said to a smiling Jerry.

"Maybe it's the salt water air and the wide open spaces." He offered.

"A sly way o' sayin' we should have a place out there."

"That never entered my mind." He said with a straight face!

Chapter Five

Eleanor's big day was here. Cleo had invited her for an early Sunday dinner and for the discussion about her offer. Eleanor mulled over what she would wear . . . *simple* was a must! She settled on a beige knit dress with a wide, soft mesh belt made of a woven bronze-type metal. It was expertly tailored and pointed up her figure. The only jewelry she wore were two emerald clips; one on each side of the dress neckline. She added her gold watch and a pair of open-toed bronze-like shoes. Brian had styled her hair in a bouffant page-boy and it was very becoming and really showed the beautiful color at its best. He was curious as to the occasion for the hair-do but didn't persist when she didn't elaborate or give him any reason. As she exited her taxi the driver was all eyes!

Entering the handsome building Eleanor was very impressed with the posh lobby. It was subdued luxury and oozed of prime taste. The elevator took her up to the fifteenth floor then she took another elevator that serviced two penthouse apartments; on her way up to the top of the building she looked into the mirror and said aloud; "if you are going to have an apartment in New York it's best to have a penthouse with a private elevator!" The door chime had a modulated, pleasant tone.

"Welcome, Eleanor; please come right in; you look exceptionally lovely dear, I'm very proud of you."

She wore a golden silk dress that was definitely couturier; her hair was in an up do styled by her own capable hands, and diamonds!

"Cleo; you look breath-taking! That gown is stunning and the diamonds!"

"You know they are a girl's best friend, Eleanor." They were laughing.

The apartment had a large, high-ceilinged living room. Tastefully furnished and with glass walls overlooking the city; a panoramic view from the large terrace was the frosting on the architectural cake!

"Oh, Cleo, this is surely heaven!" Eleanor's honest admiration was obvious.

Manny, Cleo's fiancé, approached them; he was a solid looking man about six feet tall and well-dressed in casual clothes. He was a bit swarthy; his strong features seemed chiseled in place. It was his eyes that struck Eleanor; they were dark and deep set . . . she had the feeling he could read her thoughts! Though thinning a little at the crown, his pepper and salt hair added an aura of dignity. All in all he was mighty impressive; they made a stunning couple.

"At last I get to meet Eleanor! He gently pressed her out-stretched hand.

"My pleasure," Eleanor said, smiling; "and may I congratulate you on your coming marriage . . . you couldn't have a lovelier bride."

"Thank you, dear, and I quite agree with you. Come and let me fix you a drink; let me guess; a dry martini on the rocks?"

"Right on the money." Eleanor was laughing; *now I'm sure he's a mind-reader*, she thought. There was another guest; Cleo took her arm, guiding her.

"Eleanor let me introduce our attorney and friend; Gordon Madison."

He had risen as they approached; a bit over six feet and lean and athletic-looking plus a wavy head of silver hair; Gordon made quite an impression. Dressed in a beautifully tailored dark blue suit and exuding confidence (he even had a light sun tan) Eleanor tingled as he took her hand.

"I've heard so much about you . . . it's a very pleasant relief to meet you."

"You have me at a disadvantage; I've not heard a word about you."

"Well we want to change all that!"

Manny handed her the martini and they seated themselves on the very comfortable chairs.

"But no business talking until after dinner!" Cleo commanded.

The houseman passed a tray of exquisite hors d'oeuvres. They had a couple of rounds and got acquainted; Eleanor was very impressed with Gordon and he was decidedly interested in her; a little something Cleo was hoping would happen. Gordon was a widower and a Texan; he needed a lovely Titian-haired wife!

After a perfectly planned dinner they had coffee in the living room. No drinks were offered because they had business to discuss; the celebrating would come later. Gordon outlined details and gradually unfolded the plan Manny and Cleo had thought out and he answered all of Eleanor's questions. She was receiving a very nice salary and a monthly percentage of the net profits. It was understood Eleanor would have control of the operation of the salon. If she wished to make alterations or do any expensive decoration she would need to consult with Gordon. All of her contacts would be with Gordon; not Cleo or Manny. They were planning on making extensive trips and wanted no part of business. Gordon was looking forward to this alliance and had asked Cleo if Eleanor was married or involved. Upon hearing she was a widow he already saw a common ground. It had been mentioned during their talk that Manny owned the building where the salon was located. Later she would learn that Manny and Gordon did real estate development and they owned the building Cleo lived in. Eleanor was over-whelmed by the offer. She had never aspired to making the kind of money now being offered to her. On the surface she was cool and in perfect control of herself.

When Gordon offered to meet with her attorney and go over the offer with him Eleanor said.

"I'm satisfied with what I see; we have just met but I feel I can trust you. If I'm wrong . . . I'm wrong, but I don't feel that I am."

"Thank you, Eleanor; I'll make certain that trust is well placed." Gordon pressed her hand firmly; sealing his promise.

There would be contract signings at Gordon's office and Eleanor would take over the first of November. Before Eleanor went home Cleo invited her to the wedding on Christmas day. She would be the only one from the salon invited as it was going to be a small wedding. After the church ceremony the reception would be catered at the penthouse. "We're having about fifty people; Gordon will be best man; my sister will fly in from San Diego to be my matron of honor." And knowing Cleo it would all be done in excellent, comfortable taste.

Gordon saw Eleanor to her taxi; "I have your phone number, may I call you? I'd like to take you out for dinner and get to know you. We are going to be involved in the business sense and it would help if we felt comfortable with each other. I've enjoyed your company immensely tonight."

"I enjoyed meeting you as well; call me soon. Good night, Gordon."

"Goodnight, Eleanor, I've really enjoyed meeting you."

"It's very mutual, Gordon." He watched the cab pull away; waving.

Eleanor had asked Cleo if she could discuss all this with Brian. Cleo knew how close they were and she empathized with Eleanor understanding she needed to talk to someone about it. She thought for a moment then spoke.

"Wait until we have signed the contract; which will be soon, then tell him. I don't know when I'll make the announcement in the salon; I was going to have announcements printed to mail to the clientele but I've decided against it. I will have one made up and framed on an easel in the reception room. Very soon after we sign contract I'll have an early morning meeting of all the staff and give them the news. Then we will all get our heads together and plan a celebration in your honor!" Eleanor hugged her; her eyes brimming with tears.

After locking her locks she undressed and put on a robe. Putting on water for tea she went to her bedroom and brushed her hair back and secured it with a wide band. Taking some cream and astringent with balls of cotton she went back to the kitchen and started removing her make-up. In between her ablutions she made the tea. "Oh, how I wish I had Brian here! I am bursting to scream about this!" She was talking aloud and her face was flushed with the excitement of the evening. If Brian walked in this minute and saw her condition he would have no trouble getting to the reason. She had maintained a cool head all evening but now the whistle had blown and she was unwinding. "Could this be happening to her?"

They met at Gordon's office that Wednesday at six in the evening. Even though he had everything ready it took two hours. His secretary had served coffee but now it was all over and Cleo and Manny made a hasty exit pleading a dinner date. Gordon congratulated Eleanor;

"What do you say; do you have time to have dinner with me for a little celebration? It's the start of our 'kind of partnership' you know . . . it should be celebrated." He took her hand; "please, Eleanor!"

She put his hand in both of hers; "Oh, that would be lovely, Gordon; to be honest with you . . . I'm hungry!" They laughed together and he hugged her.

While she freshened up; he made reservations at the Monsignor. It was a plush place, softly lit and handsomely appointed; neither ate heavily and both eschewed having dessert; smiling. They lingered over coffee and brandy; he was very proud to be accompanied by such an attractive companion. He was learning she was just as attractive within that lovely exterior. Gordon had a couple of affairs since the death of his wife but they were not satisfying to the soul. Both were attractive, intelligent ladies; sophisticated and well informed. He was a good catch and he knew it; satisfaction in the hay was not enough for his kind of marriage. The present mode of sophistication was not Gordon's need; he was a country boy from Texas, brought up on a small ranch outside of Dallas. His father was a lawyer who became wealthy by getting involved in oil leases. The marriage between his parents was one of love and partnership. They were best friends; devoted to each other for many years. After his mother died of cancer his father faded away in a year . . . he couldn't wait to join his lifelong friend. Gordon's marriage had been satisfying until it became evident that she did not want children. He discovered she had her tubes tied *before* they married! To him it was a betrayal. They had one serious row about it; then he gradually retreated to a guest bedroom. On a vacation cruise with her sister she drowned in a rip current.

He still owned the family ranch and he loved to get away and relax there. Although he was sixty-three he looked fifty and he kept himself in shape. A membership in the N.Y. Athletic Club assisted him in keeping fit and afforded the acquaintance of interesting men. Not to mention the wealthy clients he gathered; in fact, that was where he met Manny!

"Where are you?" Eleanor put her hand on his.

"Daydreaming." He shook his head; "You need to get home; let's go."

"That wasn't just a dinner, Gordon, "it was an experience! What a lovely place; everything is perfection, a very subdued perfection. It's quiet yet the diners were all having conversations and the china seemed to be sound proofed."

They were in the taxi and he chuckled at her comment.

"Acoustics; dear, properly done, just like their food."

"That was part of the experience; I enjoyed that intermezzo of lime sherbet in that exquisite little crystal stemware. They were so delicate! I've never had anything like that. Thank you so much for an exceptional celebration."

"I hope we have many more; I feel so at ease with you, Eleanor, sincerely."

"And I with you; I feel like I've known you for a long time."

They were in front of her building; he told the cab to wait. At the entrance he took her hand. "If you're free Sunday I want to take a ride upstate to see some old friends. They live in a wonderful old house built during the Revolutionary War. I'd love to have your company and I know you will like these people. I'd planned on leaving about eight in the morning and having breakfast along the way."

"The foliage should be turning . . . I'd love to go with you."

"Oh, that is wonderful," he was delighted! "Casual dress; I'll take everyone out to eat. I tell Dotty not to cook but we will have to see what she decides. In any case, they don't stand on ceremony. I'll call you Saturday about seven and reconfirm . . . is that okay?"

She kissed him on the cheek; softly. "Roger that," she smiled.

He hugged her and told her to go in; he took off.

It was almost eleven; she wondered if Brian was up. He was probably home because the next day was his twelve hour stint. Opening the connecting door a crack she listened and heard music. He might be in bed; he often left his music on while he slept. Softly she called his name and she heard a 'hello' from the living room. Jumping up and tossing his magazine aside he went to the door.

"Who's that knocking at my door?" He sang and he hugged her warmly.

She kissed him; "Can I bend your ear for a bit?"

"You don't bite, do you?"

"Not on Wednesdays." As usual; they were laughing.

"I have news for you, darling," He hoped it wasn't about Jerry.

"Do we have a drink?" He walked to his bar.

"A little brandy . . . you will need it!" Oh, God . . . it was Jerry.

He handed her a snifter; they sat, facing each other.

"I signed a contract with Cleo tonight; I'm the new manager of the salon. She is getting married!" He sat back in his chair and almost spilled his drink.

"Give me a minute; I'm speechless!" Eleanor was beaming;

"I've been aching to tell you but I was sworn to secrecy until the contracts were signed. They've given me a wonderful deal and a free hand."

"They? Who's they?"

"Manny and Cleo . . . he is her fiancé; he owns the building the salon is in."

Brian rose as did she and he hugged her with much gusto. He had his senses back and he could now let her know how thrilled he was. She filled him in on the details; describing Cleo's penthouse and covering everything right up to the dinner. Brian watched with great pleasure the exuberance she radiated.

"Pause a moment, precious one; I have a question. Exactly who is Gordon?"

"I told you; he is their lawyer and I will be dealing with him. They are to do nothing but travel and enjoy his money . . . there seems to be an awful lot of that. He also owns the building the penthouse is in; Gordon is his partner in that."

"Gordon . . . do you know you light up when you say his name?"

"Oh Lord; something new for you to act silly about!"

"No, no, my manager, au contrere; there is nothing silly about Monsignor! He bowed a slow, graceful bow; we are talking class, dear, high class. I've been there and was very impressed; especially with the intermezzo!"

"Oh, wasn't that petite crystal stemware a show-stopper?"

"El, my dear, I have never loved you more than I do right now."

She checked to see if he was putting her on . . . he wasn't; there were tears in his eyes. Putting his arms around her he hugged her and held her close.

"I think both of our lives are blossoming, El, luck has come our way."

She joined him; they were both bawling. In a few minutes they were laughing and he re-filled their drinks and she told him more about Gordon. He was careful not to make any smart remarks; when she described him she glowed and this time she was glowing about Mr. Right. Brian envisioned her in the penthouse opposite Cleo; he did not say one word about this fantasy because it could very well happen. Gordon was sixty-three . . . he didn't have a lot of time and Brian was quite sure he knew it! He vowed to keep his mouth shut and watch things develop; he had to keep her hair in that page boy style; Texans like page boys!

Nora was going upstate to a shrine in the Mohawk Valley area with a bus-load of ladies from her church on a retreat.

"What are you girls running away from?" Jerry had asked; twitting her.

"Satan, o' course;" she snapped back; "and an opportunity to pray fer your ilk; maybe we can get the Lord's grace inta' yer soul."

"Well be sure you bring enough beer along; they only supply holy water!"

She wanted to kill him! "Smart mouthing about the Lord is blasphemy!"

"He understands me; we have a private relationship."

"Indeed! So private that He knows nuthin' about it!"

He drove her to the church where they were boarding the bus and hugged her on her way. He was going out East with Brian and

Tony to set the railroad ties in place as a retaining wall. Working out a sketch of an idea he had for the wall had taken a good bit of his spare time. It looked pretty good and he was proud of it. Brian had managed the Monday off so there were three days to work on it. Tony liked his plan and they assisted Jerry and followed his design. By Sunday afternoon it was almost finished and the result was first rate.

"You've done some job on this, Jerry;" Tony voiced his appreciation, "we would be nowhere without your help and your idea." Brian agreed.

"I liked doing this and I have two great bosses; they can both cook!"

Brian chuckled; "we were helpers . . . not bosses!"

Toward the middle of Monday afternoon the wall was finished. Next week-end they were bringing planters and there would be geraniums along the top in the summer and vines cascading down the sides for as long as they lasted. Now that the wall was finished the next structure was going to be a lean-to type car port for three cars. They were getting the place shaped up.

"We have to start thinking of a name for the place and put a sign out at the beginning of our road." Brian was looking directly at Tony; "like they do in East Hampton. To put your name out there is too ordinary . . . we can't have that!"

"Why don't you have a naming contest and give a prize to the winner?"

Jerry was kidding but Tony thought it was a great idea. "Good idea, Brian?"

"The contestants would want to see the place in order to name it; we would need a turnstile at the door!" Tony's eyebrows were up . . . "Amen!" he cried.

They accomplished a lot that week-end and had dinner at Kincaid's late Monday afternoon. About seven in the evening they headed back to the city; the traffic would be light on a Monday. Eleanor had not been mentioned the entire week-end; Brian had a feeling that Jerry would not be seeing much of her. Brian knew something that Jerry did not know; Jerry, on the other hand, knew something that Brian did not know . . . and he never would!

Jerry was working the following week-end; they went out East alone and did some work around the cottage. By three o'clock Tony suffering with wander lust and he went outside to talk to Brian.

"I think we need to go and consult with our man in Montauk. We can have an early dinner and catch up on the latest gossip. Let's not bother to cook at home; what do you say, Brian?"

"Wonderful! Do you think there will be any new gossip?"

"Do monkeys eat bananas? You *know* there will be!"

They showered together and dressed and were on their way.

"It's almost November and you can see the difference out here already," Brian was driving, "it gets dark earlier and there are fewer people."

"I'll bet Montauk is still buzzing," Tony opened his window a little and lit a cigarette. "You want one?" He held up the pack where Brian could see them.

"No, thanks." He opened his window also.

As they came into the village Tony was proved correct. The motels had many cars parked around them and the restaurants were all busy. As always, the fishing tackle store had several vehicles in front.

"You called it, Tony, the place is buzzing!"

"Wait until we get to the docks . . . that place will be jumping!"

And so it was; they were lucky to get a parking place. As they walked toward the entrance Brian noticed a couple getting out of a station wagon. Even for honky-tonk Montauk these two were real characters! He was a tall man in cowman clothes. His chino-type pants were tapered and inside his hand-tooled boots. They gleamed in the sunlight and they were expensive boots! The silver belt buckle also glistened and the belt was now let out many holes wider than when he was young. His hand-tailored shirt was as western as you can get; and you know, the hat had to be a Stetson! But his lady! Brian pretended to adjust his shoe so he could get a good look. Tony was already in the bar and he was wondering what the hell his buddy was doing. She had a dark mass of blown-out curls (close to fuzz); at best she was five feet tall and weighed nothing. Her long sleeved ruffled blouse was gold and white polka dots and the red mini-skirt was bouffant and barely covered her scrawny backside.

Brian entered the bar and walked toward Tony; he realized they were coming to Kincaid's! He was thrilled.

"What the hell are you up to? You should see the look on your face; you look like you've been here for three hours! Tony was incredulous.

"I can't talk now; watch the door."

He greeted Bob and ordered a drink and behind him he heard Tony's muffled voice;

"Mother of Christ! What is that?"

They had made their entrance and Bob, at the piano, broke into a country tune and she went over and gave him a big kiss.

"It's a good thing he drinks." Tony whispered to Brian. Brian laughed and was looking at her make-up. The artificial lashes must have had three coats of mascara; every time she raised or lowered them her whole face seemed to go up and down. She wore ankle length white boots that were studded with rhinestones; he imagined her line dancing and flouncing the skirt all over! They did, in fact, belong to a line dancing group. Brian had never seen such a tiny waist on an adult; he was willing to bet that her escort could button his collar around her waist. This was Randy and Darlin' June from Ditch Plains; their Montauk summer home. They wintered in El Paso, Randy's birthplace. He had a ranch there and much family tradition. He provided Darlin' June with a small apartment in town; she was not a part of his tradition. Randy was a widower with two married children and they all lived on the ranch in separate homes. He visited Darlin' June often and kept her contented; which meant they went shopping. The lines in her face couldn't be hidden with make-up; Darlin' June had slid past sixty without knowing it. However; other people noticed but they took her at face value. Randy dropped a lot of money in town; that always makes you welcome.

Darlin' June had drifted down to the piano after Randy handed her the vodka and tonic with a squeeze of lime. Brian was now positive she wore a wig and she had shelled out big bucks for it! It was human hair of Bavarian quality and if it were dressed properly would have looked beautiful. She was talking to Bob at the piano and he was looking through his music; suddenly Brian realized that she was going to sing . . . naturally; she would sing country! He told Tony.

"Good Lord she will empty this place out!"

Kincaid approached them; he had a booth ready and two menus in his hand. They followed him and brought there drinks along. "Beef stew is the special and we also have striped bass."

Tony held his arm; "Who are those two in the western get-up?"

"They are a story; I'll sit with you after you have eaten."

He went to get a waiter for them. And Darlin' June began to sing; a whining tearjerker about a lover who was cheating on his loved one. They could hear a few of the diners saying 'oh, no!'

"They must be regulars and they've heard her before."

Brian was laughing at Tony's remark; "they were definitely groans!"

"Do you think she's studied voice?" Brian asked Tony.

"For sure," he answered, "in a barn!"

They had their dinner and Bob came to have a drink with them. He gave them a run-down on the 'westerners' and before they knew what was happening he went and returned with Randy inviting him to join the party and ordering a round. Randy occupied one side of the booth. Bob got a chair and sat at the outside edge. Bob had asked Brian and Tony to sit next to each other; Randy needed room for his Stetson! He greeted them in true Texan fashion and totally controlled the conversation. He didn't ask them one question about themselves but gave them a complete history of his forbears and included many historic heroes as intimate friends of his kin. When he finally was taking his leave he got around to mentioning Darlin' June; he stood, overshadowing the table.

"She's not much to look at but she gives terrific head."

He went back to the bar; Bob was doubled up, laughing. Tony just shook his head and the waiter came with a tray of drinks on Randy. That was the last they saw of them that season but in June they returned and she sang again.

On their trip back to the city they relived their meeting the 'westerners' and they were still laughing.

"I'll never forget his parting shot;" said Tony.

Brian went to the salon Tuesday morning and there was a notice in the day room as to a meeting the next morning at eight-thirty a.m.

'Please be on time' it ended. There was much speculation among the staff; Brian and Eleanor eyeing each other knowingly. Eleanor hid her excitement until she and Brian stopped to have dinner on their way home.

"We're not celebrating tonight." Brian cautioned. He told her what they accomplished over the long week-end and mentioned the quality of help that Jerry gave them. She showed interest; but not in Jerry and that pleased him no end. His concentration was on Darlin' June and Randy; she almost choked on her wine as he described their get-ups and she had questions galore about them. The time seemed to evaporate; there was so much to talk about. She didn't mention Gordon's invitation. After the trip there would be more to talk about . . . indeed! They arrived home; Eleanor entered her place through his apartment. They had talked enough and soon the privacy of home was beckoning.

"Tomorrow is a big day for you."

He hugged her and kissed her goodnight.

Justine, the maid, was usually the first to arrive at the salon but today Cleo was in the reception room when she entered. Justine could smell the coffee and there was a large tray of miniature Danish set up on the table with a small vase of flowers.

"Madam Cleo; I could have helped you . . . I could have come earlier!"

"There wasn't that much to do, dear, thank you all the same."

Justine noticed the draped easel with a 'do not touch' sign on it. She looked askance at Cleo. Squeezing her shoulder Cleo said. "It's a surprise." Justine let out a small squeal and clapped her hands; she felt she was in on it.

The staff were all punctual and witty comments were being bandied about concerning the easel . . . especially the 'do not touch sign'. There were additional comments about the Danish and how delicious they were; they disappeared fast. When they were all seated Cleo went to the easel and quickly slipped off the drape. The announcement that Eleanor was now manager of the salon garnered what sounded like one big common gasp. Edith almost wet her pants. Had this news come before the advent of Tom; she might have been envious but now she was delighted for Eleanor. She never quite liked Cleo and this gave her a friend in court. The staff congratulated Eleanor and since they were all fond of her it was good news for everyone. Cleo asked them to get their heads together and choose a suitable evening after work for a celebration dinner. She said she would make arrangements in a place close by. And the party was on Cleo! A burst of applause followed that announcement. There was to be a breaking-in period and Cleo would be on hand to assist Eleanor in the running of the business. Eleanor would no longer be styling and it would be necessary to move her clients to other stylists. This was going to be accomplished between Eleanor and her clients. Cleo cautioned that she wanted no interference from anyone and no 'grabbing' of crème de la crème clients. There was some tittering but Cleo's stern face subdued it in a hurry. Justine unlocked the entrance door and they went to their stations. Not before giving hugs and kisses to Eleanor. Edith was very demonstrative and Eleanor was almost embarrassed by the show of affection.

Most of her clients took the news in a gracious manner; they were all fond of her and happy for her promotion. She assured them that she would always be available for consultation should a question arise about their hair. Some took it as a personal affront and they went elsewhere. It was a whole new life for Eleanor; Cleo gave her a generous check and suggested a few places to shop for smart, suitable attire for her position. She tapped Eleanor's cheek;

"We don't want to out-dress our clientele, dear; you're very attractive you must be careful. This was good advice and Eleanor took it. She had good taste

Gordon called Saturday and relayed his plans and asked her if they suited her. They were very methodical and she had no questions.

"I'll be down on the street in front of the building in case there's no place to park."

He appreciated her considerate nature. "Thank you, Eleanor; I'll see you in the morning."

Eleanor was downstairs about two minutes when he pulled up and parked. He gave her a hug as he greeted her and told her how lovely she looked. Gordon looked pretty good himself; in an iridescent, pale gold Porsche. After stowing her bag he opened the door and handed her into the snappy sports car.

"I know it's a beautiful car, Gordon, but what make of car is it?"

"You've brought up one of my favorite subjects. I should warn you; I can go on about my wheels like other people go on about their kids. I've even been known to give the manual to my passenger while I give a boring discourse."

"I'm a willing listener but spare me the manual; I wouldn't be able to hide my ignorance. I know very little about cars; I don't even know how to drive."

"Maybe you could learn in this one." He smiled at her.

"I'd be petrified! I'd be so afraid I might scratch it!"

He squeezed her hand, laughing and proceeded to expound on the wonders of his machine. They were on the Throgs Neck Bridge before he came up for air.

"I warned you how I am about this machine. Never hesitate to shut me up when I get started. Don't be polite; you'll suffer!" He didn't have a relapse.

Pine Plains was in Duchess County located in upstate New York. It was hilly and rolling and excellent for farming. Especially dairy farming and there were several of them. It was good for growing apples and there were acres and acres of orchards. Frank Cochran had been in the banking business and had taken an early retirement; with his wife Dotty they had searched this area for a place to live. Frank was an accomplished painter and had traveled through India and painted exotic objects. He was especially absorbed by Bengal tigers!

There was a reason for the early retirement; Frank had a serious illness that left him addicted to his medication. Dotty had a career in surgical nursing and could be sympathetic to his problem. The medication prescribed by his doctor was not enough for him but they were able to get additional doses and Dotty administered the injections. She was able to keep his habit under control.

They were having lunch one day when they over heard a conversation about a place for sale nearby. The women were getting ready to leave and Dotty followed them outside. Willingly they gave the location saying there was no phone. "Just go there and knock on the door," was the advice, "be prepared . . . she loves animals! We should warn you she's a might eccentric."

Saying 'good luck' they went tittering away; wishing they could see this meeting. Frank and Dotty found the place and fell in love with its history. The house was built during the Revolutionary War and judging from the quality of the construction they must have been ship builders. But the owner! The property was over-grown but Frank could see the underlying original design of the place. The kitchen door was wide open and Frank knocked.

"Anybody home?" He called out. There were three chickens inside!

"Wipe your feet!"

They were startled by the admonition and entered; dutifully complying. She was sitting at the table which was strewn with an indescribable confusion of things.

"I'm Frank Corcoran; this is my wife Dotty. We heard your home might be for sale and we are interested; I have been ill and have had to retire. I am going to need rest and quiet and this seems to have that."

"It certainly does. Find yourself some chairs and sit down."

They were surprised at how well-spoken she was . . . it was unexpected.

"People call me Miss W . . . you might as well do the same. I have two hundred and seventy-five acres; mostly apple trees, I don't bother with them. I live in the kitchen with both doors open all day long. The animals come and go; I never feed them except for Julius, my cat. These animals; including the chickens, never use my house for a toilet; that's because I don't feed them and also they respect me. Two years ago my dog Laddie passed on and I have found it too hard to live here without him. I have erected a mausoleum on the property; it is made in the style of a cathedral and I keep a kerosene lantern lit in there every night. Whoever buys this place must agree in writing, to keep his lantern lit."

There were tears in her eyes and the Corcoran's were not dry.

"I think that is a beautiful tribute, Miss W, we would agree to that."

"I had no idea you had so much property; does it require much upkeep?" Frank was concerned about this; it could be an expensive problem.

"I don't do anything. The locals use the apples and they care for the trees. Their cows and sheep and a few goats keep the grounds close cropped."

She sent them down to see the cellar telling them it was carved into solid rock; that was the foundation the house was on!

"We call it a cold cellar," she added.

The entrance to the cellar was outside at the back of the house. They were looking out over a valley; the house was on a rise and it had an extended view. "How could this house not have a back porch?" He asked of Dotty.

He was astounded by the cellar! There was a small stream running through the rock the entire length of the house. The builders had chiseled steps starting high at one end and gradually getting lower until they were ground level at the other end of the house where the stream exited and was directed in different directions for irrigation. Each step was ground down to six or eight inches in depth and earthen crocks were kept there to keep food cold. The steps filled up with water to the depth they were ground and the crocks were immersed in the openings. It was sheer genius! "This is some ice box!" He hugged Dotty; "We must have it."

They went back to the kitchen and worked out a deal with Miss W. To their surprise the contract signing was in the office of a New York City estate attorney and it was there they learned that Miss W came from very fine lineage but had been involved in a scandal with a married man ending up by her banishment to Pine Plains many years back. There was a quick closing; the only thing Frank requested of Miss W was permission to electrify Laddie's lamp. She was quick to agree to the idea. "I was thinking of doing that," she said, in a far away voice.

They had a wonderful time restoring the house. It had four fireplaces; one in the master bedroom. There were all kinds of treasures in the place. She had lived in the kitchen for many years and Frank discovered the walls were papered with newspapers dating back many, many years! He had a local handyman remove them with care and they spent many hours reading the papers.

Miss W left no will; her upkeep was covered by a family trust and would continue as long as she refrained from disgrace. Some of the old timers remembered when she first came to Pine Plains; she had two saddle horses and she use to ride, in smart riding attire, through the meadows and orchards; jumping fences and hedges with her luxurious dark hair pinned back billowing in the wind. She talked to very few people; mostly tradesmen and she bore her exile alone. Except for Laddie; with him by her side she didn't need a shrink or any other companion. He had lived twenty years; a long life for a dog; love kept him alive. But she did have taste. As the Corcorans went through the house and allowed light were there had been none for so many years; they discovered wonderful antique furniture and while it hadn't been cared for in so long a time, it had not been abused. Every day was a treasure hunt! Frank and Dotty were not aware of it but they were hand-picked. Miss W had turned away many would-be buyers; especially developers who would bull-doze the orchards and rape the land. Most important; the buyers would have to respect Laddie's grave and the glistening in their eyes did not escape her. She knew they would love the place as she had.

Frank and Dotty acquired a dog . . . for Frank and a cat for Dotty. They spent hours trying to come up with suitable names; looking in books and asking friends. The solution? A dog named Laddie and a cat named Miss W!

Gordon drove into the circular driveway. The place was a paradise of all sorts of greenery. Shrubs and great trees and flowers everywhere. This is a place built on love Eleanor thought. She was greeted by a lot of that as she opened the car door; Laddie, a black Lab was giving her a royal welcome. Miss W slept!

Frank and Gordon brought in the bags and Dotty put her arm around Eleanor; walking her into the house. Laddie hesitated as to which team he should follow; he decided on the ladies . . . they were much better with treats.

In the living room they chatted and Eleanor was filled with admiration of the fine antiques. A large painting of a Bengal tiger hung over the fireplace. She felt drawn to it; the eyes seemed absolutely real!

"This is a magnificent painting, Dotty; I think he is breathing!"

"Oh; you are in the will, dear; it's Frank's favorite of all his work."

"He painted it? Gordon mentioned he was retired from banking."

"Painting is his real love and now he has time for it. We traveled in India and Bangladesh; he photographed the tiger then painted him from the photo. We have several more around the house; there's one in your room."

Dotty had the gift of making people feel right at home; she had a genuine warmth that seemed to wrap around you and tell you that everything was fine. But there was more to her obvious affection toward Eleanor . . . Gordon never brought any of his lady friends to their home. They had met him in the city many times to go out for dinner and see a show. He would have the current girl friend with him but she and Frank knew there was never anything serious. When he asked if he could bring Eleanor they were all agog! Gordon told them what was happening at the salon because they knew Cleo and Manny. Frank had cautioned Dotty not to be all atwitter and ready for a wedding. She poked him and said she knew better.

Frank was making Bloody Marys and Dotty took Eleanor to her room.

"If you want to put on jeans or anything you're comfortable in; please do. We believe in relaxing; when we lived in that city we were afraid to step out in public unless we were dressed to the nines! It was awful." She had a great laugh.

"I'm okay as I am," smiled Eleanor, "I'll just freshen up and join you."

"Well you certainly look lovely; I love your hair. See you anon."

Gordon and Frank were out on the back porch; she joined them and took a drink.

"What a lovely lady Eleanor is; I just warmed right up to her and you, darling, are going to put her in your will. She loves the tiger in the living room; she is positive he's breathing!" They all laughed. Gordon felt proud.

"I just had to look at her and she was in the will; you're going to have to go back to work. I'm going to leave her everything!" Frank needled her.

"Gordon tell that one what divorce lawyers will do to the likes of him."

"I'm neutral; I don't handle divorces. I believe in love."

Frank looked at Dotty as if to caution her; that was an opening line for her. Eleanor came into the porch and began exclaiming over the view.

"Frank is going to take you on a tour later; he is the tour director."

"And Dotty will then show you all the things she is sure I will forget!"

They were full of fun and their affection for one another was charming. Eleanor was so glad she had come. Gordon was quiet but he never took his eyes off her. Dotty was making mental notes; she was convinced Gordon was in love!

They got into their jeep and the foursome toured the property. A year after they had moved in a fruit broker called on them and was interested in leasing the apple orchards. He mentioned he had asked Miss W if she had any interest but he was dismissed with a firm "get off my property!" But Frank was very interested in the proposition. The broker would take over the care of the trees and picking the fruit. He would be responsible for maintaining the grounds around the orchards as well. Frank and Dotty were to receive a percentage of the net profits. At the end of the fiscal year the account was sent to Frank's C.P.A. for approval and the check they received was very satisfactory. Another unexpected surprise was the arrival of tenants at their door to pay rent. It seemed there were four houses on the acreage that no one knew about at the closing. Miss W did not attend the closing; she was the one would have known. After fine tooth combing the old deed Gordon had located the houses. It was a legal mystery solved!

"Gordon has always been of great help to us." Dotty smiled at him.

"You two have wonderful instincts," Eleanor said enthusiastically; to think of how this place looked when you purchased it and how it is now takes a lot of imagination and courage. So much can go wrong!"

They smiled at each other, "plenty of things went wrong; you tend to forget them as time passes and you are getting so much enjoyment from the home." Frank shrugged his shoulders and Dotty gave him a kiss. They were back at the house.

Gordon wanted to take them out for lunch and Dotty was insisting that she had lunch all prepared.

"I didn't fuss; it's a cold lunch!"

"If you promise me we will go out for dinner; I will shut up."

Dotty kissed Gordon; "then shut up!"

Laughing; they went in to have lunch.

The week-end seemed to have just evaporated; they were on their way back to the city and had chatted incessantly about their wonderful time.

"They are both so charming; they're different, but they are together."

Gordon was touched; he reached for her hand. "A perfect description of them!"

"They think the world of you . . . that says a lot for you, Gordon."

"I could use some good public relations; I tend to be a recluse."

She laughed; "Oh, I really find that hard to believe; in fact, I don't believe it!"

They arrived in the city a little before nine.

"Too late for a night cap?" There was a touch of pleading in his voice.

"If we really just have one, remember; I'm starting a new career."

He pulled up in front of the Monsignor and a car was just leaving.

"I can't believe the luck!" He parked; expertly.

A smart waiter led them to a quiet table. The lighting was soft and romantic and that is what Gordon wanted. He didn't have the luxury of a long courtship; he had things to say right now. Frank's last words were; "Don't let her get away!"

It was a glowing Eleanor who entered the salon on Monday! Cleo arrived shortly after Eleanor and they started planning their day over coffee.

Gordon had told her of his affection toward her and he asked if he could see her regularly. He was very precise in telling her his intentions were serious and was warm and affectionate in relating the qualities she possessed that he needed. She was not coy; she told him she was drawn to him. It was the truth.

Between learning the rudiments of her new job and seeing Gordon as often as she would allow; her time was limited. Brian complained that he never saw her; she had not confided in him about Gordon. Edith was absorbed with Tom. Jerry was not in her thoughts. Nora was on her mind and she called her to keep in touch explaining about her new position. Nora congratulated her and wished her luck; the sinking feeling Nora had was a sadness that had gradually let her know that Jerry was not going to have a life with Eleanor. In their many phone calls Eleanor had never mentioned Jerry; and Jerry made no mention of her in any of their conversations. Nora asked no questions; but she brooded.

It was getting close to Thanksgiving and Eleanor had accepted an invitation to celebrate it with Frank and Dotty. The invite came from Dotty, not Gordon. This told her he had been in touch with them about seeing her. Eleanor was pleased to realize he had confided in them. Dotty had been busy with her match making and she told Gordon he should pop the question when they were up in Pine Plains. "Give her the ring at Christmas; we'll have a little celebration up here and it would be lovely to have both of you as Christmas guests." This was a bit stronger than a suggestion; despite Frank's continued admonitions to keep out of their affair. *If I listen to him they will never get together!* She mused.

Brian asked her about Thanksgiving and she told him she had plans.

"Will I be intruding if I ask you where you are going?" He smiled.

"I'm going up to Pine Plains . . . with Gordon."

"You'll forgive me darling; I don't know where that is."

"It's upstate; in Duchess County; he has friends there."

"I take it you've been there before?"

"Yes; once, Gordon wanted to visit his friends and he asked me to go."

"So; you are seeing Gordon and you don't want to discuss it; right?"

"I would really appreciate that; for the present."

"My lips are sealed; I wish you to have whatever you want."

She hugged him; her eyes were glistening; "Mr. Wonderful." She kissed him.

Brian and Tony had been taking Jerry out East every week-end. He had made arrangements with the 'euchre-playing' lady to stay with Nora. There were no more objections from Nora. If he was out there working with them it kept him out of the gin mills in the city. The proof was the way he looked. His color was healthy and he was sticking to beer only. His body was firm and trim and he really looked good. Nora was having more hacking coughing spells than ever and she swore her friend to secrecy. It was better that Jerry was not there. He had not told her yet; he had put in his papers for retirement to be able to spend more time with her. He wanted to work on her to agree to spend the winter in Florida. After doing more research he learned they could rent a place at a very modest price and he could see no reason for her to stay in the city.

Brian had completed the real estate salesman course at night and was now putting in time on week-ends at Ed Gorman's office. He had completed a few summer rentals and taken a deposit on a lot sale. He was very encouraged and Ed was delighted with his progress. The clients liked him; that was so important.

Tony had put out some feelers to Gino about buying the bar. He would need no cash down and Tony would work out a time payment schedule that he could handle without pressure. Gino would have no cash to put down because his daughter was planning to be married soon and his money was being spent there. He was interested; he knew what money the place took in; and since his daughter was pregnant; he knew he was going to need money! She was his only child; he had raised her alone after divorcing his addict wife. She was Daddy's girl!

They finally came to terms and without telling anyone, Brian included; they signed the deal with a mortgage-like arrangement. Tony had a trust and his lawyer made the papers part of the trust. If anything happened to Tony; Brian would become the trustee. He would tell Brian soon. Tony was going to stay on until Gino was familiar with the workings of the business. He needed to get to know the salesmen better and they would be informed that Gino was the new owner and that it was very confidential. Tony was closer to his goal; now he had to get Brian out of that salon and they could live out East permanently.

Jerry asked Brian and Tony to come to Nora's for Thanksgiving dinner. She wanted to cook and he said she would like to have them join her and Jerry. Since they had no plans; Brian had told Tony that Eleanor had been invited elsewhere; they accepted. Tony had perceived that Jerry and Eleanor were no longer an item and he never mentioned her in Jerry's presence. Brian had not mentioned Eleanor's involvement with Gordon and was waiting for the green light from her to do so. They had a delicious dinner at Nora's and they noticed some of the spark had gone out of her. She wasn't as sassy as usual.

"Nora doesn't look too well; I think doing that dinner might have been too much for her."

They were on their way home to Brian's apartment and Tony was talking to Brian. "She wasn't nearly as sassy as she usually is; from what Jerry tells me she's always one ahead of him."

"I think it's Eleanor . . . she wanted a match for Jerry; she thought Eleanor would make a different life for him. He really is on his good behavior around her. She seemed interested in him, too. I think that's over." Brian sighed.

"Do you know something I don't know?"

"Not really."

"I'll let it rest."

"Thank you," murmured Brian.

Eleanor's Thanksgiving was quite different. There was only the four of them but Dotty had hired a local lady to help prepare the dinner and serve. It was not an attempt at elegance it was for ease and convenience and to give Dotty the maximum time with her guests. Hilda, the helper; also cleared the table and cleaned up in the kitchen before she went home. She still had time to go to her daughter's for dinner and she had been well paid for her efforts.

There was a welcome fire dancing in the fireplace and the living room was fragrant with the scent from the logs. Dotty had lit her Tiffany lamp and the room had a warm, soft glow. Frank was serving coffee and brandy and they settled back to digest a gourmet dinner. Soft music completed the picture and the ambience was heart warming. Eleanor eyed the tiger; she was sure he moved! After an hour had passed Dotty pleaded being tired and they went up to bed.

In their room Frank hugged her and said; "You were tired; some joke."

"If I left things up to you Gordon would still be talking about that car!"

"Well; he loves his car!"

"He's in love with Eleanor; that's more important!"

"You think it's that serious already?"

"I think," dear husband, "that tomorrow we will hear they are engaged!"

"You think you engineered that already?"

"I am positive! Now, let's go to bed; and don't tell me you ate too much."

He went to her and took her in his arms; in a trice her night gown was off. He was kissing her with a passion that had not diminished over the years.

They had a light breakfast in the morning and went for a walk through the orchard. Eleanor and Gordon were holding hands and Dotty shot Frank a meaningful look. After twenty minutes or so they paused by a pond where a pony was drinking. It never paused and was obviously at home with humans.

"One never has a camera at these times; it really is a picture."

"I'll run back and get my easel and brushes, Eleanor," teased Frank.

"Why not grab your camera, genius," Dotty was grinning.

They were all laughing and suddenly Gordon put his arm around Eleanor saying; "Now!" He looked at Eleanor; "we want you to know; we're engaged!"

Frank caught Dotty's triumphant look as they hugged and congratulated them. He should never doubt her capabilities; she wanted this to happen and happen it did! She immediately wanted to plan a party for them but Gordon stopped her and said they would do something in the city. Most of the guests would reside in the city so it made sense that the celebration be there. Frank and Dotty could stay with Gordon.

"We're thinking Christmas Eve," Gordon concluded.

"Oh, that is lovely," cooed Dotty, "he'll never be able to forget it, Eleanor. And the present can't be considered a Christmas present!"

Frank tapped her on the head, gently. "That's enough, old girl; enough!"

As it turned out; Cleo and Manny threw the party in the penthouse.

Sunday evening Eleanor heard Brian's door close; she knocked on the connecting door and stuck her head in.

"Are you decent darling?"

"Reasonably," came the reply.

She came and hugged him; he saw the glow emanating from her.

"Out with it; it must be earth-shaking!"

"It is, darling; I'm engaged!"

He was struck! "This is the big bang!" he hugged her. "No pun intended."

She slapped him, playfully; "How dare you!"

"I was thrown by the announcement! After all . . . sweetheart; I presume it's Gordon; whom I've never met."

"You will; just give me time."

"Give you time? Honey; you pulled this off in jig time!"

"What a beastly thing to say! I'm overwhelmed by it all, too."

He hugged her again; "You know I'm putting you on . . . relax!"

"Step up to my bar;" dear fiancé, this calls for my best brandy!"

"Dare I?" She waxed coy.

"Dare you not?" He almost spilled the brandy from laughing.

They talked longer than they should have . . . they couldn't stop! They would regret it in the morning; but a reviving shower usually did the trick.

Jerry's co-workers had planned a retirement party for him and the day had arrived. He had gone back to having a shooter occasionally but only when he was at a bar alone. Subconsciously he wanted people to think he was still on beer only. It was being held at a restaurant owned by two retired cops. It was no place for anyone but a policeman to be. The conversation was either the 'job' or women. The 'job' was discussed at the outset and as the drinking increased women became the topic. Jerry was generally well-liked and they had received enough money from the guys 'chipping in' to purchase a handsome wristwatch. He had taken a personal day off the next day to recuperate. It was quite a bash!

Jerry had not driven to the party in his car; Tom had picked him up and he was going to take a cab home. Tom had left fairly early for reasons known to all. Now Jerry was quite drunk and he decided to walk a bit and sober up a little. He didn't want to go home to Nora smashed. But deep down he had a hidden reason to walk and his footsteps took him to one of those dark side streets where he sought his secret satisfaction. It would take a while; but it would happen.

A little past three o'clock Nora was awakened by a severe coughing spell; she had somehow slid off her pillows and was lying on her back. She got to a sitting position with a great deal of difficulty; she couldn't breathe and the hacking shook her whole body. There was only about a tablespoon of her medication in the bottle; earlier she had been coughing a lot so she doubled up on the dosage. She was able to get the medicine down but the cough was relentless. At this hour Nora thought Jerry would be home and she didn't want to wake him. She went to her bathroom and closed the door; taking a thick bath towel she folded it and pressed it against her face to muffle the sound. Standing by the bath tub she pressed the towel firmer as the cough worsened; a fainting feeling was coming over her but she failed to realize it. Facing the bath tub she leaned against it for support; she was leaning into the tub and gradually she fainted; falling forward into the tub. Her feet were off the floor and her face was pressed firmly into the towel. Nora was fighting for air; but she was weak and helpless. Gradually she stopped breathing; thin blood vessels could not stand the pressure and one by one they ruptured. In this ignoble position this lovely lady died.

About five o'clock Jerry staggered to the front door; with difficulty and profanity, albeit in a low voice; he managed to get inside. He started for his room when he noticed Nora's bathroom light under the door. As he approached he saw that her bedroom light was lit. He called her name twice; a serious dread was forming within him and he opened the bathroom door calling her name. What he saw horrified him; he tried to call out her name but only a tight gasp was audible. He knew she was dead; he had enough experience with that! He caved in on his knees, beside her begging God to say this wasn't so. His head was touching the floor; his right hand clutched the hem of her robe; as though trying to pull her back to life. He was filled with the greatest pain he had ever known!

He knelt there sobbing and cursing himself for not being home; he gradually drifted into a stupor until finally his sense of duty took hold and he knew he had things to do. Nora had instructed him in this department.

He went to the leather box in her dresser draw and opened it. Inside were four envelopes; the top one bore his name. He sat on her bed and read it.

Jerry dearest;

No matter how bad you feel now do as I ask and right away. Go to my bank where you have made deposits for me and put things in my safety deposit box. You are on my signature card and can make withdrawals. The key taped to the card board in this box is for the safe deposit box. Take everything out of the box; take the bank book in this box; in this dresser draw is an empty black zipper bag, take it with you. The two envelopes with money in them are for you. It is all the rent money you paid me. Jerry, dear, having you with me was such a loving comfort I couldn't take rent from you. He broke down; sobbing and heaving.

The letter went on; the envelope marked Thomas Sullivan is for my lawyer; he goes to my church, his address is inside; but you have taken me there and met him so you know where to go. His phone number is in his envelope as well. He will arrange my funeral; I have instructed him as to my wishes. You will have my home to use as you see fit. Mr. Sullivan will explain the trust to you.

Jerry, my boy, it lets me die with pleasure to know I can leave you with security; I know the life you grew up in and none of that is your fault. I want you to know that I had no real life until you came along. God sent you, I'm sure; I could not have had a son any better than you. Take care of yourself and don't have me worrying from my grave; thank you for all the lovely things you did for me and all the pretty flowers. Have masses said for me.

Love,
Nora

The words disappeared as the tears blurred his vision; he sat on her bed and gave in to his grief; his hand gently stroking the coverlet. As soon as it was a decent hour he would call Thomas Sullivan; Mr. Sullivan was going to get an early arousal! He had to get some sleep! One look in the mirror brought a groan. Taking care of her wishes would keep him occupied for a while; but the time he spent before he came home haunted him. If he had come straight home he might have prevented this; it would continue to haunt him and being retired and having money was going to give him too much time to grieve . . . in the bars. He vowed he would never make another trip down those dark streets. He would do that for Nora; he felt he owed her that.

He made it through the funeral in pretty good shape; at the wake he refused to go out for drinks with his buddies. Jerry was amazed at the attendance; she seemed to have touched a lot of people and he was touched by the many mourners who came on his behalf. Before they closed the casket the undertaker removed her wedding ring and gave it to Jerry as per Nora's instruction. The church was filled with people and the floral arrangements would have pleased her no end. He was sure she was sitting up there on a fluffy cloud; drinking a beer and clucking away at the fanfare for her. He smiled; his eyes filling with tears. He did not see Eleanor at the funeral parlor; they met outside of the church. She offered her condolences; she and Brian had sent a beautiful arrangement. He thanked her; they shook hands and he was called to other guests. Nora did not want any kind of luncheon or party of any kind for the attendees; *it was not proper... not at all!* She did not want a celebration of her departure.

Thomas Sullivan met with Jerry in his office and explained her affairs. He gave Jerry receipts for the money he had spent from the escrow account he held for her. He took him through the workings of the trust and Jerry found out that he was paying no taxes on his inheritance.

"Nora had some very good advice before I took over her affairs; she made good investments, Jerry, I think you are in for a surprise." Jerry was astonished at the worth of her estate; he never dreamed he would have that kind of money.

"I'm floored by what she's accomplished," he whispered; how did she do it? She got nothing from her husband; I know that!"

"She worked for people who gave her expert advice. One of her clients even put money in her account with her to get her started. People loved her; I loved her. Every time I saw her name in my appointment book I knew I was having a good day. When she closed my door, leaving; I was still laughing."

Jerry made arrangements to have Tom Sullivan handle his affairs; he changed nothing. He had to take some time and absorb all this; he was bewildered.

He dropped out of sight for two weeks; Brian had tried to call him but he was never home. He was retired now; so his other phone numbers were of no use. They wanted to bring him out East for a change of scenery. Both of them were aware of how he felt about losing Nora and they sympathized with him. If he came out East he could do some work and walk on the beach and perhaps feel better. Jerry was home and he was hitting the bottle. He didn't bother with beer; he was drinking whiskey right from the bottle most of the time. He remembered to keep eating; walking to nearby restaurants and getting take-out food. His appearance was bum-looking; he was unshaven and generally messy. The daily shower was still a ritual . . . mostly to wake up.

One morning he answered the phone; it was Brian.

"Jerry, we've been trying to reach you for two weeks; have you been away? We are worried about you."

"I've been in and out, Brian." His voice was raspy.

"From what I'm hearing you've been in and out of the bottle!"

"Don't get on me, Brian; I'm too down to handle it."

"I want to help you; if you're drinking alone that is a bad sign; you need friends now; the bottle is not a friend. Come out East with us this week-end and get out in the air and get some exercise."

"I don't think I can make it, Brian,"

"Yes you can; you have three days to dry out a little and get in shape. If you need laundry done or anything like that; Tony will come and take care of it."

"I'm the one who needs laundering; I haven't shaved in two weeks!"

"Well start by shaving every day and wearing clean clothes; don't tell me you haven't showered for two weeks!"

"I'm not that bad; I've showered and I've been eating."

"Why don't you let Tony pick you up Thursday and then we can leave Friday evening from Tony's apartment. You can bunk on his couch."

"I don't want to be a pain in the ass, Brian."

"I'd be the first to tell you if you were; start shaving and Tony will call you and tell you when he is coming. And, Jerry; answer your phone! Bye . . . bye."

In spite of how he felt Jerry smiled; he really did want to go with them. He had already showered but he showered again. He used an electric razor to remove the heavy beard and twenty minutes later he shaved with a safety razor to get a clean shave. The need of a drink was gnawing at him; he went to the kitchen and filled a shot glass one-third full. Then he filled it with water. Taking only a sip at a time he made it last five minutes. That was quite an accomplishment considering how he had been gulping it right from the bottle. He felt better. Now if he could keep doing that and gradually decrease the amount of shot glasses he would be in pretty good shape by Thursday. Tony called and said he would pick him up Thursday afternoon about four o'clock. He didn't chit chat and hung up shortly.

Tony and Jerry waited until Brian came from work; then they went to the bar. Jerry had a few beers which he nursed; he was not talkative and they didn't press him. He certainly wasn't himself or he would have had many questions as to the reason Gino seemed to be running the bar. Tony fixed dinner; then he went behind the bar so Gino could have a dinner-break. He sat by himself and did not join Brian and Jerry. When Mario; Gino's helper, arrived they went to Tony's apartment and got ready for the Friday night trip. As soon as Brian came from work they would take off. Brian had a friend call and make a phony appointment which would be canceled at three-thirty; that would give them an early start. He didn't like doing it but with Eleanor just beginning her new job he didn't want to be asking favors so soon. The staff might consider it favoritism and he wasn't sure what Cleo would think; he wasn't giving her the opportunity!

Brian took a cab from work and as soon as he was inside he announced that he would take a quick shower and be ready to go. Jerry helped Tony load the wagon and in a short time they were off. But not off and running; the week-end traffic had begun and progress would be slow until they were well out in Suffolk County on the Expressway. After the usual stop to eat in Hampton Bays; they continued to the cottage. The lights were lit and the place looked very inviting. The weather was still warm enough for the plants to thrive and the retaining wall was an attractive entry. Jerry and Tony unloaded the car and Brian got a fire going. It was chilly; but the heat was on and the place was not uncomfortable.

"You've really done a job on this place . . . it looks terrific!" Jerry was truly impressed with what they had accomplished since he had been here.

"You had a hand in it, Jerry; we don't forget that." Tony patted his back; "we get a lot of compliments on that retaining wall!"

"That is the truth." Brian agreed, "the Gospel truth."

They went out on the deck and lit cigarettes; Brian offered to make coffee but no one was interested. He purposely didn't mention drinks. It was after eleven and turning in and getting some rest was unanimous. They went to their rooms; Jerry was non-plussed at how matter-of-factly they slept together.

Surprisingly Jerry went to sleep in a short time; he awoke about four and went to the bathroom. Coming into the living room he lit a cigarette and poured a glass of ice water. He was aching for a shooter. There was a stirring behind him; it was Tony.

"Early kidney call, Jerry?" He smiled at him.

"Yes, a regular thing with me."

"Me, too; I hope it's not a sign of old age!"

"We never will admit to that, Tony!" They chuckled.

Tony noticed Jerry was edgy; "Feel like you need a drink?"

Jerry nodded; "I'm afraid I do."

"Let me fix you something; it might help. I'll have one, too."

He went to the kitchen; taking two high ball glasses he filled them with ice and poured club soda half-way. He added several drops of bitters and twisted a slice of lemon in the glass and stirred.

"Try this."

Jerry gingerly took a sip and rolled it around in his mouth; he smiled. "It tastes like a drink!" He marveled. "I can't describe it."

"Neither can any body else!" Tony was laughing. "But it refreshes."

"It's good for 'hot coppers' I can tell you that!" Jerry had perked up.

They sat in the living room and talked; Jerry became very confidential with Tony and even told him about the inheritance. He had not even told Tom; his partner; whom he did not see much of lately.

"Have you thought about what you're going to do; like investing?"

"Nora had good financial advice and she made excellent choices; the portfolio brings in nice dividends which she put right back into investments. She really lived on her Social Security. I'm leaving that alone."

He explained the irrevocable trust and Tony was familiar with it. He had one with Brian as trustee. He related what she did with the rent money he had paid her; he broke down in sobs. Tony almost joined him; there was a stinging in his eyes.

"I'm sorry, Tony; I didn't want to do that."

"You should cry for her; she was wonderful and she loved you. Don't apologize for that; she deserves your tears; grieving is necessary."

Jerry had two more drinks; he made the third one himself; Tony hoped he had shown him the way to avoid shooters. They returned to their rooms.

The next morning they were all up early; Brian started a pot of coffee and turned to them;

"Let's take a short walk down the beach while the coffee is brewing. I'll fix breakfast when we get back."

"Sounds good to me," said Jerry. Tony was out on the deck.

After breakfast Tony laid out several things he wanted to take care of and they each pitched in and assisted. Jerry was making a brick base to stack the fire wood on keeping it off the ground. He decided to make two of them one at each end of the retaining wall. Tony gave his okay to the idea and Jerry had both of them finished by Sunday afternoon. Jerry advised them not to put any weight on them until next week. The bases were at right angles to the walls which were about sixteen feet apart as one approached the cottage. When the logs were stacked neatly on them it created an inviting, rustic entrance to the cottage. All this was keeping Jerry occupied and drinking only a few beers. There were no trips to Montauk and they had all their meals at home. Eleanor was not mentioned.

They were back in the city late Sunday night and they took Jerry home. He certainly looked better and as he thanked them he told them he felt better. He was invited to join them next week-end and he said he would call.

Monday morning at the salon Eleanor's party was the main topic of discussion. They were booking appointments so the day would end about four. The restaurant was a short walk from the salon and the reservation was for five. That would leave enough time for 'freshening up' for all. Cleo told them that Eleanor requested there be no gifts. "Please honor her request." There was the usual 'buzzing' among the staff but the arrival of clients sent them all scrambling to their stations. Eleanor and Cleo were going over the method of ordering supplies and they were totally absorbed for the day.

Brian and Eleanor went home together and had a night cap at Eleanor's. They talked about the coming party for a while and then he asked her about her engagement.

"Cleo and Manny are hosting a party for us at their penthouse; I am so overwhelmed with all this . . . suddenly I'm in the middle of all these sophisticated people and, I might add, wealthy people! I'm feeling a bit inadequate; Gordon assures me I have no reason to be. I love his friends upstate; they are down to earth and so much fun!" Seeing her so animated filled his heart with joy.

"Listen, darling; you are made of pure platinum; don't think for one second that *anyone* is better than you! Gordon is no fool; he is surrounded by so-called sophisticated women in this city and I'm sure the hooks were out for him; but he wants quality. Quality, my dear; is your middle name."

She squeezed his hand; "You're always there for me."

"When is this announcement party going to happen?"

"Christmas Eve."

"*Christmas Eve?* That's one way to pare down a guest list! People are tied up with family things. Whose idea was this?"

"It's not going to be a big party; we figure about fifty people. I hope you and Tony will come; I'm not telling Edith about it. My sister is the only relative I have. Inviting any of my former in-laws would be awkward. I'll send out announcements after we're married."

"When is that big day going to be?"

"We don't know yet; that will be a small affair as well."

"I'll talk to Tony about it; I'm sure he will want to come to your party. If he doesn't want to go I'll come alone . . . or bring Edith!"

They laughed as she screamed and ended in a hug. He headed for the door.

The following evening Brian went home after work and showered and changed clothes. Grabbing a cab he went to Tony's and planned to have supper there. When he entered Gino was behind the bar; Tony must be in the kitchen and Gino pointed that direction confirming his guess. He went in; they greeted each other;

"Meatballs tonight are you interested?" He uncovered the pot.

Brian stuck his head over it and inhaled. "You bet I am!"

"Go out and get a seat; I'll be there in a couple of minutes."

He went to the restroom and washed up; putting deodorant under his arms. Then he joined Brian at the bar. Gino had served Brian a drink and came to see what Tony wanted.

"Just a beer, please, Gino." Tony replied.

"It's nice to hear you say please," twitted Brian; "now I'm pleased."

"Listen; he owns the place now; I have to be polite." He poked Brian.

When they had finished eating Brian filled him in on Eleanor's party. He asked Tony if he would go with him;

"It's Christmas Eve; I want to be with you."

Slowly he shook his head; he had no intention of going to that party.

"That is not my scene Brian, I would suffocate. Hear me out! You go to the party; I don't think you will stay late. I will get everything ready to go out East; when you leave the party, take a cab to my apartment and we'll take off. I'll get some sleep while you party; just call me."

"But Tony!" Tony held up his hand; "You have to go! We'll have the rest of Christmas. You will regret it if you don't go; I insist that you go!"

"I'll go; but I'm going to leave as early as I can."

"I'll make you a promise, Brian; I'll go to her wedding; but not the reception. Will that be okay with you? Don't ask me to do what I can't do."

"That will be fine and she will understand; thank you, Tony."

Tony squeezed the nape of his neck; "you are most welcome, partner."

They discussed Jerry's situation;

"I think he might be drying out, Tony; he was good over the week-end. He needs to keep busy."

"He's got Christmas ahead of him; that is a tough time for drinkers who are brooding. He's retired now and Nora willed him a lot of money. He has time and money; that is a bad combination for unhappy drinkers."

"She left him a lot of money?" Brian was impressed; "I wouldn't have thought Nora had a lot of money."

"He told me; we both were up for an early trip to the loo and we talked for a while. She had an irrevocable trust with a very good portfolio and he is the sole heir to it. The house is his; there's no mortgage on it, and all of the rent he had paid her she saved and it was all in cash in her safe deposit box. And she had a bank account and his name was on the signature card. The bank book was in the safe deposit box, too."

"He's rich!" Brian said excitedly; and don't forget the furniture and other antiques she has. That will add up to a tidy sum. I hope he doesn't go ape."

"He wouldn't be the first one to drink up a fortune." Tony looked sad.

"We should bring him out East as often as we can. He loves to work and he has good ideas. Maybe he will get a little place across the harbor and we can visit him by boat; when we get one." Brian was all enthusiasm.

"We will; in the spring, we wouldn't use it in the winter, we can look around in the mean-time. I think we should get a pram with a small out board motor. We could even get an electric motor; they are very quiet." Tony was eager.

"I didn't know they made electric boat motors; and what is a pram?

"It's a flat-bottom boat and both the bow and the stern are straight and they go slightly upward at each end. They're designed for shallow water and the harbor has a lot of that. One about fifteen feet long should do it." Tony smiled.

"You've got me all excited now; you know so much about everything!"

Brian was poking him and the guys at the bar were watching them carry on.

The Monday for Eleanor's party came and it went off very well. The staff was happy to have Eleanor in charge and assured her of their support. Cleo was a gracious hostess and she made a warm, humorous speech which she kept short. Expressing her appreciation of their loyalty and capability Cleo made them all feel good. There was no mention of her marriage. Edith was in excellent spirits and she looked sensational; wearing a fitted knit raspberry-colored dress that clung to her new figure she was an example of a woman in love.

Brian and Eleanor went home in a cab and went to her place for a night cap. "Come in the kitchen and be bartender; I need to sit and relax."

"Does a tall, cold gin and tonic sound good? A twist of lime, maybe?"

"Right on the money, honey!" She flashed him a smile.

He busied himself making the drinks; she excused herself to change into her robe. She returned her hair brushed loosely framing her face; a general ease about her.

"Here you are, Madam Manager; and may I drink a toast to thee?"

"Sit down and stop that nonsense! It was a nice party and it's over."

"Excusez-moi! I'm just feeling festive and you deflated my balloon."

"I will really stick pins in you; you'll end up a cushion!"

"In French cushion is almost pig."

"If the shoe fits, darling; curl up your tail!"

They were laughing and he pretended to slap her. After rehashing the party for a while, both giving Edith praise for her appearance and good humor; Brian related to her how Tony felt about going to her engagement party.

"Whatever makes him comfortable; but I am happy you will both make my wedding. That is important to me; I want you both to know Gordon."

He began telling her about the rentals he had made and how Ed was very pleased with his progress. And he had sold a lot! His first sale. She was happy for him.

"I might be asking you for long week-ends this winter; I'd like to put more time in the office. I really love the business, El; I think I'm made for it."

"I'm sure we will be able to work it out; nothing is impossible."

"I'm going to tell you a secret; Tony sold the bar to Gino."

She gasped; "that is wonderful; I'm not really surprised; Tony wants to live out East and I don't blame him! And that's why you want long week-ends; I'm going to lose you!" She hugged him.

"That won't happen; we'll always be in touch."

He was very serious about that statement; her friendship was important to him. They finally said good night and parted with uplifted spirits.

Brian called Jerry and lined him up for the next week-end. He was a little hesitant but Brian leaned on him and he agreed to go. He wanted to check on the brick work he had done anyway. Brian decided to tell him that Eleanor was going to be engaged. Tony was in agreement; they shouldn't have to feel they couldn't mention her. It was an enjoyable week-end and they accomplished a lot. Jerry drank a few beers and also a few of 'Tony's Special.' He had picked up some bitters and club soda for use at home. When he was told about Eleanor he said it was wonderful for her and she was a fine lady who deserved the best. He promised to come out again the following week-end. They had ordered the material they would need and it was enough to keep Jerry busy. His years of working in the CCC and getting experience were paying off.

Gordon had been seeing Eleanor as frequently as she could make the time. He took her out to dinner so often she was forgetting how to cook! They were leaving the Monsignor one evening and he asked her to come to his place for a brandy. "I'd like you to see my apartment; if you're going to live there with me you might want to redecorate." He smiled as he opened the car.

"That would be a bit cheeky I think; in fact it would be an insult."

"I wouldn't feel that way; seriously, I want you to feel free to do what you wish. I haven't done any redecorating since I moved in. Why don't we wait until you see it?" She agreed.

It was a co-op overlooking Central Park. Eighteen floors up with eight large rooms and a lovely terrace. Eleanor just drifted through the place voicing one superlative after another. He had eclectic taste and no decorator had palmed off any exotic clap trap on him.

"Redecorate indeed! She poked his chest; "you were toying with me!"

He took her in his arms and kissed her; longingly.

"I wasn't; I swear to you I meant what I said."

"It's beautiful, Gordon; you have some wonderful paintings."

"I'm not one for modern art; if I'm going to hang something on my wall I want to enjoy looking at it. I don't want to have to try and figure out what it is."

He selected two snifters and poured the Courvoisier. He had turned on soft music while she was looking the place over. They sat on the couch and talked for a while; he began making love to her and she responded warmly. She trusted him and felt a deep security in his arms; he had previously told her he loved her and thought he was never going to find someone like her. Their passion became heated and he led her to the bedroom. They undressed quickly and he embraced her pressing his body into hers; she was filled with desire.

"Gordon; "she whispered, I have to tell you; I haven't had a man since my husband died; I might be awkward, please understand."

"You've told me something wonderful." His voice was husky.

He picked her up and gently settled her on the bed; she was amazed at his strength and was keenly aware of the muscular frame of his body. His regular work-outs at the athletic club got results . . . there were no love handles to be found. Sliding his body across hers he lay next to her wrapping her slender body with his. Gordon kissed her softly, gradually becoming more passionate; his hands seemed to be caressing every part of her body at the same time . . . his lips explored every crevice and she was hot with wanting him. He had excellent control and he made love to her until she was screaming for him to take her! Slowly he made his entrance; in short hard thrusts he tantalized her gradually increasing the force. She locked her legs around him demanding more and more; he was now satisfying his own desire and pounded into her powerfully. She climaxed gasping and he did likewise; roaring like a lion! They lay there for a long time; he on top of her, his head buried in the fragrance of her hair. Eleanor was completely spent; she had never had such a blanket!

The next morning they fixed a light breakfast together. Gordon had a houseman but he did not live in. There was a bistro table and chairs by the glass wall overlooking the terrace; they sat there eating. It was too chilly to use the terrace. He was having his breakfast with one hand; the other was on her arm or shoulder or her thigh. He had to touch her! The topic was on one subject; he wanted her to move in; pronto! Eleanor was over-whelmed.

"Gordon; I need some time to do that, getting my things together and . . . well, all of the details of moving, even if it is only clothes; it's a big operation for a woman!" She was shaking her head at him; he kissed her.

"You don't have to do anything but give instructions; I know an expert moving company that will have your things packed, carefully, in jig time. They have equipment that will dazzle your mind. One item is a long garment bag that stands erect and is on casters; they wheel that thing into your bedroom and fill it with your clothes on the hangers and take it to your destination here, in the master bedroom and into your walk-in closet. They have similar things with drawers and do the same routine. There are two double dressers in the bedroom plus other furniture for storage. That bedroom has been waiting for you; don't keep it in its lonesome state any longer; please!"

She smiled, wistfully; "I'll bet you have never lost a case in court."

"Not many," sweetheart; "but if I lose this one it will break my heart."

She was in his arms, kissing him, she sighed; "it looks like Eleanor is moving!"

Brian was dismayed when she told him the latest development.

"I could grow to dislike that guy very easily; what's his hurry?"

Gordon would have had a concise reply for him; "I'm sixty-three!" Eleanor was moved as quickly and expertly as promised. Gordon took care of the moving expenses; in fact she never saw a bill. When she attempted to tip the movers she was told it was all taken care of. In addition to that he insisted on taking over her rent payment and told her not to give up the apartment until she felt comfortable doing it. This kind of attention left her dizzy; and it was just starting! Gordon knew he had found a woman with principles . . . a gold mine!

It seemed like it happened over-night; Christmas Eve was two days off. Cleo and Manny were hosting the party but they included Eleanor and Gordon in the plans. Cleo had wonderful taste and was a born organizer so everything was pretty much left to her. Eleanor was having a dinner dress made and was very excited with the process. It was an Empire line of chiffon in folds of ice blue, mulberry and silver. The high waist was circled with a wide band of crystals. Having a gown fitted to you from its inception should happen to every woman at least once. At the final fitting she looked at herself in the full length mirror and tears rimmed her eyes. *It was so beautiful!* The girls in the fitting room gathered around her and gushed over how she looked. Eleanor swept her hair in an updo fashion and they chorused "Oh; yes!" She had crystal earrings that covered the ear lobe and a thin choker-like necklace of tiny diamonds. She would wear no rings; leaving room for the ring he would put on her finger.

Brian was getting ready for the big evening; he missed her being near to him. He realized he was planning to make the move out East and would be doing the same thing to her. "Both our lives are moving in different directions." He said to his reflection. He took a cab to Cleo's and was on time; most New Yorkers arrive 'fashionably' late so he hoped he'd have some time with Eleanor. The lobby made quite an impression on him as did the ride in the second elevator that serviced the two penthouses. "My Eleanor has turned into Cinderella with the right sized foot!" He mused aloud. The door to the penthouse was open; a side table under a beautifully framed mirror held a show-stopping bouquet. Brian admired Cleo's talent. Just as he was thinking of her she appeared; looking like a million bucks. "Welcome Brian; say hello to Manny, my fiancé." They chatted as they entered the living room Brian exclaiming over the interior. Eleanor came toward him; Gordon on her heels. She looked stunning! Gordon beamed with pride. Not even Cleo could out shine his girl; she was a knock-out!

"Oh, I'm so glad you came early; I've wanted you to meet Gordon and have some time to get acquainted." Brian raised his brows as usual; his eyes were slits. "Early? Do you think I would arrive at a soiree *early*?"

She was laughing, so was Gordon; "a thousand pardons, darling."

Cleo arrived with a martini; "Did I guess right?"

"Perfect Cleo; your usual touch."

Gordon liked him immediately and reacted to his humor. "I've heard a great deal about you and I hope you won't hold it against me for stealing your wonderful neighbor." They shook hands.

"I'm not over the shock yet; I'm numb."

Eleanor excused herself for a moment and Gordon and Brian could talk.

"I hear you have a place in Amagansett, Brian, I have some friends who have homes out there and in East Hampton. It is a beautiful part of Long Island."

"I love it; we're on Napeague Harbor; next to the Art Barge."

"I've seen the barge; some of my friends know Victor very well. I didn't go inside; they were having classes the day we were there."

"We are east of the barge; right next to it. We've been remodeling the old cottage that my friend bought some years ago." Brian explained.

"It's a perfect location; the privacy must be wonderful." Gordon added.

"It is . . . and the wild life there is a study in itself. All kinds of birds!"

Eleanor returned and they chatted; Eleanor telling Gordon about the cottage. Gordon went to refresh their drinks. There were servers; but he showed what a gentleman he was and the extent of his considerate nature.

"You look gorgeous, darling, and you have a winner! And he is sexy!"

She blushed and Brian knew all he had to know; Gordon was fantastic in bed!

The place was quite alive with guests now and they had to make their rounds. A good guest makes the rounds also and chats with people. Brian did this very well and was enjoying himself. There was an elegant buffet on a perfectly laid table; Cleo really had a special knack and the food was delicious and served so it was easy to eat. At nine o'clock Manny called everyone to order and made the announcement; each guest held a glass of champagne and Gordon slipped the ring on her finger; Eleanor gasped; as did many guests. It was a seven caret solitaire set in platinum. It certainly made a statement! Manny gave the toast and everyone milled around congratulating the couple. A wife of one of the guests told her husband he should have gone shopping with Gordon; it got a laugh from the crowd but the husband was thinking of the gem he had given his mistress!

Christmas was on a Friday this year and Brian had arranged to have Monday off. Monday and Tuesday would not be busy at the salon but Wednesday and Thursday would be wild because of New Years Eve. He had waited until they opened their gifts at the party; he had sent his a few days before. Saying goodnight to Gordon and Eleanor he was making his exit; he paid his respects to Cleo, Manny was engrossed in conversation so he didn't disturb him. It was almost nine thirty and he was delighted; he hadn't expected to leave so early. He called Tony; who was also delighted, and went out to hail a cab. Arriving about ten; Tony had the wagon parked in front of his apartment. Everything was stowed in the wagon; Tony had a thermos of coffee; "Do you want a cup before we take off?" Brian had changed his clothes and was ready to roll. "No, thanks."

They were on their way by ten thirty; it was Thursday night and traffic would get lighter as they traveled. Having a long week-end was uplifting and spending Christmas at the cottage was something to look forward to. Tony had arranged to have a tree delivered to the front door and the trimmings were already at the cottage. They were on the Expressway moving very well; Brian had been relating the happenings at the party when he paused;

"I guess you didn't hear from Jerry."

Tony shook his head; "Not a word."

"I guess he'll be on a bender for a week. I hate to see him fall back."

"You're beginning to treat him like a patient, doctor."

"Oh, you didn't put your wit to bed yet! Want a cup of coffee?"

"Please; I can be bought cheap; a cup of joe will do it."

"I have to keep you bright-eyed and bushy tailed."

"I can think of other ways; want to hear them?"

"Sail your ship onward, captain; you're not in port yet!"

Brian turned the radio on keeping the volume down.

"Will that make you drowsy?"

"No not at all; it sounds nice."

They road in silence for a while; drinking coffee and listening to the music. Suddenly Brian spoke his thoughts aloud.

"Seven carets in platinum!"

"What the hell are you talking about? You got brandy in your cup?"

Brian was non-plussed; "I was thinking of Eleanor's ring . . . seven carets!"

Tony poked him; "that's coffee money to him; but it does show he cares for her."

"They are in love, Tony; she's a lucky girl . . . he's a stud."

"How do you know that? Don't tell me she told you!"

"No; my God, never! I can tell; I have ESP"

"You better take something for it before it spreads."

They were laughing as Brian put the coffee things away.

After driving about two hours the traffic had thinned out markedly; they were making good time and agreed not to stop in Hampton Bays. Getting to the cottage and putting up the tree had top priority. At last they were driving up their winding driveway relishing the lights of the cottage beckoning to them.

After the wagon was unloaded and the food put away they set about putting the tree up. They had a new, bucket-type tree stand and Tony wanted to put sand in it to make a heavy base; Brian wanted to fill it with water to keep the needles from falling too soon and it was decided to stop and have a drink and discuss the matter. Tony solved the dilemma; he inserted a large tin can in the stand and almost filled it with water. Then they put the tree in the can and blocked the tree securely; now Tony filled the stand with sand up to the rim of the can and every body was happy. In fact; they had another drink!

The tree was placed under the circular stairway; it was about twenty feet from the fireplace and could be readily seen from outside between the glass walls. It made putting ornaments on top easy because they could reach there from the stairs. No ladder was necessary. That was a good thing considering how many drinks they were downing! Tony called a halt and said he was hungry; they went into the kitchen and he made an antipasto. The Christmas music meant more to each of them; they were having their first Christmas together.

The tree all trimmed; they admired their handiwork, they went outside in front of the house and over to the deck on the harbor side. Their tree looked beautiful; there were numerous tiny lights that reflected colorfully off all the ornamentation. Shaking hands they congratulated each other and went inside and had another drink! It was almost two o'clock; Brian's family always got together for Midnight Mass and would be home now celebrating Christmas Eve. He was calling them and he beckoned to Tony to join him; he introduced Tony to them on the phone and Tony could hear the music in the back ground. They had a warm conversation for about a half hour and Brian turned to Tony and hugged him. His eyes were teary and he assured Tony he was just so happy. Tomorrow would be their time to open presents and Kincaid was going to open his place at one o'clock for his clientele who had no place to go at Christmas. They had gifts for him and Bob and were planning to eat there; if he was sober enough to cook.

Everyone thought he was so thoughtful for opening; Montauk business was just about shut down. The underlying truth was that he couldn't stand being home with his screaming wife and the three kids who screamed with her! If ever there was a man who should have remained a bachelor; it was Robert Kincaid! Brian and Tony began to realize they were sagging; they went to bed and slept.

About ten o'clock they were in the kitchen having breakfast. It was a clear day and the harbor was a sparkling blue. It was cold outside and a good day to have a roaring fire in the living room. The smell of the logs added to the holiday spirit. After breakfast they exchanged gifts and relaxed in their robes; a fairly good wind had come up and the harbor was frothy with white caps. Brian had spread the breakfast leftovers on the shore and a myriad of gulls were fluttering and clamoring at the buffet. Standing at the glass door they sipped coffee and watched the avian maneuvers; Tony said; "it's simply disappearing!" Even though it was a bright morning the Christmas tree was lit; it still brightened the room. Brian had hung a big, festive wreath on the front door and that was the extent of the decorating outside. Slightly after three they headed toward Montauk and made their way to Kincaid's. Most of the vehicles in the parking lot were pick-up trucks; Tony noticed Henry's truck and was surprised.

"That's Henry's truck; I wonder what he's doing here."

"Do you think Techla is with him?" Brian asked.

"We'll soon see; "Do you think Bob will be playing?"

"Where else would he be?" Brian rationalized.

They entered and were regaled with many 'Merry Christmas' wishes from all over the place. Bob was just starting to play a set and broke into a lively 'Hail, hail the gang's all here.' Kincaid was on his way to greet them; both arms outstretched. After the good wishes they noticed Henry and Techla at the bar and immediately went to greet them. They were dressed up; Henry in a suit shirt and tie and Techla in a pretty dress and showing the results of a trip to the beauty salon. She had make up on and looked like a different woman. They had a Christmas drink together and many laughs; Techla being a spectator.

By four o'clock the place had filled up; the spirit was contagious and the *spirits* were flowing. Brian and Tony met some people who lived on the other side of the harbor and they mentioned how they noticed all the activity at the cottage. One couple knew the original owner and filled them in on some history of the place; including a bit of rum running! Tony sang a few songs and that seemed to open an inroad into everyone's good graces. They were having a lot of fun; it was totally unexpected; they had thought it would be just the two of them most of the week-end. They would have been happy with that arrangement; but this was a wonderful bonus. Between six and seven there was a marked thinning out of the crowd; some of them had been celebrating non-stop since Christmas Eve. Henry and Techla were still there and were now sharing a booth with Brian and Tony. Tony was on his way back from the rest room and Bob told him he was going to close the place around seven-thirty; "Before somebody starts a fight." Tony called Brian from the table and asked him how he felt about inviting some of the people back to the cottage. Henry told me that Techla wanted to have us come for supper but he doesn't want her to cook today. I think eight would be enough. I'm pretty sure the two Bobs would come; Kincaid doesn't want to go home. We have plenty of food." Brian was all for it.

As expected the two Bobs were happy to accept; Tony offered to give them a lift home later on. Henry and Techla were delighted; Techla had heard so much about the changes to the place she was anxious to see it. The couple from across the harbor was coming and so were their neighbors. At seven Bob announced he was closing and his customers had learned to leave promptly as he was known to throw people out bodily.

By seven-thirty they were all outside and Kincaid; with a large bag under his arm was forming a convoy of the cars. Off they went to the cottage and their first party was at its inception.

The entourage filed into the cottage and words of praise were coming from every corner. Brian started a fire and Kincaid took his package to the kitchen. He took out a half of Virginia ham and a bottle of vodka; there was a variety of food he had cooked that day and would make doing a buffet very easy. Bob the Scot helped making drinks; though every one had been drinking all afternoon, there wasn't a sign of anyone being drunk. Brian turned on the music and the party was in full swing. The mix of people was a spicy stew of humanity and there didn't seem to be a minute without laughter. Techla had drifted through the house and was filled with admiration. She was especially taken with the new kitchen and Henry was being prodded to redo their kitchen.

"You're making trouble for me!" He complained to Tony.

It was comical the way Techla had to go to Henry to have him translate what she wanted to say and with a few drinks in her she was uninhibited and very demonstrative. She also became very affectionate and was hugging every body when she had difficulty communicating; Techla was the life of the party!

By ten o'clock the party began to break up and they all started to say good night. Henry took the two Bobs with him and Tony was relieved of his promise to drive them back to Montauk. All of a sudden the place was quiet; Brian had turned off the music and there was complete peace.

"It was unexpected; but it certainly was a great day and a real merry Christmas; Brian, I think it was the best Christmas of my life."

"They were such an interesting group; I had so many laughs from the expressions I was hearing; especially from the folks who live across the harbor. They seem to have a language of their own." Brian was shaking his head.

Tony continued; "they must have realized we lived here alone and nobody seemed to care about that. I felt completely at ease."

"They accepted us as we appeared; 'nice people'; just as we accepted them and welcomed them into our home. You have to learn to forget you are homosexual, Tony, and live your life as you do. You happen to be very decent!"

Tony came and hugged him; "My best present is having you in my life!" They went to bed shedding a few happy tears.

Jerry Foley was having quite a different holiday; there was plenty of drinking but no merry making. He had laid in a supply of food; mostly cooked take-out and an ample amount of whiskey. He got started Christmas Eve and had a continuous performance ever since. He was numb for the holiday and that is what he wanted. It was Monday evening and he was still drunk; he had kept the door to Nora's room closed since her death and had not entered it. Now he was sitting on her bed stroking the coverlet and crying. The more he thought about his inheritance the guiltier he felt about not being home when she needed him. If he had been working it would not be as painful; there would not be this awful guilt! Only he knew where he was and it burned a hole in his soul. Would he ever be able to get it out of his mind? He didn't think he could. He lay on the bed in pain.

Gordon and Eleanor spent Christmas Day alone. Their engagement was a great success and Frank and Dotty left for Pine Plains very early as they had a holiday commitment there. They also wanted to give Gordon and Eleanor some privacy. Frank was reminded of her match-making ability all the way home! Gordon asked Eleanor if she wanted to go out for dinner and she declined.

"We can scare up something to eat right here. I've looked in your refrigerator and there is plenty to work with. I'd rather stay in and have a fire going and just be alone with you. That will be a wonderful Christmas."

He took her in his arms and held her close; "You are my wonderful Christmas."

They were still in their robes and would stay that way all day. Together they fixed a light breakfast and were sitting on the couch having coffee.

"How would you like to get married on Valentine's Day?

He continually surprised her; and he reveled in doing it.

"This is so sudden!" She teased; what can a girl say?"

"A sensible girl would say 'yes'; wouldn't she?"

"Well; I certainly want to be sensible so I'll say 'yes'!"

He drew her close and was kissing her deeply; their robes landed on the floor and Gordon continued to bring her this wonderful new satisfaction.

The holidays passed; everyone doing his own thing. Jerry was still drinking; Brian and Tony had driven over to see him New Year's Day and he refused to open the door. He promised he would go out East with them on the next week-end and would call them Thursday evening to confirm. They had to go along with him; breaking the door down made no sense. Brian had worked out a deal with Eleanor and he no longer worked Saturday or Monday. He put floor time in Ed Gunther's office every Saturday and Sunday; signing up several good summer rentals had impressed Ed tremendously, clients repeatedly told him how satisfied they were with the way Brian handled things. *He tells the truth*; was a common compliment and a very important one. Toward the end of January Brian sold three high-priced lots and the commission checks began to increase in amount. Tony was thrilled and started hinting about getting Tuesday off, too.

Gino was getting the hang of running the business and Tony thought it would not be long before he could leave permanently. He wanted Brian to make the move with him. Now that Eleanor was gone it was going to be an easier decision. Brian loved the real estate business and riding around looking at listings was giving him an education as to where the different localities were and what they were named. He had a map on his front seat and he familiarized himself with streets in the different areas. When they went anywhere together Brian now did the driving; he knew short cuts and seemed to know where everything was located. Tony was very proud of him and called him his star pupil.

"I believe I'm your only pupil," came the sly thank you.

They had Jerry coming out regularly and he kept reasonably sober. He couldn't be left alone too long before he would start hitting the shooters. Tony knew he had a bottle in his room but he made no comment; not even to Brian. Tony realized something deep was bugging Jerry and so far; he couldn't shake it. To suggest he see a shrink was like shoveling snow against an avalanche.

The month of February had arrived and now the wedding was almost upon them. The plans were all in place and Cleo had been of great assistance to the happy couple. They were happier than anyone knew; Eleanor was pregnant and her doctor told her she was healthy and had no reason to worry about being forty-ish. Gordon was walking on air! He prayed that he would have a son; he did not mention it to Eleanor. His first wish was that mother and child be safe and well. If anything happened to Eleanor . . . he could not let himself think about it.

Although Eleanor had complete faith in her doctor Gordon prevailed upon her to see a highly regarded gynecologist in New York. She complied to keep him happy and received an excellent report. They elected to tell no one at the present time. Cleo would be the first they would tell and it was after the wedding. She would turn out to be a valuable friend and when Eleanor had to stop working she would take over and the business would progress without a hitch. Cleo made the change from business associate to close friend smoothly and without fanfare.

Valentine's Day dawned a bit cold but bright and sunny. Cleo was the maid of honor and Manny was best man. They had offered the penthouse for the reception but Gordon could not impose on them and he and Eleanor arranged the festivities at the Monsignor. Gordon pulled out all the stops and it was going to be plush! He wanted his bride to cherish the day, always; and she certainly would! The ceremony would be in a small old church not very far from the reception. Eleanor was a Catholic but had not been a regular at Mass for many years. She had gone to confession and being pregnant, religion was starting to mean more to her. Gordon never thought about religion and whatever Eleanor wanted suited him. Cleo had closed the salon for the day to give the staff the opportunity to attend the wedding. It was scheduled for one in the afternoon.

Eleanor wore a floor length dress of pale peach lace and a bolero top. The seamstress created a tiara-framed hat of the same material with a nose-length veil. Cleo's dress was floor-length; dark blue in color and made of silk. Her hat was a Juliet-type of the same materiel. There were about a hundred guests and the ceremony was not very long as they did not have a Mass. The organist played the Ave Maria as Eleanor came down the aisle on the arm of her brother-in-law. It was simple with a touch of elegance and that was Eleanor!

Tony changed his mind and went to the reception; it was a sumptuous display of Gordon's love for Eleanor. Gordon had been a prime guest at this restaurant and the management demonstrated its appreciation of his patronage! To say the least; *'A good time was had by all!'*

It was a Thursday and Brian had taken Friday off so they had a long week-end to go out East. Jerry was going with them; when they stopped to pick him up around five-thirty he got into the wagon needing a shave and looking bleary-eyed. Compared to his well-groomed hosts; he looked like a bum! They had decided not to mention the wedding and they had changed their clothes.

"You must have spent hours doing your toilet, Jerry, you never looked more radiant." Brian wanted to emphasize his condition.

"I feel like a toilet so I might as well look like one." Jerry was aloof.

"Let's not start the trip with nonsense, fellows;" Tony interjected, we have a long way to go. Take a nap, Jerry, you can always clean up."

"Thank you, Tony, as always you're very considerate"

He curled up on the seat; using his bag for a pillow and was not heard from until they stopped in Hampton Bays for coffee and a bite to eat. He took his bag of toilet articles into the rest room in the diner and immerged looking quite presentable. It was a rapid transformation and they were impressed. He sat down and looked at Brian;

"Do I meet with your approval?"

"Entirely, sir." They had their first laugh.

Arriving at the cottage they unloaded the wagon and went inside. Between the three of them they brought everything in one trip.

"Want me to make a fire?" Jerry had lit a cigarette.

"Good idea; we can put this stuff away." Tony was feeling good.

Jerry went outside to bring in more logs and inspect his brick work. He breathed in the crisp, salty air and was beginning to feel better. He went back inside and busied himself with the fire. Tony made drinks and handed Jerry one of his 'specials'; Jerry got the message and thanked him. Tony *was* considerate.

"That front entry really looks good, Jerry, we had people here Christmas Day and they all admired it; even though it doesn't have the geraniums now it still has that 'welcome' effect." Brian was taking a cue from Tony to ease off Jerry.

"I'm glad it's still standing." Jerry didn't know what to say.

He felt lucky to have these two friends who didn't ask questions. He picked up his jacket and walked toward the glass door;

"I'm going for a walk."

They made no comment and busied themselves putting stuff away.

"Don't pick on him, Brian; not even in fun. He's got something heavy on his mind and it has nothing to do with Eleanor. I think it's Nora but I have no idea what it could be. God knows he was good to her."

"I realized what you were doing and I'll follow suit. I'm so used to dueling with him that I do it automatically. The kid gloves are on!"

Jerry came back commenting on the chill and said his good nights. They told him to sleep as late as he wished and had a night cap and went to bed.

The three of them slept late; it was almost eleven before Tony came into the kitchen. He was the first to start functioning; Jerry was next; showered and dressed. Tony was in his robe.

"Look at you; all cleaned up and dressed yet!"

"Want me to go to the bakery and pick up some fresh bagels?"

"Great idea; I'll get the keys to the wagon."

Tony came back; Brian trailing behind him, also in his robe.

"You must have had your vitamins, Jerry; you look like you're raring to go!" Brian was pouring a glass of juice.

"Well; at least as far as the bakery. Need anything else?"

"No; I'll have breakfast ready when you get back."

"I can smell the coffee." Jerry said over his shoulder; "See you later."

"He certainly can bounce back;" Brian was a little in awe, "and quick!"

"Let's try and keep him rolling." Tony had his fingers crossed.

During breakfast the subject came up concerning Jerry buying a place out there.

"Are you still thinking about getting a place across the harbor; Jerry?" Tony put the question to him.

"I do think about it. I'd like to do that and have a small place in Florida in the winter. Many guys on the job do that and then they retire to Florida. You can buy nice mobile homes and they are low-priced."

With all his money he's talking low price; thought Brian, aloud he said; "Let's take a ride over there later on; we've never explored that area; we can look for 'for sale' signs. I hear there's a bar at the shore where you can rent row boats Brian was all enthusiasm.

"Maybe they rent out board motors, too; we could do that until we have our own boat." Now Tony was showing a lively interest.

"Well, let's go looking!" Jerry jumped on the band wagon.

About two o'clock they took off in the wagon and took Napeague Meadow Road over to Lazy Point. They passed the haphazard collection of trailers that were nestled in the dunes across from the cottage.

"This place looks charming at night and at a distance; but who would want to live there? It's a slum!" Brian's expression was utter disgust.

"Not me!" Groaned Jerry and they drove over to the other road.

It was narrow and it wound its way along the shore. There were small houses of every description and some definitely home-made. The lots were small and they were built one after the other on the water front. This pristine location had been abused by mankind; but how could this happen? For years there were no restrictions and it was considered undesirable because a half mile south of it was a huge waterfront factory that ground moss bunker; a very smelly fish into fertilizer. The company had ocean-going barges that delivered the fertilizer down south to the tobacco grower's farms. When the factory was processing; the odor blanketed the area for miles. Those who could stand the smell lived there for very little cost. It had one redeeming grace; there was town water supply and no need for wells. Getting potable water so close to the sound was just about impossible. In recent years the factory closed and was torn down; people began buying the old hovels and remodeling them. Uninformed owners sold those water front properties for a song; they thought they had reaped a bonanza buy doubling their money. In fact; they had given the property away for a song! You could still pick up bargains there if you didn't opt for waterfront; actually the waterfront homes rarely came up for sale; if they did there was always a friend or relative waiting to buy it. Realtor signs were non-existent.

Tony made a turn around some high dunes and in front of them was the boat rental place. There was a make-shift parking area and to their left; away from the sound, were a half dozen trailers lined up and occupied. These were rentals put there long before zoning and were grand-fathered in. Facing them was a two story square building; it defied architectural description and was thirsty for paint. A rectangular sign over the door said MULLINS BAR & RESTAURANT.

"I have to see this!" Tony was all excited; "Who owns this?" The only neat thing around were the perfectly lined up row boats; twelve in all and the shack next to them. It was painted white with black trim and had a small sign that said 'rentals.' They went inside for a drink.

"Step right up gentlemen and name your poison."

Spoken by a tall, pot-bellied man with thinning grey hair and the ruddiest complexion any of them had ever seen. They selected stools and ordered. The interior of the place was spick and span and there were several tables and six booths. Tony noticed how clean the bar was especially under the bar. This was a good sign. Each of them ordered beer and it was fresh and sported a creamy head.

"He keeps his pipes clean!" He whispered to Jerry. Jerry nodded.

He came back with the change and introduced himself; another Bob! Tony introduced Jerry and Brian and himself and told him about the cottage.

"Oh, you're the city people who bought that place; you're goin' to have a hell of a time getting water there; I guess you know that already."

Tony had his number immediately; a know-it-all!

"We catch rain water and we take baths in the harbor." Tony would tell him nothing about the well on railroad property! Mullins got a kick out of his answer and laughed heartily; he was missing a few teeth and was unabashed about it. Brian went to the juke box and was delighted with the selections; he played two.

"Who picks out your records?" He asked Mullins.

"I do." He responded; his nose in the air, daring a criticism!

"First class, Mister Mullins; first class." Brian held up his glass.

A young man entered the bar from upstairs; he was short and stocky and Jerry could tell he was a bit retarded; it was his pig-like eyes.

"Mom wants to go to the stores; she wants me to go with her."

He spoke with a strange kind of accent; like his father. It was local and it was called Bonac after a section in the Springs part of East Hampton Town.

"Well get in the truck and go with her! His voice was loud and harsh.

"Do I have to?"

Mullins came around the bar like a zephyr and grabbed him by the neck.

"Get in that goddam truck; now!" His son scooted out.

"Sorry gentlemen, that's the only way to move him; his mother can't."

"Well he certainly moved!" Tony observed; and they all laughed.

"You know, you should come over on Saturday night; there's always a good crowd. A lot of dancing; they all like to dance."

That's why the good selections on the juke box! Brian didn't think he made them.

"We have good home-cooked food; my wife does the cooking."

He bought a round of drinks; *he's a good business man; thought Tony.*

"Any good buys ever happen around here? Like a small place; I just retired from the city police department and I'm alone; I don't want a big place."

He shook Jerry's hand; "My father was on the city force . . . he got killed there."

"Sorry about that;" Jerry was sympathetic.

"Well to tell the truth; he was in bed with a thug's wife and got caught!"

He pounded on the bar and roared with laughter. It was the truth!

"To answer your question I usually hear about stuff before anybody else. Right now I know of two places that could be had; one belongs to someone I like a lot and I hate to see her leave. The other belongs to a son of a bitch I hate so I'll tell you about that one. I'd like to see the last of him! I don't look for no commission; real estate is not my business." He described the place, emphasizing the good condition it was in; "the owner did all his own work and he is a master craftsman. He'll be tough to bargain with; but I know he wants to move to Florida. His mother died and left him a place there . . . free and clear!"

"It sounds interesting; how could I see it.?"

"Not with me; he'd burn it down if I went inside! He doesn't like me any more than I like him. The only time he comes in here is when I'm away and my wife is behind the bar. I'll draw you a map so you can drive by and look it over; he goes to seven o'clock mass on Sunday so that's a good time to stop and look around. Nobody will tell him you were there; his neighbors hate him. If you like it from the outside keep coming around until you see him puttering about; he is outside a lot even in cold weather. He's a Swede; he doesn't know that it's cold!"

Once again he pounded the bar and roared at how funny he was! He drew an excellent map and handed it to Jerry.

"I hope we'll be neighbors."

They left the bar telling him they would be back to sample the home-cooking.

Brian was going crazy with curiosity; "let's see if we can find this place;" he asked Jerry for the map and then asked Tony for the car keys.

"We're going to see our salesman at work;" teased Tony.

It didn't take him long and Tony and Jerry were impressed with his skill. They drove buy and the name Anderson was by the driveway. It was in apple pie order and keenly maintained. It stood out from the other places; they looked dingy by comparison. Tony told Brian to head home.

"If you really want to see the inside, Jerry, I suggest we come over on Sunday after the mass when he is home. I would knock on his door and tell him you heard this place might be for sale and if it is; ask if he will show it to you. If he asks who told you; say you were talking to some lady in the market and she mentioned it and gave you directions. We will stay in the wagon unless he invites us in."

Jerry agreed to his idea; he liked the look of the place.

Sunday morning after breakfast they piled into the wagon; it was about nine-thirty.

"This should be a good time to see if he's there," reasoned Tony, "if he went to seven o'clock mass he has had plenty of time to come home and have breakfast. From what Mullins said I don't think he's the type to hang around after mass and chit chat with the old ladies."

Brian was driving and he had no trouble returning to the place. There was no vehicle in sight;

"looks like he's not back yet; let's drive around this area a little." Tony had turned around to speak Jerry.

"We might bump into someone we can ask for information about the place," Jerry was leaning forward.

Brian circled around the area; it was windy and chilly and not a soul was in sight. Smoke curled from many chimneys and it appeared that everyone was snug inside and staying there. Brian went back to Napeague Meadow Road and turned south. They had never been over here; the sight where the fertilizer plant had been now had a decent pier and several large boats were tied along it. Next, as he drove, there were recently built modern homes along the waterfront. They were not close together and seemed to be on one or two acre lots.

"Somebody is spending money in this area!"

Tony asked Brian to pull over and park.

"Look at the size of those houses! And there are a few more farther down; on the opposite side of the road! Drive down there, Brian, I think I see a sign."

"I see it," said Jerry, "it might be a builder's sign." Brian agreed.

He drove down and parked in front of the houses; there were four very large homes and had to be on two acres each. There were no large trees; this was the meadow area on the waterfront. The vegetation was scrub pine, beach plum and a variety of wild bushes, including blackberries. Deeper into the land, many acres, owned by the state; grew wild cranberry bogs. It was Mother Nature at her best; roaming and scurrying through all this; a potpourri of wild life gave it animation. They got out of the wagon and walked around one of the houses; peering in the windows and glass sliding doors.

"Luxury plus," commented Brian; "I would love to sell one of these!"

Jerry looked at Brian; "How much do you think they would go for?

"In the six figures; that's for sure." He responded.

"Maybe you have them listed at Ed's office," Tony suggested.

"Only the builder has a sign here; I imagine he has his own staff."

"The workmanship is first class." Brian said with admiration.

"Jerry, you would look good in one of these houses; you'd have plenty of company, I'm sure of that!" Tony was squeezing his shoulder.

Jerry smiled. "I'll take that over-sized garage and live happily ever after."

Brian had written the builder's name and phone number down and when he went to the office he checked and they did not have the listing. He discussed it with Ed and was told to try and get the listing. When he returned to the cottage Tony and Jerry were rearranging the firewood and were deeply involved in how the logs looked best. He called out of the car window.

"I'll be back soon; I'm going for a short ride." He drove off.

Jerry looked at Tony quizzically. Tony smiled; "he's going back to the houses,"

As he approached the houses Brian saw a white pick-up truck in one of the driveways. His heart beat a bit faster; *could this be the builder?* He walked to the front door and was just about to knock when it opened wide.

"Can I help you sir? I'm Sam Anderson; I built these houses, are you looking for information? I have brochures in my truck."

Brian shook the outstretched hand and his was lost in it! This was a *big* man; he was at least six feet six and was well-developed; even with his clothes on you where aware of his physique. He had curly blond hair and chiseled features.

"Hello, Mr. Anderson, I'm Brian McHugh and I am an agent with Ed Gorman's office." He produced his business card; he prayed he didn't show how nervous he was. "I drove through here earlier and saw these magnificent homes and I was wondering if you did any listing with brokers."

"I don't as a rule." He could tell Brian was new at the game; ordinarily he would have dismissed him with 'no; I never do' and bid him good day; but there was something likable about Brian's demeanor.

"I thought I knew all the staff at Ed's office; are you new there?

"I guess you could say I'm brand new," Brian smiled, "I've been working week-ends for about six months and my friend and I are planning to move out here permanently, soon."

As soon as he heard 'my friend and I' Sam knew they were a couple; he had built many homes for gay people and for the most part he enjoyed working with them. There were exceptions; but the heterosexual world had more than their share of exceptions! Brian briefly told him about the cottage.

"You have a dynamite location there!" Sam had his hand on Brian's shoulder; I'd like to see what you've done to that place."

Brian immediately invited him back to the cottage and he readily accepted. He followed him home and Tony saw them coming and told Jerry.

"Brian's bringing some company; I'm going to clean up a little."

"I'll finish up here; then I'll be in." Jerry continued working.

They pulled up and parked, heading toward Jerry.

"I like the shakes," said Sam.

Brian introduced them and Sam admired the wall and the brick work.

"If you ever want a job, Jerry, come and see me; I'm serious!"

Jerry thanked him and turned back to finish up; they entered the cottage. Sam was very complimentary about the remodeling and he asked who did the job. When Tony told him it was Henry, Sam nodded his head as he spoke;

"You could not have had a better pair of hands; and that includes mine. Henry is a craftsman and takes pride in his work and his word."

Brian led the way out on the deck and Sam looked out over the harbor and then he turned to them.

"If you only had a tent here; this view is still worth a million."

They went back inside and Sam decided to give Brian a three month listing on the houses. They called Ed to confirm the arrangement which would be written up and signed in Ed's office. Sam had certain stipulations that Ed agreed to; one being a reduced commission, which was common practice. Ed was thinking of future business and he was delighted with Brian's coup! He had to get together with Tony and get Brian moved out here! Brian went back to the houses and they toured all four of them; Sam gave Brian a master key that opened each house and left him writing up listings.

"Thank you, so much, Sam; I really appreciate this opportunity."

"Brian, if you can sell me; you can sell anybody. And you sold me!"

They shook hands and said good bye . . . Brian was not touching the ground!

Back at the cottage he was filled with excitement telling them he got the listing on all four houses.

"No other brokers have the listing; oh; I have to sell at least one of them! I have to show Sam I can produce."

"Take a couple of weeks off and come out here and spend your time at the houses; if someone comes along like we did you will be right there to show them the property. You should have all the necessary papers in case they give you deposits!

Tony was just as excited as Brian. He added; "don't forget your lunch."

That brought a hearty laugh from Jerry and they immediately joined him. That night as they lay in bed Tony continued to insist that Brian take the time off.

"This is where your future is going to be; you can show Ed and Sam what you can do. Can you imagine how Ed will feel if you sell just one of those houses. He'll jump for joy! To say nothing of the commission you will make. You are going to need your own car, Brian, and it has to be a nice one if you're going to be taking clients out to look at properties. Take two weeks of your vacation now; they won't mind."

"What about my clients? They depend on me . . . many of them have been coming to me for years! I just can't up and desert them."

"Suppose you got very sick; what would they do . . . stop getting their hair done? No way; they would go to a different stylist. You're planning to leave them when we move out here . . . what's the difference when it happens?

They made the trip back to the city leaving late Sunday night. Brian drove the first half and Tony took over after a coffee stop. He had not mentioned anything about Brian taking two weeks off while Brian was driving; now he got back on the subject and it nettled Brian but he didn't show it. He really wanted to do it. His sense of loyalty was being torn in opposite directions. He couldn't argue with Tony because he made sense; but he felt timid about asking for the time on such short notice. When you work by appointment and clients book you for their regular needs and often special affairs; where they must look their best, you develop a reliability of being there when you are needed. These women have always appreciated Brian's dependability and the quality of his work and they showed it in their generosity. Some stylists took time off by pretending an illness but Brian could not do this. Whatever his decision; it would be an honest one. They dropped Jerry off at his home and decided to stay at Brian's because he had to go to work in the morning and would need his clothes. Before they went to sleep Brian had promised to ask for the two weeks off.

The next day Tony called Ed Gorman and asked him to keep his eye open for a nice used car for Brian;

"I'm talking 'cream puff' Ed, something he can take clients out in and not feel ashamed of the condition and a good running car that won't be breaking down on him. He's going to take two weeks of his vacation now and concentrate on Sam's houses."

"Talk about perfect timing, Tony; I have your car! Some friends of mine have an elderly relative who just died in Florida and her grandson inherited her car but wants no part of it. He drove it up here and only arrived yesterday; it's a Buick Park Avenue in show room condition and has only been driven forty-six thousand miles. The grandson drives a Porsche and wouldn't be found dead in a Buick! He wants to move it fast; I know you can get a good deal on it. He inherited a ton of money along with the car; the car is a drag on him now."

"Ed, buy that car for me; tell me how much you settle for and I will send you the money Western Union. Have him sign the title and it will be in Brian's name. I'll give you his full name and use the Amagansett address."

"Tony! I'll pay him with my check and you can reimburse me when you are out here; never mind Western Union. I'm so happy that someone I know is getting this car; wait until you see it."

"Thank you, Ed; we might be out there tomorrow night. Brian is all excited about those houses."

"He really pulled out a plum there; Sam thinks a lot of him. We have to get him out here permanently; Tony."

"I'm working on it; he's taking two weeks off; that's a start."

They said their good byes and Tony would have a tough time not saying anything about the car; he wanted to surprise Brian.

Brian came to the bar directly from work. He was all excited; he had gotten the time off! He hurried down to the end of the bar where Tony was talking to Gino. Tony stood up and ushered him into the kitchen.

"I know; I can tell you are off for two weeks! Tony hugged him.

"When do you want to leave to go out East?" Brian asked.

"Tonight of course; we'll get ready and take off!"

"You mean now? Brian was incredulous.

"Yes; I mean right now! We will go to my place and I'll pack, then we'll go to your place and you pack. We have a lot of clothes out there; we don't have to bring much. I have the wagon here in back of the bar. If you're hungry I can fix a hero to take in the car. If you can wait; we will stop in Hampton Bays and eat something there. But, let's get going!

"I can wait to eat; let's get going!" They hugged again, laughing.

Tony had briefed Gino that this might happen so he was not surprised. He let them out the back door and locked it.

Soon they were on their way; it would be slow going for the first half of the trip. Tony told Brian to put his seat back and take a nap. He put some music on low and said that was all the company he needed; knowing Brian would say he had to stay awake and keep him company. He obediently put his seat back and in five minutes he dozed off. Tony decided he would do all the driving this trip.

They stopped at the diner and were surprised to see Ed and his family there; they were just about finished with their meal. After greetings were over Tony asked Brian to get a booth and he would be right there. As soon as he left the table Ed told Tony he had secured the car. They could go to the Bureau and register the car tomorrow and get the tags. Tony was delighted; they made a date to meet at ten in the morning.

"He doesn't know about the car." Tony whispered.

"I surmised as much;" Ed said, smiling; his wife joining in.

"Thank you so much, Ed; you've done me a really big favor."

He hurried to join Brian and have dinner. They ate without much conversation and were soon on their way. Brian offered to drive but was told to finish the nap that he started. The cottage was completely dark as they parked; the cleaning woman always left lights on for them on Friday and Tony had not thought to call her. He kept the headlights on until Brian got inside and turned on the outside lights. They had one drink and opted to turn in early. Tony was bursting with his secret. He had to hold out somehow; but he ached to tell him.

Tony had told Brian that they were meeting Ed to look at five acres of land that could be had at a good price.

"I don't want to buy anything right now; but I'll look out of courtesy to him. I'm still waiting to hear from that developer who got us so excited about the land deal. Ed says it's going to happen; we have to be patient."

"All I can think of is how I am going to sell those houses! I want to sell all of them and Ed's other salesmen are going to be hot on them. I have to get the key from Ed. I suggested we hide it on the property but he said no way."

"Brian; when you get the key today have one made to keep on your key ring. Nobody has to know that you have it."

They met Ed in a restaurant parking lot on Montauk Highway. He was parked next to the Buick and it was beautiful. A four door sedan; light beige in color and shining like the sun. He had the two front doors open and as they approached the car Tony steered Brian to the driver's side. Ed walked over and handed Brian the keys; "happy motoring and lots of luck."

Brian was bewildered and Tony was beaming! It was dawning on Brian at last.

"You're kidding me!" He yelped . . . is this for me to *own?*"

"Have a happy career, partner; and sell a lot of real estate!"

Brian hugged Tony and his eyes were glistening; he sat in the car running his hand over the fine upholstery and moving the steering wheel.

"Start the damn thing up; I want to hear that engine!" Tony yelled.

Brian turned the key and you could hardly hear it; it really purred!

"Exactly as advertised." Tony smiled and shook Ed's hand.

"Take it for a ride around the lot, Brian; you can't go on the road yet."

Brian started off a bit gingerly until he was away from all the cars; he was over-joyed. He drove for a few minutes and returned to Tony.

Tony took the paper work from Ed and wrote out a check; he was amazed at the price. Ed could have added on a thousand dollars and it would still be a bargain. Tony was well aware of this and he would remain loyal to Ed.

They drove to Riverhead and took care of the transfer. Ed had assured them the car was safe in the lot and he had permission from the owner about the car being parked there. They returned and put on the plates and entered the restaurant and had lunch. Later; Brian followed Tony home and they left the wagon and took the Buick for a ride to the lighthouse. It carried so smoothly; it was easy to handle and the appointments were luxurious. When they were at the lighthouse he slowed down and pulled into the parking area and stopped. His eyes were brimming with tears and he turned to Tony and hugged him. He didn't speak; he couldn't. Tony wept along with him. They sat for a while looking at the ocean and the assortment of boats scattered around.

"Let's go home, partner," Tony squeezed his shoulder.

"You drive; you have to feel how this handles."

"I would love to! You have to give it a name; so we can christen it."

"I'm going to call it 'Valhalla' the Viking's heaven!"

"Valhalla?" Tony shook his head; "whatever moves you, partner."

Brian went to the houses in the morning and started his vigil. He had called Sam and learned which bank was the best to recommend if a client asked about mortgage possibilities; Sam gave him additional information that might be helpful. There was a pause; then Sam continued.

"Brian, I want to tell you something that must be between you and me; I need your assurance that you can keep something absolutely confidential."

"I know I can do that, Sam." Brian's voice was solemn.

"Okay; if you get a customer who is affluent; and I think you are able to recognize that quality in people; I will take back a mortgage for no more than five years. I will give them an attractive interest rate but they must be financially sound. You have to be careful how you offer this to them; if they can't afford it you will insult them. It will be a balloon-type mortgage and the monthly payments can be made in an amount that is comfortable for them. At the end of five years whatever amount is unpaid is due in its entirety. It is good for people who don't want to get involved with a bank at this time; it gives them time to look for suitable financing in the future. That is for your ears only!"

"Thank you, Sam, I want to deliver for you; I really do!"

"I know you do . . . you're made of good stuff. Good luck and good bye."

Brian was elated with the confidence Sam had in him; he *had* to produce!

The first day was uneventful; one young couple came by and looked at every house and picked them apart. They rode in a broken down pick-up truck and looked like they bought gas three gallons at a time. He was very polite and answered all their questions and was very relieved when they 'went for a beer'! He stayed until almost dark; Tony had come over about eleven o'clock and brought his lunch so they had lunch together . . . the highlight of the day!

The next day he left early and Tony had some paper work to take care of regarding the bar. The phone rang and it was Ed Gorman;

"Tony; can you come to my office now? It's important; that developer has been in touch with me!"

"Edward; I am on my way!"

He hung up; got the car keys, and was out the door like a gazelle. It seemed to take forever to get there and anyone who got in his way for more than two seconds was expertly cursed; sailor-style! He breezed into Ed's office; his secretary told him to go right in; he was already through the door! They shook hands and Ed poured two brandies . . . it was a little early but it seemed very appropriate; not as a celebration; more like a nerve tonic!

"It took time but it is worth it . . . he has dumped our problem broker! He discovered that he was manipulating this deal behind his back to eliminate any other brokers from participating. His name is George Treadwell and he is a very fair man to deal with. He can't afford to limit himself to one broker; he would miss out on too many opportunities! It could cost him hundreds of thousand dollars; so, he wants your acreage and I told him your conditions and he is interested. I assured him that you did not want to be involved in the way the development would be designed and that was very important to him. To shorten this story; he wants to arrange a meeting with you and me and his attorney to discuss how we will do this. I know his attorney and he is a first class real estate specialist and he will not try any sly tricks on us. He is totally above board. I have been talking to my attorney and he has given me a profile of what we should ask for; we will have to pay him for his advice; but his interest will not extend to the actual deal. I know we can rely on Treadwell's attorney; that will save us a lot!"

"My ears are ringing!" Tony had his two forefingers in his ears. "Is this really going to happen? I had just about given up on it!"

"I told you it was a waiting game; I never dreamed we would be this lucky. I figured we were going to have to wrestle with that bastard through this whole deal and on into the selling of the lots. We are rid of him! And what is wonderful is that he died by his own hand!"

Tony raised his snifter; "Here's to a most welcome suicide!"

Ed raised his glass laughing all the way."

Tony had to control his speed; he was so eager to tell Brian that he just wanted to jam his foot to the floor and push the wagon for all it was worth! He parked by the houses as a car was pulling away. He was glad Brian was alone. They almost crashed into each other in the doorway; Brian was on his way out to greet him and Tony was racing in to break his news. Tony hugged Brian.

"It's happening, Brian! It's happening! I just came from Ed's office; the deal with the developer is *on!* And not only that; he got rid of that rotten broker and there's no one else involved."

Brian could hardly breathe; he had to pry himself loose. "Are you sure? You don't have to negotiate first?"

Tony was annoyed that Brian wasn't jumping for joy; he didn't want questions!

"Will you please show a little enthusiasm? We're on our way to big bucks and you look like you lost your last dollar!"

"I just want to be sure of what happened; of course I'm happy about it."

Patiently Tony went over the details and gradually Brian looked like he would explode with joy. *Finally,* thought Tony.

Brian half-closed his eyes; "now; may I please talk about my exciting news?"

Tony regarded him quizzically; "what news?"

"A car left here as you arrived; it was a young couple whose parents are looking for a house in this area. They want new construction not old and charming; they were very excited about these houses and they are bringing their parents here tomorrow morning. The girl told me their parents have plenty of money; *'Don't let my father fool you; he always talks with a poor mouth. Concentrate on my mother; she makes most of the decisions'* those are her exact words; she pulled me aside from her brother when she spoke to me."

"That is very good news; you better take a leave of absence from the salon and concentrate on your new career."

Brian totally surprised him. "I think you're right; this is going to need all my time and it really is where my future is heading."

Tony was hugging him; "I don't believe my ears! I certainly love what you are saying, though. Maybe we are ready to make the move out here!"

"What about Gino; can he run the place on his own?"

"I think so; if he needs my help I'll drive in and give him a hand; I'm going to keep my apartment; the rent isn't high and we'll have a place to hang our hats when we go to the city. I know you have a long lease but I think your landlord will be glad to let you out of it because he can get a higher rent for it."

"Oh, he sure could! I've done a lot to that place; he hasn't seen it since I moved there; I didn't want him to get any ideas about raising my rent."

"He can't raise your rent if you have a lease."

"I don't trust landlords; they are tricky . . . and they have lawyers who are even trickier!" He was so positive!

Tony just hugged him again and smiled; he was overjoyed with what he heard.

The next morning Brian went to the houses early. He brought cleaning things and went over kitchen counters and bathrooms and gave everything a sprucing up. Sam had a couple who kept his properties in condition but Brian felt the need to give them a going over in the prime areas. He went through all four houses touching up; he also had polished himself up a bit. Then he waited.

By eleven o'clock he was sure the girl had been talking through her hat and was just having some fun. He was downcast and even turned the radio off that supplied him with great music from a station in Connecticut. He heard voices; and ran to the front door. Walking toward him was the couple and their parents were in tow. The father noted his Buick and felt a pleasant financial glow; he had a lot of General Motors stock! They exchanged introductions and Brian wisely did not try to elicit their general information; if they showed interest that would be the time to ask questions. He took them on a tour of the house they were in; handing a brochure to the father. They seemed quite pleased; the youngsters very enthusiastic; the mother was complimentary and daddy was non-committed. He did not exert any pressure; instead he suggested that he open the other houses and allow them to inspect them at their own pace. He gave them the brochures for the other houses; handing them to the son to make him feel important. This was a good move; he took a livelier interest and was at his mother's side with his comments. The sister tagged along with daddy and tried to rouse some enthusiasm in him. His only comment so far was; 'too expensive'!

Brian had explained to the wife that all the acreage behind the four homes was owned by the State and was never going to be developed. He mentioned that the home farthest to the east was almost surrounded by the preserve due to its configuration. This afforded wonderful, natural privacy. He compared it to his own cottage on the harbor; she was very impressed.

They took a long time to inspect the houses; spending the most time at the one with the great privacy. The wife came into the house where Brian waited and said;

"We're going to get some lunch and talk; when I want to spend a lot of money it is best my husband have a full stomach." She gave him a warm smile; "I love the end house; all that privacy appeals to me and the homes are extremely well built. I am very interested, Brian; we'll be back in about two hours." She asked for another brochure for the end house and went to lunch.

"Bon appetit;" Brian said to her as she exited; she waved.

He was on pins and needles! He wished he had a phone so he could call Tony and suddenly he realized in his excitement this morning he completely forgot about bringing his lunch! Well, he could not leave the house for a minute; that would be too risky. Five minutes later Tony pulled in with lunch in hand. He could tell that nothing was missing from the refrigerator when he made his breakfast; he knew Brian had forgotten to make his lunch. He could see Brian's excitement.

"Tell me all about it before you bust wide open!" He was laughing.

"Tony! I think I have a real interest in one of the houses."

He filled him in on the details and Tony was elated. He spread out the lunch on the kitchen counter on a towel he had brought; he knew there could be no crumbs here!

"What kind of a car were they in; was it upscale?"

"I didn't notice; but the wife was wearing very upscale clothes and the diamonds on her left hand and encrusted in her watch told me all I had to know! She also had very nicely coifed hair."

"Well you should be good at reading the ladies . . . God help them!"

Brian poked him; "The husband might be a problem; I sure hope he has a good lunch! She said he is better on a full stomach when she wants to spend money."

"From what you noticed about her it sounds like she knows what to do."

"She's very nice, Tony; she has a beautiful smile."

"She has a lot to smile about; she has a rich husband! Listen, Brian; it's natural to be all excited about this; but prepare yourself; if it doesn't pan out I don't want to see you fall apart."

"I'll be okay; I know it's a shot in the dark."

"That's a good attitude; if it happens; we will celebrate!"

They finished lunch and Tony made sure he left the counter spotless; he called Brian over to where they had lunch.

"Do you want to inspect this area? I don't want to leave a mess."

"Go home and count the lots you are going to be selling!"

"You are going to be selling them, partner, I'll supply them!"

Tony gave him a hug and a kiss and wished him luck; "You can do it, kid."

On the way back to the cottage he asked God to make it happen for Brian.

It was a little after three when the car pulled into the driveway; now Brian noticed it was a Cadillac and a very classy looking one! Brian had obtained their names from the wife before she departed for lunch. Valerie and John Laurie; she seemed to have a trace of a British accent; he did not. The children were not with them. The builder had placed a round table and four chairs by the sliding glass door that looked out over the meadow. Brian asked them to be seated and John Laurie got right down to business.

"Valerie is in love with the end house and I want her to have it. I want you to level with me and tell me if the price is firm or do we have some wiggle room?"

"As far as I know from Mr. Anderson the price is firm. But there is nothing to prevent you from making an offer; he has four homes here and none have been sold . . . if he gets one occupied it may make selling the others easier. As the first buyer you have that advantage; but I would caution you not to make your offer so low as to be insulting . . . he will think you are not a serious buyer. If you want him to put in any extras he might be tough with his prices."

"Brian please call us by our first names; it is more comfortable. We will listen to your advice on the offer." Valerie attempted to soften her husband's ways. "John," she continued; "you wanted to ask Brian if the builder offered any kind of financing." She looked at Brian; "Is there any?"

John was annoyed with her interference; he felt she weakened his negotiation.

"I didn't feel we were at that stage yet; but maybe we are."

Brian sensed his pique and quickly explained the five year mortgage option and he sensed that John was interested. His questions made sense and pointed up his knowledge of finance. Brian was relieved that so far he had been able to answer all his questions. He asked if he could prepay the mortgage without penalty and Brian assured him there was a codicil that guaranteed that. John sat staring out at the meadow and Valerie winked at Brian; John stood up and stretched.

"Let's go through the house once more." He walked to the door.

They returned and sat at the table; they had worked out the offer in the house and Brian filled out the papers and John gave him a check for one thousand dollars.

"I'll call you as soon as I have talked to Mr. Anderson."

They shook hands and John said; "Make it happen, Brian; for Valerie's sake."

"I know he will!" She hugged Brian and he sensed the scent of violets.

They drove off; Brian waving to them. He went inside and picked up the check and began dancing around the room. It was after five and cocktail time!

Brian pulled up in front of the cottage and parked. He was anxious to get the carport erected so his car would be sheltered.

Taking his attaché case he flew into the house calling for Tony. The Buick was so quiet Tony had not heard him arrive. Tony came out of the kitchen and was almost mowed down by Brian.

"I've got a deposit on one of the houses!" He was yelling and flushed.

"Take it easy;" Tony hugged him and tried to calm him down;

"You'll have a stroke or something." He held his shoulders firmly.

"Congratulations partner; I knew you could do it!" He kissed him.

"You make the martinis and I'll fix an antipasto."

"I want to tell you about the sale!" He was squeaking.

"And I want to hear all about it . . . with a drink; by the fireside."

"We don't have a fire going!" Brian was exasperated.

"When you've made the drinks; light a fire. I'll be ready by then."

Tony was deliberately talking in soft, modulated tones to calm him down.

"I'm ready to bust wide open and you want me to do this stuff."

"That's exactly why you should; throw some cold water on your face."

Brian turned and sped off to the bathroom and splashed his face furiously. He felt better and he lit the fire when he returned to make the drinks. Tony was ready.

"Now, partner; let's sit by the fire and you can tell me all about this."

Brian gave him a hug smiling from ear to ear. "I'm okay now; I am subdued."

Laughing; they carried everything to the table by the fireplace. Tony proposed a toast and it was the last words he spoke for quite a while. Brian covered every detail of his day and how the sale evolved. Tony was thinking that someday he would have these sales and never mention them . . . it would be all in a days work. He gazed at the fire as Brian spoke and his thoughts were of a bright future and he had someone wonderful to share it with. *I can't believe it is happening to me!*

Jerry Foley was looking in his bathroom mirror and seeing one hell of a mess! Unshaven, un-showered and unfit to be in human company; even a faithful dog would shy away. He wished he were out East; working on the carport. The idea of being out there moved him to call the bar and speak to Tony. Gino informed him that Tony was out East and he didn't know when he would be back. Jerry called them and Tony answered the phone. There was a little small talk and then Jerry asked if he could join them. He said he would drive there in the morning if it was okay with them. Tony asked Brian; who gave it the nod and he suggested that he come out by train and they could all ride back together.

"You could take the Fisherman's Special; it leaves very early in the morning and gets to Montauk at five a.m. That means you would get to Amagansett about four-thirty or so. It would save you a long drive by yourself. I'll meet you at the station; that's no problem."

"I'll call the Long Island Railroad and get the information and I'll get back to you; it's a good idea."

"Jerry; we're going to be here for two weeks so bring what you need. By the way; Brian sold one of those houses today. He'll fill you in when you get here; be prepared for a long listen!" Brian shot him a look.

"That's great news; tell him I send my congratulations."

Jerry called back in a half hour and said he was all set for the train ride. He was told he would be in Amagansett just as Tony had said."

"Okay Jerry, don't eat too much we'll have breakfast at the cottage."

Jerry was suddenly alive with energy and he packed a bag and then set about getting himself in shape. He would take a cab to Penn Station; he called and made a reservation for one telling them the train he had to be on. His blood was circulating and he was all excited about his trip. His hangover was forgotten!

Brian and Tony discussed Jerry for a while and decided to go to bed early and set the alarm for three-thirty. It was kind of exciting to be meeting the train so early. Suddenly Tony grabbed Brian's arm; he looked startled.

"Brian; there's a bar car on that train! He might be bombed on arrival!

But, he wasn't; they looked him over and he was just fine. Actually he had slept most of the way and the conductor had to rouse him to detrain.

"How was the trip?" Tony put his bag in the trunk. Jerry made no reply.

"Where did the limo come from? These are beautiful wheels!"

Brian held up the keys; shaking them. "It's my first car and I love it."

"Well lots of luck; you should sell a lot of real estate with this!"

Jerry envied the life these two guys were making for themselves; not so long ago he would have judged them scornfully but his attitude had completely changed. They were really the two people he was most comfortable with out of all the people that he knew. It was a five minute ride to the cottage and Brian started making breakfast as soon as they got home. Tony lit a fire and soon the smell of coffee and bacon wafted through the place. They sat at the table after eating; they had coffee and cigarettes and were watching the dawn slowly break and change the entire scene outside.

"I'd like to start building the carport; do you think we could get the lumber today?" Jerry was speaking to Tony.

"I'm sure we can; we can go to the lumber yard in Amagansett; it's a short trip for them to deliver. I can help you; Brian will be at the houses all day. We can go there at noon and bring lunch for the three of us. He'll probably have another house sold." He tousled Brian's hair.

"If there's a car there don't stop; take a ride and have your lunch by the water. I can eat later. I won't be in the house I sold; you'll see where my car is parked. Sam has decided to include the appliances with the houses; he gave that deal to the Lauries; so I'll be having a refrigerator to keep some lunch and I can make coffee for my clients."

"He's moving in, Jerry; pretty soon he'll have his clothes over there and I'll never see him!"

"I don't see any danger of that happening; he doesn't love his job that much!" Jerry stood up; "I'm going to take a walk down the beach; what time does the lumber yard open?"

"I think they open at eight but if we get there at seven-thirty they will take our order." He went for his walk.

"He seems to be doing okay," Tony addressed Brian, "if he made that long train ride and stayed out of the bar car I'd call that an accomplishment."

"Let's keep our fingers crossed; we can ease up on our drinking and not make opportunities for him to drink," Brian suggested.

"We don't run a monastery here, partner; let's live our lives a little."

"I didn't say we should stop drinking! Just ease up."

"I guess I could do that; I was thinking we might take him to Kincaid's for dinner tonight . . . does that fit into 'easing up'?"

"Of course it does; he'll probably just drink beer."

"He can hold a lot of beer and not get drunk." Tony laughed.

"He can drink beer for breakfast!" Brian shuddered; "that's not for me!"

They tidied up the kitchen and went to shower and get dressed. Jerry came back from his walk and did the same. Brian headed for the houses and Jerry was showing Tony a sketch of the carport and he liked his plan. They went to the lumber yard and placed their order; delivery was promised before noon.

The carport was finished in three days; they decided on a gravel flooring so very little cement work was necessary. The carport was an extension of the retaining wall and was at a right angle to the house. You could drive straight into it from the driveway; there was room for three cars and they had used the cedar shakes to match the cottage. It looked great and very professional.

"You could start a business out here Jerry. You really know what you are doing. We have very little lumber left; that's good figuring!"

"Thanks, Tony; I have to do something; I'd like to go back and see if I can nail that Swede down and take a look at his place."

"Why don't we go there and if he's not there we can leave a note and have him call us and make an appointment."

"That makes sense, Tony; this hit and miss stuff will get us nowhere."

"When we go over to have lunch with Brian we can go look him up."

Tony and Jerry went to find the Swede and again, he was not there; they left the note and there was no word from him until Friday morning. He asked Jerry many questions; especially as to how he knew his place was for sale. Finally he agreed to show them the place on Saturday morning. He instructed them not to bring any children or pets with them.

"You would think this guy was showing you the Taj Mahal;" Tony commented after Jerry related his conversation; he will probably make you take your shoes off before you enter."

"You're going with me; aren't you?"

Tony nodded; "If you want me to; sure I'll go with you."

"I'll feel better with some moral support; and you might think of things to ask about that I wouldn't; I need help dealing with this guy!"

"We can't let an old Swede get us down, Jerry; just act independent."

Saturday morning they took the wagon and went to see the Swede; he was outside raking around his home. Jerry introduced himself with a hand shake; then he introduced Tony. Tony immediately informed him that he lived in the area and told him where his house was located; there was a noticeable change in his demeanor and he became cordial.

"That's a beautiful spot where you are; you have good clams on that beach. I used to go there years ago and I picked beach plums there, too."

He gave them a tour of his 'big' little house. There were only three rooms and a bath but they were three large rooms; the kitchen had a brick fireplace and a ceramic wood-burning stove was expertly installed in it. The stove was of European design and while it had a small fire box and required very little small cuts of wood to operate it; it heated the entire house comfortably . . . and cheap! There was plenty of room for a long table and chairs and the appliances were up-to-date. It had a gas range and there was a large gas storage tank off to the side of the house but near the road for easy servicing. He had screened the tank with lattice work. The living room wall facing the dune had an eight foot glass sliding door and another window at each end. A stone patio filled the area between the house and the dune and he had created a very private spot with comfortable out-door furniture. You could do some nude sun bathing in absolute privacy. Jerry was very impressed; it was in 'move in' condition. The bedroom had one long wall of louvered door closets and on the back wall a Murphy bed was installed. It had floor-to-ceiling shelves on either side; it was spotless! Jerry was sold!

"Just bring your clothes and groceries; Jerry; everything else is here."

"I agree Tony; it's perfect for me." He had no intention to bargain.

"How much are you asking for it; Mr. Bergensen?"

"I'm not asking; this is my price." He handed a folded piece of paper to Jerry; he did not feel it was any of Tony's business to know the price.

"I will pay you all cash with a bank cashier's check. Is that agreeable with you? I'll give you my personal check for five hundred dollars deposit right now. Do you have a lawyer here in town?"

Bergensen was thrilled! He could be in Florida sooner than he thought. "I have a good lawyer and he knows this property well; if you want to have your lawyer too, that's your business. We could split his fee if we just use my lawyer; he's very honest, he is a good Catholic."

Tony smiled at the down-to-earth delivery of his statement; it was gospel truth!

"That suits me; I will want a termite inspection; I'll pay for it. If there is any termite activity or damage you will have to pay for that. That must be in the contract. Do you agree?" Jerry extended his hand.

"I never heard of anyone around here having termites . . . I'll agree."

They shook hands; Jerry gave him the deposit check and asked for a receipt;

"Why do you want a receipt?" He felt insulted.

"I'm giving you five hundred dollars; I need a record of it."

"Well, I don't have any." He wasn't sure he should sign anything.

Tony stepped in; "Call your lawyer and explain what is happening."

He moved quickly; he made the call and was told he must provide a receipt. His lawyer told him to get the buyer's name and address and bring it to him and he would prepare the contracts. His office was in his home.

Before Jerry went back to the city the contracts were signed. Bergensen insisted on an 'as is' sale and Jerry finally agreed; he would be glad that he did. The attorney said he would notify him of the closing date and he expected it to be in the near future; Mr. Bergensen was anxious to get to Florida and his attorney was going to be glad to see the last of him!

Jerry decided to go back to the city by train and arrange for the check and other details. He also wanted to look for a station wagon; he was in the market for a new car and now that he was going to have a home out East the wagon was the most practical wheels to have; you were always hauling something when you lived out there. After he was settled in he was going to have Henry build a garage attached to his house. There was a new excitement within him and it took his mind off his inner naggings and he had a purpose now that challenged his mind. He was making sketches of a garage and other ideas popped into his thoughts and took up all of his time; he drank occasional beers but the whiskey bottles gathered dust. He looked good. He was prepared to buy a new wagon but Tom Nesbitt told him of a good buy in Hampton Bays. A neighbor of Lucille's parents lost her husband and she couldn't drive. He made arrangements to see it.

Chapter Six

Gordon and Eleanor were spending week-ends with Frank and Dotty and their friendship was deepening. They had included them in their secret; that they were expecting and Frank and Dotty were jubilant. Especially for their friend Gordon; they felt he deserved all this; in fact, he was over-due. Eleanor was making it happen and they loved her; it was wonderful that she was someone they could genuinely care for; to have to pretend to like someone he chose would be a task . . . they would do it; he was their friend. On some week-ends Frank and Dotty would come into the city and they would see a show or attend some function Gordon had to appear at. Eleanor was experiencing a part of New York that she heard about from her clients . . . now she was a part of it. Between the social whirl and the new job she had no spare time. Whenever they could; she and Brian compared notes at work. Edith was in a world all her own and she was sixteen all over again. She had stayed with her diet and exercise and she had a figure any eighteen years old would envy! Tom was deeply involved in this relationship and they seemed to need only each other. He never told Edith but Lucille finally confronted him and he told her the truth. She was devastated.

"I had my suspicions; but when you hear it from the horse's mouth it's a whole different ball game. I never expected to hear you tell me what I'm hearing; I guess I should admire your honesty; but frankly I'm not impressed. Suddenly I am supposed to face the fact that wedding vows and years of what I thought was love, and having children; don't add up to much when it comes to being more accomplished in bed. I know I have my religion to thank for that; of course I thought it was your religion, too." She was taut; determined not to cry.

"This was no sudden thing; you must know how I was starved for what I need. I don't give a damn what priests are telling you is wrong. They are telling you what you can't do; but they don't practice what they preach and that is becoming more public every day! I have needs that are *natural* and the church is losing souls by the thousands because the laity of today is intelligent and can do their own reasoning. You don't see Catholic families today with six or more kids because the parents know that God does not provide! Daddy has to provide; plus contributing to the church so the hierarchy can live luxuriously. I don't see any resemblance between the hierarchy and the Man who rode into Jerusalem on a donkey! They are supposed to carry on His ways of teaching; we are getting *their* interpretations . . . there isn't any similarity. They will spend hours meeting with each other expounding on catechizma; they love to say that word; how many of the laity are discussing that subject? The laity is discussing the criminal closing of Catholic schools in poor parishes because they can't afford them; while the hierarchy wastes millions of dollars; *money that is not theirs*, on pedarist priests! You are willing to let these men tell you how to make love to your husband and what is worse; how *not* to make love to him! They tell you that you must get married to keep yourself away from carnal sin; then they give you limits on your conduct in bed! The hierarchy of our church is mired in pomp and hypocrisy and they are just as bad as the crew we have in Washington!" He was riled.

"So you want a divorce I suppose." She could hardly breathe.

"I want no such thing . . . I'm still your husband; neutered to your specifications. I intend to take care of you and the children as I always have; we must never argue in front of them; I hope we won't argue at all. I will try to be here whenever you need me; I've just had another promotion that will enable me to do more for you. I have increased the payment into their education fund. I will try to keep your life much the way it was . . . I would think you would be relieved not to have me making sinful demands on you."

He knew that was a cheap shot; but he had to make her understand that he was driven to this situation; he didn't go looking for it. He couldn't believe he was talking like this to the woman he had loved so much! He firmly believed it was destroyed by the ignorance of his religious leaders. Tom could not face her; he did not want to see her pain. He was no longer in love with her; but he still loved her.

"Thank you for thinking of my welfare, excuse me; I'm going to bed."

The kids were in Hampton Bays with their grandparents; he went to see Edith.

Cleo decided that Eleanor was now able to manage on her own and she formally announced her retirement and her coming marriage. She and Manny had changed their wedding plans and made the decision to be married in Rome. They wanted a small wedding without a lot of ceremony. It would be in the latter part of May. When they arrived back in the States there would be a reception for them at the penthouse. Cleo had the party all arranged and getting dressed would be her biggest chore. After they were wed she would call Manny's secretary and the invitations would be mailed out. It took a bit of social paring but they were able to keep the guest list down to fifty. Cleo stuck to her decision not to invite the staff at the salon; it was not an easy choice to make but she did it. Eleanor would come as Gordon's wife and not as a staff member. The staff was quite contented not to have to attend; it was one expensive gift they were relieved of buying.

Gordon and Eleanor took Manny and Cleo out for lunch and then they drove them to the airport for their trip to Europe. They had decided to tell them about their coming event informing them they were the first to hear the news. Lunch was finished and they were having coffee and brandy; Gordon looked at them across the table and raised his snifter; they followed suit expecting the toast to be to their wedding.

"Here's to my wife who is going to present me with my first-born!"

Cleo gasped and clasped her hand over her mouth; Manny's mouth just fell open! He jumped up pumping Gordon's hand; Eleanor was beaming and Cleo was hugging her; tears welling in her eyes. Then Gordon raised his glass again;

"And here's to two wonderful friends; a safe journey; a happy marriage and come back to us as soon as you can."

Now Eleanor joined Cleo in the tear shedding and they all had a few moments of showing their affection for one another. They dropped them at Kennedy and returned home. Both of them felt tired; but it was a warm, relaxed kind of feeling. Gordon sat on the couch and she came and curled up in his arms. There wasn't any conversation; her head rested on his shoulder; he loved the scent of her hair. In a short time they dozed off; quietly growing within each other.

Jerry took the train to Hampton Bays; he had made arrangements with the son of the owner of the wagon to meet him there. They went back to the house, Jerry driving the station wagon; it was everything Tom said it was. He did not haggle because the price was right and he would not embarrass Tom by trying to chisel a few bucks off the price. The son accompanied him to the Bureau in Riverhead and he registered the wagon and got the plates. After dropping the son back at his home he headed out to see Tony and Brian who were expecting him. He called and told them he had made the deal and asked if they needed anything.

"Just get out here and show us your wagon! You've got your closing tomorrow and today new wheels; we have to celebrate, man!" Tony was elated.

"I'm on my way, I have to watch this baby; she wants to fly!"

"Well, you don't have to worry about getting a ticket; not one of theirs!"

They hung up; Tony relayed the news to Brian.

"He needs some positive things right now; and it will keep him busy.

We're losing a good worker, Tony!"

"I'm sure he will help us any time we need him; that place he's buying doesn't need any work done. Henry is going to build his garage and I think he has some finishing up to do on our carport; he will take care of it; I'm sure."

"It will be nice having him out here; he's better company now than he ever was; he use to pry into our business and it aggravated me. He doesn't do that anymore." Brian was looking very serious.

"He's been through a lot lately and we have been good friends to him; I think he appreciates that. He doesn't seem to have any close friends from the job; except for Tom and he's kind of wrapped up right now." Tony grinned.

"Wrapped up? I would say hung, drawn and quartered! Edith has him in her clutches and she aims to keep him. She has gotten herself in shape and she is dynamite-looking! Her entire demeanor has changed; she is all sweetness."

"That should make everybody at the salon happy; at least she's not complaining about everything," Tony was laughing.

"That is the truth; she is even happy about Eleanor's promotion!"

Tony gave Brian a knowing look. "Tom must have the key to her inner soul."

"I've never heard it called a key before; but he certainly must have it!"

They were laughing hard and the sound of a horn got them outside to see the station wagon. It was an Oldsmobile Vista Cruiser and it was in prime condition; Jerry was standing near the back of it, he had all the doors open and the rear access lifted open. It was a subdued gold color and it was beautiful!

Tony shook his hand; "lots of luck with it, Jerry; it's a cream puff!"

Brian poked his head inside and exclaimed; "that is some radio; super sound!"

"We'll take it to Montauk later; dinner is on me!"

Jerry closed it up and took one small bag into the cottage. He had a larger bag in the wagon and he would take stock tomorrow after the closing to see what he needed. A lively excitement tingled his being and he was on a 'high'. Tony was making drinks and Jerry had a beer; he intended to stay on beer.

"I want to go over and walk through the place once more before the closing; do you want to come with me?"

"Sure, we'll take a ride; Brian, didn't you want to put some papers over in one of the houses? We can stop there now."

"Yes, I do; thanks for reminding me."

He picked up a folder and they set out for Lazy Point and Jerry's new acquisition; they stopped at the house first and then headed for Mr. Bergensen's abode.

"There he is at the back door of the house; it looks like he's trying to get that big table through the door. He's suppose to leave everything but his personal belongings . . . he sold the place 'as is' Jerry; that means the furniture too!" Brian was upset. "Stop him Jerry; tell him to call his lawyer and he will find out he can't take any furniture."

Jerry parked and went back to talk to him; Bergensen argued for a bit and then went to the next door neighbor and asked to use his phone. He returned and he was not a happy camper; the scowl on his face would scare a tiger.

"My lawyer says I have to leave the furniture; help me move this table back inside. You can go through the house and check things but I have to be in Bridgehampton in a half hour; so let's get it over with."

The place was very clean and it didn't take Jerry long to inspect it. Bergensen was openly annoyed and they were glad to leave him to his grumbling; they got into the wagon and went back to the cottage. Their celebrating mood returned.

Tony and Brian went to the closing with Jerry; they stayed outside and were surprised at how quickly he returned. He had a folder with papers inside.

"The lawyer had everything ready for me to sign; Bergensen wasn't there and it went smoothly; he will have the deed recorded and I'll pick it up here when it comes back. I have to get a box at the post office." Jerry was happy.

"I hope you have the keys; that Swede might be on his way to Florida!"

Tony was laughing as he got into the wagon; "If I were you I would have the locks changed just to be on the safe side."

"I can do that myself and I will do it tomorrow. Let's go to my place now; we can inspect it in peace. I'll get my bag when I bring you back and then I'll go back and get myself settled in. Don't forget; we are going to Kincaid's for dinner; I'll pick you up around six, if that is okay with you."

"We will have to wear our tuxedos; this is a big occasion, we have a double celebration, your house and your wagon!" Brian was squeezing Jerry's shoulder; "and six o'clock is fine."

They didn't offer to help him get settled; they sensed he would want to do that alone. They realized this was the first place he had acquired on his own and it might be an emotional thing for him.

They arrived at Kincaid's for dinner and Bob had to come out and see his wagon as soon as he heard about it. He had nothing but praise for it; he knew the Swede and had put him out of his bar a few years ago and he never returned. He got drunk and started a fight with a guy half his size . . . Bob didn't like that and he shoved him out into the parking lot and told him to come back when he could behave himself. They heard that he made a wrong turn out at Lazy Point and got his truck stuck in the sand and had to walk the rest of the way home.

"Maybe that's why he never came back;" Bob was grinning.

They christened the wagon and the house with several toasts and Jerry stuck to drinking beer and he was spacing them admirably. Brian noticed this and was glad to see him watching himself . . . he made no comment.

Jerry had called Henry and told him he had closed on his house and Henry was coming early in the morning to start the garage. The weather had been clear and he wanted to take advantage of it. They were leaving Kincaid's early because of that.

"If I know Henry he'll be there right after sunrise," Tony was the first one out the door; "and he'll be ready to go to work."

"I've got my alarm clock with me so I'll be up before he gets there."

"You have to get a phone, Jerry; we should have told Bob, he has that friend in the company." Brian wanted to be helpful.

"He can use ours until he gets one; we're not even five minutes away." Tony was generous; as usual.

"How long are you going to stay out here Jerry? I've got to go back this coming Sunday; I can't believe how fast the time has gone. The Lauries, the people who are buying the house, have some friends that are coming out to look at the other houses. Mrs. Laurie thinks they might buy one; I really should be out here." Brian looked forlorn.

"When you go back give them a month's notice and come out here and give real estate all your time. Ed says you're a natural and you know you love it; so make the break!" Tony had a few drinks in him so he was a bit heated up.

"I'm going to do it; I have to feel right about it."

They were back at the cottage; Jerry parked with the motor running.

"Want to come in for a night cap, Jerry?"

Tony was at the driver's side of the wagon; Brian was opening the front door of the cottage.

"No thanks, Tony: I better get some shut eye and shape up for tomorrow. I have to have a clear head when Henry is asking for my opinion."

"I've been there; I know what you mean, thanks for dinner."

Tony watched him pull away; waving him off with a smile.

Jerry opened the door to his new abode and flipped the light switch. He was happy to see the lamp next to the couch light up and throw a soft glow throughout the room. The lawyer said he would have the utilities changed to Jerry's name . . . it's always nice when people do what they say they will do. He put his bags in the bedroom and went through the rooms lighting the place up. After looking in the closets and dressers and other storage areas; he became aware of another side of Bergensen. There were bed linens and towels and nice blankets all freshly laundered and good kitchen equipment including an almost new micro wave oven. The entire place was spotless and there were bars of soap in the bathroom still wrapped in their paper covers. Plenty of dishes and pots and pans filled the kitchen cabinets; all of good quality and spotlessly clean! Jerry was floored; he did not expect this! He need only go food shopping and hang up his clothes; this turned out to be a turn-key operation! Soon he would have a garage for the wagon and he would be all moved in. He was thinking of leaving the wagon in Lazy Point all the time; leaving his car in the city. He could ride out with Brian and Jerry or take the train. If he went ahead with his plans he would buy a small place in Florida and sell Nora's house; he still thought of it as hers. Then he would only need the wagon and he could get rid of his warm clothes. It would be nice to have Brian and Jerry come and visit him in the winter.

This place was too small to have company and he liked that. He didn't want to ever have Tom and Edith here; if Tom was in Hampton Bays seeing his children he could come to his place and they could go out to Montauk and go fishing on a party boat. Tom could sleep on the couch; it was big enough.

He put his things away and didn't really have much to do; it was late but he wasn't sleepy. He toyed with the idea of going to Kincaid's but decided against it; he actually didn't feel like drinking. It was a clear night and he got the notion to take a ride to the lighthouse. He picked up his cigarettes and keys and off he went . . . his stereo radio playing beautiful music and his spirits lifted.

Early the next morning Jerry drove to the cottage and found Brian and Tony were out on their deck having a glass of juice. He was glad they hadn't started breakfast; he wanted them to come to his place and he would make his first meal in his new abode. He wanted to show them how the Swede left the place. After ringing the outside bell he had walked through the living room to join them on the deck.

"Good morning! I'm glad you're up and not cooking."

He told them of his plans and that he was on his way to the store.

"We'll be honored to be your first guests; what time do you want us?"

"Come at nine-thirty; would you bring some Bloody Marys, please?; I don't have the makings and it's too early to buy booze."

"Will do"; Tony assured him; "can we bring anything else?"

"No, that will be a big help and it will be all I need; I'll see you later."

He hurried off feeling a new excitement and looking forward to being a host. In his eagerness to have them see his place Jerry completely forgot that Henry was coming this morning. When he returned from the store Henry was there and already laying out the footing for the garage. His helper had not yet arrived and Jerry told him of his plans with Brian and Tony.

"It is always good to see them," Henry paused for a moment; "you enjoy yourself and if I need you I'll knock on the door."

Brian and Tony were there promptly; Brian took over the Bloody Mary department. The kitchen was well organized; he assured Jerry he needed no help. The smell of the bacon cooking in the oven filled the entire place. Jerry took Tony on a tour of the closets and drawers showing him what the Swede had left him and how immaculate everything was;

"this is how he lived, Tony; he didn't do this for me; I don't think he liked me. I have to start the coffee; let's go back into the kitchen."

"We have to check up on our bartender," Tony smiled, "sometimes he gets to day dreaming."

Brian had a pitcher of drinks ready and he had just finished making the coffee; he accepted Jerry's thank you with a bow and said;

"that's how we do it out East."

Jerry put together a nice breakfast and they admired the dishes and kitchen ware the Swede had left. Tony was looking over the kitchen and his eyes kept coming back to a towel that was hanging down at the end of the counter; it seemed to be covering something. He put out his cigarette and went to the towel; lifting it up. The three of them hooted in chorus . . . it was a dishwasher and it was in show room condition! The Swede never used it and probably forgot about it!

Brian and Tony didn't stay too long after breakfast; they knew Jerry would be getting into huddles with Henry about the garage . . . that was inevitable; it was no place to hang around and be in the way. They said their farewells.

Tony waited until the house was straightened up and the bedrooms put in order; he lit a fire in the fireplace and asked Brian to sit with him.

"I want to talk to you about moving out here permanently; I think the time is right and I know you are having difficulty with the decision."

"I am; I hope you're not going to put pressure on me; I know I'm going to do it and I feel I will know when the time is right."

"You're worried about too many other people; I wish you would just think of us. That land development is going ahead and it will probably take a couple of years before the lots will be on the market. I would like to see you out here getting experience and having an important role in the marketing of the property. You would have your broker's license by then and be familiar with the area. It's very important. You might even have your own office; if you care to."

Brian gazed into the fire; he thought a couple of minutes before he answered. "I haven't been thinking that far ahead and you just gave me some real motivation. I can see how important what your saying really is; the simple truth, Tony, is that I should be thinking of you. All these other loyalties I've been moaning about are secondary to you and I haven't been seeing it that way; but I have my eyes wide open now and when I go back I'm giving two weeks notice and no more than that!"

Tony was hugging him. "I'm not trying to force you, Brian." He was filled with joy.

"I know you're not; you're thinking! And you are right on the money."

Tony bounced up; "this calls for a drink! How about a coffee with a stick of brandy in it? It's chilly enough for that." Brian smiled;

"It's a bit more than chilly, I'd say; and an excellent idea!"

Tony made the drinks and they went back by the fire. Now there was much to talk about and they came to the decision that Brian would go back by train as soon as possible and get things in motion and Tony would stay out East as long as Jerry was there and get some work accomplished. Tony wasn't saying what he had in mind; he wanted to add a garage for Brian's car to the carport. He wanted Jerry's ideas and he would have Henry build it. Tony wanted it ready when Brian returned. He had Brian on the phone checking the train schedule! He wrote the information down and Tony came into the living room with their jackets.

"Let's ride into East Hampton Station and pick up your ticket; we'll have to take your car; we can't be seen at the Station in the wagon!"

They were still laughing when they got into the car; both riding high.

After getting the ticket they drove over to Sag Harbor, an old historic whaling village; and had lunch in an old hotel restaurant. The quaint Victorian homes varied in size and architecture; most having been carefully restored. They were close together; having been built when this was sensible for cost and safety; and only people of wealth had large properties. The Harbor was popular with sailing devotees and some fine ships were moored at the docks. After lunch they drifted in and out of the many shops and bought a house present for Jerry.

Early morning found them putting Brian's bag in the wagon and heading for the station; they had done a lot of talking the night before; planning on the permanent move to Amagansett. Tony was hoping to have the garage finished before Brian returned and surprise him with it. He waited until the train pulled out from the station and then drove over to Jerry's place. He wanted to talk to Henry about the garage; the footings were already in place and Tony was always surprised at Henry's accomplishments, even though he was well aware of his ability. It looked like Jerry was going to have a cement floor; there was a small cement mixer parked on the street.

Jerry came to meet him as he got out of the wagon. He looked like he had been working;

"You're just what the doctor ordered, Tony, you should have first-hand knowledge of pouring and mixing cement. Italians invented it!"

"It's not something I've let many people in on; you get too dirty!"

"Come in and have some coffee; did you have breakfast?"

"Coffee is fine; we ate early before I took him to the train."

Jerry stopped and looked at him; "Brian went on the train . . . to the city?"

"Let's have coffee, Jerry, I have news for you."

Tony saw Henry and waved to him; Henry waved back too busy to talk. Jerry poured two mugs of coffee and heated them in the micro wave.

"What's going on? I hope there are no problems."

"No Jerry, it's all good news . . . wait 'til you hear."

He filled him in on the new developments and Jerry was excited about it.

"He's going to do well in the real estate business; it enables him to live out here and get out of that damn city. I'm going to buy a place in Florida for the winter and live here in the summer. You two can come and visit me any time."

"We will definitely take you up on that offer; we might even follow suit." They had cigarettes; Tony told him about adding the garage; Jerry lit up!

"You could put it onto the carport in an ell shape; it would look great."

He jumped up and got a pad and pen and sketched out an idea; Tony liked it.

"You should talk to Henry now; as soon as he finishes mine, he could start yours; while he has the cement mixer here. You know; he could stop working on mine and do your footings and cement floor then he wouldn't have to rent the mixer too long. Then he could frame mine and later finish yours."

Tony was laughing; "Easy pal, we have to talk to Henry; he might go bananas!"

"If Henry can work it so he only has to tow that mixer once; he will be very happy . . . I'm sure of that; how about another coffee?" Tony nodded.

He went out and brought Henry inside and heated three mugs of coffee. Henry went to his truck and produced a bottle of schnapps; "It is winter, men!"

Jerry put the idea to Henry and he was in agreement; as Jerry had said; he liked renting the mixer one time . . . Henry was not averse to saving money and time in one operation. It was incredible how quickly Henry and two helpers erected the two garages by dove-tailing the work. There was no sacrificing his usual perfection either; the buildings were perfect. Now Brian had a sheltered home for Valhalla; it would delight him no end. The garage was covered with cedar shakes to match the cottage and Jerry had put two cottage windows on each side close to each other with window boxes for geraniums. It looked like an addition to the cottage even though it wasn't attached. Tony was convinced that he had to make the move out here as soon as could be arranged.

As soon as Brian put his bags in his bedroom he went to the connecting door and yelled a 'hello' to Eleanor; he prayed she was home and luckily she was. She was picking up some things she needed.

"I'm still moving, Brian, it seems to go on forever."

"Come in and have a drink with me I need to talk to you and it is important. I came in from out East by train."

"Why by train? Is something wrong with the wagon?"

"No; it was quicker." He handed her a drink.

"Thank you, darling, I need that right now."

"Naturally if you have to make a faster move we will work with you; I'm going to have to lay in a supply of smelling salts for your clients . . . they will be in shock! Actually I've had three stylists who inquired about working with us and I like two of them very much. We might be able to do this quickly. I'll have the two that I like come in and do some heads as soon as they have time."

"I hate to lay this on you with such short notice; it's just that a bubble seemed to bust wide open; I've just sold a beautiful new house for a Sag Harbor builder and they have friends who are interested in buying one as well."

He told her about Valhalla and she was delighted for him; she hugged him.

"Only you would name a car! Things are happening, love, good things; I can't believe what has happened to me in a short time. I can't seem to get my breath. But I'm so happy . . . that is what is so wonderful."

"You've got the right guy; that's all it takes."

"And so have you; I told you it would come your way . . . remember?"

"Yes, miss 'I told you so'; I remember." He hugged her tightly.

"I have to get my things and head home; Gordon will be there in an hour and I want to be home before him."

They would see each other at work.

He set about preparations for the move; he had talked about subletting the apartment furnished but Tony quickly nixed the idea and told him to make a clean break. He would have to sell his furniture and he knew he could not get what it was worth. Tony advised him to get a second hand furniture guy to come in and give him an estimate on everything he wanted to sell; "get three of them!" He emphasized that the money was not important; "You'll make a lot of money."

The next day at the salon the two stylists came and did several heads and Eleanor was very pleased with their work and demeanor. They had both just moved to the city from out of town and were ready to start immediately. Brian did not have appointments and had time to talk with her. They decided a clean break was best and since Brian was on leave now he just would not come back. It was a sad and happy occasion simultaneously. Eleanor took him out for lunch and he asked her if he could have the addresses of his steady clients so he could write notes of explanation. She agreed to compile a list for him. It also occurred to him that all of his clients were wealthy and might well be good contacts for the real estate business. The lots they would be selling were excellent investments; he would enclose his card with each note. Ed Gorman had figured him correctly!

That afternoon one of the three dealers he called came and looked at his furniture. Brian told him two others were coming the next day and before he left they had struck a deal and Brian was delighted with what he realized.

"Tell those guys they were a day late and they missed a bonanza!"

He gave Brian a check for half the amount and they set a date for the removal to give him time to prepare. Brian called Tony and could not stop talking.

He contacted his landlord and explained his situation. Brian had a high rating with his landlord; he had never been late with his rent all the years he had lived there and had very few calls about problems. They arranged an appointment at the apartment the next day; the landlord had not been inside since Brian had moved in. As soon as he stepped inside he knew he could get more rent for the place. Walking through as they talked he was fair in his assessment and told Brian he would release him from his lease immediately and would give him a check for the return of his security.

"If you will stop by my office tomorrow after one; the papers will be waiting for you. Brian, if all my tenants were like you I would never have suffered the ulcer I have . . . you have been a perfect tenant. By the way, your security check will include accrued interest which has added up over the years; in your case it is a pleasure to be paying it."

"Thank you, Mr. Elders; I've loved living here and remember, Eleanor will have the connecting door removed at our expense before she moves."

"She has been in touch with me and she is planning a gradual move. It seems like you both have had big changes in your lives at the same time. Brian give me one of your business cards; I want to give you my home address and keep me in mind if you have any good deals out there . . . I'm very interested in that part of Long Island. Brian immediately told him about the development that was in the works and explained the terms which were excellent for investing . . . "and you don't have to do any maintenance on a vacant lot;" he concluded.

"I would definitely be interested in those lots; as soon as you have a brochure send it to me and I'll come out and take a look at them."

They parted company wishing each other well. Brian was delighted everything was falling into place. He had no furniture to move; he was taking a few paintings and some things that had sentimental attachments and the rest was clothes. He could leave everything in Eleanor's apartment and bring the wagon to take it all out to the cottage. He was on his way to living in the Hamptons and starting a career he loved!

Eleanor was a busy lady these days and she had grown to like Austin, Gordon's houseman, very much. He was so efficient and he kept the apartment spotless. When the cleaning people came they knew right away that they were there to work; no radios or TVs were turned on . . . Austin only wanted to hear vacuum cleaners or floor polishers. At lunch time he sat them in the kitchen and served them a nice lunch. No alcoholic drinks were permitted; he made excellent tea and coffee. Shortly after Gordon learned of Eleanor's pregnancy he had a talk with Austin and asked him if he would consider moving in as live-in help; there was a large bedroom and bath and it had a nice balcony. It was private from the main part of the apartment and it had a doorway onto the entrance foyer. He had no wish to leave the best employer he had ever had and he had already developed a fondness and respect for Eleanor. Austin had always lived with his sister and her husband so there were no complications in his move. In two days he was completely installed and happy as a jay bird.

Gordon didn't hang over Eleanor like a mother hen but he made sure she got her proper rest and knowing she had a busy day, every day; he instructed Austin to consult with her but he was to relieve her of any stressful details. Because Austin was fond of her; he was happy to do this. They didn't do much entertaining at home and Gordon tried to keep week nights free of socializing. Austin was a marvelous chef and it seemed stupid to eat out when they had such wonderful meals at home. And as far as Gordon was concerned they were still honeymooning. Once a month they spent a week-end with Dotty and Frank and it was always fun. His life was so full since he met Eleanor and all he wanted was her happiness. She had stopped drinking and smoking as soon as she knew of her pregnancy and he admired her so much for that. He was trying to quit and he never smoked in front of her anymore. When the baby came he wanted to be smoke free. Austin didn't smoke so he was the only polluter! Gordon's life had much more purpose now and it was all because he had found the woman he needed. He day-dreamed of packing in this city living and taking Eleanor and their child to the ranch; they could live a more genteel life and the child would have an out-door upbringing. Helping his child select a horse bemused him for quite a while.

Jerry had driven into the city to meet with the lawyer. He had decided to sell the house and rent for the winter in Florida; six months would be ample time to find something to buy. He would have the best of both worlds and avoid the monotony. Several of the guys he had worked with had homes in Florida; this gave him some contacts down there. He called Brian and filled him in on his plans.

"Would you like to go to Tony's for a bite to eat?"

"That sounds good; what time?"

"I'll pick you up at six; is that okay?"

"Six is fine; see you later."

Brian was down on the street and Jerry was on time;

"I was surprised to know you were in town; is something up?"

Jerry smiled; "I can't keep up with my own mind . . . it is spinning!"

"So is mine; we have something in common."

"I've decided to sell the house; I came in to see Tom Sullivan. I'm going down to Florida and rent a place for six months; while I'm there I'll look for something to buy."

"That's a smart way to buy; you have plenty of time to look the different areas over. I understand most New Yorkers prefer the East coast; I've never been to Florida so I don't have an opinion."

Brian filled Jerry in on his latest developments and Jerry was surprised at how quickly things were moving.

"Tony told me you were leaving the salon but he didn't mention you were getting out of your apartment so fast."

"He doesn't know it yet; in two more days I'll be able to go back out East. Then I can bring the wagon back and take my things to the cottage; everything is in Eleanor's right now."

"You can fill up my wagon and go back out with me; I'll be going back in a couple of days."

"Oh, that would be great! I get to ride in your new wheels."

They were at Tony's and it was quite busy; Gino and Mario were both behind the bar and they were moving! They had to take a small table; all the stools were occupied. Brian went to the table and Jerry went to the end of the bar and ordered the drinks.

"They've got you hopping, Gino," he said cordially.

"Almost all day . . . and there's no full moon."

Jerry took the drinks and asked Gino to make a tab;

"Can we get a bite to eat or is it too busy? We're in no hurry."

"I can do a meatball hero and a salad; how is that?"

"Fine . . . when you have time, Gino."

Gino went down the bar thinking Jerry should have retired long ago; he actually sounded like a human being now! They had a few beers; Mario had brought their sandwiches and shortly after they finished eating they decided to call it a night.

Jerry took Brian home; "I will call you tomorrow night and we'll plan our trip out East."

"I'll be home; goodnight, Jerry, and thanks."

The next day Jerry called Tom and arranged to meet him when he finished his shift. He would be off by four in the afternoon; they agreed to meet at a nearby Irish bar. He then called Tom Sullivan and made an appointment. That just about killed the day. He called Brian and asked him for advice about selling Nora's furniture; he forgot it the night before.

"I would have an appraisal done; your lawyer could recommend a reliable one. There are some beautiful pieces there and you don't want to give them away; Eleanor told me her bedroom suite is very special."

"I have an appointment with him today; thanks Brian, I'll let you know how I make out."

He met with Tom Sullivan and Tom advised him that the house was not part of his trust and he could sell it without any legal entanglements. He agreed that the furniture should be appraised and called a friend of his and arranged an appointment for the next day.

"After you have settled down in Florida you should think about becoming a resident; it's good for you tax-wise. I have a half-dozen lawyer friends scattered around down there; I'll have my secretary give you a list. You can try and buy near one of them; it is a good idea to have one there. They are all good and will take good care of you."

Tom also gave him the name of a realtor whom he recommended highly; Jerry had already asked him to handle the sale of the house.

He stepped out into the sunlight and was surprised that he had been there two hours; he felt a great sense of satisfaction and never thought he would be doing such things as sitting with lawyers and meeting brokers and appraisers. Nora had done all this for him; a shadow passed over his heart as he had a brief recall of that dark, dingy street where he pursued his satisfaction when he should have been home with her. Tears stung his eyes and he walked quickly to his wagon to get moving. He wanted to wrap all this up and get back out East where he could breathe . . . he felt cleaner there. Suddenly this city was like a muzzle on him; he was claustrophobic in these streets that once held excitement for him and the snugness and seclusion of his little hut called to him.

He met Tom at the bar and they greeted each other warmly.

"Well, that East end is certainly doing a job on you, Jerry; you look terrific!" Tom was shaking his hand.

"It's awfully good to see you Tommy boy; you look mighty good yourself." Each ordered a beer.

They filled in on their individual happenings; Jerry having much to tell. After almost an hour Jerry asked the question he would rather avoid;

"How is Edith; is everything going along okay?"

"Yes we're hitting it very well and it keeps getting better. I had a long talk with Lucille and I've told her I will never ask her for a divorce. If she comes to me and wants one; she's got it! I know how much her religion means to her and I will always respect that. I want to make a break with her; I can't go home and lay next to her in bed when I don't want to touch her anymore; not even for the kids. Her father died two weeks ago and her mother is alone out in Hampton Bays. I suggested that she sell our house; she can have whatever profit it brings and move out with her mom. This would be a good explanation for the kids until they are old enough to understand what actually happened. I don't want them thinking it's their fault and getting all twisted up in their heads."

"How did she react to the idea?"

"She did quite a double-take at first; then we talked and I had to let her know how much I cared for Edith and that I was never coming back. I told her she needed a complete change for her own sake. Lucille sat for a while and just stared into space; she was dry-eyed and cool . . . she scared me a little; then she said, "It makes sense; I'll do it."

"Just like that; no protest at all?"

"Just like that; the house in Hampton Bays is spacious and there's plenty of room for all of them. This way she won't have to worry about her mother and financially it works out fine. She will inherit that house and her mother has a pretty good portfolio; her future is secure. If something happens to me she gets my pension; right now I have a check sent to her automatically as soon as my paycheck is deposited. She has more security than I'll ever have. I want my kids to have a good home."

"Are you going to stay at her house when you visit the kids?"

"No; that would be uncomfortable for everybody. I'll get a motel; the kids and I can rough it together. Then I'll take a week at Christmas and stay at a motel again and do things with them; Edith and I will have New Year's and we'll celebrate Christmas early. She agrees to all this; she's told me she will never press me to marry her; I don't see that ever happening unless Lucille meets someone and wants her freedom . . . I doubt that will ever occur."

"You're just going to see the kids two weeks out of the year?"

"No, not at all; I can take week-ends here and there especially if the kids have something special that parents should attend. They're not going to have a missing father."

All the while Jerry listened to his buddy he seethed inside at the cause of all this; Edith got all the blame in his mind . . . he hated her. He fantasized that she would be hit by a bus and instantly killed or some other awful fate. He never placed any blame on Tom. Tom's voice roused him back to life; he actually startled him.

"You certainly have turned your life around, Jerry; you have a whole new thing going on; I think it's great."

"Nora gave me a new life; I never imagined she was so well off. I have to laugh at how I thought I was going to take care of her . . . she took care of me in a way I couldn't match."

"You gave her something money can't buy . . . a reason to live; she loved you like a son and you loved her and she knew it. She told me that her life really began when you moved in with her."

"I miss her, Tom; she could get me laughing just being Nora and snapping those fast comebacks . . . she was never without a smart reply."

"You have good memories; they'll come in handy someday."

"They are a big help right now; I'm glad to be getting out of the house, I can't forget how I found her . . . hanging in that bathtub."

"Time will take care of that but don't dwell on it; that's no good."

Tom looked at his watch; Edith was already at home for an hour. "I've got to go; it's been good talking with you again; when I'm out visiting the kids I'll come out to see you . . . maybe I'll see you in Florida; you never know."

"You know you're welcome anytime . . . just call."

He gave Jerry a hug and went on his way; back to that bitch thought Jerry. He picked up his change leaving a few bills for the bartender.

Jerry had wound up all he set out to accomplish and was feeling quite proud; he called Brian who had also accomplished what he needed to do. Brian called Tony and he was delighted with his progress finishing the conversation with "get your little butt back home pronto!"

Jerry came over in the afternoon and they packed the wagon; he had a lot of stuff but the wagon had a lot of room . . . everything fit in! They were leaving at four in the morning; both anxious to get back home. Tony had told Brian to invite Jerry for lunch and he would have what would really be dinner; "we have a lot to celebrate . . . all of us!" Knowing they were going to have a big lunch they ate lightly when they stopped in Hampton Bays; they had several cups of coffee and enjoyed each others company. It was about eight o'clock when they arrived and it didn't take long for the three of them to unload Brian's things. Jerry asked if they needed his help inside and he was assured everything was fine.

"Get some rest and bring your appetite back around one. And don't bring anything else!" Tony was laughing; "Especially the clap!"

Jerry drove off shaking his head and laughing. He came back about one and they each had a beer; Brian had made a New England boiled dinner and beer went well with it. They chatted about the events going on and while Brian was in the kitchen Tony and Jerry were discussing the garages. Tony stopped and asked Jerry when he was going to Florida.

"I'd like to wait until the house is sold then I won't have to make a trip back up here if I'm needed; the broker seems to think it will go fast."

"I don't doubt that; it's in good shape and very well located."

"At first I felt funny about selling it; but the memories are bad."

"Jerry, you know Nora would want you to do what is good for you; she didn't make any conditions . . . so follow your dream."

"You make me feel good, Tony; I get guilty easy."

"You have nothing to be guilty about; you were wonderful to her we all could see that and we admired you for it."

Jerry wished he could tell Tony where he was before he came home; he knew it would help him if he could talk about it. He decided to tell him.

"I can see why that would bother you, Jerry; we all have our weaknesses; I'll tell you in confidence I had the same one as you. That is definitely between you and me; but how were you to know all that was going to happen? You couldn't; don't torture yourself and remember all the nice things you did for her; Nora wouldn't hold it against you."

"Thanks, Tony; that really helps. She was so good to me."

"Remember she wanted you to enjoy what she left you."

Jerry had the sudden urge to show Tony the letter from Nora; he had not shown it to anyone. He stood up and said he had to go home and would be right back. Tony was startled; but he was out the door in a trice.

"Did I hear Jerry go out?" Brian came in from the kitchen.

"He said he had to go home and would be right back."

"Maybe he left something cooking on the stove."

"Get a grip on yourself, Brian; why would he be cooking knowing he was coming here? I'm sure he will tell us when he comes back."

"But I'm bugged with curiosity now! I'm wondering what's up."

"Good grief! What is with you? I know you need help but do you need any help with the dinner? I'm not a psychologist."

"Everything's under control; let's have a beer."

"Thank God you're back to normal; I thought you were losing it."

Five minutes later Jerry returned and handed Tony the letter. "Nora left this for me; I'm sure you understand it's very private."

Tony read the letter and his eyes filled with tears; "This is a treasure, Jerry; may I show it to Brian before he explodes? He's going to bust apart with curiosity!"

"Of course, we have to keep him together; the aroma from the kitchen tells me how necessary he is."

Brian read the letter; wiping his eyes he handed it back to Jerry. "You should have this sealed in plastic so it doesn't deteriorate; it's something you will always cherish. I think it is so beautiful. Dinner is ready we're having buffet; come and fix your plates. Tony will you open some beer, please?"

After commenting on how delicious the dinner was there wasn't very much conversation until the coffee and dessert were served. This seemed to trigger energy into the mix and they were back to light chatter and kidding each other. Jerry went home and Brian and Tony talked about his staying in the cottage permanently.

"I've got to get together with Gino and finalize our deal; I think I can leave him on his own now. He has a little trouble with the ordering of the stock but he will get the hang of it; Mario is smart and is a big help. He has to get the license in his name and he has been dragging his heels on that; I hope it doesn't turn out that he has a police record from away back or some damn thing."

"Please don't look for trouble! It's bad enough when it happens . . . don't go looking for it." Brian tousled his hair; "Think positive!"

"I think we need a nap." Tony stood up; "Come along, buddy."

About a week or so later Jerry received a call from Tom; he was in Hampton Bays helping Lucille move into her mother's home. They had things just about wound up and he wanted to ride out and visit.

"Is it okay with you Jerry? I don't want to interrupt anything."

"You come right on out; it will be great seeing you. Get a piece of paper and pen and let me give you directions; it's a little complicated the first time you come. Can you stay overnight?"

Tom took out his note book; "Yes I can; go ahead with the directions."

Jerry ended telling him to call when he reached Amagansett and he would be waiting on Montauk Highway to show him the way to his place. Tom would be leaving in half an hour. Jerry was excited with this surprise;

"I'll be waiting for you; drive carefully but hurry on out!"

Jerry figured it would take him almost an hour to get there so he left early enough to be on the highway before he arrived. He was only there ten minutes when he saw Tom coming; he blinked his lights and turned to go over the railroad tracks and Tom fell in behind him. When they entered the hut; as Jerry called it, Tom was very impressed.

"It's a regular little hideaway; even the FBI couldn't find you here! You didn't have to do a lot of work on it; was it like this when you bought it? It's in such good shape and the workmanship is first class."

"I just had the garage built and the hut was pretty much as you see it . . . it even has a dish washer!"

"It's all you need and it should be easy to take care of."

"It is; I'm still going to have a cleaning woman every couple of weeks so it stays the way it is. Brian and Tony have a very good lady and she is going to start next week. When I'm in Florida she will come once a month. She will do my laundry, too."

"Jerry Foley you have become a country gentleman; and will soon have a winter getaway in Florida and follow those ex-cops down there."

He raised the bottle of beer Jerry had given him while they were talking and toasted him. "Here's to you, pal."

"We have a great spot in Montauk where we go to eat and drink; run by an Irishman, of course; I want to take you there for dinner and I'll call Brian and Tony to see if they can join us. Wait until you meet this Bob Kincaid; he is some piece of work. I'm not going to tell you anything about him; I want you to meet him cold turkey."

He opened a closet and told Tom to put his things in it; then he picked up the phone and called Brian and they were delighted with the invitation and Brian said they looked forward to seeing Tom.

"Come early and we'll have a couple of drinks here before we go."

"We're all set; they want us to have a couple of drinks at their place before we go. They have done some job on the cottage; you will be impressed with it; I'm sure."

"It sounds like fun in Amagansett; you've made a good move."

"So far, so good; let's go for a walk and tour the neighborhood."

They pulled up in front of the cottage; the sun was low in the sky heading toward its setting. The sky was clear with only a few wisps of gossamer clouds and there was the promise of a beautiful sunset. Jerry mentioned he had designed their new garage and had helped build it.

"No wonder you're looking so good; it's beautiful! When you drive up it looks like it is part of the house. Jerry; you really did make the right move and having these guys for friends certainly helps."

"Let me tell you; they are real friends."

They walked up to the entrance and Jerry rang the school bell; smiling.

"Come right in; it's good to see you Tom; welcome to our little piece of paradise. Brian; come and take the drink orders."

"You're right there! I'm getting the snacks."

Everyone laughed; outside they had sensed the scent of a fire burning; in the house it filled the room with that wonderful odor that said welcome. Tom was knocked out with what he was looking at; the outside looked charming and snug, inside was open and spacious and the glass walls offered a view in every direction.

"This is really sensational! The view is incredible and you have nobody near you. It's one hell of a piece of paradise; believe me."

Tony took him on a tour of the place and Brian ended up with the drinks; they came in from the deck and settled down by the fire.

"I can see why you want out of the city to live here; it is so peaceful and that city is a zoo. I'm glad my kids are out here now and Lucille has them enrolled in Catholic school and that makes me breathe a lot easier. I'll be in there for quite a while; I'm definitely going twenty-five years on the job; maybe more if I land the right job."

Nobody made any comment about his family because they were aware of the Edith situation and they were reluctant to say anything. The sunset was magnificent and they started for Montauk before it was finished; Tom was right at home in Kincaid's; they hit it off immediately and he enjoyed the honky-tonk piano and the dinner.

"It's a good thing I don't live near this place; I'd blow half my paycheck coming here; it is so real and the people are such a great mix and what can you say about Kincaid? He's definitely one-of-a-kind."

"He has been such a big help to all of us; he's saved us a lot of grief, especially with getting contractors." Brian was waving a celery stick as he was speaking.

"Are you directing the piano player, Brian?" Tony grinned.

He was embarrassed; he didn't realize he was waving it. "That's my new part-time job, smarty."

"You don't have time for any part-time job; you're busy!"

Brian had a deal going on a second house; friends of the Lauries had made an offer and if Sam would give them the same mortgage arrangement they would buy it. Brian didn't want to talk about it until the contracts were signed. They didn't make a late night of it because Tom had to leave early in the morning. Suddenly Tom jumped up swearing;

"I need a phone right away; I forgot to make an important call!"

"Right in the kitchen; it's on the wall, nobody's in there."

Kincaid took him by the shoulders and pointed him in the right direction.

Jerry looked at Tony; "I bet he forgot to call Edith."

Brian winced; "Oh God; for his sake I hope not."

He wasn't gone long and he wasn't smiling when he came back.

"That was a New York call, Bob; I want to pay you for it."

"Forget about it; and I mean forget about it." Kincaid had spoken.

They took care of their check and headed for the cottage. Tom was silent. Jerry dropped Brian and Tony at their door; they refused night caps as Tom had to leave early in the morning. When they arrived at the hut Jerry began to fix a bed for Tom on the couch; Tom took the bedding saying;

"I'll do this; see if you can scare up a couple of beers."

"I can do that . . . no problem, pal."

They sat down and Jerry could see he was troubled about something.

"You look worried; is something wrong?"

"Well Jerry; I forgot to call Edith she didn't know I was going to come out to see you . . . I didn't know it myself; for that matter. I was supposed to call her when I was starting back to the city; when I did call her and I told her I was staying over she got ticked off because she had prepared food for our dinner. What burned me up was she asked me if I was staying at Lucille's and pretending I was with you. I got a bit testy with her and I hung up . . . she really pissed me off!"

"I thought she was fully aware of how you were going to be with your family; she seemed to be taking that graciously."

"She was very agreeable to it; I told her we would probably never be able to get married. That was okay with her; I have to nip this stuff in the bud . . . I can't live with nagging; no way."

"She'll be calmed down by the time you get home; are you going to the job directly from here?"

"I am now; I was going to go home first that's why I wanted to leave at four in the morning. I'll leave around five instead."

"I'll make breakfast before you leave."

"No don't do that; I'll stop at a diner and get some take out and eat it on the way. The coffee is the main thing."

"Whatever you want; it's no trouble; I'll make coffee and you can take a thermos with you. I have several of them."

"I'd appreciate that; I need my coffee in the morning. Well I better hit the sack; have you got an alarm clock?"

"Yes, I'll wake you in plenty of time; you'll smell the coffee."

They said goodnight and Jerry couldn't help feeling a bit of joy over Edith's problem; maybe it was the start of a break-up . . . Edith might be reverting to type. He would sleep well. Tom was on his way by five and Jerry went back to bed.

Now that Brian had pulled off his big surprise and was, for all purposes; permanently in Amagansett Tony was anxious about his move. He decided to drive in and stay a few days and build a fire under Gino. He called Gino to let him know he was coming; Gino was glad to hear it;

"We've been really busy and I've got some money for you and I'll be glad to get rid of it!"

"You have that much money?" Tony was laughing.

"Yes; that much money!"

"I'll see you later on; do you need me to bring anything?"

"No, we're okay; you drive carefully it will be good to see you."

Tony arrived at his apartment about eleven that morning. He took care of a few things around the place and went to the bar. He would have lunch there. Mario was there giving them a chance to sit at a table over coffee and discuss matters. Gino was uneasy about the license; Tony eyed him;

"Gino; if you have a problem with the license I want to hear it! We can't do anything if I don't know what's wrong!"

"Years ago I tried to sell a car with doctored documents; it had to do with my brother-in-law who was not too honest at the time. I got nailed for it and I did some small time but it's in my record. I had forgotten all about it and when I put in the application they notified me. Mario talked to a lawyer friend of his and he says it can be set aside; or something like that, but I need a special lawyer and they cost real money. My daughter is planning to get married soon and I am going to need a lot of money for her. That's where I'm at; I was hoping you'd wait until I had the money."

"I want to have all the legal work and the insurance out of my hands so I can relax; you have to stay on top of this business . . . you know that and I'm getting out so I won't have the headaches. I can't live out East and worry about this place." He put his hand on Gino's hand; "I have an idea; why don't you and Mario go partners on this place and put the license in his name. You can work out a separate agreement that makes you equal partners. You two get along great and there's enough money coming in here for the both of you. It will also give you a chance to take time off."

Gino looked bewildered; it had never occurred to him to have a partner. "I don't know if he wants to do that."

"Gino; you have to ask him so he can think about it; does he know about your problem with the license?"

"Yeah; I tell him everything."

"Are you both going to be here at closing tonight? If you are I'll come back and we can talk; don't say anything until we're alone."

"We'll both be here; come about two; if it's slow I'll close early."

They had lunch together and talked about their plan.

Tony came back at two in the morning and by three they were closed. Gino asked Mario to skip the clean-up and come and have a drink with them. Tony outlined his idea and Mario was all attention; he was interested and did not hesitate to say so. When Gino told him about his license problem he was hoping he was going to ask him then . . . but since he didn't say anything he assumed he didn't want a partner.

"It never entered my mind, Mario; you know I'm a bit slow."

They had a much needed laugh and Gino refreshed their drinks.

"So we'll get busy on the partnership and please don't try to do it without a lawyer. I'll pay a third of his fee, with this New York liquor board you have to have everything written up tight. Mario; talk to your lawyer friend; if he can handle it that's so much the better; if not ask him to recommend someone. Finish your drinks and I'll help you clean up." There was a mild protest form Gino that they didn't need help.

Tony was determined to stay until he was satisfied that the legal work was underway. He was happy that Mario was a willing participant and as much as he liked Gino he knew Mario was much smarter. Tony felt the details would not be overlooked with Mario involved. When he arrived back in his apartment and opened the envelope Gino had given him he was amazed at the amount of money. It was a testimony to Gino's honesty; he decided to pay half of the legal fees. While he was getting ready for bed he started whistling a tune; it was subconscious; he didn't even notice it until he began brushing his teeth. Smiling into the mirror he thought he must be getting slap-happy.

Tom finished his shift and arrived at Edith's before she got home. He showered and shaved putting on his terry cloth robe when he finished. Normally he would wait until she came in before he made a drink but the urge told him; *now*. He had only taken a few sips when Edith arrived. She was visibly nervous; he kissed her briefly and walked to the window; he spoke to her looking out the window.

"Can you give me a reason for saying what you said yesterday?"

"Would you mind looking at me if you're going to talk; I don't have a window to look out of." He turned;

"I'm looking at you."

"It would have been nice if I could have a drink, too, but I don't need one that badly. I got worried when you didn't call . . . I also fixed a dinner of veal chops which I ended up throwing out; can you blame me for being upset?" She walked to the bar and made a drink.

"No; you had every right to be upset; but the insinuation that I was at Lucille's when I told you I was visiting Jerry makes me uncomfortable with where your mind is. I won't live with imaginary suspicions and the inference that I was lying." He refilled his glass; she was crying.

"What was I supposed to think? I thought she trumped up some reason to keep you there to spite me!"

"Lucille is a classy woman; she doesn't stoop to that nonsense. She has accepted the situation and is carrying out what we planned; I have to help her; I have obligations toward her. You gave me the impression that you understood all that and you were more than willing to live with it. Have you changed your mind?"

She put down her glass and ran to him; flinging her arms around him. "Oh God no; I just suddenly felt like I was losing you especially when you didn't call . . . I'm still not sure of myself."

He picked up her drink and handed it to her; "Edith, sit down here and listen to me. We fell in love and it has caused a lot of grief. Lucille has religious convictions that are very strong; I understand them. I made the decision to leave her but I can't leave all the years I had with her. I'll always hold her in high regard; any time you think you have a difficulty believe me she is having much more. I have a cozy life here with you . . . she has three kids to cope with; I told her I was in love with you and I assured her that when she needed me where the kids were concerned I would be available. If she meets someone and can have a new life that will be good for all of us but I have to keep my word with her or I won't be able to have a life with you. If you're going to have hysterics over every little thing we are not going to make it."

"I'm sorry Tom; you have my word there will be no more of this. I understand things better; kiss me sweetheart."

He kissed her longingly his passion arousing quickly;

"Let me take a quick shower; Tom, I'll be right back."

"Make it real quick!" He patted her butt as she left.

Jerry would have to put his fantasies on hold.

Brian was now going to the office everyday; he had his own desk and file cabinet and he liked the staff and was made to feel welcome. Ed was telling him he was on his own about finding the listings the office had and going to each one and learning what they consisted of;

"You will get lost looking for them, we all do, but it is good training and you automatically will become familiar with the various areas. I find that you remember everything better with this method. I'm available any time you need help but the sooner you can move on your own initiative the better you will be at selling. I see you have a second contract on one of Sam's houses; I'm very proud of you Brian; I knew you had it in you."

"Thanks Ed; I love this business and I am getting to know the place pretty quickly; there sure are some beautiful properties out here."

He said goodbye and took his maps to go hunting down listings. There was a listing that consisted of several small lots that were part of an old subdivision on the old road that wound its way to Montauk. They were reasonable in price and as he looked at his map he realized they must have ocean views because the land was high. He was heading out to see if he could locate them. The roads through the old development were narrow and winding; the sign posts with the names of the streets were new and it was easy to locate the streets. He located the lots and though they were small they were grand-fathered in as legal. The zoning in this area was now a minimum of one acre per house. The lots were marked with yellow stakes and in the midst of properties that used several lots to build homes and none of them were close together. The area was well covered with natural growth; pine trees grew thick and wild. There were five lots in total meaning five houses could be built here. Properly placed each house would have a wonderful ocean view. And who was the one who could properly place them? Sam Anderson! He got back to his car quickly and since the cottage was only five minutes from where he was it was the nearest phone. He called Sam and luckily he was in his office. Taking a deep breath and keeping calm he explained the lots to Sam ending with;

"I think your kind of home would bring a great price here; the view is incredible and the price is right." Sam moved quickly;

"Where are you Brian?"

"I'm home, I came here to phone you; I just saw the lots now."

"Stay there; I'll pick you up as soon as I can . . . I'm leaving now."

Sam came up the road at a pace leaving the sound of crunched scallop shells in his wake; he came to a screeching halt.

"Hop in Brian; this sounds good."

Brian hopped up in the truck and they were off; it seemed to Brian that it took all of two minutes to get there. He directed him to the lots and Sam did not play it coy; the existing homes were well kept and attractive there was no risk here. He wanted these lots . . . all of them!

"I want them Brian; you saved the best thing for last; there's town water here! I don't have to dig wells. Am I the first one you called?

"I thought of you right away; you will know how to place the homes that is very important here; each house has to have a view."

"I had a feeling about you and I was right; we're going to do a lot of business; you will never regret being loyal to me. Let's get back to your house and the phone . . . I want to make an offer."

Brian was ecstatic; his heart was racing and he knew he had to settle down. They pulled up to Brian's place and jumped out of the truck.

"Are we dealing with another broker or with the owner directly?"

"We are dealing with the owner."

"Good; tell him I will pay the full price for his lots if he will give me release clauses; if he is interested I will explain the release clauses to him."

Brian called and made the offer; he answered some questions the owner had and then he asked to speak to Sam. The owner was an accountant and he was familiar with Sam's intention. They worked out terms over the phone and Sam had Brian follow him back to his office to give him a check. He would come to Ed's office tomorrow to sign the papers.

"I want to speak to Ed about something important; tell him."

Brian drove home ten feet above ground; what a lucky day it was when he met Sam! He couldn't wait to call Tony.

Sam was at the office early the next morning and the papers were signed and Brian was going to go to the post office and mail them to the owner for his signature right after Sam left. Ed took Sam aside and said;

"Brian told me you wanted to talk to me about something."

"Yes; I don't know what your policy is in your office but I would like Brian to have an exclusive on selling the houses I'll be building. I'm very impressed with him and I want to show him I appreciate his thinking of me for this property."

"All you need to do is tell me that, and you have; and they will be Brian's listing; I suggest you put a time limit on the exclusive for your own protection . . . you can always extend it."

"That makes sense; give him a year with all five houses."

The house wasn't selling as quickly as Jerry had hoped and time was beginning to hang heavy on his hands. He had started drinking again and he couldn't get Edith out of his thoughts; he brooded about the trouble she had caused and how, in his mind, she had ruined Tom's life. The fact that it was none of his business did not occur to him.

Brian had been very busy and it suddenly dawned on him that he hadn't heard from Jerry in over a week; he called him just to say hello and there was no answer. He put the phone down deciding to call him later on. Eight o'clock that evening he tried again and still no answer. He wondered if he had to go back to the city; maybe there was a buyer for the house but he was sure Jerry would have called him if that was the case. A germ of concern was growing inside Brian; he didn't like the feeling.

The next morning he tried again and had the same result. Now he was worried; he had to get to the office but resolved to stop at Jerry's place on his way home. Mrs. Laurie had called him and she had another friend who had spent the week-end at her home and was interested in looking at the houses.

"Her name is Anne Adams and she will be here next week-end; her husband will be with her. Please save some time Saturday afternoon; I'll call you Saturday morning and set up an appointment for an exact time. I'm so excited about this; she's a dear friend and I would love to have her close buy during the summer."

"I'll save plenty of time, Mrs. Laurie, they can take their time with each house; I appreciate your bringing her out, I'm beginning to think we should call that section Laurie Ville!"

"Oh Brian; that is wonderful; my husband will get a charge out of that . . . he loves your sense of humor. See you Saturday."

He was able to leave the office around four o'clock and he drove directly to Jerry's. He was relieved to see his wagon there and knocked on the door. He waited and heard no sound and knocked once more; still no reply and he tried the door and it was unlocked. He entered calling Jerry and then he stopped; Jerry was passed out on the couch and the smell of whiskey and cigarettes stifled him. He turned around and opened the door to let some fresh air in; then he tried to rouse Jerry. It took some time to get him conscious and he finally sat up groaning;

"Don't bother with me Brian; I'm okay . . . I just took a nap."

"The way this place smells you must be napping for days. In case you don't know it, Mr. Foley, *you are drunk!* And I do mean drunk!"

"I had a few; I don't deny it."

"A few indeed; do you have any cream of chicken soup here?"

"I think I do; are you hungry?"

"Am I hungry? You get up and get in that shower and then shave and try to come out looking human; don't give me any stories; just go."

It was getting chilly; he shut the door and turned the heat up. Looking in the closet he found the can of soup and began to prepare it. It was Brian's cure for hangovers.

"What the hell set him off?" He said to himself aloud.

Jerry came into the kitchen; he was cleaned up and dressed. "Do I look any better now? I think I feel better."

"Well at least you look like Jerry Foley; sit down and have some soup; have you had anything to eat in the last twenty-four hours? You probably haven't eaten at all."

"I was sleeping a lot; I know that."

"You were drinking and smoking a lot, that's for sure; this place smelled like a Bowery saloon when I came in. What got into you . . . what's wrong? Everything seems to be going so good for you."

"I got to brooding about what that Edith bitch has done to Tom's life and it just started getting to me and I hit the booze."

"You have to face reality and put half of the blame on your buddy Tom; Edith didn't do this alone. To be honest with you, it's none of your business; Tom is a big boy and he knows what he is doing. It's not the first marriage to go under; people change you can't get involved with them. I know you don't want to hear it but Edith is a different person since she has been with Tom; he brings out the best in her and if he is willing to go through all this mess of leaving his wife and kids and working all that out as fairly as he can he must be in love with Edith."

"I know what he's in love with."

"If that's all there was to it he would never have left his family. He could have her whenever he wanted to; stop thinking about it!"

"That's easier said than done, Brian."

"Finish your soup; there's some left in the pot, just warm it up for a bit. Come over later and have dinner with me; you've been alone too much. Are you sober enough to drive? I'll come and get you if you like."

"I'll be fine; what time do you want me to come?"

"Seven will be good; that gives me plenty of time."

Brian drove home and called Tony and filled him in on the latest happenings. Tony told him to keep an eye on Jerry;

"He should get some kind of a part-time job to occupy his mind."

"That's a good idea Tony; he could do handyman work for those estates in East Hampton; they would appreciate the kind of work he does. I'm going to tell him to put an ad in the paper."

They said good-bye; Brian was glad the deal with Gino was moving on. He had a beef stew in the freezer and decided to have it for dinner. When Jerry came Brian made two of Tony's 'special' drinks; Jerry drank it without comment and they spent a couple of hours together and Jerry went home. He seemed to like the idea of a part-time job. Brian had cleaned up the kitchen and was sitting at his desk looking over some papers when the phone rang; it was Eleanor;

"Hello darling, how are you? Don't answer; I know you are marvelous! Gordon and I are going to be in Southhampton this week-end and we would like to drive out on Sunday and take you two out for lunch. Are you free?"

"I'm not free but I'm reasonable; Tony is in New York but I would love to see you. I have a lot to tell you; it will probably bore Gordon to sleep. Do you think you can find the cottage?"

"Yes, I'm sure I can. If we get lost I'll call you; Gordon has a phone in his car."

"Gordon has a phone in his car? That is fantastic!"

"It's also expensive . . . but it's deductible; is one o'clock okay?"

"Sure; anytime you say; I'm dying to see you."

"Likewise, I'm sure; see you Sunday, love; bye-bye."

Brian was laughing at her sign-off; it was so good to hear her voice.

Sunday came and so did Eleanor and Gordon; she had remembered how to get there. Kudos for Eleanor! Brian met them outside and

Eleanor admired the new carport and garage; he showed her his new addition in the garage and told her he called it Valhalla.

"That's a beautiful car, Brian; I had one and I put a lot of happy miles on it; good luck with it." Gordon shook his hand.

"Thank you; come in and we'll have a drink before we go."

They gave Gordon a tour of the place and he was very enthusiastic and complimentary; he especially liked the privacy.

"You couldn't ask for more than this; it makes you relax as soon as you enter. And the fireplace is the frosting on the cake."

They had a drink and talked and Eleanor finally stood up and said;

"We better get going; unfortunately we have a six o'clock date in Southampton with one of Gordon's clients."

She was beginning to show her pregnancy a little but she wore a chic dress with a three-quarter coat and disguised it smartly.

"Where do you want to have lunch, Eleanor?"

"Brian; where else would we want to have lunch?"

"You want to take Gordon to Kincaid's; really?"

"I have been telling him about it; he's dying to go there."

"Brian; I hope you don't think I'm a stiff."

"No Gordon; certainly not, I know you are used to upscale restaurants and I wouldn't want to take you where you would be uncomfortable. However, I can promise you good food."

"I've been well-briefed about the place; that's why I want to go."

They went to Montauk; Brian insisted on taking Valhalla and being the chauffeur. He even made both of them sit in the back seat. He parked the car and even though it was cold weather the docks were busy with people. They weren't strolling as they do in summer; it was cold and windy. The three of them scooted into Kincaid's and the warmth of the big pot-bellied stove engulfed them. The piano was tinkling its honky-tonk; the bar was full and Kincaid was approaching waving them to a booth. He welcomed them as usual and introduced himself to Gordon and paid flowery compliments to Eleanor. His sharp eyes did not miss the diamonds on her finger. He recognized that Gordon was a classy guy; now he knew just how classy he was. But Kincaid was the same. The waiter came and took the drink order and left the menus; Bob had a drink with them and discussed the fresh sea food that was the day's special. He chatted for a short time and then left them to their lunch. A bottle of wine came; compliments of Mr. Kincaid; who had his own brand of class! Eleanor and Gordon both had a delicious lobster salad with a side dish of the best prepared asparagus that Gordon had ever had. He was impressed.

"Brian; I am so sorry I have that appointment with my client. I would love to sit here and just absorb this place and enjoy the company. Bob is really a trip and he is a very smart man. I know there are many nice places to eat out here; I want to come here any time I'm in Montauk. I hate to leave but we do have to get back."

He excused himself and went to the waiter and took care of the check. The waiter walked away with the heaviest tip he had ever had since he was in Montauk. Arriving at the cottage they said brief goodbyes and Gordon said they would come for a week-end soon. They were off to Southampton.

Jerry was sitting in his kitchen having a cup of coffee; he had been reading Nora's letter and the phrase about not having her worry from her grave was sticking in his mind. He was doing that to her by drinking again and he resolved to stop it. The idea of working part-time as a handyman was making more sense each time he thought about it. He finished his coffee and went into East Hampton to the local paper and placed an ad. The young lady was very helpful in composing it and she advised him to keep it brief and bold. She urged him to start it with 'retired police officer'; "that will give people a sense of security; especially women who live alone and they are the people who use handymen the most."

The best rate was obtained by putting the ad in for a month; other than leaving it in all of the time; which she didn't think was necessary if he only wished to work part-time. He was pleased with her know-how. The paper was a weekly and just about everybody read it. It came out on Thursday and by Sunday he had six serious calls. He called on all six and came up with four jobs; the other two he felt were too big and he would need a helper; something he wanted to avoid. He was delighted and called Brian to inform him of his progress; Brian shared his enthusiasm and ended the call with; "don't forget to bring your lunch!"

Oddly enough Jerry had not given lunch a thought. He felt a satisfying high with his new endeavor and in time he would discover it was going to be difficult to keep it a part-time thing. His demand would increase as word-of-mouth became the only advertising he would need. He had a small decorative chest that he kept odds and ends in and he soon had it filled with money; he was paying all of his bills with that money and his pension and other income went into savings. He was sure of Nora's approval and it did a lot for his self-respect. There was no time to drink; at least for excessive drinking.

Tony was coming out for the week-end; he was getting fidgety with waiting even though the legal work was moving ahead. He wanted the deal completed so he could write 'finished' to the bar. Gino had asked him to cover the place when his daughter got married in New Jersey; Mario was going to be an usher so there was no one else he could rely on. Tony couldn't refuse and so far there was no exact date for the wedding. He needed to get out of the city for a few days and stretch. There were things around the house he wanted to do; Jerry was going to be unavailable most of the time now. He didn't think it was right to ask his help anymore.

He left Friday afternoon about one to go out East and stopped at Ed's office on the way to see Brian. He was busy with Sam on the plans for marketing the houses. The designs were modern; the demand was replacing the old traditional houses. Buyers, especially from the city, wanted the new cube look with large expanse of glass and ultra-high ceilings; Sam was progressive; a pioneer among the local builders who were reluctant to stray from tradition. The designs brought the outdoors inside and the views were panoramic; most of the homes would be built right to the lot lines using most of the property for the house. He planned on careful excavation keeping the wild growth intact; this protected the natural appeal of the area and left little outdoor maintenance. Tony was very impressed with what was being shown to him. He continued on home his brain turning over those houses and what a good deal they were.

When Brian came home he suggested they go to Kincaid's for dinner and he wanted to see where these new houses were being built. They washed up and took off in Brian's car. When Tony saw how high the lots were and the ocean views they afforded he was sold. They got back in the car and he unveiled his plan to Brian.

"I'll buy the first house he builds and we'll furnish it; I'll leave that to you. If he gives me a good break on the price I'll let him use it for a year as a model or until the other houses sell if that happens before the year is out. We can keep it as a rental; it should bring a good price; it's a great location; near the ocean and a couple of miles from Gurney's Inn, one of the most beautiful spots in Montauk!" Brian was stunned!

"What a great idea! I can't believe he won't go for it. Tony let's go back to the house and call Sam and invite him to have dinner with us; then we can talk this over with him."

"Do you think he'd come; last minute like this?"

"He loves spontaneous stuff! He'll push that truck to the floor and be here in no time."

Brian was right; he told Sam it was about the houses and he said he would come immediately;

"I warn you, I'm hungry and I can eat!"

"Wonderful;" said Brian, bring that appetite with you!"

"He's on his way; time him and watch how fast he gets here from Sag Harbor. I think he has all the village police in his pocket!"

He arrived in twenty minutes with his usual wake behind him. He always looked as if he just finished showering and he looked so right now.

"Come in and have a drink you must be parched from flying in that rarified air." Tony could see a bond had built up between them.

"Well, I got behind some tourists and they slowed me a little."

Brian made drinks while Tony unveiled his idea; Sam's head kept nodding as he talked and when he finished he put out his hand;

"You've got a deal and a fantastic idea! I will work out a price you can't refuse; I'll cut my profit to the bone and add what I lose to the price of the other houses. You get a great house at a great price and I don't lose any money . . . it is never my plan to lose money."

The drinks were used to toast the deal and they went to Kincaid's. It turned out to be a late night and Tony sang a few songs and Sam turned out to be a singer as well. Sam stayed at the cottage that night; it was decided he should not drive . . . Brian being adamant about it.

The next morning they were having breakfast and Sam thanked Brian for insisting he stay; he had one DUI on his record now.

"I think I can do anything when I'm loaded; a big mistake."

He had called his wife and explained why he didn't come home and there seemed to be no argument; she was obviously use to it. He took off and left his usual wake along the curvy road.

"Now we have another project; pretty soon we'll need an office."

"Oh Brian; I hope it never comes to that; I'm glad I decided to come out here though; things are happening!"

They called Jerry and told him the latest development and he came over to go and see the property; he got very excited about the idea.

"I might buy one of these as an investment; I could furnish it and Brian could keep it rented for me. Would you help me pick out the furniture, Brian?" Brian was smiling;

"If you are really serious; of course I will."

"I'm dead serious, I could pay cash for the house!"

"Well I wouldn't wait if I were you. Sam will give you a better price if you sign up now; after the first houses are built the prices go up. He is raising the price on the rest of the houses where the Lauries bought; he told me that after I sold the second house to their friends."

"Which model do you think I should buy?"

"The three bedrooms and two baths house; it's a great plan and that is the most popular request for rentals."

"Okay; that's the one I'll go for."

"You want me to call Sam and make the offer; you mean it?"

"What the hell is the matter with you; you are the salesman aren't you? Or do I have to call Sam myself?"

"I want to be sure you wish to go ahead; you have to pick out the lot that you want to build on."

"I hope you don't make it this hard to buy for all your customers."

Tony was laughing; he knew Jerry was putting Brian on. "Brian; make an appointment with Sam to meet you and Jerry at the property; Sam can bring the house plans and the three of you can pick out the lot. Jerry can bring his check book and give Sam a deposit right at the site. It doesn't have to be at his office." Tony got it moving.

"That makes sense;" said Jerry; "I'm available any time."

"Let's go home so I can get to the phone!"

Brian was full of enthusiasm now; he had another sale for Sam! They met Sam at the site that afternoon and because he could build both houses at the same time he was able to give Jerry a very good price. They were there over two hours; Tony had not gone with them saying he had things to do at home. One thing he did was to talk to Gino for an hour to make sure things were moving ahead; he was losing patience with this deal. Gino was getting tired of all the questions but it did make him keep after the things he was supposed to do. He had to handle Tony with kid gloves; especially since he had offered to pay half of the legal fees. The customers liked the Gino and Mario combo and their lunch business had increased to the point were they had to hire a guy to help in the kitchen from eleven in the morning to seven at night. Gino was thinking he would like to stop sharing the profits with Tony; at the same time he remembered how easy Tony was making it for him to buy the place. Tony was coming to the city the next day; Gino had to be ready!

There were still aggravating things to come; Mario had to have a copy of his birth certificate and it had to come from Italy . . . it took two months to secure it. It was a good thing Tony was buying the house in Montauk because he spent a lot of time as an unpaid foreman of the job. The men working on the house liked him; but he had too many questions and far too many suggestions. You really couldn't get too angry with a guy who brought delicious sandwiches and cold beer to the job frequently; he also constantly kept the site picked up and tidy and when Sam came to inspect their work he was always pleased with the way the site looked. He didn't know Tony was the cleaner-upper and nobody volunteered the information. His house was taking shape and so was Jerry's who didn't come around while the men were working; he preferred to go there after they finished their days work. He was more than satisfied with the progress and usually stopped to see Brian and Tony on his way home to compare notes . . . and invariably was invited to dine. Tony didn't make any comments, not even to Brian; but he thought Jerry was drinking too much. Tony had a lot of experience with drinkers and Jerry showed signs he didn't like to see. He carried his drinks well so the average person might not notice anything. Even though he was busy with his handy-man jobs it didn't prevent him from nipping; his work was good and always completed in a timely fashion; his customers were pleased with his work and his prices; so he went on his merry way with his merry habit. He still brooded about Edith. He had never been close to Lucille; he rarely came in contact with her; but now he was her champion and he had great sympathy for the injustice caused by this bitch. He knew she lived in Hampton Bays and he passed through there many times on trips he made to Riverhead but he never made any attempt to see her. He needed her image so he could hate Edith with good reason; and hate her he did! This gave him a valid reason to drink; something every alcoholic needs. It also put him to sleep early; he did not need a social life.

Brian had been very busy; he was now putting in two hours of floor time every day at the office. That meant he was required to be at the desk for those two hours and take all the incoming calls; if they were people looking for property they became his prospects. There were four salesmen each took two hours. He had not been out to check the progress on Tony's new house and he planned on doing that on Sunday. He hadn't heard from Jerry and assumed he was busy also; he decided to call him and ask him if he would like to come for breakfast and go with him to check the houses. When Jerry answered the phone Brian began to frown.

"I'm not sure I can make it Brian; I've been busy and I feel like I've picked up a bug of some kind. I need some sack time to rest."

Brian didn't buy it; "Forgive my honesty; it sounds like you're drinking."

"Oh right away I must be drinking; I'm not allowed to be sick!"

"If I come over there now what will I see? You can't fool me."

"Okay, I'm drinking; I'm also working everyday!"

"So; I repeat my invitation; have you checked your house lately?"

"I said I've been busy . . . I haven't had time."

"I have the same problem; let's go there on Sunday."

"Meaning I have two days to shape up; is that it?"

"Let's just say you have two days to get some rest."

"I'm not an ingrate; I know you are trying to help me."

"That's nice to hear; see you Sunday at nine; bye-bye."

Jerry sat with the phone in his hand; the dial toning droning. He yawned; "I guess I'm going;" he said aloud as he hung up.

He rang Brian's bell on time Sunday and Brian greeted him cordially and invited him to the kitchen; he was careful not to look him over and had decided to say nothing about his drinking. He poured a mug of coffee;

"I'm making an omelet; I hope that's okay."

"Sounds great and it smells even better!"

"It's just about ready go sit by the fire; we'll eat there I have the table set up and I poured some fresh juice."

He brought the food in on a platter and they enjoyed breakfast without a lot of conversation. When they had finished eating he poured more coffee and they lit up their cigarettes and Brian was talking about Tony's bar;

"Mario is approved for the license but the legal work seems to be dragging and Tony wants to get it done. He's glad Mario is in the picture now because he is sharp and understands things better than Gino. Gino's daughter is getting married around the end of June and that seems to be all Gino has on his mind. He is especially thinking about all the money he is going to need. She's the apple of his eye and he wants her to have a first class wedding. Weddings get to be mighty costly; I'm well aware of that."

"You've been married that many times; have you?"

Brian caught the sly look Jerry was giving him and looking down his nose he said, with much hauteur; "You forget the clientele

I had; I went to a lot of their weddings and none of them spared the bucks!"

Jerry was laughing; as he stood up he tousled Brian's hair;

"I know how high class you are! I've always said that about you."

"I have two words for you, Mr. Foley!"

"Brian! That is not high class."

They were both laughing as they went out the door; Jerry insisted on taking his wagon and as soon as they took off Brian was tuning in the station that had such great music. It was a short ride to the site but why go without music? The sun was bright and though it was chilly the air was clear and fresh; the ocean was a deep blue and strangely calm. Gentle waves made it to the shore and rolled onto the sand; one could hardly call it surf. They parked by Tony's house and were amazed at the progress; the framing was almost finished and the design was apparent. Brian was excited and began looking over the inside of the structure. He would have to give Tony a report so he was doing his homework.

"I'm going to look at my place, Brian."

"Okay; I'll meet you there in a few minutes."

About twenty minutes later Brian walked to Jerry's house and he was up on the second floor although there was no staircase.

"How did you get up there; did you bring your wings?"

"I found a ladder; I'm coming down now."

He came to Brian; "What a view from up there! I might live here and rent out my hut; do you think I'd get the same rent?"

"You just said something very sensible; I think you should live in this house. You can fix it up the way you want it and make it your place; you can get a small place in Florida but make this your home."

"This is a lot of room for one person; I wouldn't know how to act in this place all by myself; I've never done that.

"Columbus never discovered America until he tried; look where it got him. Just furnishing it the way you want it and looking for things that you will be happy to have around you is fun. You can get a dog!"

"A dog; I'm lucky if I can take care of myself!"

"Remember me? I watched you take care of Nora; don't snow me because I don't snow easily. You have time; think about it."

"You know Brian; sometimes you talk with such wisdom I think you must be seventy years old; why is that?"

"When you have it figured out you will be wise too."

"Where does that leave me now?"

"It leaves you otherwise!"

Jerry reached out to grab him but Brian moved too quickly; "I'll give you otherwise!"

He chased Brian back to the wagon; Brian jumped in; laughing.

"Do you have plans for the rest of the day?"

"I have some things I should do but I don't feel like doing them."

"Let's take a ride over to Sag Harbor; I've only been there once and it looked interesting. We can have lunch later on."

"Have you been to Shelter Island? We could take the ferry over."

"No I haven't; let's go . . . put on some music!"

They went to Sag Harbor and parked at the docks;

"Let's walk around and look at these boats, Jerry; some of them are beautiful, the owners live on them instead of buying homes. Many of them spend the summer here and winter in the Caribbean or Florida. The sailboats seem to prefer the Caribbean."

They walked along the pier admiring the variety of vessels.

"It looks like a nice way to live but I think I'd rather have wheels for transportation; I've heard that boats need a lot of work and they eat up money faster than you can print it;" Jerry was smiling.

"Oh I'm sure they are a lot of responsibility; and you certainly have to know what you are doing. I wouldn't want to get on a boat with someone who wasn't seaworthy." Brian seemed very serious.

"So let's stay a couple of landlubbers; now that you're in the real estate business we should be land lovers."

"Let's go look through some of the shops, Jerry; they have some unusual things. They are different; you don't see them everywhere."

"Let's go; you are always educating me and I need it!"

As they browsed through the stores Jerry saw things that piqued his interest and he felt he would really like to have them.

Brian commented; "If you decide to live in your new house you could collect things and enjoy them all the time; you could select furniture that suits you and not be concerned with what is good for tenants. It would be a whole different ball game." Brian watched for a reaction.

"You have me thinking about it; I'm just not sure that I need that much space to live in . . . my hut is so practical."

"You're going to be living out here and meeting people; it's nice to have a home you can invite them to . . . one you are proud of! If you decide it is too much to take care of you can always rent it."

"That's a good point; how about lunch?"

"You wouldn't be changing the subject; would you?"

"Not at all; we have to talk during lunch, don't we?"

They walked along laughing; Brian had suggested the old hotel. Lunch was pleasant; they came out into the sunlight Jerry was stretching and praising the excellent meal.

"What about our ferry ride; did you forget?"

"No; it's not far and it is a short ride over to Shelter Island. I think you will like the Island; it has very little commercial area and many beautiful homes . . . you'll see."

"Maybe you'll sell me something; you know I'm easy."

"I don't know if we have any listings there; it's a small island and the local brokers might have everything tied up."

Jerry got a kick out of the ferry; he hadn't realized that they were going to drive the car right onto the ferry he had never seen this type. He was very surprised at the Island; it was not flat and it was thickly wooded. As they drove along the shore road he saw the mix of homes; some were estate sized on the waterfront and others, tucked among trees, were ordinary-type summer homes. The terrain rose up as you left the shore and the homes on the opposite side of the road had wonderful views of the harbor. Brian was right; he thought it was beautiful.

"What about the winter months over here; does that water freeze?"

"Well, a great many people only stay for the summer; I think that stretches out past Thanksgiving. The ferry cuts down its schedule and I understand that it sometimes doesn't run at all if the weather is bad; I guess if you are a year-round resident you learn to cope with it. There are stores and gas stations and restaurants so nobody starves."

"It's a nice place to visit but I don't think I want to live here."

"I think the people who live here want you to feel that way; I hear they are kind of clannish."

"I'm going to park here by the water; let's walk a little"

They got out and the breeze was brisk and chilly; the sun was warm but when the wind came across that expanse of water it was mighty cool.

"I think it will be a short walk, Brian; it's a little wintry here!"

"I'm with you; this jacket is warm but the wind goes right through it! You should see your face, Jerry; it's all rosy from the chill."

"So is yours; let's get the hell back in the car!"

Back in the car Jerry put the heater on high and they warmed up.

"I think we should head home; Jerry, I'm feeling guilty about the work I brought home."

"I've really enjoyed today; we should do this once in a while. Have you ever been over here with Tony?"

"Yes; we went exploring now and then; especially when he was teaching me to drive, we use to find all the back roads with no traffic."

"Gino must be driving Tony nuts right now; that license sure is taking a long time."

"Thank God Mario is in the picture; it's moving along now. All Gino can think about is his daughter's wedding; she's his pride and joy."

"When is the wedding; is it soon."

"No; it is months away and Tony has promised to run the business so they can both go; Mario is going to be an usher. After that they are on their own; Tony is coming out here for good. Ed Gorman thinks the lots will be ready for sale by early summer; the whole development won't be done but the first section should be ready; weather permitting."

"Tony will want to be around for that; I know."

"It's a wonderful thing for him; he was so smart to put his money into that land long ago when it was cheap. Ed has given him excellent advice and he has brought about this development. He told me he was sorry he didn't ask Tony to go partners on that land but a broker can go broke getting into too many deals!"

They were almost to the cottage and the late afternoon was getting cold;

"Is your place warm enough in this cold weather, Jerry?"

"For sure, Brian; it's snug and he built it into the dune out of the wind. He really knew what he was doing; I'm comfortable there."

He was pulling up to the house to let Brian out.

"Do you have anything home for dinner; I have frozen stew I can give you if you don't feel like cooking."

"Thanks; I have leftovers I just have to heat them up."

"I enjoyed the day, Jerry; think about living in your new house."

"I'm thinking; thanks for getting me out of the hut."

He drove off waving; Brian wondering where he would end up. He went into the house and made a drink and called Tony; they talked a bit and Tony told him he was coming out for the week-end and would go back to the city Tuesday. Brian was delighted with that. He went to his desk and he really felt like getting something done.

Tony arrived at Brian's office Friday afternoon and stopped to say hello; he was alone and Tony gave him a big hug.

"What time are you getting off?"

"Anne will be back in twenty minutes; she's going to close up."

"Good; I'll stop at the farm store and pick up a roasted duck; we can whip up a salad and forget about cooking."

"You really get some great ideas!"

"I'll have a fire going when you come home; plus a martini."

"I'll have to make sure I don't get a speeding ticket."

"Take your time; but hurry."

Brian came home and they were sitting by the fire talking about Jerry.

"He's drinking, Tony; now he is blaming it on Edith and what she has done to his buddy."

"I know he is, I've been watching him; he is good at hiding it because he can handle a lot of booze."

"I have been busy, I sold another of Sam's houses; it had been some time since we even talked on the phone. I couldn't get in touch with him so I drove over there and he was one hell of a mess! He was still doing his part-time work and the people didn't seem to notice it."

"He's good at shaping up . . . long enough to fool the average eye."

"I suggested he live in his new house and not rent it; he can easily afford to and it would keep him busy and give him a sense of pride."

"I would like to have been a fly on the wall and heard that suggestion; I have a feeling it sounded like a command." Tony grinned.

"It was nothing of the kind! I repeat; I suggested he have a real home with things in it that he liked."

"And how did he take this *suggestion?*"

"He's thinking about it . . . seriously; or so it appears to me."

"Would you help him furnish it?"

"Certainly; we already discussed that." "At first I thought he would never do it; now I'm not so sure.

You can be very persuasive; look how many years you told all those rich ladies what they should do." Tony was smiling.

"There's no comparison here to a woman's hair-style."

"*You even told them what cars they should buy!*"

"Watch yourself Mr. D.A.!"

Tony was laughing; "Brian! Let's eat; I'm starved."

Later they lay on the sofa in front of the fire covered with an afghan and fell asleep listening to music.

Tuesday morning Tony drove back to the city; he was dreading going back and silently he renewed his vows to build a fire under Gino so he could be free of all this. He watched with pride the way Brian was moving along in the realty business and made vague plans for an office of his own when he became a broker. The important thing was for him to get good experience and working along with Ed Gorman was the best place he could be. He visualized the day when they could do land developments on their own; and if the lots started selling well he intended to look for more acreage to develop . . . he saw a bright future ahead. Gino beware!

Jerry received a phone call from his broker and he had a serious buyer for the house. They were a couple whose daughter had married and moved to Long Island so they were relocating from Ohio and were interested in a quick sale. They were paying the asking price and were interested in buying some of the furniture. He called the people who were waiting for him to do carpentry for them and explained his emergency; promising to return as soon as possible. He also called Brian. The couple were delightful people and made no attempt to bargain about the price of the furniture; Jerry had it all appraised and he showed them the appraisal; the couple agreed to a price, purchasing almost all of the furniture. Of course there were a few things he wanted to keep in remembrance of Nora. Once again Jerry was stunned; everything involving Nora was a boon for him. Against his lawyer's wishes he was allowing the buyers to move in before the closing; they were such nice people he couldn't see any reason not to make their transition easier. Luckily for him there were no complications; and now he had more money to be amazed with! He brought in a second hand dealer and sold everything the couple had not taken. Driving back out East he continued to be confounded by his good fortune. The sale of the house enabled him to make the decision to live in the new house. He would rent out the hut . . . maybe to one of his retiring cohorts.

He stopped to see Brian before going to the hut; he saw smoke curling from the chimney so he knew he was home. He rang the bell several times.

"Have I got news for you!" he boomed as Brian let him in. "You won't believe it!"

"Try me;" Brian smiled as he quickly closed the door.

I sold the house and everything in it!"

Brian gasped; "Already; is it a signed deal?"

"Signed and sealed; including the furniture!"

"Jerry; Nora is up there taking good care of you."

"That's exactly what I think; are you buying?"

"I certainly am; this needs a celebration."

He went to the kitchen and filled two beer goblets.

"Doesn't this occasion rate a shooter?"

"No; it does not!"

"Not even one?"

"Not even one; end of story Mr. Foley!"

"You're a mean one; you are."

"Keep that in mind."

"If I told you more sensational news could I have one?"

"If you mention a shooter once more I'm shooting you out!"

"I was just kidding with you."

"I wish I could believe that . . . but I don't!"

"You win; I've decided to live in my new house."

"Honestly; you're not kidding now?"

"Right hand to God; remember, you promised to help me furnish the place; I don't know where to begin."

"It will be a pleasure; you'll have fun . . . wait and see."

Brian couldn't understand why he hadn't kept Nora's furniture; it was beautiful and antiques worked in modern homes. He said nothing.

"Let me take you to Kincaid's for dinner; since you're helping me that is the least I can do."

"That's very nice; I'd love to go."

"I'm going home to clean up; I'll be back in an hour; okay?"

"I'll be ready, Jerry; promise me there'll be no shooters."

"I give you my word; I won't spoil the dinner."

"Thank you; you'll thank me in the morning."

Jerry went home feeling good and Brian sat by the fire amazed. He was back in the hour and looking fresh as paint; they took off to Montauk and had an enjoyable evening. Jerry was full of enthusiasm about his house and Brian loved to talk about houses!

When Jerry came back to his hut it was almost eleven o'clock; he was only home about fifteen minutes when his phone rang; it was Tom.

"I hope I'm not waking you up, buddy; I just finished a tough shift with some overtime and I'm feeling sorry for myself."

"You know you have my sympathy; I know where you're coming from. I have to say I don't miss any of that crap . . . life is beautiful."

"I knew I'd get some sympathy from you; that's why I called, I do miss you, you know. This will keep me from sitting in a gin mill."

They talked for half an hour and Jerry hung up feeling good and happy that he was of help to his old side-kick.

Someone else was concerned about Tom; he had called Edith and told her he would be late and she knew from his voice he was very tired. She fixed a light supper that she could warm up quickly then she soaked in the tub and made herself desirable selecting a delicate, refreshing scent. When he came home she greeted him warmly but not passionately; she sensed that this was not the time to make any demands on him; he was obviously very tired.

"You look all in honey, go take a nice hot shower; I've turned down the bed and after you've had a few hours sleep we'll have a bite to eat we don't need any chatter right now; you get some rest."

"Thank you sweetheart; I am bushed." He went to the bathroom.

Three hours later his bladder roused him and he came into the living room and found Edith watching television. She had dozed off. He kissed her brow and she awoke immediately.

"Feel better, love? I know you didn't need any rocking."

"I feel like I slept for ten hours; but you aren't getting any rest I hate to do this to you; you have to stand on your feet all day."

"I have broad feet; they match my shoulders." She got up from the sofa and took his hand; "come on we'll have a little something to eat. If you want a drink I'll join you . . . make mine the same as yours. If you don't feel like having one I'll make some tea."

He smiled at her; "maybe just one; I want to be in shape for later."

"You're not too tired?"

He turned her around and opened her robe then he opened his; pressing their naked bodies together he held her closely and kissed her deeply. He was quickly getting aroused and she trembled.

"I think we better have that light supper," she whispered.

The fact that it was almost four in the morning didn't bother Edith.

After eating they had cigarettes and talked for a short while then Tom stood and took her arm gently steering her to the bedroom. She put some music on and they slid onto the satin sheets. Facing each other his hand softly and slowly traced the curves of her lovely body; she kissed him and their tongues sought each other. He was already fully erect and he pressed close to her, undulating his strong body against hers; her lips found his nipples; something that gave him a thrill he couldn't describe. Then she lowered her head and gave him a sensation he certainly could describe! Her expertise was unmatched and he was wild with passion.

"Oh baby! I love it . . . I love it so much!"

He had to pull away fearing pre-ejaculation; his lips explored her body and he reciprocated satisfying her and leaving her gasping and screaming for him to take her . . . slowly he entered her pausing just inside of her; he undulated back and forth teasing and tantalizing her. Edith's body was heaving up to his demanding all of him; her legs locked around him. Suddenly he began thrusting into her his powerful body ramming home what she was aching for; she had several orgasms and now with a final surge of power he reached a resounding climax and slowly settled on top of her. He was still in her and they lay there in an unbelievably sweet after-glow; his face was buried in her hair and she slowly and gently massaged his buttocks . . . Edith was in another world. They lay entwined this way for quite a while; Tom finally eased off the bed and went to the bathroom; Edith neatened the bed and as he came into the bedroom she went to freshen up. He was stretched out on his back and Edith slid in next to him and cuddled close; a restful sleep enveloped them and they unconsciously continued to share the magic of their love-making. There was no question that they were physically made for each other and if Edith continued to be the new Edith; it looked like a permanent match. There wasn't much hope for Lucille's future and she was quick to accept her situation; could she ever be open to a new relationship was going to be the big question for a while. She just might end up surprising a lot of people; especially herself! Tom and Edith had many of these 'wee hours' interludes and if this was being disturbed . . . disturb me; thought Edith!

Eleanor was progressing toward motherhood nicely and she had a husband who couldn't have been more attentive; the staff at the salon were as excited as a family might be about the coming event. They were so solicitous of her condition that she had to have a meeting and diplomatically ask them to back off. The important thing was her health and the doctor assured her that she was in a-one shape. Managing the salon was no drain on her physically and it gave a big boost to her morale. She kept in touch with Brian by phone and after talking it over with Gordon; she asked him to be godfather to the baby.

"Eleanor; you've really caught me by surprise! You know I have a couple of god children already but this one would be very special; it's quite an honor and I will be delighted to accept."

"That is wonderful, darling; now for a little more news; if it's a boy we are going to call him Brian; Gordon isn't saying anything but I know he would love to have a son."

Tears stung his eyes; he really didn't expect this and he was overwhelmed. He wanted to speak but couldn't; finally the words came; "Eleanor, you got me that time . . . I was speechless! I'll have to tell you how I feel some other time; right now I'm numb!"

"You've made me very happy, Brian; Gordon is very fond of you and is delighted with the whole idea."

"Well that is going to be some christening; the baby is really going to have two godfathers; Tony will get into the act, I'm sure."

"What a lucky child we are going to have!"

"Keep in touch, El, I've been very busy but that news can wait until we talk next time; good-bye and you take care of yourself."

"I will darling; give my love to Tony; goodbye for now."

Brian was elated and he would call Tony and relate the news.

Tony had his own news and it was annoying; Gino was running into more complications and Tony was getting suspicious of his motives. He had come to the conclusion that Gino was trying to delay closing the deal on the bar until after his daughter's wedding. He was obsessed with this wedding and it seemed that everything else was on the back burner. Tony had a sense that Mario was a bit annoyed with Gino also; and Tony toyed with the idea of suggesting that

Mario proceed without Gino and if Mario wanted to he could form a partnership later on. The years of their close friendship gave him pause and he was holding back on such a serious move. Tony wanted to get his life in order because there were so many wonderful things happening; he had been putting pressure on Brian to make the move and now Brian was completely ensconced out East and Tony was being hung out to dry. He was fond of Gino but it was time to put some serious pressure on him; even if it meant turning the deal over to Mario and letting them come to their own terms. He arranged a meeting with Gino and Mario and though it got a bit heated in spots they came to an understanding that time was of the essence and Gino got the message! It ended on a friendly note and they had a drink on it. Tony went back to his apartment feeling he had made progress. The next day he and Brian exchanged news and Tony told him he would be home in a few days. He thought that soon these trips would be over and he could really get settled out East; after all; he had a life to live! Even Jerry was making more progress in that direction than he was. He had to laugh at the way he and Brian were concerned about Jerry while all the while Jerry's situation was improving steadily. Pretty soon Jerry would be telling them about his place in Florida; inviting them down for a swim!

The winter was finally over and spring came in its usual glory. It was especially wonderful near the ocean because it was warm enough to walk along the beach without wearing a parka. Gino had finally gotten his act together and Tony was officially retired from the bar business. His last performance was coming up on the last week-end in June when Gino's daughter was getting married. Tony could not wait for this celebration to take place and had sent a generous check to speed the betrothed on their way. The marriage was taking place on a Sunday and Tony had agreed to work that Monday as well to let them recuperate from the festivities. It was no secret that Italian weddings were well-celebrated! Jerry's house was finished before Tony's due to some changes they had made in their plans; he was already moved in and had rented his hut to a retired cop he had worked with. Jerry was still progressing . . . and still drinking!

Brian and Tony were busy furnishing the new house and preparing it for rental; now that this event was getting near they felt some reluctance in doing so because it looked so beautiful. Tony cautioned Brian that he had better hand pick the tenant!

The week-end of the wedding arrived and Tony went into the city on Saturday to let Gino and Mario take off early.

"I really appreciate you coming in today Tony with all the time we've had to plan this thing there's still a lot of last minute stuff."

"Even after it's over there will be things you forgot; don't worry about it Gino; when you give people plenty of good food and booze and lots of music they don't notice the things you worry about. If they do they are the kind of people not worthy of concern. Just be sure you have fun!"

The three of them toasted the bride and groom and Tony was left back at his bar with an assistant he had never met. He enjoyed seeing his old customers but he still loathed being there.

Sunday of that week-end found Brian hard at work doing last minute things at the rental. He had rented the place to a doctor and his wife from July through Labor Day; he had gotten top dollar and felt sure he had a quality tenant. They were in fact, interested in buying and he had already made an appointment to show them some properties. He finally decided he was going to need help and he called Jerry.

"Hi Jerry, it's Brian and I'm getting bogged down on having our house ready for the tenant; could you give me a hand . . . are you free today?" He took a while to answer;

"Is this Brian? What's up, pal?" Brian blanched.

"Yes, this is Brian . . . how are you Jerry?"

"I'm afraid I'm a little bombed; just a little."

"Jerry, I'm bringing some things over to the rental now; I'll stop by to say hello. Don't tell me it's not a good idea; I'm coming!"

He hung up quickly and hurried out to his already packed car. He pulled up in front of Jerry's house and rang the bell. It was several minutes before Jerry came to the door.

"Brian, I'm not exactly prepared for company; don't come in."

"I'm not company, I'm the Salvation Army; move over!"

He forced his way into the house and even with all the new things he had put into the place it looked like a pig sty.

"You ought to be ashamed of yourself Jerry; this brand new place looks like skid row! What the hell is the matter with you?"

"I told you not to come in . . . you invaded my privacy."

"You are drunk . . . you actually stink of booze!"

"Don't insult me Brian; you're trespassing on my property."

"Oh, are we a legal eagle today? You get in that shower and you shave and clean yourself up even if you cut your throat. I'm going to try and shape this house up and oh, God; air it out."

"I don't feel like taking a shower . . . so I won't"

"Don't hand me that! Get in that shower . . . good hot water!"

"You're badgering me; that's against the law."

"I'll be battering you in a minute; that's against the law too but no jury would ever convict me for sobering up a drunk!"

"Stop calling me a drunk!"

"I will when you are sober; now go!"

Jerry turned with a hang-dog look and made his way to the bathroom. The fog was beginning to lift and he felt embarrassed. He came back into the living room, which Brian had made fairly presentable, and looked cleaned up . . . but the eyes were reddened slits and belied any semblance of sobriety. He felt miserable and looked pathetic.

"I'm going to take you home and fill you up with chicken soup and you are going to help me finish getting our house ready. I will work all of that booze out of you and you are going to straighten up and stop ruining your life! Nora should see you now! Wouldn't she be proud of her wonderful detective? She would be in tears!"

"Don't go there . . . don't do that to me."

"I'll do anything that will get you off that damn booze!"

Back at the cottage Brian heated some cream of chicken soup and began to ease up on Jerry. It was amazing how quickly he could start to pull himself together and even his eyes were looking better.

"I really need your help to get this house ready; Tony is in the city taking care of the bar for Gino; his daughter's wedding is today."

"Why didn't you call me yesterday; I would have eased off."

"I thought I could handle it alone but it's piling up on me. They are arriving late tomorrow afternoon."

"I'll help you; we'll get it ready on time."

"I'm sorry I yelled at you . . . I hate to see you that way."

"You were right; I needed it. I've got to get off the goddam booze. I've got everything going for me; I should go to AA."

"That's something to consider."

"I was hoping you'd say I didn't need it."

"If you can't do it on your own you need help; that's elemental."

"Oh, is that what it is?"

He was coming back to his usual self. Brian arose and readied the soup.

"After a gallon of this you'll be fit for duty."

He placed a small bowl of croutons on the table.

"I know you don't feel like eating; these are light . . . I made them."

Jerry placed a few in his soup, stirring it slowly.

"You're supposed to eat the soup; not toy with it."

"I'm marinating the croutons; don't rush me."

"God forbid! I'll put some more things in the car."

"No, stay with me; I might want more soup."

Brian sat with him and he ate four bowls of soup.

"Now, what do you want me to do?"

"Just follow me and help me; you'll catch on."

They worked non-stop until dark and the house was ready.

"Well Jerry; the least I can do is make you a hot dinner."

"I'll buy that; I really feel like eating now."

It was June but the night was cool; Brian lit a fire and prepared dinner. It was all cooked and just needed heating; no cocktails were mentioned and V-8 juice with a little horseradish and lemon juice sufficed. They ate by the fireplace and later had coffee. Jerry was in a serious mood and he began talking about his life in the orphanage; a subject he never discussed with anyone. They were sitting on the floor in front of the fire and he poured out his soul relating some sad experiences. Then he started telling Brian about the janitor who bullied the young boys and who had taken a fancy to Jerry. The account went to an afternoon when Jerry was fifteen and was in the toilet by himself and he was in a booth masturbating. Suddenly Roy Stillwagon, the janitor, was looking down on him from above the divider; he had a sneering, knowing smile on his face and he crawled under the divider and was facing Jerry who was frozen with fear.

"I knew you had some nice equipment on you . . . I just knew it!"

He took hold of Jerry and stood him up then he sat down pulling Jerry's pants and underwear to the floor. Taking hold of his now flaccid penis he began to massage it and created an excitement Jerry had never known. With the excitement he also felt a great revulsion because he hated him.

"I wanted to smash him but I was afraid of him because he was a figure of authority to us kids. Then he got down on me and I was caught in a thrill that was unbelievable; he was an expert and I came very quickly. I kept my erection and he continued doing me until I had another orgasm. He tongued my balls and I was erect again and he emptied me. He warned me if I told anyone he would deny it and say he caught me jerking off in front of a younger boy. I was scared and I said nothing to anyone. For a year he cornered me and had me when he wanted me. I wanted to kill him; yet I was addicted to his ability. Finally, I ran away when I was sixteen and I've been on my own ever since. I've never told this to anyone . . . I was so ashamed; but I thought you would understand . . . I wasn't afraid to tell you."

Brian had tears in his eyes and he looked at Jerry with sympathy; "That was an ugly experience; especially when you were so young; it's something you'll never forget."

Jerry's eyes were stinging with tears also and suddenly he threw his arms around Brian hugging him and saying his name over and over. It didn't take long for the sympathy to turn into passion and a long pent up desire was turned loose. Their clothes were off and they were totally uninhibited in their union. When it was over they were both silent; overwhelmed with what had occurred. Each had his own thoughts.

"Stay in the guest room, Jerry; I need to be alone right now."

He gathered up his clothes and went to the master bedroom. Jerry did likewise and made his way to the guest room; he was remembering the day he had messed things up with Eleanor and wondered just how much of a misfit he really was. Everything was happening too fast; he had not recovered from what just occurred with Brian . . . he had to admit he was the aggressor and that confounded him. The fact that he relished it was also hard to digest; what the hell was he all about?

Brian was sitting on the bed staring into space; what had he just done to Tony? He knew he could never tell him; it would shatter him. How he was going to make it up to him would take time; he knew this could never happen again, he thought the yen he had for Jerry was burned out but it had only been smoldering. The swiftness of the whole thing baffled him and Jerry's participation was going to be difficult to forget. This was such a huge mistake! A few hours later it would all become a more unbearable situation.

Business at the bar had slowed down, which was not unusual on a Sunday; and so shortly after midnight Tony let Steve, the helper Gino had provided, go home early. He had cleaned up the kitchen and rest rooms and there was just some simple tidying-up for Tony to do. About two o'clock he informed the two remaining bar flies that it was time.

"Go home to your cribs, little ones, it's time for the sandman."

Amid the usual grumbles they picked up their change and departed leaving no tip for this mean barkeep. Tony locked the front door after them and began putting out most of the lights. After hiding the cash in the freezer he made a meatball hero take home wrapping it securely in foil and putting it in a brown paper bag. He went out the back door in the darkness and had just finished locking the locks when they descended on him. Four dark figures came rapidly out of the four winds and each knife expertly found its mark; Tony never knew what hit him. Snatching the paper bag, in their warped minds it was filled with money; they dissolved into the night. Tony slumped amongst the trash cans a bleeding heap of dying flesh. He died in the ambulance for a meatball hero; his killers were never found. Just as he was beginning to live . . . it was over.

The police called Gino back from New Jersey and the celebrating was over. He agonized over losing his friend muttering constantly that it was because of him this happened. Mario tried to comfort him and it fell to him to call Brian because Gino was out of it.

Brian put the phone down and fell back on the bed in a heap of shuddering sobs. He found it hard to breath and he seemed to ache everywhere. Jerry had not heard the phone but he was awakened by Brian's sobbing. He hurried to his room calling his name and was very worried when he saw the condition Brian was in. Racing into the bathroom he soaked a towel with water and squeezed it damp-dry; quickly he wrapped Brian's head in it and covered him with blankets. It took a few minutes to get the story from him and he moaned in utter disbelief when it unraveled. They waited until eight in the morning and called Gino to learn what had exactly happened. Jerry did the talking and asked the right questions because of his police experience. He called a couple of his former contacts in homicide and ended up calling Tom. Nobody knew anything; except that Tony died almost instantly from wounds that were meant to kill. These killers had killed many times before.

Brian had gotten through the funeral and the police and the lawyer; it was hard to believe a month had passed. Jerry had been a big help and Brian was far from reconciled with all that had occurred; he thanked God for his job because its demands forced him to concentrate on the real world and other people. When he realized what Tony had bequeathed him it only made getting over it more difficult. Then Eleanor had a healthy premature baby and he had to go through the godfather bit when it was a chore instead of a pleasure. He felt eighty years old. Jerry was on his way over to see him and he had sounded a little strange on the phone though it could be his imagination. He heard the wagon pull in.

"Hello Jerry," Brian greeted him at the door.

They had never discussed what had taken place between them since that awful night.

"Hi, Brian, if you've got a little time I'd like to talk to you."

"Sure I have time; can I make some coffee for you?"

"That would be nice; I've only had one cup today; I feel incomplete; kind of waiting for the other shoe to drop."

"Well, I guess I can at least drop a shoe for you."

Brian brought the coffee out on the deck and they sat at the table looking at the harbor.

Jerry sipped the coffee and looked at Brian; "I need to talk about us; I think we have a shoe hanging and I would like to let it drop even if I don't like the outcome. Can you talk?"

"Yes, I agree with you we have to get out in the open with each other. I've made my peace with Tony; that is for me to live with."

"I have had a lot of time to think about myself and where I am at; you help me really see myself and I've been working hard in the daytime and thinking at night. I can also say I've only had a few beers in over a month and there is no booze in my house. I've put hard liquor out of my life . . . it's just not for me. I'm over fifty years old and there is no one in my life; there never has been. Now I realize that you are the closest person to me . . . I'm hoping that you can feel close to me. I don't think I'm gay, I don't know what the hell I am; but I know now I have a strong feeling to be with you. It all came out in me that night and I've had to try and face up to where I'm at. I've been around you and Tony for a long time and I watched you grow together and when I stayed here I use to wonder how you could live together and sleep together and not worry about what people would think. The fact was nobody seemed to care; it really amazed me. After a while I stopped being nosy and making snide insinuations and I realized I had two of the best friends I've ever had. I kept my brain soaking in alcohol and I didn't think about who I was. It was Nora's passing that woke me up; I still feel she would be alive if I had come straight home that night."

"Jerry, Nora was dying; she knew it, you didn't want to face it."

"Well, I guess we each have to live with something; I'd like to do it together. Do you think you could go for that? Maybe not right now; but do you think you could live with me like you did with Tony?"

"Yes, I know I could and I don't think we should wait; I need someone, I need to talk about things with someone I feel close to."

"I need that too; I hate being alone, Brian."

"I think we could build a life together; you could get a real estate license, Jerry; you would be a good salesman. You don't realize it but you have already had experience in your own real estate deals and that is subtle education. I know I will have my own office after I become a broker; I am going to look for a commercial property in East Hampton and buy it now. I can rent it until I'm ready to open my own office. Later on after you have had enough experience we could open another office in Watermill, I love that village; you could be the broker there. We would then cover real estate from Southampton to Montauk; that would keep us busy. You need more than a bed to sustain a relationship, Jerry."

"Brian! You have my head spinning; but I feel the excitement."

"There's one more serious thing we need to talk about, Jerry; it is very important to me that we have an honest, open relationship. Holding things back because you don't want to hurt someone only deepens the hurt. If you have something to say you have to say it."

Jerry stood and put his hands under Brian's arms; he picked him up out of the chair and hugged him; "I agree, Brian."

Brian added; "If one of us feels he has to walk . . . he walks."

Finis